KEEPING WATCH

Bantam Books

NEW YORK TORONTO LONDON SYDNEY AUCKLAND

LAURIE R. KING

KEEPING
WATCH

Grateful acknowledgment is given for permission to reprint "September 1, 1939,"
copyright 1940 and renewed 1968 by W. H. Auden, from W. H. AUDEN: THE
COLLECTED POEMS by W. H. Auden. Used by permission of Random House, Inc.

KEEPING WATCH
A Bantam Book / March 2003

Published by
Bantam Dell
A Division of Random House, Inc.
New York, New York

Book design by Glen M. Edelstein

ISBN 0-553-80191-0

Manufactured in the United States of America
Published simultaneously in Canada

To all the children who fight in wars not of their making

Thanks to John Tiley, who tried to make sure I took the right equipment with me into the green; to Jason and Jeff of Media Associates in Mountain View, who put Allen's equipment up in the tree; and to Nathan King, gamer extraordinaire.

And with thanks to all the men and women who wrote about their experiences in Vietnam, that those of us who come after might understand.

And for those who like to know the meaning of words, a glossary of war terms lies at the end of the book.

I and the public know
What all schoolchildren learn,
Those to whom evil is done
Do evil in return.

—W. H. Auden
"September 1, 1939"

Before

Chapter 1

ALLEN CARMICHAEL BALANCED ON THE PRECARIOUSLY SLIM BRANCH OF the vine maple, pawing aside the soft new greenery and cursing the incompatibility of most trees with the human body. Particularly a six-foot-one-inch human body with a stiff leg, working its way through a sixth decade. Too old for this kind of stunt, he grumbled to himself. No doubt about it: It really was time to turn this side of things over to some younger maniac.

The house over which he was keeping watch—or rather, which his machines had been watching for him—lay slightly lower than his current treetop perch and at the other end of half a mile of well-maintained driveway. It was a solid house, big, with double-glazed windows and a lot of fake stone wrapped around a confusing number of rooms and a three-car garage. The sort of house Allen disliked, even without the things that went on inside it. Showy, unsuited to the climate, "Tudoresque" (whatever the hell that meant), and with no personality to show for its vast expense. It was also irritatingly well situated for defense. With good reason, Allen knew, but it made life no easier for a man trying to pry it open.

He downloaded the information stored in the treetop receiver, gave it a new battery, and paused to check the area around the tree for on-lookers. He was grateful, always, when his targets were not dog own-ers. Remarkably few of them were—for the simple reason, he'd always supposed, that dogs demanded a kind of affection they had no time for. Their interests lay elsewhere.

He clambered down through the unfurling April leaves, reaching the ground without breaking any of his middle-aged bones, and set off for the motorcycle buried in some bushes half a mile away. The sur-veillance on AmberLyn's stepfather was nearly finished; time to break up the party.

LATE THAT NIGHT, BACK IN HIS BARELY FURNISHED RESIDENTIAL-HOTEL apartment, Allen Carmichael dropped his pack on the kitchen table and got himself a beer. Half of it went down his throat before he both-ered to shut the door on the fridge.

He set the bottle down next to the pack and shrugged off the leather biker's jacket he wore, taking it to the apartment's single closet, where he winced at the smell of cat piss that wafted out. He worked one of the flimsy hangers into the coat's shoulders, hung the heavy gar-ment up gingerly on the chipped paint of the metal bar, and closed the door, then remembered the smell and left the door ajar a few inches so his clothes wouldn't be quite so pungent in the morning. Sitting on the end of the wobbly mattress, he picked open the laces of his scuffed steel-toed boots, placing them precisely under the corner of the bed, then unbuttoned the grubby, paper-thin flannel shirt he wore and tugged it free from his jeans. He pushed the garment into the dresser drawer that he used in lieu of a dirty-clothes hamper (unconsciously adjusting the ill-fitting drawer so it lay precisely flush to the frame), then scratched his grease-rimed fingernails through his scalp, loosing hair matted by the day's headgear of knit cap and helmet, before stretching hard in an attempt to rid his body of the day's tiredness. The attempt was not a success.

He walked out of the bedroom, limping slightly, dressed in stock-ing feet, jeans, and the spotless army-green T-shirt he had worn be-neath the plaid flannel. In the apartment's tiny bathroom (which was still pretty grim even though he'd got down on his hands and knees the day he moved in and scoured every surface) Allen ran the rust-stained basin full of cold water, splashed and dried his face. He used the toilet, then went back to the basin, using hot water and soap this time to scrub his hands, his bearded face, and the back of his neck. He'd rather have taken a shower, to rid himself of the indescribably oily feeling of his day, but he knew he'd really need one later and he couldn't permit himself to have two showers in one evening—a little compulsiveness was okay, but let's not let it get out of hand. So he washed his face and hands, and when every inch of exposed skin was clean and glowing, he arranged the thin, damp towel foursquare on the peeling chrome of the bar and switched off the light.

At no point had he looked into the dim mirror over the basin.

In the kitchen again, Allen frowned at the contents of the refrigerator, glanced over the meager supply of pasta and canned goods in the cupboard, and in the end fried up a pair of thick ham and provolone sandwiches with tomatoes and onions on week-old bread. He carried his plate with the remains of the beer into the cramped living room and propped his feet up on the massive pseudo-wood table in front of the musty sofa, allowing the greasy food and the mindless television to carry him through to the half-hour break.

With a sigh, and another beer, he then sat down to his work.

In the arc of experience that had brought him from a scorching runway in Saigon to this fetid apartment among the winos, Allen had picked up a number of skills. Primary among them, then and now, was the ability to disengage. Going through the pockets of a long-dead enemy soldier, dropping down to check a bunker they'd thought was empty but which a fragmentation grenade had proved was not, watching a brutal interrogation, loading a ville's weeping inhabitants into a Chinook like cattle—you had to stand aside mentally and let your hands and eyes do their job. Like a flak jacket on the emotions, disassociation made it possible to carry on even if you were hit.

Now, it made it possible for Allen to watch his illicit videos of blond, curly-headed, six-year-old AmberLyn McKenzie with the least possible involvement of the mind. If he stopped to let it all in, if he allowed his eyes to dwell on the child's face or let his ears hear her stepfather's clever cajoling, he knew damn well that he'd put down his beer and just go murder the bastard. Which wouldn't help anyone, least of all that little girl whimpering on the television screen. Instead, he fast-forwarded parts of what the bedroom spy camera had recorded, although truth to tell, it was rarely the actual rape that got to him on these sorts of cases. No; the part he found truly unbearable was, he'd long ago decided, the very same part that the pedophile loved the most: the seduction. Most pedophiles weren't interested in merely overpowering a child, but rather found their greatest pleasure in the game of domination, keeping the child just this side of outright panic by first discovering and then manipulating each particular victim's individual needs, fears, and nobilities. The subtle interplay of threat and cajoling, pressure and affection, always hit Allen the hardest: the terrible intimacy involved, a predator's complete understanding of his prey, a knowledge such as, more often than not, no other human being in the child's life came anywhere near to possessing. It was this terrible familiarity with the victim's very soul that made Allen crave the simplicity of murder.

When the bedroom tape was over, he got himself a third beer by way of reward before settling down with a pad of paper to watch the scenes from the three other cameras he'd planted. He made the occasional note and replayed one or two parts before labeling the recordings precisely and sealing them into a padded mailer; only then did he go and take his shower. Afterward, he sat in the dark room for nearly an hour with his feet on the table and his fingers laced together over the front of his fresh T-shirt.

Thank God this time there was a mother. It made life so much easier, having an adult to take charge of the child once he'd gotten the victims free—even if the mother was a large part of the child's problem, which was usually the case. But at least Allen didn't have to act alone, at least he avoided the soul-withering need to ingratiate himself into the child's life like the molesters he watched. He always felt . . . cleaner, when there was a mother on board.

A few minutes after midnight, Allen got up to fetch a cell phone from his bedside table. He thumbed in the numbers and put it to his ear, standing at the bedroom window and looking through its dirty glass at the deserted street below. As he'd expected, the phone was answered after the first ring. He spoke. "Tomorrow, I think. He'll be out of town until late. So plan A looks good. Everything ready at your end? Fine, see you then."

He closed the phone and climbed between the clean-smelling sheets, where he slept the sleep of a middle-aged adrenaline junkie on the eve of action, whose only dreams were cool and green and quiet as April leaves.

Chapter 2

THE BOY SAT WITHOUT MOVING BEFORE THE MULTICOLORED SCREEN OF his computer, head bowed, pulling the room's silence around his bony shoulders as if harnessing the billowing cloak of a superhero. As if by wrapping himself head to foot in the fabric of silence, he might become invisible as well.

The boy thought of his cloak as *The Quiet*, imagined it to be woven from ever-shifting tones of gray and blue, mistlike colors of peace and invisibility. He was, in truth, still nearly halfway convinced of its actual existence, a portion of his heart even now almost certain that if only he could concentrate intensely enough, like some Chinese martial-arts master—if he could just find the precise area in his brain from which *The Quiet* flowed—he would be able to trigger it at will, pulling it up over himself like a blanket so that he simply winked out, into another dimension or something, vanishing from the world's sight.

He knew this was nonsense, of course. He was twelve years old now, and he'd lost his belief in fairy tales a long time ago. The problem was, sometimes it seemed to work. Sometimes he'd sit really, really still, so motionless he could feel the blood slowing in his veins, hear his mind turning within its skull; when he reached just that right place, he could reach in and summon *The Quiet*. He would feel its cool fabric brush lightly across his skin and snug down against his clothes, as firm and protective as a mother's arms. When that happened, when he got it right, Father's footsteps would continue on past his door, as if he had lost sight of the boy wrapped in his cloak of silence.

Other times, however, the boy would just think he'd got it right. He'd sit without moving a muscle, his breath so low it did not hide the slow *lub-dub* of his heart, stilling his mind until he felt *The Quiet* begin to creep up over him, clothing him in the knowledge that tonight's footsteps would go on by, since he was not there for Father to see. Only, incomprehensibly, the approaching footsteps would turn and come through the shattered doorway, and the real world would crash over him with the shock of a bucket of ice water.

He'd seen a television program one time about a dog trainer, and although the woman herself was stupid and ugly he'd left it on for a while because he couldn't take his eyes off one of her dogs. It was a small brown-and-white animal with soft-folded ears and intelligent black shiny eyes—a terrier, she'd called it. It was a compact dog, sharp of feature and round of belly, just the right size to fit into a boy's lap and wriggle around to lick his chin with that pink tongue, but the woman acted like it was a lab rat or something. The terrier had been mistreated by its owners, she'd told the camera—and he knew just what she was talking about, oh yeah. But, she said, from the terrier's point of view, the worst part was not the physical abuse it had suffered, or even the lack of affection. It was the unpredictability of it all, the way the owner would one day kick the dog and another day pick it up and feed it treats and spoil it, so the poor animal (those were her words: *poor animal*) never knew what to expect. That was what had made the dog vicious, so that he couldn't be trusted not to bite.

The dog lady hadn't said anything about the opposite result of being treated unpredictably: the hope, constant and tenacious, that insisted on whispering in the back of a person's mind, *If only . . .* If only I could find the right spot in the brain, I'd be able to enter *The Quiet* anytime I wanted. If only I could figure out what I do that sets Father off, I could stop doing it. If only . . .

Maybe it didn't work that way with dogs. Maybe dogs didn't hang on to hope like people did. Maybe they just gave up thinking that life might make sense one day, so when they looked up and saw a hand reaching out to feed them or to hit them, they just bit it without waiting to see which it would be. Because they *Couldn't be trusted. Not to bite.*

Maybe only little kids hung on to the hope that they could *do* something—like they clung to the idea of some superhero cloak of invisibility. Lately, he'd begun to think it was time he grew out of the fantasy, that basically there was not a thing he could do to avoid Father when Father was in one of his moods.

Or maybe there wasn't all that much difference between a boy and a terrier. (Great name that, somehow like *terror,* only friendly, like the dog looked, his ears cocked at the camera and at the stupid woman who hadn't even said his real name. The boy had decided the dog's name was Terry, and concluded that Terry *Couldn't be trusted* only when it came to stupid women and unpredictable owners.) Maybe, the boy thought, it was time for him to start growing up, time to become more like the mistreated white-and-brown dog.

Time for him to become vicious, and snap those sharp white teeth down into flesh and bite and tear and—

When the sound of feet came on the stairs, the boy jabbed the SAVE button on the keyboard and subsided into motionlessness, trying not to breathe, searching desperately for *The Quiet,* for the tiny button in his brain that would render him invisible.

Chapter 3

ALLEN'S DREAMS WERE CLOAKED IN GREEN, EVEN AFTER ALL THESE YEARS. The good dreams, dreams like those flickering behind his eyelids that night in the apartment smelling of cat's piss, were woven from the rich and varied greens of the islands where he had grown up: the dark, dull cedar and the sword fern in autumn, the gloss of wet madrone and Oregon grape, the brilliant tips of the springtime firs against the gray-green mounds of the distant mainland, the opal-green tint the sea took on during a clear day after a rain, the blues and greens of the small braided rug that had met his bare feet each and every morning of his childhood, all of them melding in his sleeping mind with the mind-boggling, gorgeous multiplicity of colors that had made up the Vietnam countryside, ranging from near-black to startling chartreuse, from the quiet bottle-green flavor of light under the jungle canopy to the artificially bright patchwork of the rice paddies.

Those were the good dreams.

But then there were the other nocturnal greens. He could not have said what the difference was, why one color was comforting and its close brother brought menace. He only knew that the dreams that had him thudding out of sleep into full, sweat-drenched, tight-muscled battle alert were shaded with dead tones. They might begin with the bright olive of a new guy's fatigues, a clean slate waiting for the messages of battle and blood and the permeating red earth of Vietnam, to be followed by the ominous flatness of one lone shrub on an entire hillside of vegetation, a shrub whose roots had been cut by some tunneling creature. Sooner or later he would dream the startling jade-green of Flores's eyes, and once those eyes had appeared, the shades of green worming their way into his sleeping mind bore the inevitability of decay: the weird tones of chemically murdered foliage and the blatant innocence of the vines that sprang up overnight from soil disturbed by man; the lifeless colors of the hacked-off branches used to camouflage the enemy's trucks and the yellow-green glow of terrain through a nightscope and the nauseous blue-green of suppurating infections in Caucasian bodies that had lain a week in the jungle heat. The greens would writhe and merge like jungle phosphorescence through his sleeping brain until he bolted upright, sweating and breathless at the piercing reality of a green body bag being zipped shut inches from his nose, or of eight-foot-high elephant grass curling down upon him like the maw of some huge carnivorous creature. Sometimes he would be heading back to the NDP in a Huey, the cool breeze fingering his damp hair and his M16 easy between his knees, relaxed and safe and riding high above an undulating sheet of emerald-colored crushed velvet that draped the soft curves of the earth below—only the chopper would shudder and Allen's harness would open and out the open door he would shoot, floating unencumbered over that endless green expanse of unbroken jungle, achingly beautiful and pure except that he was not floating he was falling and the jungle was rising up at great speed and the crushed velvet became individual trees reaching up for him and the ground was getting closer so close it was nearly at his eyelids and he was about to—

Yes, Allen's dreams were green.

Of course, Allen had been pretty green himself when his stiff new jungle boots had stumbled down the metal stairs from the air-conditioned Braniff jet onto the sticky tarmac of Vietnam. Wet behind the ears, clueless jerk, fuckin' new guy, a real cherry, oh yeah. What grunts so expressively called *fresh meat*. Twenty years old and out to save the world in his yearlong cycle in 'Nam, when he hadn't even had enough sense to save himself.

He could have stayed deferred, could have sat out the remainder of his four years behind a nice clean desk in a nice tidy classroom. But romantic fool, halfway through his freshman year at the U of W he'd looked around and thought, *I'm not doing my part.* So he'd enlisted, can you believe it? Turned up his nose at the student deferment and signed his name on the forms. At least his girl Lisa had slept with him when he'd come home from boot camp, so he hadn't shipped off to war a virgin.

Sometimes, in the darkest cycles of his middle-aged sleep, smells would creep in, too. Not so much that first overwhelming stench, which he would come to know all too well as the rich savor of shit barrels doused with fuel and set alight, but rather the country's other, more universal odors—rot and stale urine and clothes stiff with fear-sweat, diesel trucks and jet fuel and kerosene cookstoves, dust and animals, rice paddies and incense and the ubiquitous fish sauce the people ate, an olfactory flood that swept over him on this, his first venture into the tropics. Even now, a couple of lifetimes later, the whiff of a pit toilet or the whoop of monkeys in a zoo had the power to clothe him in the taut and twitching skin of a kid barely out of his teens, and for an instant prickly heat would flare in his crotch and armpits, sweat trickle down the muscular hollow of his young spine beneath the ghostly pack. Even on that first day, bumping in the bus with its wire-covered windows while his mind worked to convince itself that this was the act of a righteous man, a ritual of passage that would make him whole—even then, his body had had enough sense to dread the place.

He'd learned to control himself. It was twenty years or more since he had dived behind a car at a sudden clatter, at least fifteen years since he had slapped his rib cage reaching for a nonexistent rifle. But thunderstorms still made him jumpy, approaching a strange house had him scanning the surroundings for sniper sites and perimeter defenses, and on a dirt path, his eyes never ceased searching for trip wires.

And all his dreams were cloaked in green.

Chapter 4

IT WAS THE SLAUGHTER OF HIS COMPUTER THAT HAD DONE IT, THE BOY told himself afterward. If the punishment had been the usual, the boy would have just taken it as he always did, but the sight of the computer— his lifeline, his one sure competence, his only friend in all the world, scattered across the carpet like so much garbage—that was when the thoughts had started, when the spark of rebellion had begun to smolder in his heart.

Father always liked to present himself as an indulgent dad, the sort of guy who turns up loyally for back-to-school nights and science fairs (if he's not out of town on business), who tries his best to make time for the yearly parent-teacher conferences, where he impresses that year's teachers with his caring words and earnest sympathy for their hard job, who always has a donation for the sports fund and who buys the best for his kid, be it name-brand shoes or cutting-edge computer equipment. And Father was good: Teachers and parents thought he was just a great guy. None of them ever guessed that when Father looked around for someone to defer the cost, it was the boy who ultimately paid for it.

Not in money, of course—and rarely out of his skin, at least not during the school year when teachers might notice. The boy had long since grown resigned to the rituals of payment, chiefly because he had learned how to shield off the essential parts of himself from that doing the paying. But this time, with the computer, Father had got inside his shield and found his weak point, and the price had proved intolerable. The boy knew, beyond a doubt, that the next installment might well cost him everything. And thus the small, hot burn of rebellion.

The punishment started, as most of them did, in all innocence—in this case an assignment in English class. They were to write a short story, setting their scene in a kitchen and using as many descriptive passages as possible to bring life to the smells, sounds, and sensations that the characters were experiencing. The boy labored over this as he did over all writing, since his eyes had difficulty pinning down the unreliable words that lived on a page. He knew this was a problem some kids had—he'd had a classmate who'd been diagnosed with dyslexia—but he sweated to keep it to himself. Father would go berserk if he was reminded by some well-meaning school counselor that his son was not quite perfectly made. The boy got around his problem with slippery letters by memorizing thousands of words, by being scrupulous about spell-checking every little thing he wrote, and by reviewing ahead anything he might be called on to read aloud in class. So far, he'd kept this quirk of his eyes to himself, by dint of hammering his brain into order.

He spent hours on this simple assignment, making sure he had each word spelled correctly, each verb with its proper ending and not with letters that had spilled over from its neighbor. He was so focused, in fact, that he forgot to check what he was actually writing about. So when Ms. Rao took him aside after class, pointed to the part where he'd been describing the slap of a steak being dropped to the floor (he'd been trying to be a little bit funny here) and asked how he happened to know what the crack of a belt against flesh sounded like, he went straight into panic mode and froze, red-faced and terrified.

It just seemed like it would sound that way, he stammered out; he didn't know, he didn't actually know what that noise would sound like, how could he? But he shot her a glance, and his thudding heart sank to his toes. She didn't believe him. So he raised his chin and looked her in the face, cool again. "You wanted us to write descriptions that, uh, provoked a nuance."

"Evoked a nuance," the teacher corrected automatically.

"Yeah, that. You know, like you were talking about, uh, unexpected contrast being one of the things that makes a reader sit up and take notice. So I was using the contrast of something that would really be pretty bad to make you see how basically silly these people are."

And then he shut up. Knowing when to shut up was the key to a successful lie, even more important than getting the details right and looking people in the eye. The teacher's gaze of accusatory empathy wavered, and she looked down to reread the passage he'd written, doubt in every pore of her smooth brown skin. She frowned slightly, trying to look at it from the point of view he had suggested, and he could see when she got it. He relaxed, queasy at the nearness of the danger averted.

But he had relaxed too soon. "James, will your dad be home tonight?" Ms. Rao asked.

God no, he raged in despair, *don't call him about this, don't do that you stupid shit-faced woman, what the fuck do you know about anything, just give me the damn paper back and let me rewrite it, don't try to talk to Father, don't oh don't . . .*

"I . . . I don't know. I think he's coming back tomorrow, or maybe on the weekend."

"Doesn't he tell you?"

"He doesn't always know how long the projects will go on. But he always calls to talk to me at night." Which was a lie. Jamie never knew when Father would appear, where he was, never talked to him on the phone except when Father wanted to balance a threat over his head. But Father was at home today, would be home tonight unless something important came up, and he could see by this damned woman's face that he was doomed. He hated her; he wanted to drive his pencil into her neck. Instead, he took the paper and slumped off to his next class.

Jamie spent the rest of that day in the throes of cold and hot waves, so clearly preoccupied that two of his teachers asked him if he was ill. He rode his bike home, went to his doorless bedroom to sit in front of the dark computer screen, and waited for the phone to ring.

Five hours: a lifetime. Five hours before he heard the phone followed by Father's voice downstairs, five hours and ten minutes before he heard Father's footsteps on the stairs.

The Quiet refused to come.

Father carried a fireplace poker in his right hand, an antique implement of ivory and steel that normally lived in the living room. The boy had never touched it because, as Father had explained, true ivory would scorch if a child carelessly left it within range of a hot fire. Up close it was a fearsome instrument, the end of it split into two metal fingers, one straight for prodding, the other hooked back to pull. The boy went cold at the sight of the weapon, nearly whimpering in terror, but Father intended another use.

"Unplug the machine," he said softly. The boy's eyes went from the poker, to the man, to the computer screen a foot away. The ghost of his own reflection lay there, which somehow gave him the courage to protest.

"But Father—"

"Unplug it."

The boy took another look at the poker, then dropped to his knees to crawl under the desk. He wrapped his fingers around the plug of the surge protector and eased its three prongs out of the wall, then reversed out, exquisitely aware of Father standing behind him. As he got up warily to face his father, he noticed that the small green power light beneath the screen had gone dark; he felt as if he'd switched off the life support of a close friend.

Father held out the poker, handle first. "Smash it."

There was no question but that the boy should take it. The handle was smooth and warm from Father's palm, the whole thing astonishingly heavy—Jamie had to brace both hands just to raise its split tip off the carpet. He swung it wavering through the air, and let it bounce off the top of the monitor. The screen jiggled, but stayed where it was, not a mark on its sturdy plastic casing. It was Jamie who felt shattered. He couldn't do this.

"No!" he cried involuntarily, letting the poker thump to the floor. "I'm sorry, I didn't mean to write what I did, I'm sorry! I need it, I can't work without it, you can take it out on me, but not my computer!"

It was a mistake, he knew that even as he heard the words pouring from his throat. You never, ever, disobeyed a direct order, not if you expected to remain standing. But underneath this acknowledged rule was a hidden truth, deeper and ultimately far more devastating: You didn't love something if you wanted to keep it. He saw the stern disapproval arranged on Father's face, but he also saw the flare of satisfaction, saw Father realize that he had succeeded in getting inside his son's shield.

He was not surprised when Father bent to retrieve the loathsome object, nor when Father placed the handle back into his hand. This time Father wrapped his own grip around his son's, crunching the thin fingers between ivory and implacable flesh and bone; this time the boy's arm came up hard, tugging its socket at the height of the swing; this time the monitor cracked through with the harsh thud of a skull breaking, glass spurting like blood across the desk and the boy's chest. The second blow was easier. Jamie's arm went up again, and again, pounded into shreds the monitor, hard drive, keyboard, printer—all the beautiful parts of the machine he loved.

After a while, Jamie became aware that his hands alone were wrapped around the warm ivory, that Father had stood back to watch him smash and pound without assistance on the brittle plastic and the glass, reducing the motherboard to a miniature junkyard of metal and plastic, splintering holes in the wooden desk beneath. Smashing blindly, hearing the sound (a small voice asked sarcastically if he was going to put this, too, into one of his English assignments) of crunch and splinter and spatter, horrible yet horribly satisfying, and behind it a furious, high-pitched scream that he knew was inside his own brain. He pulverized the chunks, beating at the machine until nothing but the mangled shell remained. Only then did Jamie stumble back, trembling and panting, his eyes red but dry, looking down from some far distance at the pieces of worthlessness flung across the room. He wanted to smash something else; anything.

Father's hand came down onto his again; this time it was gentle. Strong fingers pried the ivory grip from his son's tingling fingers, laying the rod on top of the debris-covered desk. He picked up the chair, and Jamie winced, but Father merely flipped it over to free it from glass before restoring it to its place. He sat down on it. The trembling boy felt one hand on his shoulder and another against the back of his knees, and then Father was lifting his son up and settling him onto his lap, so that the boy came to rest surrounded by Father's strong arms.

Jamie sat rigid inside the embrace, bubbling with rage, fighting to remain oblivious to the strength and the warmth: *Not this time,* the boy swore to himself; *I will* not *give in this time.* As if he'd spoken the vow aloud, the man's embrace tightened a fraction, a gesture of both threat and affection, but Jamie held his body taut and aloof and whole, right up to the moment the strong right hand came up to rest gently—oh, so gently—on the boy's sweat-soaked hair, pressing the child's face against his heavily muscled shoulder. "Oh, son," Father murmured into his ear; Jamie's determination wavered, rallied briefly, then collapsed. He curled into Father's chest and sobbed, in submission and confusion and hatred and love and humiliation and more emotions than a twelve-year-old boy could name, much less hold in.

When Father had left him, tucked into bed with the proud kiss of a tyrant planted on his forehead, the boy lay there, cold with shame, sick with fury, glaring at the debris of his own iniquity. *I did that,* he raged at himself. *I did that, not Father.* But in the morning, even if Father was at the breakfast table, nothing would be said. And during the day, while he was at school, Howard would clean it all up—or maybe Mrs. Mendez, but probably Howard, who was there to clean up Father's messes. Life would go on; this was just another of Father's lessons that I can't tell anyone about.

Eventually, the worst of the trembling stopped, the bitterest self-flagellation died down as the adolescent body was pulled toward sleep by the ebbing tide of a long and dread-filled day. *Don't forget to put on slippers before you walk across the carpet,* he reminded himself, free-falling toward the dark bliss of unconsciousness. His palm tingled with the feel of the ivory as he passed through images jumbled like the shards of the computer: a small brown-and-white dog *(Couldn't be trusted. Not to bite.)* with its lips snarling back from snapping white teeth; the voice of Hal, the *2001* robot, slurring its protest as Dave disconnected its clever brain; a dying elephant, the one whose tusk had rampaged through a delicate machine, flailing its ears in outraged despair as the ivory-hunter's bullet drained the life from it; his own hand grasping the poker—he could feel it, his arm muscles stretching, fingers twitching where they lay on the pillow—then driving down, hard, smashing again and again *(Couldn't be trusted . . .)* upon the astonishingly fragile head of his father where it sat on the desk *(. . . Not to bite.)*.

The image of his father's shattering head startled him back from the brink of sleep. *No, that's not what I want. It was my fault; I didn't have to keep on and on.*

But he wanted me to, and he knew I would. He always knows, and there's something going on, and today was different.

But the bed's warmth tugged at him, and the images and sounds faded, and narrowed, and settled into a brief awareness that something had changed, that the evening's catharsis had broken more than the computer.

His last thought before sleep took him was bleak, yet it had a hot, angry spark at its core: *Everything I love dies. Everything, except Father.*

(Couldn't be trusted. Not to bite . . .)

BOOK ONE

Into the Green: Allen

Chapter 5

ALLEN LIKED VIETNAM AT FIRST SIGHT—NO, BE HONEST: HE LOVED IT. October 1967, and here he was, a middle-class white kid who'd never been out of the USA, in uniform, a man among men, rocking to the new Byrds album, sitting in an air-conditioned jet with a lot of other hungover new recruits, dropping from the cloud cover to reveal a great sweep of green such as even his childhood had not prepared him for, going back and back until the blue-green of the most distant reaches was indistinguishable from the sky. *Lush* was the word, he decided. As lush as a woman's body, and every bit as welcoming, and secretive. A man looked at that green spreading out into the distance, and he craved to enter it, at the same time knowing—and he'd be sure of this with one glance, even if he'd been shut in a cave his whole life and had never heard of the war—that some of the life-forms in that gorgeous lush greenness would kill a man soon as look at him.

Like some women.

Not that twenty-year-old Allen Carmichael had a whole lot of familiarity with the ways of women. Most of what he knew about the lush and mysterious side of the other half of the human race was theory gleaned from novels and locker-room talk, and from precisely five nights with Lisa before he shipped out. But it seemed right, and would last him until he had more real-life experience to replace it with.

By all accounts, this was just the place for real-life experience. Everyone knew that war made a man out of a boy. Always had.

The jetliner thudded down hard on the Saigon runway and the planeload of fresh-faced teenagers jostled and joked toward the exit. They took care, however, not to press too near the handful of men in the front seats who were returning to this place from medical or home leave, returning warriors in well-worn uniforms with medal ribbons on them, who ignored the boys' presence as completely as they had during the flight.

The warriors moved off, leaving the stewardess at the door to wish each new boy well, saying that she'd see them in a year. So eager were they all to see what lay on the other side of the exit door, not one of them looked past the short skirt and sexy makeup to notice that she did not meet their eyes when she said her cheery good-byes.

At the door, the heat slammed into them as if they had stepped into the world's largest steam bath, followed closely by the ungodly stench, an oily burning shit-smell that instantly made the eyes stream with disbelief. Allen gagged, swore, and the boy behind him nudged his arm to continue down the flight of steps. At the bottom, the heat beating off the softened tarmac was overwhelming, and as Allen shouldered his duffel and joined the olive-green ant-stream flowing in the direction of the nearest shade, he wondered, for the first time, what the hell he was doing here.

The shadow of the metal-roofed shed made not the slightest difference to the heat; if anything, enclosing the beast made it seem all the more stifling. When Allen's eyes had adjusted to the dim light, he saw that the shed was already occupied by a crowd of dirty, motionless figures—soldiers, clearly, and all of them headed out, but they had none of the high spirits he would have expected from a load of men about to board a plane bound for soft beds and American hamburgers. Even those without bandages or crutches looked severely wounded, and all the eyes watched the scrubbed newcomers with a wariness beyond cynicism. One man seemed to meet and hold Allen's gaze, but Allen didn't think the man knew he was there.

The hot day gave an abrupt shiver, reminding Allen of stepping into the meat locker at the supermarket he'd worked in last summer; he looked away, and made an uneasy joke with the guy next to him.

A reassuringly abusive sergeant finally appeared to scream them onto a series of ancient Army buses with heavy wire screens instead of glass in the windows. Allen dropped to a worn bench beside his seat-mate of the flight out, a short, sturdy PFC named Ricardo Flores. They'd been in basic together, where Allen had taken one look at those green eyes in the brown face and remembered him from high school wrestling matches—although they had never gone up against each other, Flores being a bantam and Allen at the time hovering on the edge of heavyweight. As a kid and in basic, Ricardo had been known as Flowers. On the plane, he'd been dubbed Lucy—or rather, "Loo-Si!"—and it looked like it was going to stick.

"You should've told them your name was Rick, not Ricardo," Allen said now, as if they'd been discussing the topic, which they hadn't.

"Don't matter none, just so I don't have to wear the lipstick."

"Why do you suppose they put wire on the windows?" Allen wondered aloud, when the bus had rumbled into life and driven away from the resultant diesel cloud. "They think we came all this way just to jump out and go AWOL on the way in from the airstrip?"

"Jeez, look at them girls—jumping out's not such a bad idea." Flores stood to peer through the mesh at the two slim, swaying figures in long pale dresses and wide-brimmed hats, walking the garbage-strewn roadside in front of a row of shacks made of cardboard and reed.

"Only a midget like you could fit out the window," Allen retorted, although he too admired the women until they faded in the distance.

"The wire's to keep the locals from tossing a grenade in on top of us," contributed the guy behind them. "You know—our friendly allies."

"Great way to welcome troops who've come to fight your war for you," Allen said, then stuck his hand over the top of the seat. "Allen Carmichael."

"Tim Barker, they call me Dogs. And this is Nor Petersen. Short for Norvald, but call him Pete."

Handshakes all around. Dogs was small, dark, and muscular, and spoke with the nasal accent of Bobby Kennedy; Pete was a lanky, buck-toothed kid nearly as blond as an albino, his face studded with acne and freckles. He looked as if his hair should be tousled, with bits of hay in it, and his innocent blue eyes looked out from a face about twelve years old. Allen wondered if he was shaving yet; the others already called him Farmboy.

The bus came to a cluster of smoke-belching trucks in a sea of bicycles ridden by everyone from children to old women, half of whom had some enormous and precarious load strapped on as well. Buildings pressed in on them, signs and tacked-on extensions brushing the bus's mirrors, women in wide conical hats or precarious turbans squeezing matter-of-factly to the side, uniformed men with automatic weapons seemingly oblivious to anything but a potential threat, street merchants hawking everything from peanuts to plastic bowls. This seemed to be the Saigon equivalent of rush hour, and the buses slowed to a crawl, surrounded by *cling-clinging* bicycles, rattling Lambretta scooters, hooting trucks and cars, brightly painted buses with passengers perched on the roofs and hanging out the windows, and a pair of huge, black water buffalos prodded into movement by two diminutive girls. It was like going on a school field trip to another planet: the bus, the high spirits of the guys, the day-off feeling.

Allen gazed down at the entrancing cacophony, unaware of the sweat stinging his eyes, caught up in the sheer romance of the place. Pedestrians crowded the sides of the now-stationary bus; but for the wires, he could've reached out and touched their heads. One of the things they'd had drilled into them in basic was how you couldn't tell a civilian from a Viet Cong by looks, or even an NVA from the north. He hadn't really believed it until now. Watching a man push a bicycle heavily laden with unidentifiable boxes of goods into a narrow alleyway, a thought occurred to him.

"I suppose the bottom of the bus must be armored," he said to Flores. "I mean, a grenade under the floor could do as much damage as one tossed in a window."

Flores shook his head, no more well informed than anyone else within hearing, and looked apprehensively down on the crowds at their flanks.

The air stank, not the rank and cloying stink of the airport, but of diesel and excrement, punctuated from time to time by the most exotic cooking odors his nose had ever encountered, rich whiffs of hot peppers and exotic spices. Noise beat at him and the colors here seemed brighter; ancient and modern, peace and war jostled each other's elbows: elegant brick colonial buildings next to ramshackle constructions glued together of tin and scrap wood; banana trees waved lush wide plumes over concrete-block walls topped with vicious broken bottles; an old woman rode demurely in a rickshaw, aloof to the crowds pressing near her knees, while an identical old woman bent down beneath a bamboo pole with a basket of rice at each end, her feet doing quick small steps under the heavy load. A thousand-year-old man made of wrinkles and a rag, his few teeth black from betel, sat against a wall trying to sell three bananas; a bucketful of water flew from an upper window and splashed across the back of a foraging pig; a scooter putted by with a toddler perched on the front and a cage of chickens on the back; birds had built a nest on a bottle-shaped sign advertising Coca-Cola, making it look like the Coke was foaming over. A feast of the senses, a confusion to the mind. Allen wanted to stretch wide his arms and gather in every ounce of it. This was LIFE.

However, the Army decided to place LIFE on the shelf for a while. They were issued their jungle fatigues, but it was ten days before the last of them were processed and shipped out. They cooled their heels at the base in Bien Hoa, getting up basketball games or playing poker, submitting to lectures and inoculations, sitting around with beers at night to watch the fireworks display of distant battle over the horizon, champing at the bit. They even picked up garbage for a while, since the sergeant couldn't think of anything else to do with them.

Flores went first because, despite his stature, he'd trained to hump a radio and there was a platoon that badly needed an operator. Dogs and Pete went next, together to a platoon way up north near the DMZ. Finally, four days later, Allen was handed his orders; he was surprised to see it was the same company, just a different platoon.

"Why didn't they send me there three days ago when Dogs and Farmboy went?" he complained, although he knew enough about the Army now to figure it was just the usual inefficiency.

"Maybe they didn't need reinforcement three days ago," the bored sergeant said.

Allen opened his mouth to object, then closed it again before he could say something monumentally naive. Of course he was going to replace someone who'd been killed—or maybe just wounded. This was a war, stupid.

Sounded like there'd be action there, he told himself, and felt a peculiar flutter down in his gut where glee and apprehension mixed.

The Chinook flew north along the coast, Allen's face pressed to the small, cloudy window to stare at the countryside, intensely foreign and green, to which he would give the next year of his life. (Or even the life itself—but he wouldn't think about that.) They flew so long, it began to seem that they'd soon run out of country, then abruptly dropped out of the sky to land with a jolt that rattled Allen's bones. He hauled his duffel out into a land that was still hot as hell, still stank of burning shit barrels and jet fuel, but at least wasn't quite such a madhouse of men and machines. In fact, once Allen got away from the HQ, loaded down at last with weapons and gear, he thought the country really wasn't bad at all.

Five deuce-and-a-half transports left the command post in convoy, with Allen and all his equipment in the third along with two dozen or so other replacements. The guy next to him was completely stoned, oblivious to the billows of red dust pouring in the sides and back of the truck. Allen pulled his T-shirt over his face and coughed into its dusty dampness. The stoned guy didn't bother, and soon had what looked like red frost rimed on his eyelashes and tracks of blood-colored sweat dribbling down his face. Finally Allen had to speak.

"Why don't they take turns riding first?" he complained.

"'Cause they got the lunatics up front," the other guy said.

"No, I mean, couldn't we at least take turns having a breath of air?"

The stoned grunt reared back his head and struggled to focus on Allen's face. "You an FNG, ain't ya?" he asked, and began to giggle as if Red Skelton was standing in front of him.

"Yeah I'm new, what of it?"

"You *belong* up front, then, sweetie."

Finally, the soldier on the other side of the pothead leaned forward to put Allen out of his misery. "Lost fourteen men in one day last week. VC mines the road."

And the first truck in line . . . Allen felt like an idiot. "Right," he mumbled, and pulled the stifling T-shirt back up across his face.

The other guys had a good laugh.

Bravo Company was at home today, all three rifle platoons and their weapons teams occupying the company's Night Defensive Post instead of out on patrol. In the half-light of early evening the NDP was a sunbaked, half-bald hillock covered with sandbags and canvas, set off from the rice fields, noodle shops, and refugee shacks by a perimeter of concertina wire and guard posts: home for a hundred twenty-some frustrated, crazy-ass, armed-to-the-teeth teenagers and their not-much-older officers. Children wandered around on both sides of the wire, along with the dogs, pigs, and chickens. The place smelled like a urinal and sounded like an open-air rock and roll concert, but the company had been there for long enough that most of the men's hooches had some kind of scrounged material reinforcing their canvas roofs. The hooch someone pointed Allen to was not one of those, but at least its canvas was taut and whole. It was, however, empty. He let his rucksack slide to the ground between two empty "beds" made of C-ration cardboard with deflated air mattresses on top, took out his felt-tip pen to write his DEROS date ceremonially on the cover of his helmet, and went to see if he could find Dogs and Farmboy.

He tracked them down on the other side of the hillock, in a cluster of men bent over a borrowed mess pot filled with some kind of meal they were debating over. He walked up behind Dogs and said, "Hey."

Dogs craned up and gave him a grin, although he didn't stand up or introduce him around. "Hey, man. Didn't know you were coming here."

"Second Platoon," Allen informed him. Dogs nodded and turned to stir the pot with a wooden stick.

"How's it goin'?" Allen asked.

"Oh, you know."

Allen nodded himself, as if he did know, and since Dogs didn't seem interested in pursuing the conversation, he said hello to Pete. The farmboy too was taken up with the contents of the pot; Allen, feeling more like an intruder every moment, just stood back and watched them.

There was, he realized, some subtle difference in the two men he'd met on the bus in Saigon. It wasn't just the grubbiness of their fatigues or the scabbed scratches on both men's arms. It was something in their faces and in the way they held themselves.

"You seen some action?" he blurted out, then flushed with embarrassment.

Dogs shrugged, and glanced sideways at Pete. "Farmboy here killed himself a gook on his first patrol."

"Way to go, Pete!" Allen responded, although he wasn't at all sure this was the right answer. The blond boy himself looked, if anything, queasy at the memory, but Dogs didn't give his platoon-mate a chance to put his foot in it.

"Yeah, after chow we're gonna take the kid down to the camp, introduce him to one of the boom-boom girls."

At that, Pete turned bright red.

There was, however, no move to invite Allen's participation, either to the mess in the pot or to the evening's entertainment. After a minute, he said he'd better go find his squad.

"You do that, Carmichael," Dogs told him, not looking up. "See you 'round."

The message was clear: A man's platoon is his family, and Allen had better go find his own. So he did.

In spite of the awkward beginning, Allen quickly settled into the life of a grunt. The company's NDP was in a quiet zone, and for the next week the most exciting thing that happened was the VC who wandered through every other night to toss a grenade or two into their midst, making them all turn out and blaze away into the complacent darkness. A black trooper named Cooper broke his trigger finger catching a baseball, two other men were lifted out with high fevers, and a couple of others got so short they were sent to a bigger base to await the end of their year's service. Nobody liked to dangle a man in front of Fate when he only had a few weeks left on his helmet's calendar. Even a combat zone as quiet as this was no place for a soldier with a wakening sense of self-preservation. Short-timer's jitters made everyone in the vicinity nervous.

By week's end, Allen could have done with some jitters: He'd written a hundred letters home to Lisa, and thought he'd go nuts with boredom.

The lieutenant in command of Second Platoon was a Texan named Woolf, called The Wolf by his men. The nickname was appropriate, not only because of the man's oddly large incisors, but because he carried himself with a kind of lupine authority, quiet and with an element of native threat. He had a knack of slipping soundlessly in and among his men, and his commands were well-thought-out and never contested; Second Platoon, which on the day of Allen's arrival numbered twenty-nine men, felt secure under The Wolf's rule. Allen was well satisfied.

The leader of Delta Squad, on the other hand, was something of a washout, the kind of soldier who always managed to be behind a tent when volunteers were sought, who helped himself to the prime C-rations before the carton was dumped in front of the other men, and who was generally a pain in the ass to anyone who was interested in action. His name was Bird, and if they called him Birdman, it was not because he was a hard guy. Birdman was twenty-two, acted like Allen's prissy grandfather, and had sixty-eight days left on his tour.

Delta Squad now numbered eight. Chris Adamson was a blond surfer from San Diego with gold-rimmed granny glasses, facial hair so new he only had to shave every couple of weeks, a string of genuine San Francisco love beads, and an endless stash of high-grade pot. Theo "T-bone" Muller was the son of a German butcher from Pittsburgh whose bad acne vied with a perpetual sunburn for control of his face, and whose time in basic and two months in-country hadn't managed to wear the baby fat from his cheeks. Mouse Tobin was a very large, very black, nearly professional football player from Seattle. The three were roughly Allen's age, and none had more than a dozen weeks in-country, although the fourth man, Streak Rychenkow, was the squad's oldest at twenty-three, with five months in-country. The eponymous white patch in Streak's black hair was the source of a hundred explanatory tales from falling through a skylight during a burglary to an assault with a baseball bat—all good stories, but after the third version, Allen decided the truth had to be either too boring or too embarrassing to be told. Nobody was quite sure where Streak was from or what his family situation was, although his accent was Midwestern and he carried a picture of a woman with two small children with him wherever he went.

Hal Fields and Chuck Tjader were short-timers with less than six weeks to go. Allen watched the two covertly, wondering what he would look like when he had that much time crossed off the back of his helmet; these guys looked like anyone else, just a whole lot older. Hal talked incessantly about his recent R&R in Japan, how he was going to move there after DEROS; he had a small Japanese grammar book he was slowly working his way through; Chuck was too silent to get much out of, other than he missed his wife and sometimes dreamed about the Colorado mountains.

Allen got along with the rest of the squad well enough, considering he was the fucking new guy, the cherry, the fresh meat, so none of them was about to grant him any but the most grudging friendship until he'd proved he wasn't going to get himself—or them—killed by his incompetence. He kept his mouth shut, watched how the more experienced men acted, and couldn't wait for his first patrol out into all that green.

It was Hal who told him the reason for their extended leisure behind the wire: the delayed arrival of the company's new captain. However, like captains through the ages, no sooner had this one hit the ground than he had to establish himself in the eyes of his men and of his superiors. He arrived on a Tuesday afternoon; patrols into the green began again at dawn Wednesday.

Hueys dropped the platoon off on an LZ scarcely larger than the blades, men leaping for the ground the moment the skids touched down, spreading out and making for the safety of the trees. Allen came out of the machine on Streak's heels, moving awkwardly under all the equipment draped across his person—he felt weirdly like a football player who'd barreled through a crowded kitchen and come out with his pads and helmet dangling with cast-iron pots and rattling utensils.

The Huey pulled pitch, tipped its tail and lifted off; the *whup whup* of the blades faded, and for the first time Allen heard the breath of the living jungle.

It was big. He hadn't expected that, since he'd spent a lot of hours in the woods as a kid, both in the islands and on the mainland, but this was like no woods he'd ever met. It was a living thing, this jungle, huge and aware and unfriendly, like a grizzly with a toothache. The only place he'd ever felt remotely like this was in the Olympic peninsula rain forest, an ancient place of dripping trees, muted sounds, and vague menace, but this was far, far stronger. It made him feel very small and very vulnerable.

He didn't hear The Wolf's order to move off, but Streak bumped against him in passing and he automatically fell in behind the man, trying to rearrange his grenades and the belt of M60 ammo he carried so they didn't bump or chafe. They pushed into the thick bush, unable to see more than a few feet ahead of them; Allen cradled his M16 to his chest and tried to keep Streak's helmet cover in sight. It had written on it BORN TO DIE, in a sort of Olde English script. Mouse had on his the simple BLACK POWER, and Chris, not the expected Beach Boys, but rather a lopsided skull with GRATEFUL DEAD underneath. T-Bone's held the long-winded statement that Allen had seen on a couple of T-shirts: *Yea though I walk through the Valley of Death, I shall fear no evil, for I am the meanest son of a bitch in the Valley.* The butcher's boy had written it in a spiral out from the helmet's top, and the spare magazine and cigarettes in the band obscured some of the words, but Allen appreciated the bravado.

He kept his thumb near the safety of the M16, breathing in the reassuring smell of fresh gun oil over the rich organic smells of the jungle. His head kept swiveling around: Did VC ever climb trees to take potshots at passing GIs? How the hell could the man walking point watch for booby traps in this? And if someone started shooting up ahead, should he throw himself on the ground so the guy in back of him didn't blow his head off?

After a couple hours, when they'd covered maybe two klicks and driven off every form of life in the whole area, The Wolf called a halt and they dropped down for a smoke and to suck hot water out of their canteens.

Allen plopped onto a log next to T-bone, who had been the new guy until Allen arrived, and said, "Jesus, we could be ten feet from an NVA battalion marching three abreast down the Ho Chi Minh Trail, and we'd never know it until they opened up on us."

"That's why we've got Intel, man," T-bone said.

A man needed faith, Allen reflected, and pawed through his pack to see if perhaps he'd overlooked a can of peaches, or if the dread lima-beans-and-ham C-ration that was left behind for the new guy had somehow transformed itself into fruit cocktail. It hadn't, and he raised the warm canteen to his mouth for another pull of plastic- and iodine-flavored water. One swallow went down his throat, and then the world exploded in a huge *bang* and a gush of wet. Allen flew backward off the log, certain he'd been shot through the head. The rest of the platoon dove for anything resembling cover and started firing on full automatic into the surrounding greenery. It took half a minute before the lieutenant's voice penetrated the panic.

"Cease fire, you idiots!" he bellowed. "Who's hit? And where'd it come from?"

"Me," Allen said, and then took his hand from his soaked face and blinked: There was no red on his fingers, no red at all. "I think."

"Jesus Christ, are you wounded or not?"

"Well, I thought I was, but—oh yeah." Allen found blood at last, a faint smear on his fingertips from high on his forehead. "No, it's nothing. I guess it just hit my canteen."

"Jesus, kid, you're one lucky son of a bitch," came a voice from behind a tree. Allen felt a wail of panic pushing to get out, although it was a bit late for that.

"Where'd it come from?" The Wolf persisted.

"How the fuck would I know? Sir."

"Think, damn it. There's not much point in chopping down trees with bullets."

"Uh, maybe over there? I mean, that hill at one o'clock. I think."

Not that he could be sure, since all he'd known was an explosion two inches from his nose, but the lieutenant called for a few shells in that direction. In a minute, the hill ahead of them spouted flames, just like a war movie except that the ground shifted and rolled underneath them. The men regrouped in the trees, passing around Allen's shattered canteen and agreeing that Carmichael was one damned lucky bastard. Not one of them had to say what a hole you could push your thumb through would have done had it been two inches lower.

The rest of the day, the world seemed to Allen a place of extraordinarily vivid colors and noises. He kept finding his fingers creeping compulsively back to the tiny nick at his hairline, and each time he would feel shivery in the heat. Some man out there had wanted to kill him, had actually wanted him—*him!*—dead. The anonymity of "them" had dried up faster than the canteen water on his fatigues; some human being out there had aimed his sights at Allen Carmichael as if he'd been a rabbit in the lettuce, aimed, and pulled the trigger. Suddenly the war was no longer an impersonal adventure. It was a scary thing in a big jungle.

But after the bullet, nobody called Allen the fuckin' new guy, not in his hearing.

Chapter 6

THE PLATOON WENT THE REST OF THAT DAY WITHOUT SEEING SIGN OF ANY living creature at all apart from bugs, birds, and a handful of mildewing deer droppings. The scattered gray pellets struck Allen as the most bizarre thing he'd seen all day: What the hell was a deer doing walking around in a place where men were trying to murder one another?

They reached the LZ that evening without incident and lifted out cleanly. Hot food waited for them at the company NDP, and a joint from Chris's bottomless stash, and after Streak had given them yet another story about his white patch, this one involving a jealous husband and a crystal vase full of tulips snatched up from a piano, they settled into their sleeping rolls.

Until around midnight. As if the bullet through Allen's canteen had been a shot across the bow of their little ship in the jungle, the cannonade began in earnest. Allen was wakened by a sudden convulsion of movement all around him and the shouts of "Incoming!" He fought his way out of the poncho liner and was reaching for his M16 when the earth roared and debris rained down on their hooch.

He scooped up his helmet, stepped into his boots, and ran to join the others.

"What the hell's happening?" he shouted at the figure beside him in the firing hole.

"They're coming through the wire, probably sent the mortar in to distract us," answered the voice. Allen hadn't the faintest idea who his neighbor was, just hunkered down behind the sandbags and thumbed his safety to full auto.

Thirty seconds after the first mortar, the bullets started coming, the clatter of AK47s providing background to the *zip zip whizzipzipzip* of incoming bullets, then WHOMP! and with a *takatakataka* the squad's M60 was in play, spewing ten rounds a second into the dark. In a minute flat the company was in full battle mode, with grenades and tracer bullets and the roar of what could have been a hundred machine guns, so enormous was the noise. Allen thought his heart would beat itself right out of his mouth—he could feel it even over the jerk of the gun in his arms. His senses were filled with a fury of sound so great, it transformed itself into a huge and echoing silence populated by slow-motion soldiers, incomprehensible flashes of light, and the bucking object against his shoulder, all of which seemed to have less to do with an act of war than with a hallucinogenic experience. Parachute flares transformed the landscape into a lunar expanse of bare ground and confusing motion. Was that black shape down there a VC or a member of the listening post? Was that bouncing shadow a thrown grenade or a panicked rat? Did it matter?

An hour passed like a moment, or like a month, and suddenly someone was pounding Allen on the helmet and shouting that he should cease fire. The shooting died away, and a lesser silence of groans and curses rose up. Allen fumbled to get his gun safety on with strangely unresponsive fingers; he didn't know if he felt like throwing up or standing and whooping. But he did know why it was called a baptism by fire: He'd been scoured inside and out, and was not the same person he'd been when the sun went down.

When Delta Squad reassembled itself, there were two wounds among the eight of them: Chris had a small chunk bitten out of his arm by a piece of flying shrapnel, and T-bone had sliced his foot open racing out of the hooch bootless.

Back in his sleeping roll an hour later, with dawn coming on and his heart still jumping while all his companions snored, Allen decided that the main difference between old-timers and new guys was, they knew how to sleep in a fire zone.

In the morning, one body lay in the wire, although there were signs that three or four more had been dragged, or dragged themselves, away. Of Bravo Company, there were two body bags, four wounded medevacked out, and half a dozen more treated for minor wounds. The raid had begun with the shell, but the real attack had been carried out by men crawling through the wire and tossing grenades into the foxholes nearest the wire. They had then faded away into the darkness, but for the man left behind.

Allen stood with his rifle tucked under his arm and tried not to look at the two anonymous shapes swaddled in green plastic at the LZ. Instead, he watched the captain and sergeant going through the pockets of the black-clad man. Or rather, boy: The enemy soldier looked about the age of Allen's kid brother Jerry.

Streak, standing next to him, pointed out that the kid wore the tire-soled sandals and buzz cut of the NVA.

"Not just VC, huh?"

"Nope. There's been rumors that an NVA battalion is moving in. Guess it's here. We'll see a lot more action than we've been doing."

Twenty-four hours earlier, Allen's response to that would have been one of uncomplicated approval, but now? After having his canteen shot away from his lips, then spending the night firing madly at ghosts, with a pair of anonymous green bags haunting the edges of his vision? Now he wasn't so sure.

They dragged the boy's body to a shell hole outside the perimeter and shoveled some dirt in on top of it. No one suggested that they put up a grave marker.

THE PLATOON WENT OUT AGAIN, PART OF A SWEEP IN THE DIRECTION OF A suspected VC stronghold. Allen stuck close to Streak, emulating the older man's movements and trying to figure out why he did things one way and not the other, looking wherever Streak's attention went, even though most of the time he couldn't see anything there. They walked without attracting fire, but when they got to the ville there was no one home; the cook-fires were smoking and a bowl of warm food sat on the packed-earth floor of one of the hooches, but they were greeted only by dogs and ducks. They searched the hooches for bunkers, finding two or three with small quantities of rice and a handful of U.S. Army C-rations, but the stores were not sufficient for a group of soldiers, and did not justify torching the village. The Wolf ordered them to blow the largest bunker, and while the troops sat having a smoke, the sappers laid a C4 charge and turned the hooch into a cloud of sticks and straw.

As a military response to the previous night's barrage, it left something to be desired.

The terrain opened up somewhat as they went on, through harvested paddies bristling with stubble, and small villages with duck ponds and banana trees. They spent the night in the bush—calling in marking rounds to form a perimeter, digging in through the sandy soil, setting up trip flares and Claymores. (These bore the helpful label *This side toward enemy*, a reminder that trip wires worked both ways, which nonetheless always struck Allen as comical.) Allen crouched in the black night, twitching at every jungle sound, feeling like a very small and timid rabbit cowering in his burrow, all ears and nerves.

In the bush, at night, Charlie was the predator.

The long hours crept past. Dawn edged into the sky, birds sang, cramped men stood up, pissed, and packed away their Claymores. A resupply chopper racketed in to drop them food and water, then the platoons split and continued on. Late in the afternoon they came to a ville of twenty hooches, one of which concealed a bunker stacked with big earthenware jars. The rice jars were hauled to the center of the ville, smashed, and set afire, the villagers looking on in silence. Allen wondered if the farmers hadn't just lost their year's entire crop, but The Wolf seemed to think there was too much rice for this small a ville, and he should know. They did some spot interrogations, had a few of the villagers lifted out for further questioning, and three hours later reached the appointed LZ to be taken out themselves. The patrol was judged a success.

After eating a well-earned hot meal, Allen carried his ration of beer to where Chris and Mouse sat with their backs against a small mountain of C-ration cartons. The sweet smell of Chris's joint joined the perpetual odors of urine and dust, frying onions from the cook house, and Vietnamese food from the other side of the wire, with the primal whiff of the jungle beyond. Allen opened the first can and took a mouthful of the soapy brew, feeling the tightness of his shoulders relax a fraction. The other men talked desultorily about the inferior weed in the States and the chicks in San Diego, until Allen sat up abruptly and asked, "Who was that?"

Chris was too stoned to bother opening his eyes, but Mouse had noticed the peculiar figure pass.

"That's the Snakeman," he answered. "Dude's a Lurp with the First

Cav, least they say he started out that way, but now he just kinda runs his own war, 'ports in when he has something to say, otherwise you don't see him for weeks, months even. I don't know if the Snakeman's even officially here anymore. That dude's gone bush in a major way."

The Lurps—Long Range Patrol—walked with impunity through countryside where Victor Charlie ruled supreme. They had their own way of doing things, as deep-ranging scouts always have done, but the stories Allen had heard about them always seemed to him apocryphal. Seeing the figure gliding across the compound toward the captain's tent, he wondered.

He shifted his seat so as to watch the place where the stranger had disappeared, and an hour or so later saw him emerge, making in the direction of the mess tent. The stoves were long since shut down for the night, but somehow Allen was not surprised to see activity, when he wandered up casually a couple minutes later. No cold C-rations for the Snakeman.

The man was wearing an ARVN tiger suit permeated by the red earth of the country, a brass Montagnard bracelet on his right wrist, and elaborate tattoos spiraling around both upper arms (a pair of dragons, Allen decided, although their legs were so vestigial they looked more like snakes). The stranger had shed his pack somewhere, but he still wore two bandoliers, various kinds of grenades and flares, a Bowie knife strapped to his leg, with an enemy's folding-stock AK47 on the table near his hand. His ancient bush hat was the color of the soil, his face had worn camouflage paint (or maybe just dirt) so long it had seeped into his pores, and he smelled like something dug up from the ground, strong but not unpleasant. The twin plaits of his hair were longer than most hippies wore back home, but no proponent of peace and free love had ever gazed on the world out of eyes like those. The Snakeman sat with his back to the sandbag-reinforced wall, watching Allen's approach from beneath half-lowered lids.

"Evenin'," Allen said, trying for cool.

"What do you want?"

"I'm Allen Carmichael," he said, holding out his hand. The Snakeman looked at it, then picked up his fork for the plate the cook put down in front of him. It was piled high with beans, rice, and some green vegetable that looked like spinach and had not been on the camp's menu that evening; a second plate held an entire loaf of sliced bread with pots of butter and jam. No meat, which struck Allen as strange; surely if the man was important enough to have the kitchen open for him, he ought to qualify for better than beans.

Allen retracted his unshaken hand and thrust it into the cargo pocket of his fatigues. The man's fist tightened around his fork as he watched Allen's hand; when it came out with nothing more lethal than the second half of Allen's beer ration, he resumed eating. Allen placed the can and an opener on the table, then retreated a step.

"Thought you might like a beer to wash that down," he told the man.

"Why, you underage?" The Snakeman's voice sounded rough, either from an injury or through disuse.

"Not here. You a vegetarian?"

To his surprise, Allen got an answer. "When I'm heading back out, yeah. Meat comes out the skin, they smell you coming."

"*Smell* you? Jeez, we had a dead NVA on our wire the other night, he stank like hell. How can they smell it when you eat a little meat?"

"People smell like what they eat. The Cong eat different from us—spices and shit. You don't want them to smell you, 'a course you don't slop insect repellent all over and you don't smoke American cigarettes. And you either eat their shit to smell like they do, or you eat vegetables to smell like the woods. Their food gives me gas." He went back to the food that would make him smell like the woods.

"How long have you been here?"

The fork stopped in mid-air. "Look, you want to talk, or can I eat first?"

The "first" was encouraging. Allen sat down at the next table, to give the Snakeman some distance, and looked out into the night. The cook brought the pan of beans over to slop out a second helping, the bread and butter disappeared with the better part of a pot of jam going onto the later slices as dessert, and finally the plate was pushed away, the last of the warm beer savored as if it were a fine Bordeaux. The Snakeman belched delicately.

"Got any smokes?" he asked.

Allen moved to sit across from the man, placing a pack on the table, along with the silver Zippo lighter Jerry had given him for his birthday before he shipped out. The man fitted a cigarette to his lips and lit it, then tucked the rest of the pack into his shirt pocket. The man's black-grimed thumb ran across the lettering on the side of the lighter: TO ALLEN FROM HIS BROTHER JERRY; Allen braced himself, half expecting to see the Zippo follow the cigarettes, but the stranger kindly laid it back on the table for its owner to retrieve.

"You wanted something?" the braided Lurp asked.

"You been here a long time, I'd guess. I've been in the bush about two days. I just thought I could learn something from you."

"Like what?"

"Like anything. I look at the jungle and I don't know . . ."

"You don't know shit," Snakeman finished for him.

"I was going to say, 'I don't know enough to know what it is I'm ignorant of,' or maybe, 'I don't even know what I'm seeing,' but yeah, I guess what it boils down to is, I don't know shit."

"Well hell, at least you admit it."

"So," said Allen, feeling monumentally stupid and definitely uncool, "you have any words of wisdom for a fuckin' new guy?"

The Snakeman studied him for a long minute, either putting together a response or, more likely, trying to decide if the FNG before him had sufficient potential as a student, and consequently as a survivor, for him to bother answering. Allen felt like he was having his fortune read.

Finally, the man spoke. "Okay, here it is: Never go through an open gate. In the wet, it's better to do without socks. Keep your eyes on the ground and your ears in the air. And remember, never trust a kid. Even the babies'll kill you soon as piss on you." With that, the sage of the jungle rose, picked up his rifle, and walked out of the mess tent.

As he stood up, his shirt fell open, revealing a length of black twine threaded through many leathery scraps.

Back at the squad, Allen found Chris flat on his back snoring and Mouse playing poker with Streak and Hal over an upturned C-ration carton.

"Got a new friend there, Lucky?" Mouse asked him.

"Jeez," Allen said. "That guy's definitely been in the woods too long. He's got a necklace of ears, for Christ sake."

"Half the grunts I know collect ears," Hal said, amused at the repulsion in the new guy's voice. "Other platoons, 'a course—The Wolf doesn't like it."

"That's just sick," Allen said.

"Wait'll you've been here a couple months," Streak commented. "It'll seem pretty tame."

"Do you have any ears?" Allen demanded, and immediately wished he could retract the question. Streak, however, seemed unoffended.

"I don't, no, but you see Charlie kill enough of your guys, maybe a few ears seem like the least you can do. Like the First Cav leaving a playing card on their kill sites as a message to the Cong. An ace of spades."

Mouse looked up from his cards. "Always wondered, how they do that?"

"Well, they shoot the guy and then stuff the card in his mouth."

"No, I mean, how they come up with that many ace of spades? They buy 'em by the deck? Or does the whole First Cav play with fifty-one-card decks? Seems to me kinda impractical—unless you don't got a lot of dead bodies. Maybe that's it. Message like that would sort of depend on not having a very high body count. I can see where ears'd be better."

"What I'd like to know is," Hal interjected, "how do you keep the ears from rotting? Everything rots in two seconds here, 'specially when the rains come. Leather, canvas, armpits, you name it."

Human beings, thought Allen. *A man's soul.*

"Maybe they smoke them, over a fire," Streak suggested.

"Could be they use some kinda curing stuff," Mouse volunteered. "Had this crazy uncle once, went out and shot him a deer—well, said he shot it, but I always figured he scraped it off the side of the road somewhere. Anyways, he took the thing to a taxidermy I think it was, had it stuffed, these glass eyes and ever'thin', put the fuckin' animal in his front room. But the taxi guy did a shit job on it, began to stink, my aunt made him put it out on the front porch. Neighbor kids were pretty hard on it, I have to say."

"Shit," Allen burst out, "what the hell is with you guys? These are human ears we're talking about."

"No they're not," Streak objected. "They're gook ears."

"I don't care. Can you imagine taking them home to your mother?"

"I can't imagine taking *me* home to my mother," Streak answered coldly. He dropped his cards onto the box table and walked off.

Chapter 7

SECOND PLATOON WENT OUT THE NEXT DAY, AND THE DAY AFTER THAT, AND for many days thereafter. Chuck got short and lifted out; Hal, only two days behind Chuck, wavered and finally signed up for another tour. They had two solid days of rain, and overnight, the company's hill took on the consistency and odor of a monumental cow pat.

Patrols now rarely went without some sign of the enemy: a bullet out of the heavens, the odd booby trap, once a patch of pungi-sticks stretched across a faint path, serving to keep their eyes stretched and their spines crawling. The night assaults continued, with the artillery response screaming out of the east and hammering the darkness with explosions.

Boredom and terror: A mortar came through the roof of the next hooch over one night, killing one man and tearing up two others; the next day, a careless jungle boot triggered a mine, taking off the offending leg and peppering five men with shrapnel and gore, the point man dying before the chopper could get him. Half the platoon went down with dysentery after filling their canteens in a creek, and through it all, Allen went unscathed, but for the sucker marks of leeches and the tiny nick on his forehead.

He grew used to the jungle and its noises and rhythms. He no longer had to think about where to put his feet, no longer looked around to see where his companions were. As the hours he spent in the green turned into days, then weeks, he felt as if he was developing another sense, a feeling that, even if he closed his eyes and stopped up his ears, he'd be able to find his way around.

Three weeks in, approaching a ville on a search-and-destroy, Allen's squad had the point position. There was no sign of life in the hooches ahead, although they had seen some figures working in the paddies as they walked up the valley, and Mouse, who was point man, headed for an inviting break in the wobbly fence.

"Wait!" Allen shouted urgently. The Snakeman's voice: *Never go through an open gate.* "Hold on, there could be a booby trap."

Mouse glanced at him as if he was nuts, because Allen had been too far back to see any trip wire unless it came with a painted sign and an arrow, but he stopped short and examined the ground. Allen came up beside him, and they were joined by T-bone and Chris, incongruously sharp-eyed when he had his glasses on and when he wasn't stoned.

"Shit," Chris said. "He's right. Look at that kind of a twig there. That could be . . ."

Birdman went back to report the possible trap to the lieutenant, and in a short time The Wolf was there with what he called his blow-'em-up team. The twig was, in fact, attached to an enormous mine, made from an unexploded American shell wrapped in C4. Had Mouse gone through the gate, the entire squad would have been vaporized.

"Good work, Private," Woolf said. "What's your name?"

"Carmichael, sir," Allen answered.

The Wolf nodded and went back to the operation. Chris nudged Allen in the ribs. "Sir. Sir."

"Yeah I know. What can I say? The Wolf brings out the kid in me." In fact, Woolf was the only lieutenant Allen knew who seemed to require the honorific.

"You sure enough are a lucky bastard, Carmichael. How'd you know that was gonna be there?" Mouse asked him.

"I keep my ears open when people tell me things."

"Well, you go on ahead keeping them ears of yours open. In the meantime, can I hold your hand when we walking patrol, huh?"

"Yeah," T-bone chimed in, "maybe sleep curled up next to you?"

But Allen didn't feel like a lucky bastard—he was in Vietnam, wasn't he? Besides, talking about luck invited its opposite.

FIVE WEEKS, SIX. THE COMPANY MOVED FROM ITS HILLOCK TO A DEFENSE post in the woods. It hadn't rained in weeks, but no sooner had they hacked their holes into the solid earth than the sky opened up. Leather mildewed in hours, pack straps rotted, boots fell apart mid-patrol, and ponchos developed diabolical leaks into sodden flak jackets. Allen took to leaving his socks in his pack—the Snakeman was right: Bare boots gave a grunt fewer blisters than wet wool.

Seven weeks. The rains came and went, the platoon lifted out for a few days in the bush: C-rats, skirmishes, the same old shit. The zip of bullets and the cries of "Incoming!"; in the morning the rise of mede-vacs heavy with stretchers and body bags; in the evening came the choppers bearing food, water, bullets, and new faces with clean uni-forms and jumpy trigger fingers, all the supplies necessary for the busi-ness of war. Then back to the NDP for one night or four, gaunt with sleeplessness and stinking to high heaven, to fall on the hot food and warm beer. Chris got his second Purple Heart—a pungi-stick through the side of his boot—and was shipped out to the hospital, but it didn't infect, which meant that the stake's layer of shit had been washed clean by the rain, and he was back in a week. One of the FNGs shipped in to boost their numbers, a complete virgin on his first day in the bush, caught a bullet in the spine before the sun went down.

They killed Cong and NVA and a handful of peasants who were probably just doing their job on the land but got unlucky. Allen felt bad about them, but what could he do? The first time he objected, the oth-ers razzed him—and they were right, it was naive to fret over civilian casualties in a war zone. The next day Birdman brought down an old man in a field; Allen turned his back. As he did at the episodes of grunt humor, like when four VC sheltering in a bomb-hole met a grenade, and the next morning some of the grunts posed the stiff corpses with cigarettes in their dead lips and C-rat can teacups clasped in their rigid fingers, to take Instamatic snapshots of the kill.

The patrols, company-sized, full-platoon, or one squad at a time, baked and sweated and humped their way through dripping jungle, reeking paddies, and mountain paths, in no particular direction but out and back. The new guys grew frightened, then tired, and finally thin and hard. The days and the kills began to blur together, until even the DEROS date on their helmets didn't mean shit. Just keep moving, that was all.

Even Thanksgiving, back at the muddy hillock, did not manage to strip away the lethargy Allen had drawn over himself. The slabs of turkey and watery tinned cranberry sauce the cook dished out were almost worse than if he'd stuck to beef stew. For a moment, when the mass-produced pumpkin pie was set before him, Allen was with his family the year before, home from college in a kitchen fragrant with spice, his twelve-year-old brother Jerry winning a bet by eating one of their Aunt Midge's three-inch-thick pies single-handed—after a full dinner. Laughter, fragrance, disbelief—and then Allen was back in a mess tent in Vietnam, gazing down at the taunting reminder of The World. He pushed the tired object over to Mouse and went to swipe a joint from Chris's stash.

Chris came back from his hospital rest with a new string of love beads, a fresh supply of hugely potent weed, and a lot of far-fetched stories about the hospital nurses. One evening, a week or so before Christmas, Allen was sitting beside him as they stirred their C-rats over the heat tabs and waited for night.

"Chris, you know the funny thing about this war?"

Chris snorted. "Whoa, man, don't get me started."

"Well, yeah. But really. Wars are supposed to have some kind of strategy—you know, push the line forward, take that hill, drive the enemy back. But here, what've we got? What the fuck are we after? Do you have any idea? I mean, look at what we do here: We go out, we bump around in the trees looking for people who've got nothing to do with us, and try to kill them before they spot us. Then we count up the bodies and hotfoot it away again before their big brother comes along and pounds the shit out of us. There's no front line, just hills we borrow for a while and stick an NDP on top of so we can hide behind the wire, and hell, half the time the enemy's some poor bastard who's just trying to grow enough rice to keep his kids from starving. I mean, correct me if I'm wrong, but doesn't this whole thing seem just a little fucked to you?"

Streak had been listening to Allen's tirade and started to crow with laughter. "Hey, headline in the *Stars and Stripes:* 'Carmichael Declares, War Is Fucked.' "

"Maybe Westmoreland'd read it," T-bone sniggered. "Spray-paint us a nice front line down the trees."

"Jesus, Carmichael, you've been here, what, going on three months now, and you're just discovering how completely shit-faced this war is?"

"I always was a slow learner, okay? But I mean it. The whole thing's like some kind of lethal kids' game, like—I don't know, musical chairs played with toe-poppers. I mean, I know the guy on the ground never has much of a clue on what the generals are doing, but I can't help thinking that if we'd carried on like this in the Second World War, we'd have an Emperor of California and a Führer of New York."

Mouse protested. "Maybe we only get one or two KIAs each patrol, but how many patrols the Army runnin', huh? Look at the body count, man."

"And what the hell's that mean?" Allen retorted. "You know damn well that hundred-year-old *mamasan* Birdman wasted last week got tallied as VC, and probably got bumped up to three NVA by the time Washington added up the numbers. Hell, they probably tally the dead pigs and water buffalo, too."

" 'If it's brown and it's down, it's VC,' " chanted Chris.

"Damn straight they count the pigs, man," Streak said. "Those animals are dangerous."

"Body count," Allen spat out, jabbing at the beans in his can with the plastic spoon. "How the fuck can you run a war when the only thing you're interested in is a body count? How long is it going to take us to kill off the country at this rate? Maybe we ought to just dump poison in all the wells and we can go home."

"Tell you straight, Carmichael my man, you oughta run for general," Mouse said. "You got my vote. 'Til then, you got any of that Tabasco sauce left?"

Allen subsided, although the whole idea of war by numbers still seemed to him insane, and basically as repugnant as napalming civilians or taking ears. With time, however, the methods of war-making would become so familiar he no longer questioned them, just kept on keeping on.

But the reasons behind collecting ears: Those were to become a lot clearer on his very next venture out into the bush.

Chapter 8

A REPORT CAME IN DURING THE NIGHT THAT THE VC HAD BURNED A village ten miles north. Instead of being lifted in, however, the company was to split up and sweep in that direction, in the hopes that they might meet the enemy on its way south. So off they humped along the paddy dikes, the sun sucking clouds of moisture from the earth and using it to beat into stupidity the humans below, silent but for the occasional cursing stumble into the knee-deep muck.

Just before noon a heavy tree line began to close in on Second Platoon's right hand; any troop with more than a couple weeks' experience in the bush crept out from under his heat stupor and began to eye the approaching trees warily. Sure enough, the staccato burst of AK47 fire came just as the platoon was straggling out of the dike system. Men splashed belly-down into the mud and returned fire over the paddy walls; the crack of the rifles was punctuated by the *spat spat* of bullets hitting the muck. Two men were hit before the artillery responded to The Wolf's call for a strike on the offending clump of brush. The shells came in, sending a miniature tidal wave through the paddy mud. The men waited through ten minutes of silence before scraping off the thick ooze and going up to check the sniper's site. They found only shell casings and a spider hole in the ground, so they tossed a grenade down it and then looked in, but it was empty. The medevac came for one man, the medic patched up the other wounded, and on they went.

A mile later another AK47 opened up on them, and they jumped for cover again. Another artillery strike, another empty spider hole; the only difference was, this time they picked themselves up unwounded.

The third time it happened they were spread out across a hillside of derelict terraces. Allen dove into what looked like a bomb crater but turned out to be the other half of a terrace wall, crumbling with disrepair but still running all the way to the tree line. He ventured a glance across the stones to the other end of the terrace, where he saw the Birdman ripping open someone's blood-soaked bootlaces with the point of his bayonet, cursing in chorus with the owner of the boot.

"Who's that?" Allen called across the break.

"Hal," he said, without looking up.

"Shit, man, sorry. Look, is the lieutenant there? I need to talk with him."

"We're kind of busy over here, Carmichael, case you hadn't noticed."

"Bird, I need to talk to him. Tell him I think I can get a line on the shooter."

Birdman said something over his shoulder, and in a moment Lieutenant Woolf was on the other side of the gap.

"Loot, we've got a clear line down here to the trees. We can circle around and be waiting for him when he tries to get away."

"Let the artillery do its job, Carmichael."

"They've missed him twice already," Allen pointed out.

The Wolf thought for a minute, then nodded. "Worth a try. But he's not going to hang around waiting, so we'll send him a mad minute in three, aiming to the right. See how close you can get by then."

"Just, uh, make sure the guys know that we're out there." Allen saw the lack of expression in his lieutenant's face, and knew he'd just put his foot in it. "Sorry."

"Go."

Allen gathered his squad-mates ahead of him, carrying only rifles as they crouch-ran along the lee of the terrace wall. Once among the trees, they scrambled uphill until they were even with the sniper, still invisible among a pile of rocks. Without thinking, Allen put up his hand, but no one argued with his assumption of command.

"Somebody should take a position here, in case he comes straight over. Chris?" The surfer dude was never very determined when it came to actually killing the enemy, even when he wasn't stoned; sitting and waiting was about his speed.

"Fine, man."

"Keep your head down. And for God's sake, if you shoot, watch you don't hit us."

T-bone, Mouse, Streak, and Allen continued through the undergrowth. Halfway up the hill, Mouse and T-bone dropped off. Allen and Streak were twenty yards from the pair of trees that they'd decided was their goal when the platoon opened up; with a wall of noise, bullets spat a cloud of dust on the far side of the two trees. It was their bad luck that the sniper was bright—or experienced—enough to know in an instant that there was only one reason the GIs would be firing to one side of his location.

The black-clad figure broke from the trees, sprinting directly into the hail of mis-aimed fire. Before Allen or Streak could get their sights on him, the man tumbled to the ground, then rolled, shot to his feet, and dove into a clump of bamboo. Streak snatched at a smoke flare to signal the platoon to stop shooting, but when they reached the bamboo, the sniper had vanished. The only trace of their man was a smear of blood the shape of a small hand; it looked like some child's fingerpainting experiment.

Streak slung his rifle over his shoulder and shook his head. "I was beginning to think the little fucker was a ghost."

"Well, this ghost bleeds."

"Want to go after him?"

The two young men gazed without enthusiasm at the wall of green that had swallowed up the pajama-clad sniper. "Maybe we should ask The Wolf."

But Lieutenant Woolf said no, they'd wasted enough time, they had to be at the burned ville by nightfall. The medevac was on its way, they'd be off as soon as Hal was gone. One glance at their mate's shredded ankle, they all knew that Hal was back to The World.

Their bleeding ghost, however, either hadn't been seriously hit or else had brothers. They met the first one less than a mile up the trail. This time the artillery response was successful, although the sniper's body was so torn up, they couldn't tell if it was the one they'd winged. They searched the man's single surviving pocket, tossed a fragmentation grenade into his hole, and found neither cached weapons nor additional VC. They left his remains where they lay.

Twice more that day they came under fire. Once they responded with their M16s and a few LAWs, the second time they were close enough to heavy tree growth to break for cover. Running left a lousy taste in their mouths, since by this time most of them were so fed up, they would have happily gone after the bastard with their bare hands, but the lieutenant said to leave him, so they did. The whole day had been as maddening as mosquitoes in Alaska.

"You think Charlie gets as pissed off when we won't stand and fight as we do when he *didi*s away?" Allen speculated aloud.

"Shit no, man, Charlie's the ghost. He don't get mad, he gets even."

They eventually reached the ville, a burned-out and stinking wasteland with the skeletons of hooches teetering over piles of swollen corpses with four and two legs. Nine children, thirteen women and old men, an uncounted number of dogs and pigs—all had been shot, many with a single bullet in the head, at least two days before. The stench was ungodly.

"Ah, ain't that the shits," Mouse drawled. "Now we're gonna have to clear another damn position."

Allen grunted in agreement, then started to chuckle. The rest of his squad stared at him in disbelief, which made it all the funnier. He giggled until the tears came.

"The fuck?" Mouse demanded.

"Ah hell, man," Allen finally got out, "listen to yourself. We're knee-deep in corpses with the snipers closing in on us, and you're bitching because we have to go down the road to dig in."

"Hell yes, I'm bitching," the indignant PFC retorted. "If Charlie hadn'ta shot all them damn pigs, we coulda had fresh pork chops for dinner."

They dug in, spending a restless sleep punctuated every thirty to ninety minutes by one sort of attack or another. The company's first platoon, dug in a couple of miles off, got it about eleven o'clock, and Second lay listening to the thumps carried by ground and air, hearing the frantic radio noises, seeing the flashes of illumination rounds and mortar fire as their company brothers fought for their lives. It was a relief to them all when the sky lit up with the distant artillery wading in; after that Fourth of July display, things quieted down.

At dawn, Charlie subsided back into the hills, leaving the daylight to the foreign invaders. Unslept and edgy, the platoon prepared to move out.

But not toward extraction. The Powers on High had come to realize that the amount of activity in the area meant something, although intelligence reports conflicted as to whether the enemy was local or imported. In either case, VC cadre or NVA infiltration, Saigon wanted to know, and Bravo Company was already in position to find out.

The three platoons continued north, spread out across the hills and lowlands, meeting sporadic fire all the way. Second Platoon spent most of the day climbing up and down a series of hills, and rarely an hour went by without someone opening up on them from somewhere. They stopped by a stream for a smoke and some food, but as Allen sat with half a dozen others in the shade of a tree, mechanically spooning his grease-clotted beans and wieners into his mouth, the familiar slap of a bullet hitting something solid shuddered through the group. Food cans flew into the air as rifles were grabbed, and they were all flat on their bellies before the shot had ceased to echo. They waited, but nothing else came.

Allen lay there, his lunch already attracting a swarm of ants and a rock burning into his thigh, and had suddenly had enough. If today was his day, then so be it, but he wasn't going to lie with his face in the mud for any damned gook. He stood up, brushed off his filthy flak jacket, and walked across the intervening open ground to retrieve his spoon. He cleaned it off on the edge of his shirt, put it into his chest pocket, delivered the taller half of the peace sign to the invisible enemy, and stalked back to where his gun lay, refusing to hurry.

"You crazy bastard, Carmichael," Mouse shouted, "you're gonna get yourself killed!"

"When your time's up, it's up. I'm sick of being a rabbit. Fuck 'em, I say."

"Carmichael," came the voice of authority from behind. Allen swiveled and looked into The Wolf's face. "You feel like committing suicide, let me know, we'll leave you on point or give you a nice isolated listening post."

"Sorry, Ell-Tee, he pissed me off is all. I thought I'd lost my favorite spoon." He pulled the disreputable object out of his pocket as illustration.

"Looks to me like you lost more than that," Woolf said.

Allen followed the lieutenant's gaze to the place the rest of the squad had so rapidly abandoned, and saw that their leader, Andy Bird, was still there, stretched peacefully on his back with his C-rat and spoon clasped firmly in either hand, resting on his belly. It took a moment for Allen to realize that the Birdman's chest was not moving.

"Ah shit!" Allen lunged for the Birdman's legs and hauled him back to shelter, felt for a pulse, called for a medic even though he had known, as immediately as the lieutenant had, that there was no life left to save. The medic shook his head, more at the small and nearly bloodless chest wound than to indicate a judgment, and sent two men off to fetch a stretcher.

Bird had been due to leave the bush in three days.

The Wolf was still standing at the edge of the clearing. Allen looked up at him, questioningly.

"Who in your squad's got the most time?" Woolf asked.

The men looked over at Streak. Not only was he the longest among them in the bush, but Streak knew what he was doing, was neither gung-ho nor cowardly. They'd be okay under him.

Woolf's eyes traveled to the man with the white patch on his scalp. "Look's like it's you, Rychenkow."

Streak thought about it for a minute, shrugged, and picked up his gun. "Okay," he said. "Let's move out."

The spoon episode changed Allen's nickname from Lucky to Crazy—although given the backwards logic of Vietnam, they meant much the same thing.

The sniping went on, as ominous as a cockroach in the kitchen: You just knew that there had to be a whole swarm more of them in the woodwork. Cigarette or water breaks were taken crouched behind the thin trees, open ground was to be gotten over at a fast trot, and the lack of sleep brought alternating bouts of lethargy and hypersensitivity. The whole of Bravo Company ached, for sleep or for action, it hardly mattered which.

Mines came next, clear evidence that the enemy knew where they were and where they were heading. With the first trip wire, the platoon's progress dropped to a near crawl as booby traps were disarmed or blown up, and the next trap watched for intently. Meanwhile, snipers continued to harry them, they were running short of both food and ammunition, and night was coming on. The Wolf called a halt early in a site that would be defensible, although the resupply choppers wouldn't be able to reach them. There they dug in, spending the dark hours under sporadic torment, with a mortar attack at one in the morning, ten or twelve shells pelting down all around them but miraculously killing no one. The sniper's attentions resumed at dawn.

Allen's fingers fumbled to open his second-to-last can of C-rations, clumsy with exhaustion and nerves. He stared down at the greasy lump of ham and limas, and decided he'd rather starve. He put the can down on the ground and dropped his filthy, sweat-caked head into his hands.

"What's the Vietnamese for 'Harassment and Interdiction'?" he asked nobody in particular.

"What I wanna know is, when we gonna H & I they asses?" Mouse retorted. "This shit sucks, man. I feel like a white rent collector in Harlem on a Saturday night. Not really welcome, know what I mean?"

"Nobody loves you, Mouse," T-bone lamented.

"Everybody loves me, asshole, just not Luke the Gook."

"Luke loves us all," Chris said. "He just loves us better dead."

"He gonna find us dead, we don't get resupplied," Mouse complained. "You gonna eat that C-rat, Crazy?"

"I thought I could, but I looked at it and thought I'd rather eat my bayonet. You want it?"

"Sure. Lima's my fav'rite. Reminds me of my mama's cooking."

So worn down were they, not one of them reacted to the outrageous concept of any human female producing the slop in that can.

THE LIEUTENANT HAD SPENT THE NIGHT STUDYING HIS MAPS, AND PLOTted out a change of course that led them away from the mined trails and into terrain that grew clear and flatter as they went on. They picked up speed, outrunning the mine setters, although the snipers soon found them again. Just after noon they swept into a ville that clearly hadn't heard they were coming. A pair of armed figures burst from a hooch and sprinted for the trees—too far away for the rifles, although several grunts opened fire anyway. One of those was Allen, who was so pissed off at the ghosts that he'd happily waste some bullets just for the sake of the noise.

The Wolf called them into line and sent them to searching the ville. They ordered the weeping women and half-naked children out into the village square, and the nervy platoon took out its frustrations on the huts, merrily smashing pots, gouging the floors in an ostensible search for bunkers, and tossing grenades into any minor depression they came upon. One of the other squads was headed toward the thatch with a torch when The Wolf caught them and sent them to round up the livestock.

Even here, however, he had problems controlling the men: One soldier gunned down a young male water buffalo that was placidly chewing its cud in the river. And then the villagers were wailing about the buffalo as well, and one of the GIs made an obscene comment about the animal's equipment, and suddenly out of a clear sky rose a cloud of sexuality, encompassing the entire platoon. An electrical current crackled back and forth across the clearing as the platoon of young and severely frustrated males realized that they had several presentable women in their hands, and no one to object. One man reached out and dragged a villager to her feet, and had his hand inside the woman's shirt before the lieutenant noticed what was happening.

"What are you doing, Malone?" The Wolf's cold voice cut through the hectic glee like a whip. Malone's hand dropped away from the woman's breast, but his other hand kept hold of her arm as he turned to stare insolently at the platoon leader.

"Thought I'd question her."

"You speak Vietnamese now?"

"I didn't reckon we'd do all that much talking, Loot." A couple of the new guys laughed nervously at the joke, but no one else; this was The Wolf they were dealing with.

"You didn't."

After a long minute, Malone's hand let go of the captive arm, and the air's electricity flickered, and guttered out.

Lieutenant Woolf held the gaze of each of his men until he was certain that the urge to atrocity was dead. "Save it for the whores, boys," he said in the end. "These women don't deserve that."

"They've been sheltering VC, Loot," someone groused.

"And they'll probably lose their land because of it," Woolf answered evenly. "We're supposed to be the good guys here. Never forget it."

That night, twenty-year-old Allen Carmichael lay bundled inside his poncho liner, unable to take his mind off the picture of his countryman's hand inside the woman's blouse. His eyes replayed the motion, his hand felt the warm shape as if it had ridden there itself. He told himself that he would never have raped the woman, assured his self-respect that he would have stopped Malone if The Wolf hadn't. But although he was dead certain about the first declaration, he could be none too sure about the second. He too had felt the electricity, he'd been aware of the lust for savagery.

When battle couldn't be joined against the enemy, sometimes the definition of enemy had to expand.

Chapter 9

BY THE TIME ALLEN HAD BEEN IN-COUNTRY THREE MONTHS, HIS MIND held a lifetime of savage images. A three-year-old child burned to raw meat, burned beyond pain, stumbling blind and bewildered through the napalmed ville; a stack of what had once been human beings, now half a ton of squirming rat food; the belt buckle of a fellow GI, still fastened to the stubs of its belt on both sides, sitting in the middle of a path where it had been blown free of its wearer; a weirdly flattened NVA who had fallen from the sky onto rocky ground, a quick means of encouraging his fellow prisoners on the chopper to talk. Men bled impossible amounts; men were impossibly violated by various kinds of metal; men died in silence from tiny wounds while others screamed and screamed and refused to die. Allen had seen so many weeping women that their tears had no power to move him; weeping men were harder to take, when they were his own, but even those had become more of an irritation than something that wrung the guts. He had seen so many Vietnamese smacked around and beaten that the sounds did not even make him look around.

For a while, the everyday horror had festered inside Allen's mind. For a few days after Christmas, he had felt as if he would burst with the memories, swollen as a corpse about to spill itself out onto the earth. For a time, he had almost wished for the release of pressure, looking for ways to cause his mind to break up, thought about just pulling a grenade pin and hugging the thing to his heart.

In the end, the buildup had simply leaked out of him, leaving him a functioning shell. The vivid dreams of raining belt buckles and his foot coming down onto the trigger of a Bouncing Betty ceased to torment him, and during the day he grew accustomed to seeing men he knew were dead walking or sitting with the others: blink hard enough, they went away. As for fear, it was a tool, adrenaline cranking up the perceptions. It could even be a thrill—like the sheer, heart-pounding helplessness of coming down into a red-hot LZ, when the zip and clang of bullets made your balls shrivel up behind your navel, until you set down in an orgasm of terror, finding release in a stream of heavy-laden men pouring out the back of the chopper. Exhaustion, pain, filth, it all got converted into *bau,* pronounced as if it were a Vietnamese word, a joke-adaptation of *business as usual.* Tedium? Turn off the brain and hump the pack. Horror? Let the eyes glaze over. The bright and shining terror of an FNG make you want to just bash him on the head and put him out of his misery? Don't sit near him, don't ask his name.

More and more rarely did he stand back, reflecting on how strange it was that he didn't find the war intolerable, or even particularly awful. He wasn't even afraid of death any longer, looked unmoved on horror, and only the rare pulse of his body's fear told him he was still alive. Life was a long stretch of tedium broken by the fierce joy of battle.

And joy there was, now that he was learning the language of the jungle. In the bush, as the thud of rotors faded, the men would stand motionless until sounds returned: the buzz of insects, the cry of birds, the hiss of the radio. Then slowly they would move out, hunting the enemy, seeking out his hiding places, offering themselves to him as a snake hunter might offer his hand to coax a rattler from his den. And the smaller the group, the more Allen liked it—being stripped down to a night ambush party of three men carrying nothing but M16, canteens, and a Claymore was an experience so intense, it was like being drunk, or in love. Saigon was far away then.

Allen learned the bush, his senses screwed tight to the brink of madness: the chill back-of-the-neck sensation that meant Charlie was watching; a sure conviction that the path ahead held a booby trap; the sixth sense that kicked in when you could feel—*smell*—the enemy with a kind of internal radar. Nights were the best, keeping watch, when only your alertness stood between your brothers and death—he loved them then, his brother soldiers, loved them like he'd never loved Lisa, or his parents, or even Jerry. He discovered that he had a knack for ambushes, working with Streak and Mouse to triangulate a suspected hole in the ground and wait for Charlie to stick his head out, and he developed rituals the night before a patrol—laying out his boots just so, repacking his field pack, covering two sheets of paper with a dutiful set of entertaining lies to Lisa; they became a kind of meditation. He ate less meat, used mud on his exposed skin instead of the Army's insect repellent, he eyed everyone other than his platoon-mates with close suspicion.

He didn't grow braids, although he did toy with the idea of transferring to recon, so he could spend more time in the green. Away from all the crap. And he didn't rape women or collect ears himself, but once he'd sighted down on an old man plowing a paddy with his water buffalo, just to see what it was like to play God. And sometimes, after particularly brutal days, he even began to understand those twin urges of domination, the fierce desire to cap mere killing with calculated savagery against the enemy, assaulting his women or hacking off parts of his corpse. Rape and mutilation were extreme versions of pissing on the enemy: If nothing else, they made crystal clear just which one had survived the battle.

Three months in-country, and Allen's eyes gazed on the world from the other side of a chasm. Whenever he shaved in his murky steel mirror, he concentrated on the cheeks and chin, because he knew that if he looked farther up, he would see that look the journalists liked to call the "thousand yard stare," the expressionless face of an old, old man who no longer dares focus on anything close by. Allen concentrated on the face below the cheekbones, because a part of him did not want to acknowledge what he in fact was.

A twenty-year-old cold-blooded killer.

THE CALENDAR CHANGED TO 1968, AND PARADOXICALLY, WHILE ALLEN'S own tensions simplified and leveled out, the pressures on the country around him grew. While Allen learned to move quietly in the land he was coming to know, Charlie was growing more and more blatant. It was almost as if he could smell blood in the water, as the growing drag of antiwar sentiment at home made even the rawest recruit suspect that the U.S. wasn't going to be in the country long enough to win. The Wolf took on a haunted look, and his determination that the men under his command would fight an honest war was grim now instead of dignified. Things happened even in Second Platoon that wouldn't have earlier, blind eyes were turned on the unjustly dead. Someone told Allen that life would calm down once Tet, the Vietnamese New Year, started. He replied that he'd be more than ready for it.

During a day inside the NDP, Allen was mending a ripped cargo pocket on his fatigues when he looked up to see Ricardo Flores, the whip of an antenna snapping back and forth over his head, bright green eyes sparkling in a grinning face. Allen dropped his clumsy needle to throw his arms around this figure from a past life and pound on the little guy's tightly muscled back.

"Hey Flowers! Or do they still call you Lucy?"

"Don't know what I'm going to do when I go home and my mother calls me Ricky," he admitted. "How you doin', man?"

"Counting the days, Lucy, just countin' the days. What're you doing here, anyway?"

"They had to do some shuffling at the regiment I was in, putting some platoons together, that kinda shit. We had two romeos, you guys were one down, so here I am."

In other words, his company had had such heavy losses, they shipped in an entire new platoon to fill their numbers.

"It's great to see you. You with the Second Platoon, then?"

"First."

"Second's better, Lieutenant Woolf's better'n most of the generals."

"Hell, Carmichael, *you're* better'n most of the generals."

"True. Hey, I should tell you, Farmboy's in your platoon. Remember him and Dogs? Dogs shipped out last month, lucky bastard, some kind of liver thing."

"Yeah, I remember them, from the bus. So the farmboy made it this far—I'da thought he'd get hisself stomped by a water buffalo or something."

"Not yet. So where you been?"

"All over." The green eyes took on a haunted look and shifted away, which meant that he didn't want to talk about it. Fair enough.

"Well," said Allen, "anyway, welcome to Bravo Company. You need me to show you where your platoon is?"

"Nah, I got it. See you around, okay?" And Flores left Allen to his mending.

Two days later, Tet began.

But instead of the breathing space of peace that past experience led everyone to expect, the celebrations set off a paroxysm of violence that ran from the delta to the demilitarized zone. VC and NVA alike rose up from one end of the country to the other, even in areas assumed to be secure. Saigon in the south came within a hair's breadth of falling, the Marines in Hue to the east were awash in blood, battalions near the DMZ came close to being overrun. The grunts hunkered down and met the enemy, and it was a close thing, but by the end of February, it was apparent that the Tet offensive had stalled. Westmoreland claimed a victory on his way out the door, but when Walter Cronkite came to see for himself, he declared to the American people that the war was lost. The men on the ground figured both authorities were right; at the same time, they knew it would be a long time before anyone recognized it.

In early March, Allen's platoon lifted out for five days of turnaround time near the coast, hot food, cold beer, real bunks, and above all, someone else to stand guard. The five days passed in a welter of fistfights and fucking and they returned to their part of the jungle more tired than when they'd left.

Still, it had been a change, and had let them take a small step away from the craziness.

AND THEN THERE WAS WHAT WAS CALLED "FRIENDLY FIRE": ARTILLERY WAS given wrong coordinates, overheated guns misfired by one or two degrees, gunships laying down white phosphorus were given incomplete information or failed to see the smoke markers. Whoever came up with the phrase no doubt did not intend its flavor of bitter irony—that came from the victims.

Late March; raining. First and Second Platoons had been out for the better part of a week, slopping through the deluge, trying to keep their M16s dry, looking like mud men, the noise of the rain on their steel hats deafening them. The point man in the next squad up had his bush hat on, no protection from flying steel but it kept the rain out of his eyes and gave him a chance to hear something other than pounding rain. Still, not even he heard the gunship coming up the turgid, red-brown stream. Allen's squad was picking its way through the waist-deep water, rifles over their heads, when the Slick came upon them. The gunship had taken ground fire in this same place three times the previous day and its crew was antsy; when it swooped around a curve in the stream and saw heavily draped men carrying burdens, the gunner opened fire.

The Huey had turned and was taking a return pass before one of the men in Alpha Squad managed to free a smoke canister and set it going. Fortunately it was one of the yellow ones, visible even in the half-light of the rain and the streambed, because the helicopter bearing down on them abruptly pulled up and sailed past; the gunner stared down appalled at his handiwork, like a god who has mistakenly summoned lightning against his own priests.

Of the twelve men caught crossing the stream, four were down, two trapped underwater by sixty pounds of equipment. Allen flung his rifle in the direction of the bank and splashed after the nearest spread-eagled figure. He grabbed the man's foot, then his own boot went out from under him and he went down, bouncing along the stream bottom until he fought clear of pack, grenades, bandoliers, and flak jacket, staggering upright, gagging and coughing as he tried to shout for help, but when he dashed the water out of his eyes, all he saw was the downed man in the fast-moving center of the stream, gaining momentum. He waded after the figure, slow as a bad dream, then flung his helmet aside and dove in unencumbered. Ten, fifteen strokes, and he had hold of the boot again. He clawed at belt, equipment, anything. The body seemed determined to head for the distant China Sea but, cursing and choking, Allen managed to get the senseless weight turned faceup.

Streak.

Allen hawked the mud from his throat and roared, "For Christ sake somebody help me—Streak's hit!"

Then Chris was there, lifting Streak's head out of the swirl while Allen took the feet; using the water itself as a stretcher, they struggled against the current, back to where the bank ran with blood. Hands reached for Streak, dragging him onto the rocks, fumbling to release his web gear while Allen ripped at Streak's flak jacket and yelled, "Medic! We need you here, right now!"

The medic appeared at his shoulder, kneeling beside the still body, resting his fingers on the skin under Streak's jawbone. Then, inexplicably, he was straightening up and moving away, back to the man he'd abandoned. Allen grabbed his arm, hard.

"What the hell you think you're doing? This man needs you."

"What this man needs, I can't give. He's dead, Carmichael."

"He's not dead, he's just stopped breathing. Give him some artificial respiration or something, get the water out of his lungs."

"Carmichael. Look at him. He's dead."

The medic's patience forced the meaning through.

Streak? Their shortest guy, their platoon leader, nerves-of-ice Streak? No. Not possible.

But without the muddy water, with the wide bandoliers stripped from his chest, Allen could see that the words were true. The blood oozed, without the pressure of a heart to pump it: For eleven months, Streak Rychenkow had survived all Charlie had to throw at him, only to fall to a bullet made in the USofA.

That was not the whole of it, either. Allen looked up from Streak's slack features to another face startling in its contrast, a face so contorted in pain and fear that he failed for a moment to recognize it. Farmboy Pete, helmet tipped back from that blond and tousled head, legs in the water, freckles stark against skin gone monstrously pale. He was trying to get his hands onto his belly where the medic was working; two men were struggling to hold his wrists while Pete writhed and gulped for air, his eyes locking on to Allen as if to a life ring. Allen splashed over to his side, and one of the bloody hands shot away from its keeper to grab Allen's arm.

"Don't leave me, Carmichael, don't leave me here."

"Nobody's going to leave you, Farmboy, you're safe now. The medic's going to patch you up and it's off to the hospital with you, nice, clean sheets and plenty to eat, all those pretty nurses, don't worry." Nonsense phrases poured out, nonsense because it did not seem possible for a man to lose that much blood and survive to the medevac's arrival. "Can't you give him some morphine?" he asked the medic.

"Any more might kill him."

It was on the tip of Allen's tongue to ask why that wouldn't be the lesser evil here, but with Farmboy's blue eyes holding his, he could not. All he could do was wait, and listen to the gulping quieten, and watch the eyes' focus go farther and farther away. The kid was still alive when the medevac came. It was only the drugs, Allen told himself, that made him seem close to death.

The gunship's friendly fire had taken Streak and another short-timer from Alpha Squad just behind them on the bank, given T-bone a bullet in his buttock, and left Farmboy . . . wherever he was. They shoved the four men into the medevac with as much gentleness as they could, and watched the chopper take to the air.

"Not enough that Charlie's shootin' our asses, now the First Fuckin' Cav's got to take its turn." It was Mouse, more bitter than Allen had ever heard him. "Suckers think we can't aim better'n Charlie, put a hole in they gas tank?"

"They know we're not going to do that, Mouse. They've got us by the balls—we're not going to shoot at the guys who bring us food and haul us out."

"Maybe *you* not gonna do that, Crazy. They better damn well not count on this boy not to get 'em in my sights."

"Frag a chopper, man?" Chris exclaimed. "Dude, that'd be bitchin'. Get their attention, know what I mean?"

"They sure as shit think twice about shootin' at our asses—eatin' this fuckin' mud while they sittin' up there, nice and dry."

Allen didn't like this talk, not the way Mouse was saying it. Things had to become pretty grim in a company for the men to talk about fragging a hated officer, "accidentally" loosing a round or grenade in his direction during a firefight. But this company had no such hated officers, and open war breaking out between the grunts and the helicopter crews would be a catastrophe.

"Look, Mouse, fuck 'em. Let The Wolf tear the chopper boys another asshole. He'll do it righteous, you know that."

Even Mouse had to pause at that, considering what their lieutenant's response was going to be, having his own men shot down by some jumpy-fingered gunner. Mouse's bulked-up shoulders relaxed, and the open rage faded from his face as he began to imagine The Wolf lighting into the gunship crew, The Wolf closing in on the hapless First Cav gunner, eyes gleaming and teeth bared; every man there pictured it with anticipation. "He better, man, you know what I'm sayin'? He just better. Streak was good people, fuckin' hell."

"Who better what?" spoke the voice of authority, and Woolf was there, his eyes already angry.

"Nothing, sir."

"How many in your squad now, Carmichael?"

Allen did a quick head count: Mouse, Chris, and he were the only members of the squad as it had been when he first shipped in; T-bone would be gone for a while, by the looks of it; and there were a pair of new guys who'd been with them eleven days.

"Five, sir."

"Okay, I'm dropping Bravo Squad until we're reinforced, I'll be putting two of them in with you. What're your DEROS dates?"

Allen found he was fourth down, even though he'd served less than half his time, following Chris, Mouse, and a guy recently transferred into Bravo, one of the few soldiers Allen had seen here who looked older than twenty. The guy's hair was even thinning—he'd have looked like an accountant playing at Army Reserves if it hadn't been for the eyes.

"Okay, Garrison, you're squad leader," Woolf told the man, but the accountant shook his head.

"I'd rather not, sir, if you don't mind. I've been here long enough to know that my strength is not in leadership, you might say. Besides, I'm off to R&R in a week."

"Take it now, Garrison. We'll shuffle when we get back to the NDP."

"Yes, sir."

The Wolf's gaze went to the other squad members. *Funny,* Allen thought, *you always expect his eyes to be yellow.* "You men okay with that?"

"Sure, Loot."

The lieutenant shook his head. "A person would think this Army was a democracy or something," he said, and walked away.

The squad stared openmouthed at the retreating back.

"Did The Wolf just make a joke?" Allen asked.

"Hard to imagine," the accountant said. "You're Carmichael? I'm Gregory George Garrison—they call me ThreeG." They shook hands, and went off to amalgamate their two squads.

But the Army didn't seem to be in much of a hurry to bring the platoon in. Over the next two days, pressing forward into the green, no one seemed to know what they were doing out there, and they would have suspected that the company command had forgotten about them had they not responded to radio requests for artillery and supplies. Allen found himself walking next to Flores the morning of the second day, and heard how The Wolf had used Lucy's radio to call in the report of the gunship's friendly fire.

"Sweet Jesus, I'm glad it wasn't me on the other end." Lucy said it with admiration. "Just listening made me want to crawl off and shit my guts out under a tree. Thought my radio's tubes'd be melted down. That gunner better arrange himself a quick bullet in the foot and get lifted out right quick, else he's gonna find himself in lots of little pieces."

That cheered Allen, and left Mouse with a bounce in his step when he relayed the conversation to him. The rain even let up for a while, enough to tuck their ponchos up over their shoulders and steam in the sun.

They came to a small ville around two in the afternoon, five hooches, six ducks, and a bunch of kids wearing shorts or nothing at all, most of them with sores on their legs and scalps. The closest thing they found to a bunker was a suitcase-sized hole under the family sleeping area, covered with a board: a rat-resistant store for rice, but nothing being hidden from human attention. The ville's papers were in order and the people were friendly, so the GIs distributed a few chocolate bars and cigarettes, the medic smeared the worst of the kids' sores with ointment, and they moved on. One kid tagged along for a while, a handsome boy of about eight, formally dressed in both shorts and an adult-sized T-shirt that had once been printed with a picture of the Eiffel Tower. It was more hole than fabric and the ragged hem came to his knees, but it was clearly a thing of pride. Allen figured the kid was hoping that if he hung around the GIs long enough, one of them might give him another T-shirt. The boy skipped up and down the line, chattering merrily in his pidgin English, and because he was cheerful, because his scalp was relatively clean from scabs and his face was animated, the weary, dispirited grunts put up with his presence. Eventually, though, he decided that these GIs had given all they could be talked out of, and between one tree and the next, he was gone.

That night, the enemy fell upon them.

The platoon was dug in on a piece of ground marked on the maps as Hill 117, nicely softened but with enough drainage in the soil that their holes did not turn instantly into bathtubs. Allen was not the only one to fashion a cup from one C-ration tin and cut a stove from another, heating a cup of cocoa over a chunk of burning C4—the air was cooler here on higher ground, and the hot drink was welcome. Chris lit a joint and handed it back and forth with Mouse, offering it to Allen but not taking his refusal personally.

Allen took first watch for their stretch of the perimeter. It was an odd night, the jungle quieter than usual, without the usual shift and rustle of the wildlife. The clouds cleared for a while, revealing a quarter moon lying peacefully in the blackness. Something about its distance made him think of home—not the dry California valley where he'd lived the last few years, but his real home, the string of islands lying in the straits between Canada and the state of Washington. Jerry and he used to sneak out on moonlit nights, creep down to the dock and climb silently into the family rowboat. They'd go out into the strait, draw the boat up onto one beach or another, maybe make a little fire and cook some hot dogs. That must be why he was thinking of those nights: The moon had been like this the night he and Jerry shared a can of watery cocoa heated over a fire on the cove beach at

Sanctuary, one of the uninhabited islands everyone said was haunted by ghosts. Cocoa, silence, and ghosts; yes, that was Vietnam all right.

Shortly before the end of his watch, he heard the *thump* of a flare, followed by the pop overhead and then the wavering light. He brought his rifle up, hearing the line of M16s similarly responding to the alarm. Two guns fired, but there was no answering fusillade from the night, and after a minute Allen thumbed his safety back on; somebody probably heard a wild pig, or a rat.

Still, there was a sensation as of the jungle holding its breath, and it made him edgy. On the stroke of midnight, Mouse, who had an extraordinary sense of time even if he never wore a watch, stirred in his sleeping trench, paused to take a piss, and shambled over to the fighting hole the squad had dug for itself. Hearing every sound the big man made, from the rustle of the poncho liner to the last spatter of drops hitting the ground, Allen nearly laughed aloud. When Mouse climbed down beside him, Allen put his head close to his squad-mate's and whispered, "I was getting all freaked out at the bad vibes, nearly talked myself into sending up flares to check for VC in the wires before I realized it's only because the damn rain has stopped."

"Know what you mean. I kept wakin' myself up with my breathin'."

"Well, everything seems okay. Alpha Squad sent up a flare a while ago, but nothing there."

"Maybe Charlie's spooked with the rain stoppin', gone home to wash his socks. Sleep good, man."

Allen went back to his hole behind the sandbags. Before he lay down, however, he studied the darkness again: There were people out there, he could feel them. Still, there was nothing he could do sitting here. Might as well sleep.

It began an hour later with a scream, a sound of distilled mortal terror that jerked every man upright, hair on end and gun in hand, a sound that seemed to last a lot longer in the memory than the two or three seconds before the grenade exploded. A man in Alpha Squad had been peaceably in his hole, either dozing or staring out into the night, when a grenade dropped out of nowhere and he had felt Death rolling around between his boots. That explosion was followed rapidly by three more, then *Move move MOVE!* and a mounting wall of noise, bursts and firing and yelps of pain. Allen caught a snatch of Flores shouting into his radio and braced himself for the resulting artillery, but for what came, there could be no bracing. Two of the shells came to earth twenty feet from the perimeter, the concussion slamming into any person still above ground. There were four men in the fighting hole Allen's squad had dug for two, a press of elbows and gun butts, and the sides of the hole half collapsed into them with the incoming shell. All four crouched over each other's knees and shoulders, hands gripping their helmets. Allen, squeezed in against Mouse, had a crazy image of what a passing bird would see: four round rocks jammed together in a hole. Then the third shell landed, nearly on top of the first; for several long seconds, he couldn't think, couldn't even breathe.

Did he imagine a high, panicky voice screaming instructions to correct the distant guns? He must have imagined it, he couldn't have heard anything in the cacophony of explosions, screaming men, and gunfire that followed. Flares and smoke filled the air, flashes of launched grenades shot more or less blindly into the dark, the flares throwing dancing shadows from the trees, shadows that hid the enemy. Both sides flung death at each other across the cleared ground; inside the perimeter, men died.

Years later, when Allen happened to step into a discotheque with its pounding music and pulsing strobes, he was instantly snatched back to that night in the jungle. The flash of shells and sweep of tracers, the weird harsh light of the flares, the heat and confusion and the noise of all-out battle overwhelmed the senses, leaving a man with no choices but to curl up in a fetal position, or rise to his feet and hurl mad defiance out at the terrifying dark with all the breath in his lungs and all the ammunition in his possession.

One of their radios was still working, or perhaps the distant artillery had found its error. The next rounds hit lower ground; one thin scream, indistinct words over and over again, proved that the response had been to some degree effective. The attack slowed. After a few minutes, Allen eased over the top of the sandbags so the others could shovel out the dirt that had collapsed in. He heard ThreeG calling for a damage report, and he answered that his guys were okay. The hole closer to the misfires had not fared so well.

"They're dead, Carmichael," came a choked voice. "We're all fucking dead, oh fuck, oh God, we're dead."

Allen squirmed over the ground, dragging his gun after him. He couldn't see a thing, not until another flare went up, and even then all he could make out was a black hole until a hand shot up and seized his, scaring him half to death. Its owner pulled himself up until the gleam of wire rims was inches from Allen's face.

Allen turned to hiss over his shoulder, "Mouse! I need a hand here, man."

Mouse was there in an instant, the whites of his eyes the only thing visible, but his strength hauled Chris up from the hole. The surfer's hands came up automatically to straighten his glasses, his skin pouring out the musky aura of old marijuana.

"Where you hit, man?" Allen asked him.

"Everywhere, shit, I can't feel my legs. No, wait," he said, and kicked first one boot, then the other. "Did I move them?"

"Damn right you moved them, asshole, you kicked me in the face," Mouse objected.

Allen had been running a tentative hand over Chris's body, feeling for breaks in the fabric of the uniform or for warm pools of blood, praying he didn't encounter some really gross protruding organ or bone fragment. The cloth had soaked patches, but seemed to be whole.

"See if you can crawl," he suggested. "We'll take you down to the medic."

Instead, Chris braced himself on their shoulders and stood up, swaying but obviously intact. "Shit," he said. "I thought I was cut in half."

For some reason, the statement struck Mouse as funny, and he began to emit a gurgling sound. "Really sorry to disappoint you, dude," he finally choked out, and crawled back over to finish digging out the collapsed fighting hole.

The other two men in Chris's hole, however, made no effort to stand. One would never stand again, since most of his head was gone. The other man lay groaning quietly, one arm twisted and useless. He also seemed to be bleeding, although it was hard to tell what was his and what had belonged to the dead man. Allen patted the guy's good shoulder and told him, "You hang in there, man. I'll get you a medic, he'll give you something that'll make you feel better. Chris, you think you can go find us some kind of stretcher? Tell the medic to come when he has a chance?"

"Sure. Shit, man, I thought I'd get my ass medevacked outta here."

"We just love you too much to let you go," Allen told him, and dropped into the hole between the dead and the wounded. The limp corpse in the bottom of the hole was a bitch to move, and would have been impossible if Allen had had to think of it as a person, but treating it as a really awkward wet log with sprawling extremities meant that he could just shove away at the thing, propping his shoulder under it, cursing it all the way up the side of the hole until it flopped onto level ground. He scrubbed his hands on his shirt and left the body lying along the top of the hole; when shooting resumed, he didn't think the guy would mind reinforcing the sandbags for his squad.

It didn't take long for the shooting to start again. He could still hear the rapid clink and scrape of the entrenching tools in Mouse's hole when the rattle of an AK47 brought his M16 up to prop on the body of the dead man. Who the hell was it, anyway? He'd have to check the tags when it was light, he thought, and then he was too busy.

If it hadn't been for the gunships, Second Platoon would have been overrun—give them their due, First Cav might have twitchy fingers when it came to their own side, but the bastards had balls. Near dawn, the besieged platoon was an island in a lake of fire, napalm on one side and mortars on the other, but once the jets came in, ripping the air with the sound of a stupendous bolt of silk tearing and leaving in their wake the superheated mushrooms of serious firepower, Charlie called it quits, and left the shaky GIs to lick their wounds.

They got the emergencies off in the medevacs, then the priorities and the body bags, and when the wounded were safely off their hands they went outside the perimeter to see what the enemy had left for them.

Most of them were NVA, with tire-soled sandals and flat-top haircuts. They went over the dead like ghoulish scavengers, emptying pockets, gloating over information (and, occasionally, souvenirs), feeling nothing at the sight of the dead but satisfaction that it was someone else.

Allen, standing with his M16 in his arms while the sergeant rifled a man's pockets, noticed a patch of something light in the bushes.

"Another one over there, Sarge," he said. Sergeant Keys used the dead soldier's AK47 to lift up the branch, revealing a crumpled figure even smaller than the men they'd been seeing on the battlefield.

"It's a kid," Keys said.

Allen went down on one knee.

"Hang on." The sergeant put out a hand to stop him. "Under the bushes like this, damn thing could be booby-trapped."

Allen nodded, and bent his head to examine the front of the child's garment without touching it.

The boy wore a long, ragged T-shirt that had once been printed with a picture of the Eiffel Tower.

"Ah, damn it," Allen said. "This kid followed us from that last ville."

"Followed us, or came back?"

"He disappeared during the afternoon."

It was all he needed to say. The two men gazed at the dead child who had brought the enemy to their wire. The Snakeman's words ran through Allen's mind like a song's refrain: *Even the babies'll kill you. Never trust a kid. Even the babies'll kill you.*

What remained of Second Platoon was finally lifted out that afternoon, abandoning the hard-fought hill to its dead guardians, one of them a handsome child who had gleefully scrounged chocolate bars from the passing Americans.

But Hill 117 wasn't quite through with them.

One by one the Hueys lifted off. Someone on the ground gave them a farewell fusillade, pings off their side that made the men inside cringe, but which did no harm.

Except for the round that passed through one small but vital part of the last chopper off the ground.

Allen was in the air when he felt the man beside him go stiff, and he whirled around, thinking his companion had taken a bullet through the floor. But the man's face and outstretched hand had Allen whipping back the other way, leaning to see out the Huey's open door, past the gunner to the copter behind them. The last Huey leaving the LZ was in trouble; every man there knew it was the one in which Lieutenant Woolf was riding. It faltered and tipped in the air, its stuttering rotors fighting for control, then tipped farther. A figure separated from the dying ship, jumped or shaken loose, and then the machine gave a shrug and dove after him, falling from the sky like a dropped house. The jungle where it came down erupted, a huge paw of flame that reached up for anything else it might grab, stretching out and out—until with an inaudible *pop* the cloud of flame collapsed back on itself and winked out, leaving only a wide circle of black vegetation and the first exploratory tendrils of smoke.

The body of the door gunner was the only one later recovered from the smoldering wreckage. Even it was charred beyond recognition by the heat of the fire.

Chapter 10

BRAVO COMPANY'S CAPTAIN CAME TO THE PLATOON THAT NIGHT, OFFERING up his words of praise for their valiant actions and the company's mourning for one of its fallen leaders. Second Platoon stood in silence while he talked to them, because The Wolf would expect them to show respect, but that was as far as it went. The captain looked at their closed faces and their postures of reserve, and saw insolence.

Chris dug out his stash and they all got hammered, so high that they were still buzzed the next morning. Sitting in a tight group in the mess tent, the squad chowed down mechanically until Mouse threw down his fork.

"I'm gonna go find me that fuckin' Huey gunner. Anyone wanna come?"

"Mouse, you can't do that, they're based about ninety miles away from here, you can't just take off," Allen told him.

"You gonna try an' stop me?"

"Mouse, you'll get your ass thrown in the brig. You'll get a dishonorable discharge."

"Fuck 'em. And fuck you. I'll go myself."

"I'll go with you," Chris offered. Allen stared at the pacific surfer in surprise. "Hey, I can't let my bro' here go alone."

"You ain't no brother 'a mine, man," Mouse retorted.

"Sure as shit, man. I'm turning into a black man," Chris declared, and lifted his shirt to display the purple-plum blotches that covered half his torso. "I'm even darker under my pants. Dig it—I'm gonna be as black as you, Mouse. Want to see?" He stood and laid his hand on his belt buckle, but the table was loud and unanimous in discouraging the display. He sat down to finish his eggs.

"Come on, guys," Allen pleaded. "You two do this, that's the end of the whole damn squad. No offense," he said to the new guys.

"Then you better come too, Crazy. Keep us outta trouble."

Allen looked from the black face to the suntanned one, and saw only conviction. "Shit," he said, with feeling.

"That's my man," Mouse said. It was the first time he'd grinned in days.

They would have to wait until night to be relatively certain of finding their crew at base instead of in the air. Mouse had found out that the gunner's name was Perry, which could have been either a first or a last name, and he knew where Perry was serving—one of First Platoon's soul brothers had caught a ride in the man's gunship a month or two before and had recognized the face looking out the door over the streambed. Mouse dug up a friend in the transport crew who would allow them to stow into the back of his deuce-and-a-half, so long as they left him out of it if they were caught. To Allen's relief, talk of fragmentation grenades had been replaced by plans for a good old-fashioned beating: The threat of discharge was one thing; the brig for life was another.

However, as the day wore on, Mouse took on a mood of expansive gaiety. Allen, watching him joke with men he would have cut dead the week before, began to wonder if this was the big man's way of dealing with the loss of their lieutenant, and his apprehension grew, along with the conviction that when the time came, Mouse was not going to stop at a mere beating. He hoped that some hitch would come to delay the plans for revenge, even that one of the squad would rat on them, but when afternoon came and the night convoy set off, there was room for the three of them in the last truck. *Shit,* Allen said to himself. *Shit, shit, shit.* And went to borrow a handgun from Flores, just in case.

No operation laid out in Army headquarters went off more smoothly than Mouse's ill-conceived plan. No one challenged them as they left the company perimeter, checkpoint guards seemed blind, and the three strangers slipped into the First Cav base as slick as wet trout, where they asked a few questions, then walked straight into gunner Perry's tent.

Only problem was, the gunner wasn't there, just three men playing cards and drinking beer to the Mamas and the Papas.

"Little Greggie? He's not here," the dealer told them.

"Shoot himself in the foot, did he?" Chris asked.

"What? No, he's fine. Came back from the last mission, cleaned himself up, took off. In a truck, not taking off, you know." The card players snickered at the joke; the grunts did not.

"Where did he go?" Allen asked, feeling Mouse bristle.

"See a man about a dog," the first player replied, and took a swig of the beer—or started to take a swig of the beer, except that Mouse was suddenly at the guy's throat. Cards and beer flew in all directions as the others upturned the makeshift table and went for their weapons—but Allen was there first, fumbling the borrowed sidearm out of his clothing.

"Hold it," he shouted, keeping the heavy revolver pointed halfway between the two men. "We just want to know where your buddy went, and then we'll be gone. Mouse, the guy can't answer if you don't give him some air."

The big hand relaxed a fraction under the clawing fingernails, and the man choked out, "I don't know where he went. I swear. He's been moping around here for days, I told him to go get himself laid or something."

"So he's gone down to the camp for a whore?"

"Why'd he clean up for that, put on his good shirt and ribbons, for Christ sake? He was looking for a ride, said if he wasn't back in the morning to cover for him if I could."

"Fucker's gone AWOL?" Mouse said incredulously.

"Fuck if I know, I'm not his baby-sitter."

Mouse looked about to shake the man like a dog with a rat, but Allen grabbed his shoulder. "This isn't getting us anywhere, man. Let go."

After a minute, Mouse did so. The man stumbled rapidly backwards out of reach, his hands nursing his throat, coughing. "You bastards are in real trouble here. I'll have your heads for this—"

Allen put his gun away and started pulling Mouse and Chris back. At the tent flap he gave the two men a firm push, then turned back to say, "Before you go reporting us, maybe you should have a conversation with your friend the gunner, find out what this was all about. Tell him the guys he met crossing the river the other morning want to have a word with him."

The three invaders walked away with dignity, certain the card players would come after them, but they made it without incident through the camp and to the gate. At Mouse's insistence, they ripped through the Vietnamese encampment, from one end to the other, ignoring the cries of outrage and the offers of "Boom-boom, GI?" and "Good fucky-sucky, okay here." Their target was not to be found in any noodle shop or boom-boom girl's bed, and none of the vendors or customers would admit to having seen him. It was frustrating, particularly for Mouse, who ached to beat up an enemy, any enemy. Allen and Chris had to haul him away from two confrontations; the third time, when he stood in a bar full of First Cav men and called them cowards, even Chris had to admit they were getting nowhere but into the promise of full-body casts, and they made their exit. It took them most of the night to hitch their way home, trudging through the company wires to the smell of breakfast cooking. Allen was famished. As they walked back toward their hooches, they passed one of their platoon going in the other direction. He raised an eyebrow at their condition, but said merely, "There's somebody looking for you, Carmichael. I think he's in your hooch."

"Who is it?"

"Don't know. Kid in a First Cav uniform, looks like the mascot."

The grunt walked on, leaving Allen staring at Mouse and Chris. They marched across the camp to Allen's hooch, jostled to get into the small space, and woke their visitor.

He was just a kid—as full of fresh-faced innocence as Farmboy had been, small enough to have given his recruiting officer pause. The gunner stumbled up from where he had been sitting against the wall, blinking at their entrance, all but rubbing the sleep from his eyes like a child. Even Mouse, who had come to the hooch with his fists clenched in readiness, hesitated.

The boy straightened his jacket and his shoulders, and stepped forward with his hand out. "My name is Greg Perry. I'm the guy who shot at your squad Tuesday morning. It was a terrible mistake. I have no excuse for my actions. I've admitted full responsibility, but my CO gave me permission to come here and tell you myself how sorry I am before I'm taken into custody."

He stood before them, hand out but clearly braced for their rejection. He was practically on the edge of tears.

What else could they do? Allen stared at the outstretched hand, let out a deep breath, and shook it. After a minute, Chris followed. Mouse looked at it, but in the end screwed up his face and muttered, "I can't, man. Friend of mine died in that river. I can't tell you that's okay."

"I understand. If you want to hit me, go ahead. I won't report you."

In the face of that, even Mouse had to retreat.

"Nah, man. You gonna have problems enough, don't need a broken jaw on top of 'em."

They watched the boy put on his hat and set it straight. When he saluted them, it was all Allen could do not to return it. Greg Perry walked past them out of the hooch. His hat came to Mouse's chin.

"Ah, fuck it," Mouse said when the kid had left them. "Just fuck this whole fucking war, anyway."

THREE DAYS LATER, AT A QUARTER AFTER NINE ON THE FIRST SUNNY MORN-ing in some time, Second Platoon's new lieutenant arrived. The jeep passed through the gates and climbed the hill, and the man in the razor-creased uniform dismounted from the vehicle to plant two shiny boots on the worn soil. The sergeant was nowhere in sight, and the of-ficer surveyed his new command from behind a pair of impenetrable black lenses. The men were sprawled around the compound, soaking in the warmth like so many large, grubby lizards. The Beach Boys ex-tolled the virtues of California from several speakers, courtesy of the Armed Forces radio, with a Hendrix guitar solo beating their harmony back from the corner where the black troopers congregated and Frank Zappa doing his thing from inside the next bunker. The newly arrived officer seemed to expect his platoon to leap instantly to its collective feet, but after the last week, the platoon would take its revenge where it could, and it ignored him. One corner of the newcomer's mouth pulled up briefly, then relaxed.

As chance would have it, Allen was among the soldiers nearest to him. He'd been trying to figure out why Chris's rifle kept jamming whenever it heated up, and was so closely involved with the project—prodding delicately with the cleaning rod, searching for rust—that he was unaware of the arrival of Authority until its polished boots in-truded themselves into his line of vision. He blinked, looked up into his own reflection in the dark glasses, and was struck by an irrational crawling sensation up the nape of his neck—what his grandmother would call someone walking on his grave.

"Soldier, do you know where your sergeant is?" The man's voice was light, educated, and quiet, which might have made for a pleasing combination but for the indefinable quality of scorn that it carried, as if the person he was addressing had all the intelligence and self-awareness of an ape. Allen got to his feet, more from wariness than from the respect due an officer, and held on to the gun with his right hand.

"Yes, sir. I think he went to see about our shipment of LAWs."

"Well, you go find him. Tell him I want him in my quarters at ten hundred hours."

Allen looked over at the other men, who were doing nothing more strenuous than writing letters, and mentally shrugged. "Okay, sir. Ten hundred hours."

"Did no one teach you how to salute, soldier?" the quiet voice asked. It sounded as if he was asking, *Did no one teach you to wipe your ass, moron?*

Allen stiffened. He was already in an irritable mood, even more so than usual, a combination of frustration at the damned gun, the underlying suspicion that in the hands of a more enthusiastic owner the thing wouldn't be jamming, and the fact that Chris himself was just sitting there watching and crunching his way through the M&Ms from about ten sundry packs, to say nothing of the dose of malaria prophylaxis they'd swallowed that morning, singing through his teeth and skull like feedback. And now to find they'd sent as The Wolf's replacement a man like this—for one brief fraction of an instant, his hand felt the urge to raise Chris's gun and try out its firing mechanism on the man, but he squelched the feeling before it started, smoothly and obediently transferring both cleaning rod and M16 to his left hand so he could snap out a salute. If the guy wanted his rank pointed out for a nearby sniper, who was Allen to argue?

The new lieutenant studied Allen. He surely couldn't have been aware of Allen's brief flare of animosity—Allen himself had hardly known it was there—but still, he stood for a moment, smiling oddly at Allen, before he turned on his heel and walked back to the jeep.

Allen let out a breath, glanced at his watch, then squatted down to show Chris the suspect point in the feed; halfway through his demonstration, he felt a cool tickle up the back of his neck. He looked around. The officer was sitting motionless in the jeep, watching him—waiting, it seemed, for his order to be carried out. It was oh-nine-twenty; it would take Allen five minutes to hunt down the sergeant and thirty seconds to deliver the order, which left him more than half an hour of leeway before ten hundred hours. But the lieutenant sat waiting and so Allen pushed the gun into Chris's hands, telling him that he'd be back to finish it in a minute. As he walked off up the hill, he heard the jeep start up and move away.

He found the Sarge gassing in the cook tent, and told him their new loot wanted to see him at ten hundred hours. Allen hesitated; he got along fine with Sergeant Keys, but he couldn't exactly tell him that their new loot had made the hair on the back of his neck stand up. The Sarge'd think he was nuts. In the end, he just added weakly, "The guy's got real pretty polished boots."

"Figures."

"You know him?"

"Of him. Name of Brennan."

"What do you know about him?"

"Not a thing. Has your squad got itself sorted yet?"

"Not really. Lieutenant Woolf was going to reorganize when we got back. Garrison's off on leave."

"Who's squad leader 'til he gets back?"

"Well, Chris is."

The sergeant's look said it all. "Who's next? Mouse?"

"Yeah."

"How would he feel about being leader?"

Mouse would be fine as a squad leader if he made up his mind to get along with the others instead of growling at them, but it would be up to him. Allen said something of the sort to the sergeant, who nodded.

"Okay, I'll think about it, have a word with Lieutenant Brennan."

Fifteen minutes after he'd gone in to see the new loot, the sergeant was rounding up all the squad leaders—including Chris, until decisions were made—to inform them that a new regime had begun. It would start with haircuts, clean shaves, no sideburns, and regulation Ts instead of the rock and roll T-shirts half of them wore. The squad leaders looked at each other with apprehension, and went to do as they were told.

When the sergeant came past, Allen called out to him, "Hey Sarge, has this guy ever been in the woods before?" He was voicing the concern of them all: If Brennan was new to jungle warfare, the platoon would be teaching a green officer the nitty-gritty about his job. Not an ideal way to begin.

"He's been sitting a desk for a while, but he's been here since sixty-five, and yeah, he's spent time in the woods."

"But he still wants haircuts."

"He wants the haircuts, he wants the men and the grounds cleaned up. And that volleyball net down. Now."

"Shit," someone muttered.

"And Lieutenant Brennan's not too keen on obscenity," the sergeant added.

"Well, fuck me Brenda," someone else said aloud.

Allen stifled a laugh, but it wasn't very amusing. The men felt bad enough at losing The Wolf, and to have the man replaced by an REMF was going to prove hard to swallow. The others were thinking the same, because after they were dismissed, Mouse, walking in front of Allen, said very clearly, "Boys, we got us a rear echelon motherfucker."

But they scraped off their whiskers, stuffed the more offensive T-shirts back into their duffels, and at one time or another, most of them managed to pass by the platoon's canvas HQ in order to lay eyes on their new lieutenant. Strangely enough, considering Allen's first gut reaction, most of the guys thought he'd work out great.

It was funny, Allen reflected that night as he stared up into the darkness. You'd think men as hard-pressed as these would be so glad to rest in the relative safety of the company NDP that they'd drag their feet at anything threatening to push them outside the perimeter. Still, even if he didn't like the man, he'd give him a chance. He had to admit, life in camp was so boring it made his skin jump. If surface tidiness for an REMF was the price to pay for getting back out into the bush, then shave he would. Hell, he'd spit-polish his jungle boots if the bastard wanted him to.

Out in the bush, that was where he belonged.

LIEUTENANT BRENNAN—NOW PERMANENTLY KNOWN AS BRENDA—HAD his platoon assembled on the clearing used by the supply choppers. Most of the men hadn't been at full attention in many weeks, and their bodies had forgotten how. The sergeant howled at them until they were more or less rigid—cheeks smooth, hair cropped, pants bloused into clean boots—then gave them permission to stand at ease.

The lieutenant stood before them, hands clasped behind his back, eyes invisible behind his black glasses, waiting for their attention to settle. Allen prepared himself for the standard lecture taken from an officer's handbook, under the heading "Speeches for a Company in Need of Discipline." All around him he could feel his mates arranging looks of attentive receptivity on their faces, locking their eyes on the man while their ears shut down and their minds were free to wander.

They might have granted him their conditional approval, but no loot new to the bush was going to command anything but the most surface obedience, not until he had proven himself.

The trim figure stood waiting. The platoon went quiet, and still he stood. The speech on Discipline and Pride did not begin, and one by one the eyes of the men came back to him, wondering what was going on.

For the first time, Allen noticed how small the man was, a good head shorter than Sergeant Keys. His features were delicate, with high cheekbones and narrow nose, but for his mouth, which was surprisingly wide and full. Dropped into a prison yard, Allen thought, the guy wouldn't stand a chance. Maybe that was why Brenda spent so much time on his physique: His upper body looked like it could do a hundred one-armed push-ups without breaking a sweat.

Only later did it occur to Allen to wonder why he had equated that proper military figure with a prison yard.

The black lenses hiding Brennan's eyes never wavered in the sunlight. The lieutenant stood like a statue while his men examined him, as they all began to wonder why he wasn't speaking, as their restlessness shifted into uneasiness. And only then, the instant before the first head turned to consult the man at its side, did Brennan move.

He reached up to pull off his dark glasses, revealing a pair of icy blue eyes, the irises so pale they seemed alien, or artificial. In the sunlight, the pupils were invisible, exaggerating the weird brightness of the blue. The eyes touched down onto each man in turn with a psychic tingle, as if they were some kind of a weapon with an electrical charge. It took a long time for him to make a reading of the thirty men now under his command.

Finally, he spoke, his light voice so low those in the back had to strain to hear. It may have been a deliberate technique, to get his troops to pay close attention in spite of themselves, but it certainly invoked a feeling of intimacy. It felt as if he were murmuring directly into each ear. What he said came as a surprise.

"You men have had an eventful few weeks. I trust that each of you is now fully committed to paying Charlie back. From here on out, this platoon will go hunting the enemy. From this time forward, I am your mama and your papa and your grade school teacher rolled into one, and when I say 'Shoot,' you don't even say 'Where?' Each confirmed kill earns a man an extra ration of beer and a free day back at base. I trust we understand each other, gentlemen. We will leave at oh six hundred hours. Dismissed."

The glasses went back on, and the man was gone before anyone else could move. As Allen watched the trim lieutenant stride off, he was aware of the hum of talk around him. The others seemed eager to begin, pumped up by the promise of revenge.

So why did he feel as if a sleazy man in a bar had just muttered a proposition in his ear?

That night the Sarge came through, carrying a paper with the new squad assignments and leading two new faces who'd arrived on the night chopper. Bravo Squad was being re-formed, so the men who had been with Delta since the debacle at the river picked up their bags and split. The new faces were an FNG named deRosa, a swarthy boy with delicate hands and the eyelashes of a fashion model, and an Oregon logger named Penroy who was halfway through his second tour of duty. No one argued with Penroy's assignment as leader. The squad now consisted of Chris, Mouse, and Allen, de Rosa and Penroy, and Tim Balsam and Joey Thomas (who'd been with them for less than two weeks, and were known collectively as Tim-and-Tom). They'd also be getting another newby in a day or two.

Later that evening, Allen went to welcome Penroy and offer to show him around. Penroy had been in Saigon, and he thought Walter Cronkite was right, the war was lost. Then Allen asked him, "You hear we got a brand-new lieutenant?"

"Heard we had one, haven't met him yet."

"Little guy named Brennan, weird eyes and polished—"

"Brennan?" Penroy swiveled to look at him, the shirt he was stowing forgotten in his hand. "Cal Brennan?"

"Don't know his first name. Sarge said he'd been in-country since sixty-five, but he's been sitting a desk for a while. Why? You know him?"

"Of him." The new guy turned away.

"What have you heard?"

"Nothing. Just . . . Nothing."

"Is there a problem with the guy? I mean, everybody else seems to think he's okay, but I've got to say he gave me the creeps."

Penroy muttered something that Allen didn't catch, and he wouldn't repeat it when Allen asked, but it had sounded like "Sensible man."

"Hey Penroy, look," Allen persisted. "Tell me what you know."

"Well, the man lost his platoon."

"Lost it? What do you mean, like, misplaced it out in the bush?"

"I mean they walked into an ambush. Three men and Brennan came out. And when they went to get the bodies, they only found one—parts of one, and two mismatched boots. That's the story, anyway. Twenty-six men and their equipment got swallowed by the green, not so much as a dog tag left behind. Nobody could prove it was Brennan's fault, and the three guys with him swore he was a great leader, but they put him on a desk anyway. Guess he talked them into letting him back into the woods."

Allen thought about the possibility that desk duty had taught some caution to the man with the strange eyes, thought about warning the others, and reluctantly decided that starting off with the entire platoon braced against the lieutenant would only make matters worse for everyone. "Might be better if the rest of the guys don't know."

"They'll find out, soon enough." Allen thought that the newcomer sounded grim.

Bright and early the next morning, the platoon assembled at the landing site, waiting for the Hueys. A heartbeat before the first vibration of the air heralded the choppers, Brenda walked up. He waited until the men were looking at him, and he raised his voice to give them his own version of an inspirational talk.

"Men," he shouted over the sound of the approaching rotors, "I am your mama and your papa. Let's go kill us some gooks."

If he expected the gung-ho cheers of a football team, he was disappointed, but the men happily waded through the flying red dust and prepared to be lifted far in-country. A long, cold ride later, they set down in one of the most inhospitable valleys Allen had ever laid eyes on, wide and exposed and bordered by heavily forested hills; the whole place reeked of VC. His squad hit the ground running, to meet up in the tree line. Brenda strolled away from his chopper like a conquering hero, and Allen wondered if he was the only one watching who fantasized a nice, tidy sniper bullet out of the green.

But in Vietnam there was no God, and Brenda made the trees unscathed.

The valley was reported to be sheltering men and supplies for an assault. No one seemed to know just where this information came from, and certainly the first couple of villes showed no sign of it. The planes came down and laid a strip of fire on the far side of a ville, the inhabitants came running out, and after the grunts sat them down and went off to check for VC and weapons, Brenda and the translator worked their way through the old men and women. Brenda had some of the villagers lifted out for further interrogation, but the only thing to indicate VC presence was a pair of rusty grenades and a rifle older than any man there.

At the second ville, a kid of around eight tried to ingratiate himself with the GIs; it was Chris, to Allen's amazement, who turned his gun on the kid and ordered him to *didi mau*. The child turned obediently and sprinted back in the direction he had come; only when the boy had joined the cluster of villagers did Chris put up his gun. He glanced at Allen, gave a shrug, and went on with overturning the ville.

That night their new lieutenant went through and corrected the digging of foxholes. Delta Squad was occupying two holes laid perpendicular to the perimeter, and Brenda didn't like it. However, rather than ordering the sergeant to have it changed, or telling the squad leader, Penroy, Brennan's eyes sought out Allen.

"I want these holes turned ninety degrees. Only one man in them would have a clean line of fire. I want them set parallel to our perimeter."

"Sir," said Allen, "if we lay them parallel to the perimeter, we're vulnerable to snipers from that ridge over there." Indeed, a single machine gunner would be able to take out the whole squad just by lining up with Brennan's holes and holding in the trigger.

"That's what mortar's for, soldier. Redig those holes."

Allen nearly retorted that it was reassuring to know that mortar would avenge the deaths of Delta Squad after they had been mowed down, but he bit his tongue and pulled out his entrenching tool. The lieutenant waited until they had started digging to his specifications, then left them.

"We not gonna sit in these here holes, now are we, Carmichael?" Mouse was stabbing petulantly at the ground. However, in Brennan's absence, Penroy reclaimed authority.

"Brenda's right," he said. "We join up the ends, that way we'll keep both options open."

The ground was rocky, and Allen didn't believe that the resulting L-shaped holes were what the lieutenant had in mind, but by dusk Brenda had other things to worry about than making the squad fill in the offending leg.

The night was hard. It was as if the countryside was a living thing, rallying its defenses against a thorn in its side, isolating the foreign body and bringing in blood to fight the infection. If you looked at the platoon from the air, Allen decided, you'd see a growing red welt all around it, puffy and ugly. And growing uglier with every passing hour.

The medevac helicopter had a hot LZ in the morning; the platoon moved off as soon as the wounded were away.

And halfway through the morning, they came to the elephant grass.

Elephant grass was hateful, terrifying stuff, a sea of head-high blades edged with flexible razors, tall enough to cut a man off from his companions as effectively as a bag over his head. Worst of all, Victor Charlie knew every square inch of it. While the grunt flailed around, blind and isolated and trying to keep from being flayed raw, entire companies—regiments—of VC could be hiding in the holes that flanked the trails and the trenches that threaded off in all directions. Charlie heard you coming, he knew just where to lay an ambush, and you had absolutely nothing to shoot back at unless you happened to fall off the trail into his lap. Elephant grass was the substance of nightmares, alive and malignant; it was the reason Agent Orange and napalm were invented, and Lieutenant Brennan marched them straight into the heart of the biggest, thickest, tallest patch of grass any of them had ever seen—acres of the stuff, like an expanse of mutant rice paddy.

Lacking heavy earth-moving equipment, it was all but impossible to push through the wet, high grass. The platoon was forced to use the faint trails used by the locals—the same locals who knew they were coming. Allen was point man for the squad when a battle broke out somewhere ahead, and all they could do was hunker down on the trail and hope the bullets passed over their heads. Mouse squatted onto his heels, lit up a cigarette, and stared morosely at the wall of green pressing in on them. Chris sat on his pack and played with his M16's safety. Penroy took out a tin of tobacco and rolled himself a smoke, but did not light it. Allen listened to the dueling M16s and AK47s up ahead, punctuated by grenades and shouts, and tried not to feel like the grass was about to wash over his head and drown him. He'd never had much of a problem with claustrophobia; however, the thick growth overhead, moving to and fro in the slight breeze, began to resemble the tentacles of a huge sea anemone, wafting with the tides and waiting to curl in on their prey. He took his eyes off the grass and looked at his neighbor, and saw the little new guy sweating, his dark eyes wide and staring at the narrow strip of blue sky between all that green—Jesus, Allen thought; if they didn't move soon, the guy was going to freak out completely.

"Hey, uh, deRosa," Allen said. "You ever have to mow the lawn when you were a kid?"

The guy tore his gaze from the far-off sky. "What?"

"The lawn. Your folks make you mow the lawn when you were a kid?"

"Yeah. I used to do that."

"And maybe take the old mower down the street to the neighbors?"

"What the fuck you talking about, Carmichael?"

"Did you?" Allen insisted.

"Sure, sometimes. The old fart in the next block had this huge yard, couldn't do it himself 'cause he had the emphysema or something. What's that got to do with shit?"

"You ever think at the time all those lawns might be planning their revenge? Like, 'We got this big brother named Elephant Grass, one day when you get in his neighborhood, he's gonna pound you stupid.' "

Allen had hoped he might laugh, but deRosa just stared at him as if he'd sprouted a second head.

"Jesus, you're nuts, you know that, Carmichael?"

Mouse spoke up. "Why d'you think we call him 'Crazy'?"

The shooting from in front had slowed to a sporadic crack now and then, all from M16s. Mouse dropped his cigarette butt to the ground; the squad shouldered their packs and continued on into the field.

They came out of the grass in the afternoon, walked up a finger of ground, and, half an hour later, prepared to enter another field. Allen trotted forward to talk to Sergeant Keys, out of the lieutenant's hearing.

"Sarge, we're not going to spend the night in that stuff, are we?"

"Looks like."

"Oh sweet Jesus, won't someone tell him what that means?"

"Lieutenant Brennan's big on not giving way to the enemy," Keys replied, but Allen could hear the apprehension in his voice. This was the Sarge's third tour here; like Allen, he knew exactly what they could expect.

"Are you having a problem, Carmichael?" It was Brennan, his face striped beneath the black glasses where the grass had whipped him, his uniform crumpled, but his back still straight, the generous mouth still quirked in private amusement.

"If we dig in out there, sir," Allen told him, "a lot of us are going to die."

"This is war, soldier. Men die."

Allen tried to control his voice. "Not uselessly, sir."

"You think what we're doing is useless?" Brennan didn't even sound threatening, merely interested.

Of course it's useless, you stupid piece of shit, Allen wanted to scream. *You should know, you've already lost one platoon—this whole fucking war is useless.* "If we give ourselves to the enemy in that grass, then yes, those deaths will be useless."

"Soldier—" the sergeant tried to cut in, but Allen overrode him.

"Sir, there's no way we can guard a perimeter in there. They'll pick us off one by one."

"Losing your nerve, Carmichael?" Brennan asked lightly.

"I'm concerned with losing men. Sir."

Both corners of Brenda's mouth curled up. "You have something to say to me, soldier?"

"No, sir. Just that there's no point in risking men's lives for no reason."

"Are you refusing this order, soldier?" The glasses really were impenetrable; all Allen saw was himself, his distorted face motionless.

Allen shook his head and turned away, muttering to himself through clenched teeth, "Man, you go a long way in explaining the high death rate of new officers in the field."

That, finally, got through to Brenda. He barked out, "Carmichael!" Allen turned back, to see the man's slim hand come up to yank the glasses away from those ethereal eyes. "Was that a threat I heard, Carmichael?" He sounded almost happy at the thought.

"A threat?" Allen repeated, startled. "No, sir. All I meant was . . . Oh, never mind."

He turned and walked away, feeling the touch of his officer's pale gaze on his back, aware that he'd probably just made matters worse.

Chapter 11

WHEN IT CAME RIGHT DOWN TO THE REALITY OF NIGHT IN THE GRASS, however, either Brenda's nerves gave way or his platoon's feet grew wings, because they hacked, shoved, and sweated their way through the field in record time, emerging well before dusk at the coordinates of the next ville.

Most of them emerged, at least. Ten minutes up the trail, a guy from one of the other squads trotted up.

"Anyone here seen Dixon?" he panted.

"Don't know him," Allen told him.

"Little guy from Jersey?" Mouse asked. "Mole on his face, really shitty poker player?"

"That's him."

"Ain't seen him since we stopped for lunch."

"He's missing?" Allen felt the stupidity of his question as soon as he'd asked it. Why else would the guy be searching the platoon for him?

"Nobody remembers him coming out of the last field."

The elephant grass could swallow a man with ease. Hell, it could swallow a damn army.

"Aw fuck," Mouse said with feeling. "Sucker owes me ten bucks."

"I am not going back in there," deRosa declared flatly.

"The Loot's sending Dixon's squad."

"Thank you, God," said Chris.

"They lost him, they can find him," deRosa said.

But Dixon's squad-mates, though they pushed nearly halfway through the vast field before they turned back, found no trace of him.

In the meantime, the rest of the platoon dealt with the next ville. The artillery did its stuff on the far side of the hooches, the villagers washed out toward them, Brenda and the translator turned their attentions on the more likely suspects. A Huey landed to throw out food, mail, and the squad's other FNG, a complete virgin who looked scared to death. Penroy, who spoke some Vietnamese, was assisting with the interrogation, and told Allen to deal with their new guy, a skinny black kid with a Georgia accent that flowed like honey. Since everyone was pushing hard to finish checking out the ville before they found themselves digging in for the night in the pitch black, Allen just told the kid to stick with Mouse and not touch a thing.

It wasn't twenty minutes later that Allen heard Mouse's raised voice, climbing higher in a frantic tumble of words, and Allen knew in a flash what the sound meant. FNGs were so absolutely clueless, he should've made the kid sit on a log, he should've kept the guy with him and watched him every instant, he should've tied the poor bastard to a—then came the *whomp!* Penroy abandoned the prisoners to come running, and men began popping out of the hooches to see who'd got it.

"Mouse!" Allen was bellowing before the air cleared enough to see where the hooch had stood. "Mouse, oh God damn it—Medic!"

He skidded to a halt before the smoking pile of sticks and dust. Somewhere in there was at least one body. Although, judging by the extent of the damage, there would be no nice neat corpse to retrieve. There would be pieces of new guy, and assuming the stupid kid had followed the other half of his orders and been sticking close to his more experienced squad-mate, somewhere under there would be Mouse. "Medic!"

And then, like a spirit rising from its grave—an enraged spirit bellowing obscenities—a portion of the hooch floor shook itself upright.

"Ah, fucking hell," the dark spirit shouted furiously. "You stupid shit, ain't got the sense of my retard cousin, 'What's this?' the lil' fucker says. Ah, Crazy, you ever give me a new fucker to baby-sit again, I'm a gonna shoot you dead, swear to Jesus."

Mouse stood bent over, hands working to clear the dirt from his eyes. Allen tried to help, pulling the wounded man's hands away so he could pour water across his face, but Mouse only struck out in anger, nearly knocking Allen's canteen to the ground.

"Stop it," Allen ordered, but when the curses continued unabated, he pressed his canteen into Mouse's hands and let the man pour the water himself. Eventually the eyes were clean and red, and, Allen was glad to see, whole. In fact, other than a bloody gash on his arm and a scattering of punctures on the back of his legs, Mouse had come through the booby-trapped hooch unscathed. "You okay then, man?" Allen asked, lightheaded with relief. Mouse continued to grumble and curse, so he repeated his question, then finally he grabbed Mouse's shoulder to get his attention. "Are you okay?"

Mouse shook his head, sending a drift of dirt and straw down his flak jacket. "Can't hear a fuckin' thing, Carmichael," he said loudly. "Stone deaf—I'm gonna have to join the fuckin' artillery." Allen and Penroy looked at each other, and the leader went back to his interrogation. Allen walked over to see what else the booby trap had done.

Charred hunks of flesh were scattered over a twenty-foot radius. The new guy's helmet was still strapped under its chin, but one of the shoulders had no arm, and the torso lay in two pieces, separated at the waist. He must have bent over to pick up some provocative object, the trapdoor of a hidden bunker or a gun sticking out from under the family's bed, the sort of thing anyone with an ounce of experience would treat with great respect. Thank God he hadn't taken Mouse with him.

"Anyone know the new guy's name?" Allen asked, although he really didn't want to know. Nobody spoke up, so he turned to Mouse, who had come over to scowl at the damage. He shouted in Mouse's ear, "He tell you his name?"

"What?"

"Name?" Allen said, shaping the word with his mouth and nodding at the remains. He really didn't want to dig through that to find the dog tags.

Mouse got the question, but shook his head to express both ignorance and disgust. "And that," he said loudly, "*that* is why they're called 'new meat.'"

Watching the big man spit on the ground and walk away, Allen felt a familiar rising sensation inside. A few months earlier, the result would have been nausea, and he would have bolted for the shrubs to vomit out the brutal joke. Now, what rose up was a laugh, black as the blood-soaked earth of the hooch and every bit as corrosive on the throat. He laughed until the tears came, then mentally slapped himself, and went to help bag the chunks of new meat, so that what was left of a boy named Paul Michael Stevens might be returned to a family on the other side of the world.

He was glad, in the end, that he'd come across the kid's name—if Stevens had died without anyone there knowing who he was, it would feel as if he'd never existed.

The next day they left the burned-out ville and turned north. The platoon medic had picked out the bits of shrapnel from Mouse's legs and buttocks, dousing them with iodine and slapping some bandages on the larger holes. Mouse's hearing improved slowly as the day went on, but the others resorted to rudimentary sign language or scribbled messages to communicate with him. No one wanted to shout in a VC jungle.

Their goal was a large ville two hills over, a ville that Intel had decided was too close to a branch of the Ho Chi Minh Trail for comfort. The entire area had been declared a free-fire zone; their orders were to clear the ville of its innocent inhabitants.

At first it went according to plan. Artillery barrage on the far side, gathering up the fleeing residents, initial interrogation getting them not much, then accompanying the villagers back to their hooches to gather their possessions for relocation. Some hooches had food stores larger than the family would require, so they had a rice bonfire to send the residents on their way. Hooches were torched, livestock slaughtered, same old thing. They came across a few printed papers and some sketches that might be maps, three rifles so old they might have been the first generation after the flintlock, some cartons of American C-rations, and a handmade mortar that looked more likely to take off the head of the man firing it than to actually reach a target. Everything pointed to VC, but nothing to be too worried about.

Then they pulled out of the smoldering ville, and the hills came alive at their backs. In thirty seconds they went from a nearly full-strength platoon marching away from a job well done to a collection of thirty-two targets trying desperately to burrow into the earth. Furious gunfire, far too close in for artillery response, grenade launchers and small rockets slammed down among them. Men cried out for their mothers and their medics, squad leaders yelled to restore order, no one paid any attention to Brenda, and the radio operator screamed for assistance, as unable as Mouse was to hear any answer down the line.

When the gunships responded, laying down a hail of bullets and tracers in the trees surrounding the smoke canisters, the attack ceased as abruptly as it had begun. Second Platoon picked itself up, counted heads, radioed for a medevac, and returned to the ville.

This time they probed the hillsides behind the ville, and uncovered a network of tunnels and holes that showed signs of hasty retreat. An entire underground village had lived here, larger by far than the population living over their heads, and it took them the rest of that day and most of the next to strip it of equipment and stores. They even found two wounded NVA, lying feverish in the airless dirt cave that was the settlement's hospital ward. Brenda was ecstatic at the trophies, although from the looks of them, neither prisoner would live long enough to be of much use to Intel.

Late on the second day, with the farthest reaches of the tunnels emptied out, the platoon returned to open air. They sat among the trees, grateful for air and sky, while the sappers laid their charges. They had to retreat to the other side of the ville remnants, but the men cheered when the C4 went off and the entire hillside shivered and settled into itself. Their reward was a hot meal, a flurry of visits from the colonel, Intel, and press, followed by the luxury of a night's camp without having to dig new holes.

Chris got it during the night.

They'd been expecting an attack—after all, the men who had lived in those tunnels were out there somewhere, biding their time. They deepened the holes before settling into them, made sure their magazines and grenades were instantly to hand, and dozed with one eye open.

The ghosts came on them later than they'd expected, nearly at dawn, just as everyone was beginning to think they were safe for the time. *Clever move* was Allen's waking thought the instant the firing started; men who had been waiting all night were tired before the day began. The ghosts also came, somewhat unusually, all at once, a wave of small-arms fire and mortars from all around the perimeter, giving the platoon a three-hundred-and-sixty-degree line of fire. Within half an hour the sun was lighting the sky, giving shape to the night's ghosts, turning them into small men moving across the landscape. And then they were gone, leaving Chris bleeding silently from a bullet wound through his belly, a wound that came out nearly on top of his spine. His glasses had disappeared somewhere, leaving his face strangely naked, and he came halfway to consciousness before the medevac arrived, focused on Mouse's face a foot from his, and smiled sweetly.

"Wipe out, dude," he drawled.

The black man's ears had cleared enough to hear him, or maybe he was just reading Chris's lips. "You be back on that surfboard before any of us DEROS, man."

"I don't have any legs, Mouse."

"Sure you do, man. They there, okay."

"Funny thing, a surfer without legs . . . Mouse, do me a favor and check my equipment, will you? If my dick's shot off, I don't want you to put me on that medevac."

"Your dick's fine, man, don't be stupid."

"You didn't look. Mouse, I need to know."

Without another word, Mouse unfastened the boy's trousers and peered inside, then rearranged the flap shut again. "Your dick's there. Ain't no less of it than there was yesterday. 'Course, that ain't sayin' much."

"You promise?"

"Look, dickhead, there's nothing wrong with your fuckin' equipment. And I ain't gonna give it no tug to prove it to you."

"Thanks, Mouse. Look me up sometime, when you get home."

"Yeah, right," said Mouse under his voice. "That's gonna happen." But he rested his black hand against Chris's blond hair, and stayed with him until the medic loaded him away.

The medevac took off, and the men heated their C-rations and waited for orders. The platoon was now so light, they would have been justified in returning to base to put themselves together again. However, Brenda had his ideas about what a lieutenant asked of his men, and no one was surprised when the order came to move out.

"Fuckin' hell," Mouse said. "We just gonna march to Hanoi, you figure?"

"Why not? Go direct to the source," Allen told him.

"What?" Mouse asked, and Allen just shook his head to say it was not important.

When the Claymore wires were up and their packs on, Allen looked at the rest of the squad. "Hey, Penroy," he said. "Where's deRosa?"

The others shrugged. Allen dug out a scrap of paper and wrote the question, shoving it under Mouse's nose.

"The hell should I know?" Mouse grumbled. "Ain't seen him since last night."

"He's probably gone to check on his buddy Gonsalves," Tom said, or maybe it was Tim.

"He's prob'ly off gassin' with that cousin of his, Gonzo I think his name is," Mouse said, not having heard the first suggestion.

But deRosa was not with Gonsalves, and in fact, deRosa did not seem to be inside the perimeter. They found his pack, and they found a rifle that could have been his, but they did not find him. He'd either dropped his things and fled in a panic, or he'd been taken. Penroy took the news to Brennan, who came over with Sergeant Keys to examine the abandoned gear.

"He was getting pretty flaky out there in the elephant grass the other day," Allen said to the sergeant. The lieutenant heard, and turned the reflective glasses on Allen.

"You sure seem to have a lot of problems with that elephant grass."

"Not me, but it sure made deRosa nervous."

"DeRosa. He's the pretty one, isn't he, Carmichael? Special friend of yours, maybe?"

"Special . . . sir!" Allen felt himself go red. "He's a member of my squad, sir."

"And you had to hold his hand out in the grass."

"No, sir. I only—"

"Well, there's no elephant grass around here, soldier."

"No sir, I just meant—"

"You think the man deserted under fire," Brenda stated.

Allen stared at him. Who the hell would desert out here? You'd have to be insane. "Sir, no, I don't believe deRosa deserted. I never saw any sign of cowardice in him, not even under fire, just in the grass. I think he was claustrophobic. He was okay once we got moving again, just needed his mind taken off it. So no, I don't think he ran."

"Well, we beat the bushes all around, if he was wounded and crawled away we'd have found him. We can't wait around hoping your boyfriend—that is, your *squad-mate*—comes home. Prepare to move out."

They beat the bushes for another half hour, found no more sign of this missing member than they had of Dixon in the grass, and finally, looking over their shoulders like a herd of herbivores with a lion on their trail, they moved out.

Unknown to them, deRosa followed. Or more accurately, deRosa was brought along in their wake, across the jungle floor, through the tunnels that wove among the hills, silently flitting through the green gloom in the platoon's wake. They did not know he was there until nearly midnight, and even then they could not be certain it was he. All they knew was that at 23:40, a man started to scream somewhere off in the green, an endless and impossibly high-pitched sound of ultimate agony and hopelessness.

The twenty-nine remaining members of the Second Platoon shot bolt upright, primeval hackles rising along the backs of their necks, fingers nervously working the firing mechanisms of their guns, bracing for the eerie soprano wail to repeat itself. When seven minutes later it did, they instantly wished it had not. There was no telling where it was coming from, no rushing out into the darkness to rescue a comrade.

"Fuck me," Mouse said, slapping his head. "That's worse than the ringing."

Allen leaned into him and said directly into his ear, "It's not your ears, man. There's some poor bastard out there."

"DeRosa?" Allen could only shrug, which Mouse felt even though it was too dark to see the movement. "Shit, what the hell happened to him?"

Long before the noise stopped, it was all too clear what was happening. *What kind of injuries could you inflict on a man, to make him scream like that but not die?*

Most of the platoon was thinking the same thing; thought, too, when the noise finally ceased to come at dawn, that the relief for that poor bastard out there was as great as their own. They traveled eighteen miles that day, losing three more wounded to a freshly set mine. All the while they pretended that they were doing a sweep; in truth they were interested only in fleeing the night noises. They dug in, setting up their trip-flares and Claymores, only to find that the man and his torturers had dogged their steps. From midnight until dawn the shrill sounds of torment rose and fell and echoed off the hills, until many of the men were whimpering themselves, or screaming curses into the night. All of them not actively standing guard stuffed wads of cloth into their ears and wrapped their heads in whatever they had. At three in the morning, Allen gave up all attempt at sleeping, and went to talk to Keys.

"Sarge, the loot's got to get us lifted out tomorrow. We'll go nuts if he doesn't."

"We can't do anything until morning, I'll talk to him them. He's not sleeping either, Carmichael."

It was true, the sound from the darkness would wreak havoc on the nerves of a coddled REMF, Allen had to agree. By morning, Brenda would be soft enough to agree to anything.

Again the noises died away at dawn; this time, no man fooled himself that their platoon-mate had been granted death, that night's fall would not find them again assaulted by a soul in torment. They bent over their C-rats, watching their lieutenant out of the corner of their eyes. Brennan ate his breakfast with a solid appetite, he shaved without nicking himself, and if he was aware of their collective gaze, he showed no sign of it.

"Prepare the men to move out, Sergeant," he said. The men just stared at him in growing disbelief, before he relented. "We've got an LZ twelve miles from here, one small ville to check on the way, then it's hot food and clean uniforms."

And no more sounds of deRosa dying, they all finished in their minds.

They moved out.

THIS WAS THE STATE OF THE TWENTY-SIX MEMBERS OF BRAVO COMPANY, Second Platoon, that April morning when they entered the ville the maps called Truc Tho—twenty-one teenagers who should have been bagging groceries and wondering about their chance of scoring at the drive-in Friday night, plus five men who (if they survived) would be old enough to choose between Kennedy and Nixon in November. Aside from its leader and a handful of FNGs, the platoon had been under fire more or less continually since before Christmas, four solid months of harassment by invisible ghosts with neither planes nor equipment, who lived in dark tunnels like vermin, and like vermin were proving maddeningly difficult to eradicate. Twenty-six filthy young men, their muscles aching with exhaustion and frustration, who had been in the woods for the last eleven days straight, cut off from the rest of their company, battling an unseen enemy who refused to stand and fight, yet who had sent nearly a third of their brothers off into the blue on stretchers or in bags. They had been the target of daily ambushes, been nearly overrun twice, been continually besieged by mosquitoes and leeches, had not eaten a truly hot meal or shaved or even had their boots off in longer than they could remember. They had spent their days being picked off among the bush and the high grass and their nights cowering inside their feeble perimeters, the last two of them spent in raging impotence while one of their own was slowly peeled apart by animals. Their commanding officer, a man who had narrowly escaped one court-martial two years before, was riding their lunatic energy like a kite in a high wind, pulling them on in his wake.

Twenty-six components of a bomb, primed, loaded, and about to be dropped on the unsuspecting village of Truc Tho.

The ville was firmly inside the free-fire zone, which meant: If it moves, shoot it. These niceties of definition had little impact on the women and old men trying to scrape a living on the lands their families had worked for generations; the grunts had seen this often enough to know that just because a ville was in enemy territory didn't necessarily mean it was entirely VC. Still, they moved in with an even greater expectation of problems than they normally did. The artillery laid its line of fire on the far side of the village, but unusually enough, the residents did not immediately begin to stream out in terror. There were definitely people there—smoking cook-fires, laundry draped on the bushes to dry, and a recently butchered animal hanging from a sturdy tree branch told them that—but either the inhabitants had fled before the bombs hit, or they were staying put. The platoon thumbed their M16s to rock-and-roll, and crept through the fields toward the hooches.

The point man in Alpha Squad, a phlegmatic dairy farmer named Kowalski who'd been in Vietnam for nine months, saw it first; his incredible reaction made half the platoon think he'd been hit by some silent weapon. He whimpered—*whimpered*—and dropped his gun before staggering back to retch violently. In a rapid wave out from the center, the rest of the platoon threw themselves flat and brought their guns up. They stretched their senses and waited: They saw nothing but the hushed village with a few curls of smoke, heard only the usual farm animals, Kowalski's vomiting, and the steady hum of a beehive.

And then the man next to Kowalski gave a shocked curse, and Allen craned to find what had triggered the reaction. It took him a minute to see it; when he did, he felt himself go cold with shock: What he had taken for a slaughtered pig hanging from a tree for butchering was no pig; nor was the insect hum from bees.

A small man hung by his heels from the tree branch, flayed down to muscle and bone. His skin lay in a heap on the ground beneath him, crumpled like a pair of multicolored tights. Delicate red fingers, drips still collecting at their tips, seemed to reach down for the skin; the gesture and the diminished size of the body made it look like a young adolescent, embarrassed by nakedness, hurrying to clothe himself properly again. His muscles looked startlingly like the illustrations in an anatomy book, except for the thick, shifting coat of flies.

One man after another looked, and either froze where he stood or turned to heave the contents of his stomach into the bushes. Had the ville wanted to wipe them out, it would have been easy, for shock reduced the entire platoon into immobility.

Only much later—far too late to do any good—did Allen realize that the ville hadn't wanted to do anything to them, that the people were cowering in their hooches, trapped between the VC who had done this in their ville and the Americans who were sure to revenge it. Right then, in that place, with the blood still dripping off deRosa's fingers and the buzz of ten thousand flies rising loud in their ears, no man stopped to think it through. Six months of rage and shame flooded up through Allen Carmichael's gut and seized his heart and his mind; six months of confusion and hatred and humiliation, long weeks of gut-shrinking terror and soul-withering frustration slammed together in the cleansing red emotion of savagery given a clear target. When Lieutenant Brennan stumbled to his feet and lifted his gun, as one his platoon rose with him, to smash and destroy, to avenge their fallen and restore their lost honor. The mad paroxysm took them all, although none saw that Brennan himself was the first to stop, to stand back and watch his men kill.

The chain reaction did not end until it had burned itself out and there was nothing left to kill. Until every old man had ceased to twitch, each woman had ceased her crying, every child and infant lay still. Until the ville was as lifeless as deRosa.

BOOK TWO

Home Coming

Chapter 12

THIS IS WHAT ALLEN CARMICHAEL SAW ON THE THIRD OF THE ILLEGAL surveillance tapes made of the O'Connell residence that May:

The man has been sitting for at least an hour on the black leather sofa, watching a baseball game on the television, staring nearly straight at the pinhole camera that Allen planted in the corner of the high window four days earlier. The man on Allen's screen is of average height, the chest under his loose silk shirt testifying to regular workouts, his face good-looking but nothing memorable. The features of that face are capable of considerable charm—Allen has seen this in earlier tapes—but when at rest, a slight twist of the mouth imparts a look of boredom, or petulance, perhaps even a hint of cruelty. Particularly, as now, when he is drinking.

He seems to be paying little attention to the game in front of him, for the occasional crowd roars that Allen's bug picks up have no corresponding effect on the man's expression. He frowns occasionally, and once glances at his wristwatch, but for the past forty-seven minutes his only change of position has been to walk over to the wet bar and refill his glass. He has done this three times.

Now a sound snags his attention, and his light blue eyes flick to the doorway at his side. After a moment, the lower half of a heavily built man appears, and the man on the sofa lifts the empty glass in his left hand. The figure enters the side of Allen's screen, his head cut off by the upper border—when planting the camera, Allen had to sacrifice a broad picture of the room for the invisibility of his lens—and a meaty hand reaches out to take the glass.

The figure that now crosses the room is called "Howard" by Jamie and his father, "Mr. Howard" by the housekeeper; Allen thinks he is probably the George Howard listed as an employee of O'Connell's company. He looks like a professional bodybuilder, cropped blond hair and muscles that strain his polo shirt and the thighs of his tan pants. He does not live here, although he spends most of his time with O'Connell, doing pretty much whatever needs doing, from picking up the boy at school to hauling the garbage and recycling bins from garage to street. And now, filling his boss's glass with expensive whiskey and carrying it back to him. The big man then turns, taking three steps toward the television before a movement from the sitting man's mouth brings him to a halt. Allen can't tell what has been said, since the noise from the game drowns out the words, but it makes the bodybuilder stop, then turn to go out the door again.

When the other has left, O'Connell sets his glass sharply on the table in front of the sofa and goes over to the wet bar again, this time continuing around behind it. He ducks down, disappearing from view for a few seconds; when he comes back up, he is holding a beautiful old double-barreled shotgun. He also has a pair of shells, sticking out from between his fingers like cigar stubs, but even though Allen replays the recording several times at slow speed, he cannot tell if the man has taken them from a box, or from the gun itself. He can, however, see that the man's expression is no longer bored.

O'Connell returns to his position on the sofa, laying the gleaming weapon onto the black cushion beside him. He leans forward to stand the two shells on end next to the glass, which he picks up, shooting the contents down his throat in one quick gulp that causes Allen's constricted throat to burn in response. The crowd on the television roars. The man stretches out to prop his heels on the dark glass tabletop. Allen sees that the man is wearing worn-down leather moccasins with no socks.

Then O'Connell sits upright, returning his feet to the floor. His head turns, but not before Allen has caught a change of expression on the handsome face. He rewinds his tape several times here, too, until he is certain he has seen the beginning of a smile on the man's lips.

Two figures now enter the side of the screen. The pair of tree-trunk legs continues over out of the camera's reach, taking up a chair next to the television, stretching out so that a pair of expensive shoes is clearly visible at the bottom of Allen's screen. The room's third pair of legs is naked, the feet shoeless, the thin preadolescent torso bare. The only clothing on the boy who has been brought in is a pair of snug white briefs.

The boy clearly knows what is expected of him, and without hesitation takes up a position facing his father, back to the camera, skinny white calves pressed back against the edge of the low table. Allen's gut tenses, in his hotel room miles away and hours later; his thumb hovers over the fast-forward button. But what happens next is nothing that long experience could have led him to expect.

The boy's hands come back, gripping each other at the base of the bony spine. Only then does the man move, reaching out—not for his trouser fly, nor for the boy, but for the shotgun lying on the sofa.

The father is looking directly into his son's eyes. The boy stands still, although Allen knows that he is trembling ever so slightly, because of the minute vibrations of the shotgun shells on the smoky glass. The child's chin is raised to meet the eyes of the sitting man. Those thin hands, in much the position of a soldier on parade, grip each other so hard that Allen can see the knuckles turn white, but the boy does not move. When his father holds the gun up between them, peeling the hammers back to cock both barrels, the child does not move. The man's eyes never leave his son's, not even when he lowers the heavy gun to the floor, wedging its stock between floor and sofa so that it is pointing up between his legs. The boy moves only when the barrels of the gun actually come to rest against his belly, a slight shift of position caused (Allen is somehow sure of this) more by the weight of the gun than by any psychological reaction. The pair of upright shells on the glass table jiggle, then steady.

Does their presence on the table mean the gun is unloaded?

Allen has to remind himself that this has taken place hours before, that there is nothing he can do about this episode, it's over. Beyond his reach. The boy has to do this alone.

The two figures remain in their positions for a long, long time. The weight lifter's expensive shoes are still stretched out into the room, their ankles casually crossed in the lower border of the screen as their owner, apparently unmoved, watches the tableau of father and son linked by the gun. The baseball game goes on, the crowd and the announcer roar indistinctly, and the two figures lean into each other's eyes.

Only when the first hammer snaps down does the boy react, with a sharp, uncontrollable shiver that tips one of the standing shells over. The father's faint smile grows, as if he's scored a point, but both he and the boy stay where they are, the bones under the child's skin seeming to grow ever more pronounced, until the hammer comes down over the second barrel. Another shiver, but this one does not stop. The boy is quaking now like a birch leaf in a wind, and the grin the father gives him is one of the creepiest things Allen has ever seen. The man tosses the gun aside, reaches out and tousles his son's hair affectionately, then sits back on the sofa, looking past the boy toward the blond man—or at the television, Allen can't actually tell.

The boy, clearly, is dismissed, even forgotten. The small hands behind the spine separate, then involuntarily go up to hug his naked shoulders, as if attempting to conserve warmth, or modesty. The boy steps away from his father's knees to retreat toward the door; he moves as if his feet are uncertain of their surface.

But he does not flee. Instead, in the doorway he turns to look back at his father, and he is just short enough that the hidden lens captures the whole of him. On his chest are the twin crescents of the shotgun barrel; on his face is the sickly expression of fading terror, and a flush of shame. But the face holds some other emotion as well, hopeless and confused, and Allen has to play and replay this three-second section of the tape a dozen times before he can be sure what he sees there.

It is hate, but it is also love.

Chapter 13

THE WAR LET ALLEN CARMICHAEL FREE FROM ITS CLUTCHES ON THE twelfth of September, 1968, leaving him with a Bronze Star, a Purple Heart, some medical and monetary offerings, and a pair of government-issue crutches. He came back to a country where gentle, long-haired proponents of free love spit on men in uniform and called them baby killers, and police beat up protesters at national conventions, home to the green islands of the Pacific Northwest, to a peaceful sea that was home to the intelligent black-and-white orca and the fragrant cedar tree.

Home to a place where the people were afraid of him.

He'd told his family not to come visit him in the Honolulu military hospital, not wanting to see anyone he cared about in that setting, not wanting them to see him. But Lisa came anyway, a week after he'd gotten there, showed up tentatively at the door to the ward the day after his second surgery with a bunch of flowers that looked as if she'd carried them all the way from the islands. The nurse was late with his pain meds, so he was sweating and panting with his teeth clenched against the fire burning up his leg, staring at the open door as if he could summon her there by sheer will, when abruptly his eyes reported that the sweet-faced, long-haired girl in the miniskirt was someone he knew.

He'd far rather have seen the nurse there, although the other guys in the ward were more than happy to make up for his lack of enthusiasm. At the whistles and calls, Lisa nearly turned to flee, but at that moment she spotted him, or thought she might have, and she raised her chin and stepped into the ward. Halfway there, her steps faltered again as she began to doubt her eyes, but she came on, ass-length blond hair shimmering under the fluorescent lights, legs like something from a pinup, made-up eyes, white lipstick, looking so innocent and untouched that Allen felt like weeping.

Then she was by his bedside, her fear pushed down and her uncertainty betrayed only by a slight waver in her voice when she said his name. "Allen?"

"You shouldn't have come," he told her, but it was like swatting a kitten, and he relented. "But I've got to say, you're the most gorgeous thing I've seen in about two hundred years."

Lisa blossomed into a smile, and leaned forward to kiss him, but he was afraid that if he let his jaws relax into it, he'd start to moan—and not from pleasure. So he accepted her kiss closemouthed, and she drew away, the questions back in her face.

"My leg's kind of sore," he admitted. "They operated again yesterday."

The operation at any rate gave them something to talk about, and after a while the nurse came and gave him his drugs, and things got better, if a bit fuzzy. Later he remembered Lisa offering to stay until he went home. He also remembered the look of relief, poorly concealed, when he told her he didn't want her to.

He saw her next at the airport in Seattle. He was the last off the plane, thanks to the crutches, but when he came into the hall, she was not there. The terminal was bright and noisy and whirling with strangers dressed in peculiar clothing, and in the hospital he'd heard stories about hippies spitting on soldiers. Sweat broke out under his uniform as his eyes began a recon for potential ambushes, and he found himself backing into a corner where he could see everything coming at him. The stewardesses came off the plane, and the flight crew, and he was just starting to wonder how the hell a man on crutches was supposed to hump his duffel bag all the way to the islands when Lisa came flying down the terminal, all legs and hair, to rescue him.

She didn't understand his silent mood, and became hurt at his refusal to laugh away her car problems. He dozed, or pretended to doze, on the drive north, and on the ferry used his crutches as an excuse to stay in the car. Lisa went up to the passenger deck, coming back before they docked with a paper cup of coffee for him. She was ridiculously grateful when he not only accepted it, but leaned forward to kiss her on the lips.

There was, inevitably, a party to celebrate the hero's return, all the cousins and aunts and childhood friends gathered together as if to exorcise the horrors from his past year. And Allen stood apart, watching their mouths move as they consumed food and emitted words, knowing beyond a doubt that he had nothing whatsoever in common with these people. His real family was either in Vietnam or dead; these were loud strangers who twitched and shied away whenever he made a sudden move. After an hour, when the noise was building into a crescendo of desperation, he saw his brother eyeing him, wondering and uncertain. Allen put down his drink and struggled his way to bed.

IT TOOK HIM A WEEK TO WORK UP HIS COURAGE TO SLEEP WITH LISA. HE told himself he didn't know how his leg would take it, that she was too innocent to feel comfortable in being on top, but deep down, he knew he was terrified of hurting her.

When they did manage it, and she did not bruise with the desperation of his embrace or melt from the acid emanations of his accumulated guilt, he felt that he had taken the first step to leaving Vietnam behind. As soon as he was off the crutches, he limped away from the dark identity of "Crazy" Carmichael as well. One night in October, his body spooned to the length of her back, his left hand cupped around the heaviness of her breast, he asked her to marry him.

She wriggled around to face him, and said yes.

They wed quietly in the town hall, witnessed by Lisa's parents and kid sister Nikki, two of Allen's aunts, and his brother Jerry. The following week, Allen filled out the paperwork requesting a mid-year university reentry. Life resumed.

He didn't sleep worth shit, of course; that was to be expected. And food had no taste to it and sex tended to be either frantic or nonexistent, both of which left Lisa unsatisfied. But he told himself that it took time to crawl out of the sewer. That it was normal to be washing your hands in the sink and suddenly imagine you were standing in a river washing dried blood from your arms. That anyone in his position would feel like a cracked sheet of glass rattling loose in its frame, waiting for a minor knock to shatter it to bits.

Classes started in January. The campus stank of rotting corpses—not always, just occasionally. One morning in February he glanced up in the lecture hall and knew, with no doubt in his mind, that the instant before he raised his eyes every person there including the professor had been dressed in black NVA pajamas.

In March Allen gave up driving when he spotted a booby trap in the center of the freeway, jerked the wheel violently, and missed causing a massive pile-up by inches. The bus system proved no less troublesome, because deRosa liked to ride in the back during rush hour, affording Allen glimpses of flayed skin in between the shoulders of bored commuters. In April, Allen took to carrying a screw-top bottle of vodka, which he was pleased to find kept both deRosa and the smell of corpses at bay.

The summer of 1969 found more hippies converging on San Francisco and Allen carrying a heavy load of summer classes, leaving him with only August to fill. The month of free time, which Lisa seemed to expect was going to be some kind of a relaxing honeymoon, was a dark hole in Allen's memory. All he remembered were two episodes, both involving Lisa. At the first, he was walking next to her on the street in Victoria, a dignified city across the water from the islands. She was chattering about nothing in particular and swinging their joined hands, dressed in something new and brief and bright; Allen meanwhile was—as he always was doing on any street—checking out the rooftops, windows, and alleyways for potential ambushes. Without warning, the *thucka-thucka* of a helicopter echoed down the street from the waterfront, and Allen's muscles reacted instantaneously. His right arm shot out to scoop Lisa down by her shoulders, shoving her to the ground where he crouched over her, hand slapping his side for a nonexistent gun. Her arm was badly scraped, her wrist sprained, her dress ruined, and her embarrassment so profound, she forgot to be frightened. Lisa was furious, then and when the emergency room was finished with their X rays and strapping tape. He finally had to tell her that he'd thought he'd been protecting her from a gunship. That was when she began to look at him oddly.

But it wasn't until two days before classes began that the previous September's apprehension returned to her eyes. The weather had turned cool, and they had spent the afternoon at the movies, so that Allen could be inside before darkness fell. Lisa was feeling hopeful, and flirtatious, and she did a sort of self-conscious striptease in the bedroom, tossing her clothes around to stir her husband's passion. It succeeded beyond anything she could have imagined: When Allen came out of the bathroom and spotted her red tights lying in a skinned heap on the floor, he went berserk, shouting and breaking furniture. The evening ended with her in tears and him drinking himself into a stupor. At four the next morning, he woke to her choking noises and struggles, and the realization that his hands were around her throat.

From then on, the fear was never very far down in her eyes. And Allen slept on the sofa, waking several times each night to check the doors and survey the street below. He couldn't make her happy, but at least he could keep her safe. From himself, if no other.

HE MANAGED THE REMAINDER OF HIS UNIVERSITY CAREER BY SWEATING the books and taking on a massive class load (hell, he wasn't sleeping anyway). He played on the sensibilities of two profs who weren't peaceniks to gain credits for class work he hadn't actually done. At the end of it, his college years seemed to have been spent with a scream of rage clenched between his teeth—a huge animal fury that would rise up at nothing more than the suicidal innocence of the other students as they thoughtlessly settled down without so much as a glance at the rooftops, or at the professors who thought their classes had any kind of relevance to a world in which VC skinned living men. But he clamped his feelings under iron control, and in the end, he managed to cram four years into two and a half, graduating in June of 1970 along with the class he had originally entered with, the year before he'd enlisted.

Almost as if he hadn't gone away at all.

A job followed. And another job, when that one fell through. And a third close on its heels. A weeklong fight with Lisa about having a baby (a dream, about deRosa coming to pick Lisa's newborn up with his bloody hands) ending with her moving out for a while, then returning with tears and pleas that she didn't understand why he was acting this way, what he wanted her to do, what had happened to them. . . . And another job, more fights, while the cracks in the glass façade spread, the hold on its frame weakened.

CHRISTMAS 1971: DINNER AND FAMILY AND A TREE, AND THE EVENT THAT sent the pieces of Allen's life raining down with terrifying rapidity. Afterward, he could never understand why one snide remark from one of his smart-mouthed hippie cousins should have sent it all to hell. Allen had been eating remarks like that for three years, what was one more? Maybe because he was in his own home, surrounded by family, his and Lisa's, and that self-righteous sneer from a boy too young to face the draft was the final straw. Maybe the remark itself had nothing to do with it, but only chanced to coincide with the countdown of seconds from the timer that had been pulled long ago and in another country. Allen couldn't even remember exactly what the jerk had said, only that he'd said it, leaning back in his chair and looking at his girlfriend for approval. Whatever the trigger was, the result was the same: Allen came out of his chair with the intention of taking the guy apart.

It took most of the men there to pull him off the terrified long-hair, a whirlwind of blood and shouting and the sweet and glorious release of pounding the bastard's bearded face to a pulp. Panting and huge and feeling whole for the first time since the VC bullet had dumped him into the stinking paddy, Allen slowly became aware of the rest of the crowded room, the appalled women and charged-up men, the huge eyes of Lisa's gorgeous little red-haired kid sister Nikki, the bloody nose of seventeen-year-old Jerry, who'd somehow gotten in the way of his brother's fist. His father, disappointed yet again.

A moment of stillness, all the faces turned to him; a moment eerily akin in his mind to that of Brennan looking out from the cave. A shrill sound began to sing through his brain, jangling like malaria pills, dangerous like the whine of a starlight scope when it is first toggled on. Only this grew, quickly, becoming clearly audible but directionless— why did none of the others hear it? The sound was piercing now, flooding his head, a shrieking cacophony like a whistle or a woman's voice or—or a man being tortured to death out in the green. It climbed higher and louder until all the fractures of his glass façade seemed to quiver in their frame. Then Nikki broke into gulping hysterics and a roar of emotion filled the room, and Allen felt his life shatter and rain down around him.

He turned and ran.

Back into the jungle, where a creature like him belonged.

Allen left his home, left the islands, left the state for a while, moving ever deeper into the green, burrowing deep among the splintered remains of his life, doing his best to hide from the noise and what it had to tell him. For months, years, the piercing wail of a man in agony rode his brain like a constant auditory migraine. Afterward, when the scream began at last to fade, pieces of his time in the wilderness came back to him, but never in its entirety, only as hunks and slivers that he would push around, uncertain just where each memory belonged, or how many were missing entirely.

A CLEAN-EDGED SHARD, UNCONNECTED TO ANYTHING ELSE: ALLEN WAS drunk, so profoundly intoxicated, he had come out the other side into a moment of startling sobriety. He could remember every detail of the faces around him, the wrinkles on the cop's uniform, the spicy smell of the guy's deodorant and the chewed nail on the thumb that grasped the nightstick. Allen's throat ached with the roar he was letting out, his shoulders bunched, remembering the sensation of throwing himself into battle with nothing held back, his feet recalled the intimate crunch of the grit beneath his shoes as he crouched to launch himself at the other man. Then out of the corner of his eye the thumb going tight on the nightstick, and clean bright nothingness.

SOMEPLACE WARM; PALM TREES AND SAND. SUNBURN CRINKLING THE SKIN on his face, eyeballs burning with the glare off the water, his back leaning against a wall or building, something hard. And a very young child playing with a bright red beach ball, a girl of three or four with a floppy pink hat on top of her glossy blond curls. The ball got away from her and came to rest near his feet. He stretched, an enormous distance, to nudge it back in her direction, when a shrieking harpy flapped out of the day and beat him verbally about the head and shoulders, snatching the child up and scurrying with her to the safety of their umbrella, the child shrieking too as the ball got farther and farther away. Allen thought he had somehow managed to get the red object into his hands and propel it in the general direction of the beach umbrella; he thought he remembered the child's steady gaze, her look of considered appreciation, as if they had for a moment shared some secret acknowledgment of the important things in the universe, but he could never be sure. That uncertainty troubled him, out of all proportion.

Come to think of it, he was probably drunk then as well.

ANOTHER FRAGMENT, BRIGHT AND SHARP. WINTERTIME, RAIN SHEETING down on the other side of a partially intact wall, warmed by a small fire that he fed scraps of two-by-fours and broken pallets, talking for a long time to Streak and Mouse about mountains and football and methods of keeping your feet dry. Mouse was dim, his black skin fading into the night, but Streak was as clear and solid as the boots on Allen's feet, the white patch in his hair gleaming in the firelight.

HE'D SPENT SOME TIME IN THE WOODS—THE ACTUAL WOODS—HE WAS sure. One fragment had the smell of mussels cooking in seaweed, so he must have lived on a beach for a while. But in another, he was in the deep woods with the silence and the stars and the green stretching out for a hundred miles, his possessions reduced to the small pack on his back. He'd been hungry for so long, he was probably not far from starvation, but the pains in his belly no longer bothered him. It was almost like being on patrol. Particularly when one evening he caught a faint whiff of strangers, and all his senses went wild. He slipped out of his pack, took his big knife into his hand, and crept in utter silence through the undergrowth, hunting the intruder.

There were four of them, two men and two women, disguised by long hair and hiding their NVA pajamas under jeans and Mexican ponchos, but Allen was not deceived. He squatted motionless outside the firelight as they cooked and ate their meal out of battered pans. One of the men then went over to the Volkswagen van they had driven there, coming back with a small pouch. From it he removed four white objects the size of dice. They each took one and placed it in their partner's mouth, a ceremonial gesture, then lay back on their sleeping bags to study the stars. Nothing happened for a while. Then one of the women began to giggle quietly to herself, and one of the men said over and over, "Far out, man, look at that; far out." After a while, the familiar sweet musk of high-grade pot filled the forest; at this more familiar marker, Allen stirred, and stepped out from his hiding place, knife in hand.

Only when one of the women screamed, a full-throated sound that could not have come from a VC soldier, did he pause to reconsider. His eyes finally took in the meaning of the ethnic clothing, the long hair and beards, the VW van, the terror in four hippie faces.

"I'm sorry," he told the screaming woman. "I'm sorry, I'll go now, I'm sorry."

And he went.

He couldn't be sure, but he believed that he'd stayed out of the real woods after that.

*   *   *

LYING WITH LISA, AFTER A GOOD TIME.

"Were you afraid?" she asks him, her voice low.

"Just now?" he replies, and nuzzles her. But he knows what she is asking.

"No. Over there. In Vietnam."

How could he say no without sounding insane? How could he possibly begin to explain to her what kind of fear Vietnam was, how the only hope for survival was indifference? How could he say to this good woman that the only human beings he could have spoken to about it were either dead or scattered, that he ached every day for them, that the fact she'd never been there made her forever Outside? Still, he had to give her something; she deserved that. "A little. At first."

"Not after?"

"No. I was mostly tired. All the time, really, really tired. I fell asleep on a march once," he told her, knowing the story would amuse and distract her.

But then, looking back, that memory could not have been from the jungle time. It must have broken loose from before, when he was still with her. For some reason, the realization that he didn't even know when this was from seemed sadder than anything else.

IMAGES, AS MEANINGLESS AS A DUSTPAN FULL OF BROKEN MIRROR. HEATING a can of beans over some Sterno, talking about the superiority of C4 for the purpose, passing trains rattling his very bones. Mouse's black hand cradling Chris's pale hair, compassion and gentleness such as Allen had never known outside of his platoon. Snow drifting through a broken window—a shed of some kind—collecting into a pattern on his boots that seemed somehow meaningful. A school yard in a desert, brown children and a white teacher, and a uniform come to move him off. A night under a full moon, the stars paled by the light's intensity, and rabbits moving in the cool illumination, the comfort that came from knowing an enemy could not be creeping up across that dark landscape.

THEN, SUDDENLY, A BIG SLAB OF MEMORY, VIVID AND COHERENT. IT WAS, HE thought, probably September, and almost certainly 1974, which would mean that he'd been living in the urban jungle for three years, at home with all the other animals that moved through the dark concrete wilderness under the bridges and behind the warehouses. He was in

Portland, he was sure of that, spending his days with the usual changing handful of bearded men, many in fatigues, some of whom even belonged in them. They spent their days in the parks and near the river, drinking fortified wine, which he'd found almost as good as vodka at keeping his leg from aching and his eyes from seeing too much of deRosa in the shadows.

"You seen Mac lately?" This from Todd one day. Todd had been a Marine outside Saigon in 1966 and 1967.

"Probably got picked up again," said Beanfield, a three-tour sergeant who'd left most of his left hand behind.

Mac's real name was McAllister, also a vet, although his war had been Korea. He got picked up regularly, whenever the wine freed the demons instead of keeping them subdued. He'd be out in a few days. Allen nodded, and turned his mind to dinner.

But Mac never showed. A couple days later the civilian squad was at one of their favorite haunts, a coffee shop run by a young woman whose father had fallen in the Hue bloodbath celebrating the Tet offensive. As she was handing them their to-go orders of coffee and soup, she asked, "Did you know that guy who got killed?"

"What guy?" Allen asked her.

"That homeless man that got torched. You didn't see it?" She bent to paw around under the counter, coming up with a newspaper.

It must have been a slow day for news, because the reporter had spent several column inches describing a decorated veteran named McAllister who had ended his days under a bridge, burned to death. The police suspected arson, as they had found no accelerant more volatile than fortified wine in the vicinity of the body.

"Fuck," exclaimed Todd. "Uh, sorry, Jennifer."

"Don't worry about it. Was the guy one of you?"

"That was Mac," Allen said.

"Wonder if they're having a funeral or something," Todd speculated, reading the article again.

"You could call the police department and ask," Jennifer suggested.

The men looked at each other. In their collective experience, the police department was something you avoided, not something you phoned. The girl gave them her gentle smile. "You want me to find out?"

"Would you? That'd be really great. Here, how much do we owe you?"

"Nothing today," she told them. "It's on the house, in memory of your friend."

Mac, with two years in Korea and a Bronze Star, was granted no memorial services. The local funeral parlor finished the job of cremation and shipped his ashes home to a sister in Idaho, who buried him in the family plot. His vet buddies bought a bottle of expensive California wine, propped up the torn-out article from the newspaper, and toasted it to Mac's memory; and that was that.

Except that a few days later, another homeless man was attacked, lingering in the burn ward for three days before his body gave up. Before he died, he told the police that two teenagers had sprinkled him with lighter fluid and tossed a match on him. They'd been laughing when they did it. He hadn't been one of the squad, but Allen and the others had seen him around, a gentle old man plagued by voices in his head, who slept under bridges because he hated to disrupt other people with his nocturnal conversations.

Then came a third victim, another of theirs. Gibson was a grunt with a steel plate in his head that left him with severe headaches, hearing loss, and an aversion to bright lights. His favorite underpass was noisy, but hidden from passing headlights, and that was where the kids tracked him down. He hadn't died, but he was going to be in the hospital for a long, long time.

"We've got to do something," Allen told Todd over dinner at the Salvation Army.

"Yeah, like what? You wanna clean off your M16, run a patrol?"

"Something like that. Look, Todd, the cops don't give a damn. Oh, if they spot two kids carrying a can of lighter fluid and some matches, they'll pull over and ask questions, but they're not going to beat the bushes under the freeways looking for anyone."

"Yeah, well, time to head south, anyway. San Diego, I was thinking."

"Okay, man, you do that," Allen told him, and bent over his bowl.

"Interested in coming along?" Todd offered.

"Driven out by a couple of punk kids who seem to think they're just burning the garbage? No thanks."

"So, what, you gonna lay an ambush?"

"Why not?"

"Great idea, Carmichael, handing M16s to the brain-dead and the drunk. Let me get out of town before the firefight, okay?"

"I didn't say anything about a firefight. The punks aren't shooting us, are they? One real soldier could take them. Of course, two would be better."

"You're nuts, Carmichael."

"Sure. But I liked Mac, and old Gibson never hurt a soul. I feel like . . . like there's a sniper working his way through my squad, and it's pissing me off."

That was language Todd could understand, an image calculated to bring him over. Frankly, Allen didn't want to do a solo patrol. Lurking in the back of his mind, a part of him that he'd never been able to kill off no matter how much he drank, was the hard-ass, competent grunt he used to be, a small, ineradicable seed of a personality that refused to fade away. Still, Allen wasn't so delusional as to imagine that he actually was that man. He might possibly be able to take two kids single-handed, but he'd have to count on luck. And if it came right down to it, he didn't know if he'd have the guts to go it alone. He watched Todd, and saw with relief the moment the other man gave in.

"Shit, this is just nuts. But I can't let you stick your neck out alone."

"Semper fi, man."

"Ain't it the truth, the Marines are always saving the Army's butt."

Todd and he spent the night in Allen's fleabag hotel, staying relatively sober, working out the plan. Keep it simple, they decided; punks wouldn't be expecting their victims to ambush them. Take turns being the bait. One night the Marines would take the point position, pushing a shopping cart piled high with junk around the city, pausing regularly to carry on conversations with the ghosts before openly retreating to the underpasses and bridges as the sun was going down, and all the while the Army would be following at a distance with a length of galvanized pipe tucked inside his overcoat, watching for interested kids and cutting ahead in order to be hiding near the target bridge when Todd arrived. The next night, Army and Marines would reverse the roles.

It only took six days. Allen was point man, limping along in the rain, covered head to toe in plastic bags and tattered rain gear, wrestling the awkward, clattering metal cart over the uneven ground. He'd been stopped twice during the afternoon by police warning him of the dangers that lurked under the bridges, and he'd nodded mutely and continued on his way. The daylight was fading and Allen was about two hundred yards from the bridge where Todd was waiting, thinking more about dinner than about their patrol, when he was hit by a quick chill fizz up his spine, and in an instant all his senses were tingling. He was smelling through the pores of his skin, hearing with the back of his scalp: Someone was out there, watching him. His impulse was to dive for cover, but in another lifetime, Allen had been good at laying ambushes, and now he reminded himself that although he looked like the target here, in fact, he was the hunter. He kept his head down, one more scrap of society's garbage, and continued trudging.

At the ambush site under the bridge he stripped off the plastic bags, surveyed the area closely for intruders, and then said quietly to the other half of his squad, "Todd?"

"Yo" came a reply from the shadows where the roadway met the riverbank.

"Charlie's here, man," he said. "Stay alert."

"No shit?" Todd exclaimed. Neither of them, Allen suddenly realized, had expected anything to come of this brief, final spasm of self-respect. Of course, he could be wrong—his instincts might be so screwed up by the years of abuse and retreat that he was imagining the enemy's eyes, and maybe nothing would come of it.

But he continued with the agreed-on plan and stuffed a blanket so that it looked like an occupied sleeping roll, then arranged the rest of the goods so he had a clear line of sight, since the combined noise of rain, traffic, and the sporadic trains behind them made it unlikely he would hear anything short of a full motorcycle gang. If they did come, their approach would be from the riverbank or through the train yard; in either case they would be outlined briefly against the lights. If there was someone out there. Which half an hour later he was beginning to doubt.

But there was someone out there, two someones, and they did come. An instant before they appeared, openly casting the beams from their flashlights across the rough riverbank, Allen's jungle instincts flared through his brain, and he could smell them coming, could feel Todd's location in the dark recesses, hear the rustle of the jungle green. Excited voices echoed from the concrete—not children's voices, but those of young men, with muscle in their depth. Allen eased himself back behind the stanchion, stripped off his warm but rustling raincoat, and prayed that Todd hadn't fallen asleep.

The beams zeroed in on the cart and pile of blankets beside it, and the voices went silent. They passed the stanchion, with Allen circling silently around its far side, and halted at the foot of the blankets. One of them handed his light to the other and fished something out of his jacket pocket, fumbling with it for a moment before his arms thrust out into the light beams, revealing a small square can. The stream came from crotch level, up and down across the lumpy sleeping roll. Allen crept forward, catching a strong whiff of lighter fluid, and reached the oblivious pair just as the boy with the fluid was putting the empty canister into one pocket and pulling a book of matches from another. Allen swung.

The lights dropped to the ground at the feet of the boy who had been holding them. The boy with the matches gave a startled curse, before the length of pipe slammed into him. A sharp cry told Allen he'd hit something, but not knocked him out, so he swung again in the confusing light, connecting mid-body with a crack of bone and another scream.

Then Todd was there, throwing himself across the kid, and Allen could pick up one of the fallen flashlights and shine it on the first boy he'd hit, who was trying groggily to stand. Allen kicked his feet out from under him, then took out the ball of heavy twine he'd bought specially for the purpose and bound the kid hand and foot. He did the same for Todd's boy, then the two-man patrol dragged their captives over to the stanchion to prop them up.

They were more than kids. Two well-clothed, middle-class boys, one about nineteen, the other two or three years younger, and if Allen hadn't taken them by surprise, they'd have been all over him. They had blood on their faces and beer on their breath, and they winced away from the light beams, shocked stupid but trying not to show how shit-scared they were at their pain, their helplessness, and the abrupt turn of events. Asking themselves what the hell had gone sour so fast.

Allen screwed the directional cap off one of the flashlights to expose its bulb, wedging it upright between some chunks of concrete like an electric candle. The boys could see them now, two worthless homeless men who had somehow taken over. Allen and Todd stood looking down at their prisoners, both of them wondering how many times they'd done the same with small men dressed in black pajamas.

"You think we'd let you get away with it?" Allen finally said, breaking the silence. "Two worthless little pieces of shit like you?"

"What the fuck are you talking about?" the taller boy blustered. "We were just down here checking things out, you've got no right to attack us like this. Man, you're gonna be in deep shit now."

Allen squatted onto his heels so he could look into the kid's face, letting the boy see just how much he wanted to take him apart, how easy it would be, how deeply pleasurable. The already pale face went stone white. Allen murmured, "You think that's the way it works? You think when you come into the jungle, you bring the rules and regulations of society with you? Oh, no. You're on our ground now. Nobody can see you from the river. And sure as hell nobody can hear you when you scream."

The prisoners did not like that last word one bit. The match boy with the cracked rib, the smaller of the two, was already sweating with pain and sheer terror. He wasn't far from tears, thought Allen. Not that tears would do him any good.

Without another word, Allen slowly put his hand to the capacious pocket of his overcoat, turning that side of his body to the light so both boys could see his movements. He pulled out two objects: a roll of wide duct tape, and a lighter fluid tin.

Todd took the tape from Allen and slapped pieces of it across the two mouths, then used the rest of the roll to bind them together where they sat, shoulder to shoulder. Allen waited until he had finished, and then deliberately stuck his gloved thumbnail under the plastic spout at the top of the small tin to pry it open.

The boys convulsed so violently when he came at them with the can, he was afraid they were going to knock themselves out, if not on the concrete stanchion then on each other's skull. He signaled to Todd to hold them down, then sprinkled them with the can's contents.

When he had shaken the last drops from the can, he put it away and pulled out a box of matches.

The smaller boy moaned, his eyes flickering before he fainted dead away. Todd slapped him sharply to bring him around. When his eyes focused again, Allen lit a match, meditatively let it burn out in his fingers, then dropped the twisted stick. He lit another. As it flared and settled down to a steady burn, Allen negligently flicked it in the direction of the boys. A flurry of bound legs spasmed to push away, and the match died out. Allen lit another, tossed it, and it too died. By the next one, the teenagers were beginning to realize something was wrong. They held nearly still for the last one, their bugged eyes watching it flare, fall, and die against the damp cloth of their blue-jeaned legs.

Allen smiled, and squatted down again. "Smart little prick heads, aren't you? You notice that stuff in my can wasn't quite as flammable as the stuff you used. Of course, if my friend and I'd had more to drink today, it might've gone up, but we've both been pretty abstemious." He waited a while to see if the meaning of his words would register through their confusion, but eventually he saw their eyes go wide, with revulsion this time instead of shock. He smiled. "Yep. We've just pissed all over your pretty clothes. 'Course, you seem to've pissed yourselves pretty thoroughly as well, so it might not bother you.

"Well, boys, it's past our bedtime, old losers like us. What's that?" he asked, as the younger one struggled and tried to speak through the duct tape. "Oh, right. Your names."

He made a show of finding the taller boy's wallet, taking out a driver's license, which informed him that the boy was indeed well past his eighteenth birthday. He dropped it into his own pocket before returning the wallet to its place. He didn't bother with the younger kid, just rose to his feet and brushed off his hands.

"I'll make a phone call before I go to bed, let someone know you're out here. If I remember, that is," he added. "Men as old and brain-dead as we are, you can't expect us to be too with-it. I expect we'll remember to call someone sooner or later. See you boys around."

He and Todd abandoned the shopping cart and sleeping roll they'd been pushing around for days, since they'd taken care to ensure that there would be nothing there to lead anyone to them, including fingerprints. They also left untouched the sleeping roll that the boys had soaked with lighter fluid, evidence for the police.

Out from under the noisome roadway, Allen sucked in a deep breath of moist river air flavored with exhaust. The city lights sparkled and danced over the surface of the water, pulsing with secret messages, and the light rain drifted down as God's blessing. He felt strong, tall, invincible: righteousness personified.

"Jesus, that was just far out," he said to Todd.

"I still think we should've just torched the little bastards."

"And had the police after us for murder? No thanks. And this'll sure bring those two a load of grief. Christ, I haven't felt this good since 'Nam."

"Yeah, well, don't get too attached to the feeling," Todd grumbled. "You sure you don't want to come to San Diego with me?"

"No, thanks, man. You take care, now, okay?"

They embraced, the parting of squad-mates, then went their separate ways. Allen walked on toward his part of town, filled with the glory of the night, going a mile out of his way to use a public telephone he'd spotted earlier. He told the police dispatcher that two suspects in the murders of the homeless men were under a certain bridge, then hung up to stroll through the rain-splattered shadows to his hotel, where he fell asleep, high as a kite but stone-cold sober, with a smile on his face and a mind nearly free of the sound of a man's distant scream.

And when he woke in the gray, wet Portland morning, the smile was still there. It dawned on him that he could not remember the last time he'd slept a night free of horror. Last night, he had actually dreamed of his mother, young and sitting among the driftwood on the beach in front of the house, playing with a baby. Jerry.

No deRosa's hands. No heap of dead infants.

No Brenda, with those ice-colored eyes.

Allen got up from his musty bed, unaccountably hungry. He show-ered, shaved for the first time in weeks, and walked half a mile to a place he'd never been in before although the morning fragrance had often caught at him as he passed. He ate to satiation, but when he walked out an hour later, he discovered that, far from feeling logy, his skin was as jumpy as a junkie needing his fix. He had looked in vain through the café's strewn newspapers for word of the adventure under the bridge, even though he knew it was too early. As the day wore on, he had a hard time waiting until the evening television news, and at five o'clock he was sitting in a bar where the television was always on, waiting for the early local reports.

It was, he was pleased to see, the lead story. When the police spokesman admitted to the cameras that the arrest of two local teenagers under a bridge was due to an anonymous tip, it was all Allen could do not to whoop aloud.

That was when it dawned on him: He'd thought he'd come out of Vietnam scarred but intact, but in truth, he had a monkey on his back as bad as a strong taste for grass or an addiction to pain pills. His per-sonal monkey was a craving for adrenaline, a bone-deep need for the thrill of patrol.

HE THOUGHT IT MIGHT HAVE BEEN JUST AFTER THE PATROL WITH TODD that he'd shaved off his beard, bought himself some clean clothes from Goodwill, and gone to the islands for a few days. He told himself he just needed to show his family that he was still alive, so his father wouldn't cut off the monthly allowance that kept Allen under roofs in-stead of on the street, but really, he wanted to see them. To see, most of all, Jerry.

But after four or five days, he looked out the window one morning and saw deRosa in his coat of flies climbing down from the tree with the swing in it, stepping onto a pulsating heap of dead infants and coming toward the house with his raw hands held beseechingly in front of him. That afternoon, with the thin wail in his ears, Allen headed back out into the jungle.

THEN A VERY STRANGE CHUNK OF MEMORY, SO BIZARRE HE COULD NEVER be sure it had actually taken place. If it did, it was between the patrol with Todd and the incident with the wife-beater, but he had no idea when, or even where.

As if in a dream, he was inside a convenience store holding a gun— a real gun, although it felt like a joke, since it was just a handgun, a thirty-eight. But it was no joke to the wide-eyed man behind the counter, who babbled in two or three languages his willingness to part with his cash register contents. Allen would have dismissed the brief image as fantasy, but for its clarity: the man's patchy moustache and frayed collar, the accumulation of candies and whatnots piled near the register, the feel of the bills spilling into his hand, and the physical memory of the jolt on his shoulder blades as his good buddy partner in crime (whose name he did not think he'd ever known) slapped him in congratulation.

That, and the sensuous memory of how sweet the air was that night, how alive a person felt with adrenaline kicking through his veins.

But for many nights after the robbery, he dreamed of the Snakeman, hunting the American jungles for prey.

What, after all, could a man like him do after Vietnam?

MEMORY SPLINTERED THEN, A KALEIDOSCOPE OF BONE-CHILLING WEATHER and vicious fights and at least a couple of arrests. One instant of supreme clarity involved a knife, slicing into his arm with the shock of a paper cut, but what the fight was about, and what had happened to the other man, he hadn't a clue. The pieces became smaller and smaller, a shower of gleaming fragments: flowers in a park; reading a paperback book by the light spilling through a window; belt buckles lying on the path; the taste of coffee on his tongue.

Then: It was May (a magical word, full of blossom and unfolding) and he was in some dry place, where the rains were over for the year. He was walking along a quiet street, very late at night, carrying nothing but the clothes he wore, boiling with the feelings of clamped-down rage that had ridden him all through college. Only this time, it wasn't very well clamped down, not at all.

The noise that came from the house he was passing seemed inevitable, as if he'd laid the perfect ambush and the enemy had walked right into it. The sound was brief but unmistakable, a yelp merged with a grunt. Allen paused, and was rewarded by the crash of a chair going over, the meaty sound of flesh hitting flesh, and another cry: He was listening to the sound of a man beating the crap out of someone. He turned up the short walkway and simply kicked in the flimsy door. The woman took one look, stumbled to her feet, and fled out the back door; her attacker swung his head around like a confused bull, and charged.

The moment Allen stepped onto the scene, faced with a man in a sweat-stained T-shirt and a woman with a bleeding face, he was no longer in a sad, trampled room with a drunken middle-aged white man. For all intents and purposes, Allen was back in the jungle, facing the vermin who had flayed deRosa, who had set the booby traps, who had laid the pungi-stakes along the trail. The rage swept out of nowhere and took control, as surely and completely as it had at Truc Tho, a savage release of the furies within. He wanted to tear the bastard to pieces.

He did in fact nearly kill the man, bashing joyously with fists and feet before the sight of blood dribbling onto the matted beige shag carpet jolted through him, opening a small icy vein of rationality in his brain. He froze, trembling with unsatisfied hungers, then forced himself to squat down and grasp the man's bristly face with his fingertips, to stare into the terrified, swelling-shut eyes.

"You remember this," he ordered, his voice torn with the effort of control. "Anytime you're tempted to hit that woman—any woman— remember this: I could be standing right outside your door, waiting. Next time, I won't stop."

He left the house, left the town, fleeing the rebirth of the man he'd thought he had done with. He ran as hard and as fast as he could, crawling into a black pit of memory from which nothing later came out but a sense of loss and utter hopelessness.

His next clear memory came from weeks later. He was standing at the door to his own home in the islands, looking into his brother's face.

Chapter 14

AT FIRST GLANCE, JERRY CARMICHAEL WAS NOT AT ALL CERTAIN THAT THE shambling wreck of a human being making his way up the drive was anyone he knew, much less his own brother. The figure was dressed in filthy trousers out at one knee, an equally disreputable Army jacket, and a pair of boots so sprung they were barely staying on. The figure moved with the grim determination of a man long past his limits, whose will alone kept his battered self aimed for the Carmichael door.

Jerry dropped the soapy pan into the sink and hurried around to the front hallway, where he waited for the door to open. The sound of those frayed boots hit the porch, but the doorknob did not turn. Had he been mistaken? Was this just another bum, looking for a handout? A long minute went by. At last Jerry couldn't stand it; he pulled the door open.

Allen raised his bloodshot eyes from the wood of the door—an Allen fifteen pounds thinner than when Jerry'd seen him the previous fall, a miasma of cheap drink and weeks-old sweat pulsing out of his pores with every beat of his abused heart, most of his possessions having been stolen, traded, or simply abandoned along the way—Allen Carmichael stood at his own front door in the islands, bewildered into immobility by the choice between knocker and knob.

The insurmountable dilemma of how to get through the door—as guest or resident?—was solved by Jerry, who hesitated only briefly before he stepped forward to embrace the man on his doorstep. Allen winced away from the contact, and Jerry's hands fell to his sides.

"Jesus, Allen, what the hell happened to you?"

Allen's body had delivered him to that threshold as surely as a fish headed upriver, but there the forces of instinct abandoned him, leaving him mute and shivering. Even if he could dredge up the memory, he had no words for what had happened to him, for why he was here, or how. Jerry saw the confusion on the poor derelict's face, and gently drew him inside, leading him by the elbow until they stood in the bathroom. He turned on both taps in the tub and went out, returning in a moment with a pile of clean clothes that he put on the sink.

Jerry eyed his brother uncertainly. "You need some help?" In other words, *How drunk are you?* In response, Allen reached for the buttons of his filthy jacket. Jerry waited long enough to make sure the fingers were operating correctly, then left him alone. When the splashing sounds from the bathroom had ceased, and the thumps of a clumsy man dressing had gone on for a long time, Jerry returned to lead his brother to a freshly made bed.

Allen collapsed onto the sheets like a shot steer, one leg off the mattress and the blankets rucked to the side. Jerry bundled together his brother's noxious rags for the garbage, gingerly going through the pockets and taking out a handful of change, a broken comb, and a familiar silver shape. He turned the Zippo lighter over in his hand, and a painful smile broke onto his face as he ran his thumb over the inscription he'd had the jeweler put on: *To Allen from his brother Jerry.* How on earth had Allen managed to hold on to this? He lifted Allen's stray leg back onto the bed, drew the covers up, and quietly closed the door.

FOR DAYS, ALLEN INHABITED A DARK LAND ON THE EDGES OF SLEEP. JERRY took a couple of days off work to stay with him, watching him go from a sleep so heavy it looked like death, to long muttering conversations with people named Todd and Snakeman, that concerned revolvers and lighter fluid and blood. That first afternoon, he called in the neighbor for help, to see if the retired surgeon thought Allen should be hospitalized.

The older man took temperature and blood pressure readings, and shook his head dubiously, saying that Jerry's care would probably do as well as a hospital ward.

For days, Allen woke only to the occasional violent coughing spell. He would stagger drunkenly to the toilet and, on his way back to the sheets, gulp down the glasses of water or mugs of cold, milky tea that had been left on the bedside table. He was aware of Jerry's presence, and of visits from a man who strapped a blood pressure cuff around his arm, shone a bright light into his eyes, examined the veins of his arms, and prodded various parts of his anatomy before jabbing something into his hip, but apart from those two, he was left alone. On the way back from one of his midnight trips to let a stream of dark, hot urine into the toilet bowl, he became vaguely aware that his father did not seem to be around, but as that absence was nothing but pure relief, it did not interfere with his return to sleep.

On the fifth morning the sun rose, and with it Allen. His cough woke him, although it no longer felt as if his lungs were about to rip themselves from his chest. When the spell was over, he sat among the fetid sheets, considering the pale square of the window, and finally rose on shaky legs to go and stand under a long, hot shower. A rummage through the bathroom drawers gave him a pair of nail scissors and a half-empty package of pink disposable razors. His heavy beard caught and bound in the scissors, blunted three of the plastic razors, clogged the drain, and carpeted the floor with wiry hairs, but at long last he got it off. The man who looked back at him in the mirror was a person mired in hopelessness and confusion, the hard, distant stare of the past years replaced by . . . nothing. He dabbed at the nicks and turned away before the face could begin to seep tears, and worked on buttoning up a shirt and threading his legs into a pair of clean jeans too large in the waist. He concentrated closely on navigating the stairs, bringing both bare feet together on a step before daring the next, leaning heavily on the banister to keep himself from tumbling to the bottom. He reached the main hallway without mishap and turned toward the back of the house, hands out from his sides as if the carpet was tossing beneath him. He made it all the way to the kitchen, and collapsed into a chair, nearly sending it flying in the process. He had to bury his head in both hands to stop it spinning.

Jerry put a cup of black coffee down near his brother's elbow. "You want any breakfast?" he asked. There came no answer, but Jerry turned to the refrigerator as if there had been. He took out a bowl of brown eggs, a loaf of bread, and the home-cured bacon he traded firewood for. He fried up the bacon and broke eggs into the sputtering fat, toasted the bread, and laid everything before his brother. He was just thinking apprehensively that Allen looked a little green when the seated man coughed twice, then vomited the contents of his stomach across the table. Not that there was much to vomit, but it smelled vile.

After Jerry had cleaned it up, he made Allen a cup of weak, milk-laced tea and went to the phone.

"Mrs. Weintraub?" he asked the woman who answered. "I wonder if the doctor is still there?"

"He's just out walking the dog. Is your brother awake?"

"Yes, he's downstairs. I hate to bother your husband . . ."

"Jerry, he's happy to feel useful. I'll have him come over when he gets back."

"I really appreciate it," Jerry told her. He meant it.

Jerry went back to the kitchen and toasted another piece of bread, leaving this one naked of butter or jam. The gaunt, ill-shaved stranger at the table seemed not to notice it. Jerry washed up the dishes, and in passing made the suggestion that Allen might try a bite. Thirty seconds later, in a sort of delayed response, Allen obediently picked up the mug of cold tea with both hands and tried a sip. When it didn't immediately come up again, he took another. And, Jerry was ridiculously pleased to notice when he came through the kitchen a few minutes later, his brother had even nibbled one end of the toast.

A head passed under the window, and Jerry went to let the neighbor in. Weintraub was a vigorous, balding man not yet sixty, betrayed in his profession of vascular surgery by an onset of faint shakiness in his right fingers, turned now to teaching on the mainland two days a week. He set his bag on the table, exchanged some remarks on the weather with Jerry, and accepted a cup of coffee with thanks.

"Glad to see you up," he said to Allen. Allen seemed mesmerized by a trio of seagulls at the end of the dock, and did not respond. "My name's Weintraub, in case you don't remember meeting earlier."

"He hasn't said anything," Jerry informed the older man.

"He'll talk when he's ready," the surgeon said placidly, and pulled a stethoscope and blood pressure cuff out of the bag. He took his various readings in silence, asked Jerry a couple of questions, and then sat down on the chair across the table from Allen, interrupting his gaze out the window. "Allen?" he said. "Allen, would you look at me for a minute, so I know you're listening to me? Thank you. Young man, you're in god-awful shape. Your lungs were swimming when you got here, and that slice on your arm should've been treated weeks ago. The antibiotics are helping with both those, and it did you a world of good to sleep, but now you really need to eat. You understand me?"

He waited for a response. Jerry thought in despair, *He's not going to answer; he's like an animal crawling home to die;* but in this, his brother surprised him. Allen blinked, looked down at the plate in front of him, then picked up a corner of cold toast. Weintraub took this as answer enough, and gave him another injection of antibiotic before packing up his bag. This time, he left Jerry with a bottle of pills, saying that if Allen wouldn't take them, or couldn't keep them down, to give him a ring and he'd come back with the needle.

Allen did not eat the eggs Jerry scrambled him, but he did pick at some poached egg on toast Jerry brought him at noon, and when Jerry walked through the sunroom that afternoon eating a peanut butter sandwich, Allen's eyes followed it. He ate one of his own, then a bowl of chicken soup at dinner, and Jerry felt like crying in relief.

At Weintraub's suggestion, Jerry had cleared the house of every drink stronger than beer and every pill more intoxicating than aspirin, but in truth, Allen seemed not to look for chemical escape. He was looking for something, that was obvious, but once on his feet, his search turned out of doors. By week's end, he'd moved from house to beach, spending hours in a chair whatever the weather, smoking the stale cigarettes he had unearthed in their father's study and watching the birds and the passing boats, so motionless he might have been asleep but for his eyes. At Weintraub's suggestion, Jerry made a point of talking to his brother, and although he got scant response, he found he could read his silent companion's reactions. When he told Allen that their father was away for the summer, the invalid's subtle relaxation surely indicated relief; and when various family members dropped in at one time or another over the next few days, to see for themselves the disreputable return of the most prodigal of their sons, Allen's gaze and slight withdrawal seemed to indicate a sort of bemused disinterest, reminding Jerry of a large and patient dog confronted with the antics of a kitten. Eventually the others did as the kitten might, and left Allen alone in his silence. They had, after all, seen him in difficult states before.

Within his silence, Allen was conscious only of a vast and dreary confusion pierced by a tiny spark of life, a nameless identity throbbing stubbornly beneath the wreckage of his life, like some long-buried earthquake survivor. If he was aware of others outside his skin, it was in the sense of mute gratitude engendered by his father's absence, his family's general lack of interest, and his brother's patient and undemanding presence. Most of all, he was abjectly grateful that the people

around him didn't have raw, bleeding hands, and that no rotting children had yet appeared to tug at his shirttails, asking for chocolate bars
and bullets.

Then one day, two weeks after Allen's arrival, Jerry came home
from his summer job scrubbing down boats for tourists to find the
house empty, the beach unoccupied, and the motor skiff gone from the
dock. He spent a tense couple of hours drinking beer on the beach
while the sun dropped low on the horizon before he heard the familiar
sound of the skiff's outboard coming across the water. He quickly went
back inside to put dinner together, allowing Allen to tie up on his own.

Allen's attempts at communication (apart from the long mutters
and terrible high moans of his nightmares) remained monosyllabic answers to direct questions or the equally brusque request for cigarettes,
but once he started going out on the boat, he began to put on weight.
Long hours spent on the water turned him brown. His infections
healed, his limp seemed less severe, and his hands grew steady enough
to shave him without bloodshed. Jerry took a breath of mixed relief and
resignation, bracing for the next phase—a restlessness that would end
with an abrupt, unannounced departure.

But as June turned to July, Allen gave no signs of leaving. He
seemed to be more preoccupied than restless. The inevitable Fourth of
July bangs and flashes gave him a hard time, and more than once he
retreated to the TV room with the volume cranked high, but even then
he didn't drink more than a couple of beers, and he was still there on
the morning of the fifth.

Not, however, on an evening two nights after Jerry's twenty-first
birthday, when Jerry came back late from work to find the skiff missing. And when the stars were out overhead it was still gone, although
the tide had been going out for hours, all the waters of the Georgia
Strait sweeping around their islands, rushing to sea along with anything that wasn't anchored down.

Torn between fury and dread, Jerry slapped together some macaroni and cheese for their dinner, ate his in front of the television, and
finally pulled on his jacket to go lie on the dock, staring up at the sky,
listening to the *pat pat* of wavelets against the posts, wondering how
soon he could call the sheriff's office without sounding like his
brother's fretful grandmother. Stretched out on the old boards, he
searched the heavens for a shooting star, so he might make a wish.
That he might miraculously be made older, perhaps, so he'd know what
to do about his brother. Or that Dad might come back from Europe
early and take over, leaving his latest girlfriend behind. Or that—and

then he heard an engine approaching; not the skiff's uneven outboard, something heavier.

He got to his feet, watching lights from what looked like a fishing boat round the point and turn in his direction. The big motor slowed, grumbling down to a near idle and allowing Jerry to hear a stranger's voice raised to give orders. A spotlight touched the end of the dock, guiding the boat up to the bumpers, where it came to rest with a touch so light, he barely felt it through the boards. When the boat and the skiff it towed lay alongside the dock, Allen stepped down, a cigarette dangling from his mouth and a rope in his hand. The boat's engines reversed away from the landing, and Allen pulled the rope hand over hand until the skiff was against the side of the dock. He tied it up and turned toward the house, then stopped at the sight of his brother standing before him.

"The motor finally died on you?" Jerry asked.

"Yeah."

"Who gave you a tow?"

"Ed."

Ed De la Torre, Jerry identified. An established island character, although he'd only come to the San Juans ten or twelve years before. Ed lived on his boat, a converted trawler called the *Orca Queen,* and scrounged a living taking tourists out in the summer and making illicit deliveries in the winter. He was a scoundrel and a ladies' man, living proof that not all of society's anarchists were under thirty. A nice stable guy for someone in Allen's condition to make friends with, Jerry thought grimly.

"Where'd he find you?" he asked.

"Folly."

"That would've been quite a row home, all right. You eat yet?"

"No," Allen said, not sounding too certain. He was in his shirt-sleeves, and Jerry thought he must be cold, even with the soft windless night.

"I made a pot of mac and cheese," Jerry offered. Wordlessly, Allen flicked the burning cigarette stub into the water and walked toward the house. Jerry watched his brother's retreating figure and glanced up at the stars. *I wish I didn't feel like the parent here.*

ALTHOUGH JERRY WOULD NOT KNOW IT FOR SOME TIME, THE DAY HAD been a turning point for his brother. Since Allen had left the house that morning, two things had shaken his world and stirred through the rubble, two events linked by the otherwise unimportant matter of a dead outboard motor. The events taken separately would have left no dent in the state he'd been in when he left the house that morning; following in such close succession, they set out the first steps of a path leading Allen Carmichael back to the realm of the living.

First of all, that was the day he rediscovered Sanctuary. This was a small, tree-covered, uninhabited island of about a hundred and fifty acres, the last of the San Juan chain before the Canadian border. The natives referred to it as Folly, after an idiosyncratic but long-derelict house that had once stood above its beach; the older Carmichaels tended to still call it Minke, its official name until Allen's grandfather sold it to a mainlander in the 1920s. Allen had forgotten all about the place until it rose up in front of the skiff's prow just past the end of San Juan; once he had steered the boat into the island's small cove— just about the only way onto the steep island—he cut the motor to gaze around him, wondering that anything once so important to him could possibly have slipped his mind. He and Jerry had practically lived out here as children, skinny-dipping, sunbathing, cooking hot dogs over driftwood campfires, staring up at the clouds and inventing elaborate ways of reestablishing Carmichael possession of the island. Sometimes they maneuvered to spend the night there, drinking cocoa under the stars and telling each other about the ghosts (here a faint memory of Vietnam passed over Allen's skin) that inhabited the weed-shrouded towers marking the demise of the house. Sometimes they had hiked the bald knob of mountain at the island's north end to survey the watery landscape that was their universe. And now, all those years later, Allen let the boat bump up to the narrow beach, not trusting the ancient dock, to splash ashore with the awe of a New World explorer.

He eyed the path that circled the overgrown remnants of the house and led to the island's heights, but he knew his legs would never make it all the way up and back. Instead, he set off along the more gentle path toward the island's once-magical warm springs. All the way there, following the rotting remains of the house's water system, he warned himself that things changed, that outsiders had no respect for one boy's memories, and he must brace himself to find the ugly hand of a vandal at the spring's perfection. But he was astonished to find the water serenely trickling down the rocks and through the summer-lush ferns to the crystal-clear pool. On a cooler morning, he thought, wisps of steam would still rise from the surface.

He followed the stream downhill until he reached the edge of the sheer drop-off, peering cautiously down at the tiny spit of beach and trees far below. As a boy he'd gotten up and down that rock face without too many problems; given his current state, he might make it down without breaking his neck, but he'd never manage the return climb. So he went back to the boat, yanked the reluctant motor into life, and chugged out of the cove and around the western shore of the island.

Allen's mother had died when he was fourteen and Jerry seven. For reasons Allen had never understood, their father had chosen to split the boys up, taking Allen south and leaving Jerry to join an aunt's household. But in the summers he'd allowed Allen to come back. During those idyllic two months, he and Jerry would sail all over the islands, ignoring the set boundaries to their explorations. At first they had been in one boat, but in later years they'd had two, and could race.

Then in the first week of the third such summer Jerry, eager to show his superior skills to his exiled older brother, stove in his hull on the treacherous shoals to the west of Folly. In the process of picking his ten-year-old brother off the rocks, Allen had glimpsed what looked like the entrance to a cave, returning to explore it a day or two later, when he was alone: He shared more with his little brother than most kids his age did, but that beckoning darkness in the rocks had all the earmarks of a private space. Besides, he hadn't wanted the blame when the headstrong kid disappeared into it.

The low cedar branches that had hidden the entrance from public view on his last visit here a decade earlier still did their job—and more, they would conceal a skiff as well. As he pulled the boat into the shallow pool under the branches, he remembered how low the entrance actually was—at high tide a person got soaked; at plus tides, a vigorous wave would brush the entrance roof. Right now the tide was maybe an hour from its highest point, but the hole in the rocks was in no danger of disappearing. He secured the boat to a branch and waded up to the hole between the rocks.

No graffiti, no sign of disturbance. And, damn it, no flashlight. Allen patted his pocket to check that his Zippo lighter was there, then dropped down on all fours in the water. To his satisfaction, the entrance had grown no smaller—even seemed less snug, which surprised him until he remembered himself at eighteen, the same six foot one that he was now but packing a lot more muscle. The length, rise, and twists of the passage were as his body recalled; when he felt the walls fall away, he got to his feet—gingerly, in case the roof had shrunk or grown lumps. When he was upright, he dug out the lighter and snapped it to life.

Exactly the same. It was as astounding as if his mother had appeared before him, still vibrant and thirty years old. None of the strewn garbage and condoms the island's beach had collected, no spray-painted declarations of love or possession, no smells even, other than sea and rock. After the huge turmoil of the years since he'd last stood here, to find this space timeless and unchanged was deeply disorienting.

By the pale flickering light, Allen picked his way over to the corner where the first cave ended and the next in the series of three began. The cave system reached into the island perhaps seventy yards altogether, and was dry except for the steady trickle of mineral-laden but drinkable water down one wall of the front cave. The air was cool but remarkably fresh, just as it had been all those years before.

It was almost as if the cave had waited for him to return, he thought, and smiled.

Still, he had to make certain that it was not a trap.

He ducked back through to the main cavern, walked to the middle of its uneven floor, and deliberately thumbed the cover down over the lighter's flame.

Darkness snapped down around him; Allen waited, his senses tingling with apprehension, waited for the crawl of danger up the curve of his spine, waited for the ghostly click of a safety being flipped on to fire or the quick *tink* of a grenade handle snapping open, for the jingle of dog tags or the growing conviction that a blade was closing in on the side of his throat, for the back-of-the-neck certainty that he stood in someone's crosshairs, that the impenetrable darkness was a jungle that nurtured a platoon of silent assassins. In a minute—less—the stones would begin to whisper like wind through rice, then suddenly ring with the ghost of an agonized shriek; when he snapped the lighter back into life, the childlike deRosa would be dangling before him, raw fingers reaching for his shed skin, and behind him a heap of dead and dying infants and a man with ice blue eyes . . .

And so Allen waited, for the faint rumor of the cavern's freshwater trickle to transmute into the sound of rustling cloth, for the rhythm of the waves outside the entrance to become the wind's susurration through elephant grass, for the air moving through his nostrils to stutter to a halt so his ears might strain to hear movement. He waited.

And sounds did emerge from the dark, but they were not those that he had dreaded. Standing blind with the cool air brushing his hair and the darkness pressing close against his skin, his ears began to shape the sounds of children. But the cries and voices his mind summoned were not the usual accompaniment to his nights, those choking screams and sobs of the dying. These ghostly voices were more like playground noises, nonsensical but clearly joyous rhythms: the shouts of a ball game, the cries of recess, the regulated chaos of games.

Allen waited, head down and listening intently. He stood in that position for a long time, but the sounds of the cave remained innocent, holding no menace, none at all. He sensed no VC lurking in unseen corners, no trip wires humming their siren song, calling for him to brush close. He stood unmoving in the dark belly of the island, listening to his own steady breath and the beating of his heart; as slow as the dawn, it gradually came to him that in this place, there would be no threat. Here, at long last, was one small corner of the earth that had never known VC.

He thumbed the Zippo alight, half expecting to see his cave transformed into an Aladdin's grotto of jewels and Oriental carpets. But no: only rock. He held his arm high and turned around, staring upward, like a somewhat tipsy Statue of Liberty welcoming himself to the promised land. He wanted to sing a new song, or to shout like a kid in a tunnel; instead he said aloud, "Open sesame," then giggled at the intoxicating silliness of it.

Carpets wouldn't be a bad idea, he thought—or at any rate, a sleeping bag. With supplies, a person could take shelter here for some time. The world would never know.

He extinguished the light again and followed the daylight glow to the outer cave. At the small pool formed by the constant drip, he dropped to his knees and sank his hands into the silky water, feeling the texture, intensely aware of how cool it was. He raised a double handful to his face, bathing his skin from hairline to neck; dipped again, and drank. Then he got back to his feet and went over to the low, light-filled entrance, surprised that the sun was still out. He would not have been astonished to discover that it was the following day—or century, such had been the dreamlike quality of the cave. He crawled on hands and knees through the slick rocks toward daylight, noting as he passed that the tide had risen to its high mark and begun to retreat while he was inside. He squeezed through the final barrier, climbed to his feet under the protective cedar tree, and filled his lungs with the fragrant air. He felt ten feet tall and bursting with muscle. He felt like spreading his arms and shouting. He felt like a different person from the lost soul who'd crept between the rocks two hours before. He felt like . . .

He felt like talking to his brother.

Allen carried the cave with him as he loosed the skiff's tie and negotiated out from under the branches of the tree. The cave seemed to fill him, its hollow spaces expanding to take up all the edges of his person, leaving no room for the jagged emptiness of rage. And when the skiff's outboard spluttered and died as soon as he cleared Folly's cove, abandoning him to a whole lot of open water and an enthusiastic ebb tide, he could only laugh at the absurd melodrama of his dilemma. He was too taken up with the inner vision of all that rotund potential, and the absence of menace, and the echoes of playing children, to worry about the minor threat of being swept out to sea.

The approach of Ed De la Torre's *Orca Queen* seemed almost comically inevitable. And although her owner seemed to know who Allen Carmichael was—at any rate, Ed never inquired how to reach the skiff's home dock—at first sight Allen's rescuer did not make much of an impression on a mind still wrapped entirely around the spaces of the Sanctuary cave, merely: longhaired guy in an old boat with a sweet-sounding engine. Ed came alongside the skiff, where Allen was rowing just enough to ease his craft in the direction of the last solid ground before the Pacific Ocean, and asked if Allen might want a hand. In reply, Allen shipped his oars.

While Allen was drawing in the anchor he'd let out to slow his progress, Ed rearranged the cartons of toilet paper and peanut butter on the *Queen*'s deck. He glanced at his soon-to-be-passenger, looking from him to the nylon line that ran off the back end of the trawler, then shrugged, stripped his jacket and shirt over his head, and reached down to haul in the wet thing at the end of the line. It was a weighted waterproof box, large enough to hold ten pounds of flour or any other substance that needed to stay dry, some substance that the boat's captain might find necessary to jettison with one quick flick of a knife. He set the box on the deck, then tossed its unoccupied line down to Allen.

When the Carmichael skiff was secure, Ed thrust a hand down to help the younger man climb into the *Orca Queen*. Allen balanced on his skiff's seat, but when he glanced up to check that his weight wasn't going to pull his rescuer off into the water, he found himself looking into a veritable tapestry of tattoos, the main character in which was a sinuous dragon that took up the better part of the arm from elbow to shoulder. One of the man's two long braids, brown with threads of gray shot through it, looped slowly off his shoulder to dangle over the tattoo.

Allen froze, brought up short by a weird sensation of near recognition—*never trust a kid even the babies'll kill you never walk through an open*—but when he glanced at the other arm, then farther up the man's body, the sense of familiarity faded. The other arm held no matching dragon; there was no twine necklace around the sun-tanned neck. This was not the Snakeman. And the smile beneath the oversized moustache was the friendliest thing Allen had seen in a long time.

"Thanks," he told his rescuer, and clasped the oak-hard hand to pull himself up onto the *Orca Queen.*

"Thanks" was all the conversation Ed seemed to require. The *Orca Queen*'s master seemed interested in philosophy. Maybe *obsessed* was a better word. All the way to Lopez, a slow trip against the tide, with the skiff slewing around behind them on the tow rope and darkness set-tling down, Ed played his tapes of Hendrix, Joplin, and the Grateful Dead, and lectured his passenger about the history of Taoism, the Chinese philosophy based on The Way, or The Path, which seemed to be what the word "Tao" meant. Ed had discovered that "The Way" was also an early name for the movement that came to be called Christianity, and he spent some time speculating on the possible links, historical and psychological. Or something—Allen wasn't really paying much atten-tion. One might have thought the demands of prolonged conversation would soon have had Allen eyeing the black waters off the stern, but in fact, Ed's steady stream of vocalized meditation demanded little par-ticipation from his audience. It was, in the end, very nearly restful, rather like a waterfall of words with a rock and roll accompaniment, leaving Allen free to meditate on his cave. One thing, however, did get through.

"You know," Ed said in a voice of mild speculation—they were coming past the ferry slip on Shaw at the time, with its Franciscan attendant—"Sartre said that the only real moral decision a man makes is whether or not to commit suicide." They went on for a while, long enough to clear the north end of Lopez, circle the polyplike Frost, and turn south again into Lopez Sound before Ed added, "Might be worth pointing out that Sartre didn't in the end commit suicide. Which ei-ther means that he couldn't make up his mind, or that he wasn't a very moral man."

"I wasn't trying to commit suicide," Allen told him, in the longest sentence he'd put together since May.

"Well, there's two kinds of trying. One is going after something with both hands, the other is just leaving the door open in case it de-cides to come after you."

Allen watched the dark outline of the shore go by, the lights of houses and the glow from beach fires, before an answer formed itself around the buoyant shape of the internal cave. "No, I really wasn't." *Maybe for the first time in a while.*

"That's good to hear," Ed commented. "Be a bit of a waste, seems to me, after all you've been through. I mean, hell, there's a lot of women out there, boy."

Allen laughed—actually laughed. "Women and I, it's not a great mix. Last time I slept with my wife, I tried to kill her."

"Oh yeah, I've known women like that myself," Ed told him cheerfully, and then went about the business of getting them in to the Carmichael dock.

Chapter 15

JERRY SET THE PLATE ON THE TABLE IN FRONT OF ALLEN AND LEFT THE room. Allen listened to his brother's retreating footsteps, and heard a door closing upstairs. He turned his attention to the macaroni and cheese, which had not benefited either from Allen's absence or from Jerry's irritation, but such was his appetite that he polished off every dried and chewy crumb. In truth, it tasted profoundly nurturing, like communion, perhaps, or a glass of cool water after a high fever. When he had finished, Allen loaded his plate and glass into the dishwasher, filled its container with soap and set the cycle going, then made some coffee. When the pot's gurgling turned to an asthmatic splutter, he poured the rich liquid into two cups, added milk to one, and carried them up the stairs. With both handles gripped in his left hand, he opened the door to Jerry's bedroom.

Jerry looked up startled from the desk where he was writing a letter, and watched wordlessly as Allen brought the coffee in and set the milky cup on the desk next to the pad of paper. Allen leaned up against the wall and sucked in a cautious swallow of the hot brew, and suddenly noticed across the top of his cup that his baby brother was in fact a man, bearded and wide-shouldered as their father. Jerry must be, what? Twenty? No, Christ—the kid had just had a birthday, and turned twenty-one.

The same age Allen had been when he'd come home from Vietnam.

"Is everything okay?" Jerry asked him, not expecting an answer.

"Jerry, why are you here?"

"So, you've decided to talk. Weintraub'll be happy. What do you mean, why am I here? I live here, in case you didn't notice."

"I meant, aren't you supposed to be in school?"

"Allen, it's summer vacation."

"Right," Allen said. "Right, I knew that. And, remind me why Dad's not here? I know you told me, but . . ."

"He and his girlfriend went to Europe. Jesus, Allen, you saw the postcard he sent from France. What's wrong with you, anyway? Where have you been?" He meant that day, no doubt, but Allen heard the question behind it: *Where have you been, all these years?*

"Just . . . around."

"Al, you picked up more scars in the past year than you brought home from Vietnam. Isn't it time you got yourself together before something serious happens to you?"

"I been thinking the same thing."

"Yeah, I've heard that before," Jerry muttered. "What the hell *have* you been doing, anyway?"

"You don't want to know."

Jerry's face closed down. He turned back to his desk. "Fine, I don't want to know. Thanks for the coffee."

"Jer, I'm sorry."

"Don't worry about it."

"I mean it, Jerry," Allen told his brother's back. "I am very sorry, for a lot of shit over a lot of time."

Jerry drifted around to face him. Allen sighed, and sat down on the foot of the twin-sized bed. He and his brother had slept together in this bed a handful of times, for comfort after their mother died, by necessity a few times when the house was bursting with guests. He doubted the narrow mattress would hold them both now. Even alone, Jerry must have to curl up to keep his feet from sticking over the end.

"You do know that Lisa divorced you?" Jerry asked when Allen showed no sign of speaking.

"Yeah, I got the papers in . . . somewhere. And a really vicious letter.

Who could blame her? I wouldn't have stuck by me as long as she did." Words were hard, but becoming easier, like water finding its course through a breached dike. "Thank God we never had kids. Is she okay, have you heard? Still on the mainland?"

"She's in Florida, last I heard. Miami. I see her sister sometimes— remember Nikki?"

"The kid with the incredible hair?"

"That's her. She's seventeen, and so gorgeous it's scary."

"Oh yeah?" Allen raised an eyebrow, a ghostly imitation of the easy relationship they'd had as kids.

"Not like that. She's got a boyfriend, this creep from Anacortes, treats her like shit. Why do girls put up with that?"

Allen looked down at his hands around the cup, the vivid feel of teeth meeting those knuckles shooting up his arm. He took a deep breath.

"Jerry," he heard himself say, as from a great distance. "You ever hear about a place they call My Lai?"

"Of course. You weren't there."

Jerry's sure response gave Allen pause: Jerry had been, what? thirteen at the time, yet he'd kept close enough track of his older brother to know unhesitatingly that Allen hadn't been at My Lai. "No," he agreed. "But it wasn't the only thing like that during the war. You leave men out in the woods long enough, all on their own, eating the enemy's shit, well . . . They're not men anymore. The problem there was, the brass had decided to put on a staged battle for the press, let the folks back home see for themselves what hotshots we were, only they forgot to tell the men on the ground that the whole world was watching them. When things got out of hand, there was nothing the brass could do to hush it up. Shocked indignation all around. Calley stood trial for a lot of others. The lieutenant in charge of my platoon . . . well, he got himself blown up, or else you might've been reading about us, too. And that's all I'm going to say about it. I just wanted to tell you. And I'm not saying it excuses anything I've done, except that, when you see a thing like that—when you *do* something like that—it never leaves you. You never get over it."

"Is that what you dream about? I hear you, sometimes," Jerry explained, apologetic.

"I dream about a lot of things, not always when I'm sleeping. And sometimes . . ." Allen ran a hand over his hair, trying to work out how to say what needed telling, how much to reveal. "Things happen that bring it all back. I mean, bring it back so it's like I'm there again. For the most part, it's like the whole war is just walled off, and then something will happen—a smell or a sound, a face maybe—that knocks a hole in the wall and there I am, back with the jungle in my ears and nose. It takes a while to come back again, after that happens. To build up the wall again. Anyway, I'm sorry, and I appreciate how hard it is to be around me, while I'm making repairs." He stood up to leave. "I'll let you get on with your letter."

Jerry studied his brother's haggard face, remembering how when Allen came home—on crutches, twenty-one but already an old man—Jerry'd been almost scared to be around him. His brother's face had been without expression, only the eyes darting about, watching and wary. Allen had lost that frozen look over the years, but what lived on his face now was almost worse, a slackness and incomprehension that made him look lost and ancient. Jerry had always felt bad that he'd never found a way of telling him that it didn't matter, that he still loved him, and he couldn't think of a way to do it now, either. The only answer he could come up with was not a verbal one. Knowing full well that Allen hated to be touched, Jerry stood and went over to him, and put his arms around his brother. He was just thinking in surprise, *I didn't know I was taller than him,* when he felt a tremor go through the wasted body. Jerry tightened his arms, expecting his brother to fight free; instead, Allen's arms shot around him, wrapping down hard so that his fingers dug into Jerry's shoulders. Then Allen shuddered, and now his entire body was shaking against his brother's solid frame, shaking like a man wracked by fever. He sobbed three times, four, painful, wrenching noises gasped into the hollow of Jerry's neck, and then he did break away, shoving Jerry back hard enough to send him stumbling into the desk, fleeing out the bedroom door and down the stairs.

When Allen did not return that night, Jerry told himself in resignation, *So much for getting yourself together.* His brother was gone again, disappearing into the void as he had every time before. In a day or two, some stranger would phone to say he'd found the Carmichael skiff tied to his dock, or else Jerry would get a note in his mailbox from someone working for the ferries to say he'd let Allen ride to the mainland, and maybe Jerry could drop off the fare next time he was up at the dock. And one of these times, the phone call would be from a stranger, to say that his brother had been found dead.

However, the phone call did not come, the note did not appear. Instead, forty-six hours later the door opened and Allen came in: unshaven, limping heavily, and wearing the same clothes he'd left the house in, smelling not of booze but of clean earth and salt water, his gaze clear and even. He nodded at Jerry and a couple of their cousins who were over watching TV, went upstairs to shower and shave, and came down to fix himself a sandwich. He even sat in the room with them and watched the program, although Jerry didn't think he was taking in much of it. When the cousins left, Jerry switched off the television.

"You want a cup of coffee?" he asked Allen.

"Yeah, I would. Thanks."

Allen followed him into the kitchen, laying the plate and glass in the sink. Jerry felt his brother's eyes on him as he spooned the grounds and poured the water; he wondered what was going on. Little point inquiring, though—he'd just get the silent treatment.

"What happened to the old percolator?" Allen asked after a while.

"Just up and died one day. Took it in to Tony to ask if he could fix it, he said it'd be cheaper to buy one of these. Makes better coffee, anyway. Where've you been?"

"Back in the womb, seeking enlightenment," Allen answered. Jerry didn't get the joke, but figured any answer at all was a good sign.

"Did you find it?"

Now the silence came back, and with it Jerry's despair. But when he glanced over, he was surprised to see his brother's face transformed by a deep, private smile.

Allen stared bemused at the gurgling machine, caught up in his memory of long hours of dreamlike emptiness, of listening with fascination and the first tendrils of understanding to the sounds of playing children that ran through the back of his hearing. He smiled to himself at the unformed but sure feeling that the cave was a place that would welcome him, hide him, nurture him. At the simple sense of well-being he'd gained there, which was probably as close as he would ever get to understanding enlightenment, or grace. Too much nuttiness for Jerry, however, so he merely said, "Nope, no sudden nirvana, just cold feet and an empty stomach. Tell me something, Jerry; did Saigon fall or was that something I hallucinated, too?"

"God, did it ever. Like a rock. Two, three months ago. There were pictures of helicopters taking off from a roof jammed with people, thousands of them trying to get a ride away. Some of them were giving their babies away to complete strangers, can you imagine? God only knows what happened to them all."

"I must have seen the pictures somewhere. That would have been April?"

"End of April, right. There's probably still a *Time* magazine around somewhere, if you want to see it."

"That's okay," Allen said, and accepted the cup of coffee. The end of April, Saigon had been overrun by the NVA, shutting down the futile crusade that had taken the lives of Streak and T-bone and Birdman and deRosa, cost Chris his surfing legs, taken from so many others their sanity and their relationships with the world. That was the end of April; it was early May, so far as he could remember, that he'd tried to pound the wife-beater into his shag carpet. He burned afresh with the humiliation and outrage that had taken hold of him when he'd looked up in some bar and seen those laden helicopters on the television screen, relived the shame at having alone survived one of God's huge, bitter jokes, all that death and torture and madness for nothing. But also, now, he could feel a trace of relief. His overreaction to the man's abuse had been at least in part a reaction to the news, not a clear sign that he was losing his mind completely. Not that it made much of a difference, but it was nice to know. Made him feel nearly human.

Time, then, to start acting like one. Conversation, he thought; it's what we humans do. He cast around for a topic, and cleared his throat. "You decided yet what you want to do, when you get out of college?"

"I'm going to be a cop." The defiance in Jerry's voice spoke volumes: He'd clearly been over this with their father.

Allen stared at him, seeing the number of police cars he'd so carefully avoided over the years, feeling on his arms the ghostly imprint of impatient, even brutal hands, hustling his ass into the drunk tank. "A cop, huh?"

"I've got to get off this island, Al. I feel like a rock, with moss creeping up over me."

Allen couldn't imagine his brother out of the islands. "You'll come back," he said.

"Christ, you sound just like Dad."

"Sorry. But really, Jer, you love this place."

"Okay, so I love the place. That doesn't mean I'm not suffocating here. I was thinking of joining the Army for a stretch, and then finishing college. Like you did."

Allen opened his mouth to protest: *You don't want to join up, little brother, believe me you don't want to put on a uniform and go kill a lot of small brown-skinned people who are only trying to protect their own country.* He teetered on the edge of spilling everything: deRosa, the heaped children, shame and a fatigue so great it went beyond the reach of sleep; the near-sexual release of standing with his platoon brothers and wiping out the ville; the lighter fluid boys under the bridge and the convenience store holdup (*was* it a dream?) and beating the wife-beater and everything—even that final thing, the perfect, solitary, gently rolling unpinned hand grenade—that he faced only in his dreams. But the thought of Brennan's eyes hit like a bucket of cold water on the heat of the impulse. No way he'd wish those images on a person he loved. Besides, Vietnam was over, right? The Army was out of the business of jungle warfare, for a few years anyway. And Jerry had just said he wanted to be a cop. How could he go ahead with that plan, knowing his older brother was a person who'd broken most of the laws on the books? Bad enough their father's lifetime of misdemeanors; Allen's were of a different plane entirely. Jerry would understand, Allen knew that, but he would also be torn between loyalties.

Let one of us walk a straight path, he decided. No reason for both the Carmichael brothers to be pulled to shreds because of some distant war, over now.

"A cop, huh?" he said instead. "Man in a suit, the FBI maybe?"

"Oh, right, I can just imagine me in a skinny tie working for the feds," Jerry answered him, willing to be distracted. "No, I'd like to be in a city for a while, just for the experience, and then maybe come back here, work for the sheriff's department."

"Well, I've got to say, Jer, you'll look pretty sharp in one of those uniforms."

THE SUMMER WAS IDYLLIC, A CALM PLACE THE WORLD COULD NOT TOUCH. Allen remained in the islands. Jerry spent his days at the marina and his evenings out on dates with girls local or seasonal, while Allen took over first the cooking, then the shopping, and even gave the house a more or less thorough cleaning. In early August he dug out the key to the boat shed and dragged out one of the small sailboats he and Jerry had used to explore their watery neighborhood when they were kids, and set to work scrubbing, painting, and refitting it.

Without either of them voicing either offer or acceptance, Allen made himself available to Ed De la Torre, a deckhand for Ed's licit services or assistant for the shadier times when goods or people were moved across the border. On the days Ed did not need him, Allen ran the pretty little sailboat down into the water and spent long hours skipping up and down the islands. Under the influence of sun and canvas, wood and physical labor, Jerry's cheerful conquests and Ed's philosophical reflections—and of the cave, although he went there less often than he'd have liked, fearing the watchful eyes of summer boaters—the brutal images in his mind grew paler, and his mind and memory began to unclench enough to permit some reflections of his own.

For the first time since he'd shipped out for the war, Allen's mind began to nibble at the idea of a future. *What do I want to do with my life?* he pondered one morning, steering the sailboat toward open water.

The answer was there: I want to sleep without nightmares. I want to have a purpose. I want to feel alive.

And what have I got to work with? he went on, tacking the channel between San Juan Island and Shaw. I hear voices and see dead men, and I'm paranoid as hell. On the other hand, like they say, it's not paranoia if there *are* people out to get you. Physically I'm in decent shape—amazingly so, considering the shit I've put myself through. A little money, a college education, fair brains, loads of patience, lots of practice in doing without—without food, roof, freedom. I've got good jungle skills—for all kinds of jungles—and the experience to know where the enemy walks.

Actually, he reflected, bringing the little boat about to dance away from a lumbering ferry, a person might say that just being aware there *was* an enemy out there put him one up on a lot of the good citizens of this fair country, most of whom had no idea what waited in the shadows. And of those who had learned the hard way about the dangerous creatures that moved outside of the lights, most hadn't a clue what to do about them, so that they either curled up and died, or wrung their hands and waited for someone to take over their rescue.

I am, he realized later as he lay on the sun-warmed beach of the Sanctuary cove, a soldier. Since the day I set foot on that baking airstrip in Saigon, I've never really been anything else. A fucking romantic, a soldier convinced that he's Serving Right, that he could do something about the fucked-up state of the world. Like Jerry, he realized, astonished at the connection; that's why Jerry wants to be a cop.

But Allen knew himself well enough to be certain that he would never wear a uniform again.

He was, then (this epiphany unfolded at dusk, while he was sitting at the end of the family dock, line in the water and bare feet dangling), both a romantic and a man willing and able to break the law, ferociously if need be. A loaded weapon, looking for a Cause.

Some vets in that condition became mercenaries, but Allen had seen enough of war to know that no side was right, and to pay a man to do your fighting for you made it even less right. He was not the man to become one weapon among many: On that road lay a heap of dead children and their mothers. No, what Allen wanted to be, he decided, was something less structured, more individual. Without the heavy restrictions a cop labored under, free to turn down anything he felt uncertain about. Surely there had to be people out there who needed the services of a . . . what? A civilian mercenary?

Yeah, right, he jeered at himself. Might as well buy me a mask and a cape, call myself a Crime Fighter. You've really lost it this time, Crazy, he thought, yanking the lure off his line and tossing it into the gear box. You've gone right off the deep end.

He gutted his catch, rinsed the blood and scales from his hands, and took the fish off to the kitchen to make dinner.

But he couldn't shake the conviction that somewhere, someone needed what he could do. That someone needed him. There would be some cause he could ally himself with that didn't involve breaking down the doors of wife-beaters and letting the animal rage sweep over him. Some underground of the oppressed, if only he could find them. Something linked with the cave, and Ed, and with the sounds of children playing.

Thus, Allen's summer gently passed. September came, and Jerry went back to college, but Allen stayed on, reassuring his brother that he'd drain the pipes and clean out the refrigerator before he took off. Before Jerry drove away, Allen hugged him hard, grateful that, if nothing else, the summer had brought him back to his brother.

September edged into October. The weather turned too rough to sail, so that the Sanctuary cave became hard to reach, but Allen stayed on. He split a mountain of firewood, repaired the front steps and a drooping gutter, spent the better part of a week sanding and finishing the bashed-up hardwood living room floor, all the while knowing that somehow the fractured pieces of his life were trying to reassemble themselves, that if he waited, in patience, he would know what he needed to do.

The solution came with a tiny event, a terse paragraph of newsprint in a thrice-read paper. In itself, it would have been nothing, but coming as it did after the summer's two fundamental events—rediscovering Sanctuary and meeting the tattooed philosopher-boatman Ed De la Torre—it laid the first stones in the path of Allen's life.

With Jerry gone and the islands settling into their annual liberation from the summer hordes, Allen had gotten into the habit of walking into town once a day to eat at a café frequented by locals. The woman who owned the place was a rangy ex–basketball player who led a troop of Girl Scouts. She had been in his class in junior high, and had never once asked him about Vietnam. He could have kissed her for that, and felt that buying a few meals was the least he could do to show his appreciation. Besides, she had the best pie on the island.

He tended to go when the place wasn't busy, breakfast at ten or lunch at three in the afternoon, exchanging nods with the other regulars and taking a corner table (his back to the wall—some habits were unbreakable) where he would settle in with the Seattle newspaper that had come over on the morning ferry. This particular day he glanced at the headlines, turned to the sports without much interest, and skimmed through the section in which they stuck a variety of things like book reviews and human interest stories plucked off the wire service. This day's paper ran one of the latter, the sad tale of a veteran's widow whose second husband had recently run off with their three children, only the youngest of which was his, taking them to one of the many parts of the globe where a request for extradition was met with open hands and a decade-long delay. He read every word—like picking at a scab, it was painful and irresistible—then shook his head, finished his sandwich, and told the attentive waitress that he would have a slice of that apple pie she'd offered him after all, but only if she could wrap it in some tinfoil. He then paid and walked home, end of story.

Except for the mental click that came while he was watching some mindless variety show on the television that night. In two minutes Allen was in boots and jacket, wobbling through the pouring rain on Jerry's bicycle, to pound on the café's door and ask the startled woman who peered down from the second-floor apartment if she'd thrown out that day's paper. The sleep-befuddled woman dropped the object from her upstairs window and pulled her head back inside; Allen ducked into the shelter of the café entrance to read the article again.

As he'd thought. The name of the decorated vet the bereft widow had once been married to was given as Connor Rychenkow.

Streak.

SEVENTY-TWO HOURS LATER, ALLEN CARMICHAEL CROUCHED AT THE FOOT of a neatly trimmed privet hedge in a suburb east of Los Angeles, waiting for the ranch-style house on the other side of the street to go dark. It was, he reflected, one of the oddest jungles he'd patrolled yet. The woman who lived there had visitors—a sister, guessing from the resemblance, with the sister's husband and two small kids. Kids they would surely want to take home and tuck into bed, he urged, before some neighbor walking their dog last thing at night came across the intruder in the privet hedge.

And there they were at last, one kid flaked out in Daddy's arms, the other whining and half-asleep, being tugged along after Mommy. The sister kissed the woman who lived in the house, and the visitors drove away. The porch light went off, followed by the light in the front room.

Allen didn't worry much; he doubted any woman whose kids had been taken from her less than two weeks earlier would be sleeping all that soundly.

He retreated to his car in the next block, stayed there until the golden Labs and the German shepherds had finished their business, then slipped back up the quiet sidewalks to the house over which he had been keeping watch. Sure enough, a light shone from the back of the house, which proved to be the kitchen. Through the door's window he saw the woman, seated at the table with a mug in front of her, head in hands.

She jerked up at his gentle knock on the screen. Allen took a step back from the door, far enough not to seem a threat but near enough so the porch light would fall on him. When it came on, he held his hands out so she could see he wasn't holding a weapon, then lifted one finger to his lips as a plea for silence. Through the glass the frightened face shaped the words "Who are you?"

He stepped forward so she could hear him. "I'm sorry to startle you, coming at this time of night. My name is Allen Carmichael. I knew your first husband in Vietnam. We called him 'Streak,' " he added, by way of proof.

The door opened a crack, and she studied him. "So?"

"I think I might be able to help you get your children back."

BOOK THREE

Jamie

Chapter 16

Twenty-six and a half years after the night he met Streak Rychen-kow's widow, Allen Carmichael was in a camper-topped tan Ford pickup, traveling the endless miles from central Montana to his island home above the hidden cave. Sometimes he felt that all he had ever done with his life was drive unending miles in unfamiliar cars, fly over vast spaces miles high in the air, sleep in strange beds, and look in the mirror at so many slightly wrong faces, men with dark hair or extravagant moustaches, men with obviously bleached hair and the trimmed beards of gigolos, men with nerdy glasses and protruding teeth. Twenty-six years; nearly half his life.

Over now, he reminded himself for the hundredth time that day. Each time the thought came, Allen felt the same jolt of relief and apprehension, as if someone had told a weight lifter he could let go of that enormous thing across his shoulders, but not told him how to get it off. And each time he had to reassure his apprehensive self that he'd be fine, that retirement didn't kill a man, that he'd settle into a less active life with no problems.

His apprehensive self hadn't believed it the first dozen times, and was little closer to accepting the reassurance now. But it would come, he told himself. He'd get the burden down, and after a while, he'd wonder how on earth he'd borne it so long. He would reshape himself around a future that did not actively involve him in the process of taking children away from violent adults. The cave's foodstuffs, its generous supply of games, videos, and children's clothing could be cleared away, its role of temporary safe-house for fugitives closed down. He knew he was probably going to take Alice up on her offer of a supervisory role, of making contacts with lawyers and shelters and document forgers, extending and laying down new connections on their modern underground railway, but as for climbing trees and snatching kids, he was retired from that, for good this time. Alice had dragged him back from the brink once—and truth to tell, he was glad she had talked him into it: He wouldn't for the world have missed his encounter with Jamie O'Connell. But that was over now. Jamie was safely stowed far away from his father, under the care of a good, strong, clever woman and her affectionate family.

The highway stretched out between the two hands on the wheel, unseen by anything but his automatic vision, the rest of his mind working to get itself around the idea of a new life. For twenty-six years, Allen had been a civilian mercenary in the service of abused children and their mothers, disappearing them from harm. Sometimes this required his services only as advisor or advocate, at other times as out-and-out kidnapper with his own ass on the line. His clients had been mothers with young children, and although he had occasionally helped a man disappear, there was less pleasure there, merely the satisfaction of exercising skills. It was transporting kids to safety that he treasured, the joy of watching a mother as it slowly dawned upon her that the burden she had carried for so long, the threat to her children that she alone had known was there, had been taken away. As thrills went, witnessing that expression was right up there alongside good sex. Almost as satisfying as seeing one of his clients, years later, strong and proud and transformed into steel by what she'd been through.

Twenty-six years of dealing with terrorized women and children, two and a half decades of keeping out of sight of both law enforcement and abusers, a quarter of a century of collecting, witnessing, and collating the most distasteful sort of evidence imaginable. How many hours of abuse had he watched, by means of his hidden cameras? How many whimpers and shouts had he heard through his microphones?

There was no reckoning the hours. What he did know precisely was the number of rescues he'd participated in: forty-eight, roughly two a year. He remembered every face and all the names, each identity inextricably wrapped up with tactile impressions of the case: the texture of a sleeping toddler's hair against his bare arm on an early morning ferry leaving New York; the scent of datura flowers outside the moonlit walls of a Palm Springs mansion; the sand crunching under his boots as he sprinted across the Mexican beach toward the waiting *Orca Queen*; the laugh—a song of joy and wonder—that the small blond woman named Wanda gave out when she stepped from the mountaintop cabin and saw the ten thousand acres of trees that separated her from a husband with murder in his eyes.

Strong, clear memories that made the fatigue, the rootlessness, the danger, and even the endless gut-churning surveillance tapes all worthwhile.

If there'd been just one kid like Jamie in the past twenty-six years, Allen would have felt his life justified. To have been instrumental in preserving seventy-nine kids, that felt like a gift.

Not that all the children had been like Jamie. Most had been simply a logistical problem, a potential source of disruption that he needed to keep under iron control until he had them away from danger. Most of the kids had been either so young they were unformed, or else so confused and frightened that he couldn't tell what their personalities would be. He did his job, he lodged his evidence, he made sure they were cleanly away, and then he turned his back. Only rarely had he been tempted to look up one of his rescues and see what had become of them. But Allen already suspected that Jamie O'Connell would be a different matter—not that he'd endanger the kid by hanging around to check on him, of course not, but somehow he knew that he was going to be tempted. Maybe it was because the boy had been his very last client. Maybe he'd spent a day too long in Jamie's company, and what a shrink would call countertransference had begun to establish itself.

And maybe he ought to think about other things.

With a wrench, Allen pulled his mind away from Jamie, from Montana, and from the past. That was over; he had a life to live now. He was still a young man—well, a healthy middle-aged man—and he had a life ahead of him. He'd leave Alice dangling for a while before accepting her offer, just long enough so she didn't take him for granted. In the meantime, there was his increasingly interesting relationship with the extraordinary woman who owned Sanctuary Island, to say nothing of the challenge he would face in ingratiating himself back into his extended family, finding a way of convincing his younger brother the sheriff that his long, long absence was neither sinister nor unfriendly, merely eccentric. It was June: the beginning of a promising summer.

The miles spun on beneath the truck's tires, and as they did, the myriad gossamer threads that bound Allen Carmichael to his life as a professional kidnapper grew taut, and silently, one by one, parted, leaving him, for the first time in his adult life, a free man.

Or so he told himself. In fact, a portion of his mind could not quite let go of Jamie O'Connell, a boy whom he almost hadn't met at all.

ALLEN HAD RETIRED FOR THE FIRST TIME BARELY A MONTH BEFORE, ONCE blond-haired AmberLyn McKenzie was safe with her mother over the Canadian border. And maybe that was the problem—he'd just begun to relax, only to be snatched back for Jamie; some part of him anticipated it happening again.

Relaxation did not come naturally to Allen Carmichael. Relaxation was as dangerous to a man who spent his life on the wrong side of the law as it was to a soldier in the jungle, and most of what he did in the course of disappearing people was illegal: He was, after all, a man who routinely committed breaking-and-entering, burglary (both physical and electronic), hideously illicit and often supremely tasteless forms of electronic surveillance, blackmail, assault (twice, when it had proven unavoidable), threat with a deadly weapon, kidnapping persons whose custody had been granted to others and transporting them across state lines, conspiracy, falsification of evidence, and half the offenses in the penal code. Once he'd even murdered a guard dog.

Kidnapping was a tool with a whole lot of really sharp edges to it. It had taken Allen years to refine the techniques, figuring out ways to use them without causing a world of hurt to himself and others. That first time, stealing Streak's kids away from their Cuban stepfather, had been an ignorant grab-and-snatch, and he and Ed had been incredibly lucky not to have been caught and either shot by the stepfather's pet cops—a bullet had whizzed over their heads, for God's sake—or arrested by their U.S. brothers. One time was all it took and, adrenaline rush or no, he'd had to confront the hard fact that luck just wouldn't do it. What he was doing was the equivalent of long-range patrols into a VC-infested green, and on that kind of mission, a man's luck ran out fast.

The key was not high-tech gadgetry or super-spy techniques, although Allen had used plenty of cutting-edge technology and had trained in a wide variety of arcane secret-agent skills, from lock-picking to martial arts. He was no black belt, but he'd taken a lot of classes, mostly the sort of dirty fighting that would win him no prizes on a mat but which might save the life of a client, one day. He hadn't fired a gun at a living being since Vietnam, but he practiced regularly at the range, both with a scoped rifle and a handgun. He was no master of disguise, but he could apply makeup that made him look younger or older or of a different ethnic background, and he'd practiced long hours with a coach to learn to change the way he moved. He was no race-car driver, but on a racetrack he'd mastered the controlled skid, the quick hundred-and-eighty-degree hand-brake turn, and the trick of nudging a car ahead of him into a spin.

For twenty-six years, Allen had survived by appearing absolutely ordinary while telling himself that the police forces of five countries were on his neck. In another twenty or thirty years, when electronic surveillance would become so all-pervasive that cameras hooked to central computers would occupy every city block, his job might well become impossible, but so far, he'd managed to avoid becoming a blip on any official radar. Nod a greeting to the cop on the corner and walk on by; look curious instead of guilty when a siren screamed past; drive like a law-abiding citizen who knew that the worst he did was edge up a couple of miles over the limit; with young kids, be a granddad with white hair and a Pontiac, with teenagers, wear brown hair dye and the look of a harassed father.

Normal and invisible was the answer. Sure, they could find you if they were looking hard enough; the key was not to have them notice your presence in the first place. No police force would have a gun battle or put out an APB or do a credit card search unless they had a name, a face, or a fingerprint, and all of Allen's skill over the years had gone into presenting none of those pieces of evidence. And those police forces that did have an unsolved disappearance on their books scaled the search down when they got a note from the wife or kids saying they'd run off, and here's evidence (maybe not justifiable cause, but evidence) to show the man left behind was a dirtbag. Allen had even two or three times come across cops who'd taken a cold, hard look at the facts behind a child's disappearance and chosen to turn their back on it. The letter of the law doesn't necessarily save lives.

So he'd learned the skills of urban surveillance and Internet security, false identities and how to go unnoticed by the most suspicious of men, how to disappear completely when burdened by the innocent. He'd moved through a network of small churches and women's shelters, making friends with doctors and psychotherapists who understood the necessity of going outside the law. He had set up the Sanctuary cave as a place to conceal kids and their mothers; he'd even learned how to snatch a frightened child who didn't know him, who regarded this tall stranger as just one more threat in a lifetime of them. For that, he'd had to learn to think like a real kidnapper, and he'd studied his tapes of pederasts to see how they coaxed their victim into trust. He hated it; his skin crawled with self-disgust while he was seducing a child into going with him, but he did it. And afterward he slept, more often than not unvisited by deRosa.

Thus it was that on a spring morning a little over four weeks earlier, following his fifty-second and (or so he thought at the time) final rescue mission of six-year-old AmberLyn, his biker's jacket (still emanating the gentle aura of cat's piss) stowed in the rental locker with a dozen or so other personas that he never intended to use again, Allen had been sitting on the balcony of his Seattle apartment, feet propped up, drinking a beer, enjoying the bustle of the waterfront below, and idly checking in his mind to see if he'd left anything undone. The child he'd spent most of April watching was physically fine and young enough to be psychologically resilient; copies of the tapes Allen had made were locked away both in his own safe and that of the private investigator who'd hired him in the first place; and the police would get a set of the evidence as soon as the PI was satisfied that the threads that linked her with Allen had been safely cut. The tapes and letters might not convict the bastard, but they would make him squirm, and keep him too busy to pursue his daughter. Another child safe, another creep with a heel about to crush his head. His final job well done.

So Allen sat with the gentle sun of early May shining full on his face, and thought lazily about giving Ed a call. They'd made loose plans for a fishing trip, maybe even a run on the *Orca Queen* down to Baja to soak up some serious rays and go scuba diving in the clear, soothing waters, but hadn't been able to set a date for it, not until Allen was free. Well, he was free now, free as a bird, a man of leisure, a fifty-four-year-old retiree. And none too soon; God, he was tired, tired of the life, worn to the bone. A rest would be good. Maybe he'd even start it right here in the warm . . .

The *beep beep* of the fax machine tickled his awareness half an hour or so later, and although it was not enough in itself to wake him, it did make him aware that the sun was not really very warm. He stretched, picked up his empty beer bottle from between the legs of the deck chair, and went in for a sweater, then decided instead that he'd put off a trip to the gym for long enough, and checked to see that the sweatpants and lifting gloves were still in the bag before he left the apartment.

Two hours later, the sun was low across the water when Allen let himself back in. He took a bottle of water from the fridge and unscrewed the cap as he passed through to the shower, stripping off his damp sweatshirt and throwing it in the general direction of the clothes hamper, kicking his battered running shoes into the closet, feeling aches from calves to wrists. Too long, he thought. Damn, you neglect your body for two minutes, it turns to mush on you. Although when he turned on the shower, he caught sight of himself in the long mirror, and looked over his naked body with critical approval. *Maybe not completely to mush,* he thought, sucking in his gut only a little.

The shower felt great on his skin, and he let it run hot onto the trembling muscles of his shoulders and haunches. He shaved in the shower, and scrubbed dry with one of the thick, scratchy towels Rae had brought him from Sweden last fall. His hands slowed at the thought of her, off in Switzerland, he thought it was, or had she reached Belgium by now? At any rate, she would be far away for the next three weeks, which was the only reason he'd consider going to Baja with Ed. Much as he loved the old bastard, Ed was a distant second to the marvelous woman who shared his life on Sanctuary.

And thinking of Ed, better call him and let him know the trip was on. Allen wrapped himself in the terrycloth robe that matched the towel, wadded the damp cloth over the towel rack, and went into the room that he'd set up as a study.

That's when he spotted the fax, patiently waiting in the machine's tray. He knew before he reached for it who it would be from, knew that his mind had conveniently set aside the *beep beep* in order to put off having to retrieve the thing.

"God damn it, Alice," he said aloud, scowling in irritation at the white edge of paper. *I'm finished, I told her that. She agreed—I've gotten too old for this game. I'm as near as dammit to qualifying for Social Security, for Christ sake.*

He picked up the paper from the fax machine's tray, and read the scribbled note. *How about lunch tomorrow?* it asked, without signature. In Alice's code, this actually meant dinner tonight, only it wouldn't be dinner, it would be a business meeting, and because it was a, let's see, Thursday, he even knew the place. Hell. For the first time in months, he became aware that he was craving a smoke, and pushed away the desire in irritation.

Maybe, he told himself, it would only be a review, or a distant proposal. Maybe she'd present him with an engraved plaque: THANKS FOR ALL YOUR HELP.

Yeah, right. He'd better not call Ed until he talked to her.

SHE WAS THERE WHEN HE ARRIVED AT THE RESTAURANT. LOOKING AT ALICE, you might think she was some mid-rank executive, or a teacher in a private high school. She had medium length brown hair that looked short but could be made to look longer, and the only distinguishing thing about her face was the nose, which Allen knew had been broken twice but which had been set straight by experts. The other scars, the injuries physical and mental, did not show until you knew her well. She had invested her million-dollar settlement wisely.

She greeted Allen with more friendliness than she'd have shown if they'd been in private, getting up to kiss the air next to his cheek and patting the chair next to where she sat. An onlooker would catch a long-standing affection in her manner, as if they were old friends or even relatives. In truth, she trusted Allen only slightly more than she did most men, and regarded him as a useful instrument in her cause, as replaceable as a laptop or a camera.

The waiter poured him a glass of the white wine sitting in the tabletop cooler, and they made a show of studying the menus before calling the young man back. When their salads were in front of them and the topics of weather and politics had been disposed of, she said without preamble, "There's another case come up, if you're interested."

Only if we can finish in three weeks, Allen thought. The apparent lack of concern was typical of her. When they'd begun to work together nearly ten years before, he cautiously allying his one-man operation with her only slightly larger organization, she'd made it seem as if she was doing him a favor, allowing him to help with one of her rescues; now, at least, she'd graduated to a demonstration of indifference over whether he took it or not.

He wasn't fooled. "Alice, I'm retired. Besides which, I made plans to go away for a couple of weeks."

"If you want," she said, cool as always. "I wasn't sure you meant it."

You knew damn well I meant it, he thought, then asked aloud (as she no doubt knew he would), "What have you got?"

"I'll forward you the email. The terminal it came from is in a public library, but the letter looks genuine. A twelve-year-old boy."

"Parent?"

"Father's the problem. Mother's dead."

Problem, Allen reflected, was a word loaded with reverberations. Especially the way Alice said it.

"Isn't there someone else who can take it?" Alice had a number of women who did the same thing he did, some of whom he had worked with, others whose existence he merely inferred.

She just shrugged, a ladylike gesture packed with disdain. God, she pissed him off sometimes. "How the hell did I ever get involved with you, anyway?" he said petulantly, startling the waiter, who was about to remove his plate.

She met his eyes for the first time that evening. The demure smile she gave him was a wicked thing, holding more mischief than Ed got into in a year; Allen shook his head in admiration, and in surrender. "Okay, but this really has to be the last one."

The rest of the meal passed in conversation about nothing.

Afterward, they parted at the door with another air kiss. Allen went straight home and booted up his computer. He poured himself a small Scotch, then settled down to read about Alice's twelve-year-old problem boy.

Chapter 17

THE BOY WITH THE UNDEPENDABLE CLOAK OF INVISIBILITY HE CALLED *The Quiet* thought of himself as Jamie. No one else used that name: At school he was Jim or James (if you were a teacher) or Jam, Jerk, or J-Bo (if you were another student). At home he was nameless when things were good or, when things were looking grim, *Jameson,* or even *Son.* Only his mother had called him Jamie, and she was long gone.

Jameson Patrick O'Connell had been born twelve years earlier to a mother who loved him with all her heart, as much as she loved life itself, as much as she feared his father, almost. He came thirty-eight days before his mother's due date, a tiny premature infant of less than five pounds. Despite his size, his thin-boned mother had a hard labor, and the doctor had been on the edge of calling for a cesarean when the black-haired skull finally crowned and the tiny squalling thing slipped reluctantly from the hot comfort of his mother's womb.

It was almost as if Jamie knew already, before he'd so much as drunk a breath of air with his underdeveloped lungs, that the comforts of life in the open would be few and far between. He lay in the plastic-sided, artificially heated, overly lit ICU nursery for the better part of a month while his mother's milk first came in, then dried up, and his father studied the enormous and ever-mounting bills in disbelief, vowing revenge on the insurance agent who had sold him the inadequate policy, the hospital that hadn't had the guts to let such an obviously defective infant die, and the wife who had borne him this feeble excuse for a son. He had seen the thing once, two days after the birth; gazed for thirty appalled seconds at the hairless kitten with tubes running in and out and bandages across its eyes, and left the hospital. A son was a thing to be proud of, not this half-formed lump that hadn't even the strength to yell.

That remained his attitude for the next dozen years of the boy's life. Someday, the man knew, a lot of his business would rest on this miserable creature; in the meantime, he alternated between ignoring it and teaching it the discipline and skills it would need if it grew to manhood. Mostly, he was happy enough for it to keep out of his way.

Jamie sometimes wondered what would have become of him had he been born before the days of computers. The mere thought was enough to give him the cold sweats, as if he had conjured up a nightmare creature, gripping an ice pick in its paw, that loomed over his head and threatened to put out his eyes and his ears at the same time. He could not imagine living without the screen that linked him to—everything. To the soothing rhythms of the game worlds with their crisp boundaries and electronic gore; to the Web where he harassed and teased; to the chat rooms where, every so often, he felt the honest touch of other minds. Of course, when he did that, he usually dropped out of the room. He didn't mind chatting with other gamers, but the heart-to-heart stuff made him uncomfortable. Plenty of time for relationships when he was older, he figured. For now, mastery was more than enough.

For some unknown and not-to-be-considered reason, computer equipment was the one thing Father did not begrudge him. It was funny, because Father was no techno-whiz. In fact, it never seemed to occur to Father that the computer was a way out for the boy, the one place in his entire life where he was free from the heavy paternal hand. Jamie knew with bone-deep instinct that when it finally dawned on Father that the computer was far more than a glorified encyclopedia-cum-typewriter for schoolwork, on that day the plug would be pulled, and Jamie would be isolated for good. But in the meantime, somehow Jamie always had as much power at his command as a boy could want.

More than some professional programmers, in fact. Hardware, software, phone lines, DSL, satellite connections, you name it, it dropped into Jamie's lap. He could barely wait until he was old enough to quit school, which was a complete waste of time and a constant horror socially. He only knew three kids he might, sometimes, privately acknowledge as friends, and one of those was gay, one was fat, and one was a girl. God help him if he hung out with any of them publicly. Mostly he talked with them online.

The one thing that made life bearable was his ability to get by without a whole lot of sleep. Other kids his age seemed to sleep all the time, which cut severely into their nighttime gaming hours, but Jamie's otherwise unsatisfactory little frame chugged along quite happily on five or six hours' sleep a night, less when something good was happening.

This inevitably meant that most of the online friendships he had forged were with older people, college kids mostly, and he had learned to talk the talk. He doubted any of them guessed that Masterman or RageDaemon or any of his other characters disguised a runty kid. He was great at shooting the breeze, could shoot back jokes about sex and drugs with the best of them.

The only people he wasn't sure what to do with were the creeps. They would first appear on one of the games or a chat room, but it wouldn't be long before they were trying to get you aside for a personal talk. The first few times Jamie had realized what was happening, he had shut them off in disgust, and been left feeling creepy himself. After a while, he got to spot them early, and confront them. This had the effect of making them slink away into less threatening territory, but left Jamie wishing he had someone to crow to about the victory. Last month he'd had a really good time hunting one of the creeps down, hounding his steps online and even hacking in to a couple of accounts and finding out who the guy actually was, then sending him (this, Jamie thought, was real genius) fawning but anonymous letters, with explicit language and a couple of pictures he'd picked up from a porno site—at the creep's work address. The guy had gone silent right after that; Jamie kept checking for his name online, wondering if he'd been arrested yet.

It had been shortly after his tenth birthday (uncelebrated in any traditional sense of the word, although it had not gone unremarked in the O'Connell household) that Jamie had realized the Web could be manipulated. Oh, he'd known for a long time that the names populating the Internet were just people, with all the undependability and quirkiness of their fleshly counterparts, but not until he turned ten did it dawn on him that even a weak little kid like himself could become a force within the vast electronic realm of the Internet.

That was when he began to reach out, as the saying went, to touch someone, and pretended to be an authority on some bit of stupidity one of the chat rooms was discussing, he couldn't even remember now what it was. But it had been fun, composing an opinion that sounded good and fooled the other jerks blathering away, had made him feel superior, even powerful. The day one of his invented "facts"—a technical-sounding piece about how the government was causing hurricanes over Cuba to become more devastating—came full circle and was deposited, scarcely changed, into one of his mailboxes, was a day of revelation and triumph. At home he was less than a piece of toilet paper stuck to his father's shoe; on the Web, he was an Authority.

On his eleventh birthday (an anniversary still too recent for Jamie to think of with any equanimity) the boy had been hit by (among other things) a revelation. The Web was good for a joke, but it could also be used as a tool. Or rather, the people on it could be used and manipulated to get himself out of this increasingly hazardous place.

Because the truth was, Jamie loved his father, but he also knew that if he didn't get away, one of these days Father was going to kill him.

Chapter 18

ALLEN KNEW NONE OF THIS ABOUT THE BOY, NOT FOR A LONG TIME. THE first of Alice's forwarded emails read simply:

my mother's dead. my father hurts me
soemtimes I want to die too
deadboy

The fourteen words touched Allen's senses like water on a dry sponge, expanding them, leaving them thirsty for more. A boy, Alice had said—taking the signature at face value, or was she seeing behind the lines on the screen? Allen, too, heard nuances: rage twisted into self-contempt, the writer's disgust for his own weaknesses. **deadboy** was a personality with these first three declarative sentences, but how much of that was Allen's experience, and how much a projection of himself? The message had come, according to Alice, from a public library in San Jose,

California, using a Yahoo account with the name **deadboy**. The letter had originally been sent in early March, but it floated around for eleven days, washing in and out on the electronic tides like a note in a bottle (and, Allen thought, no doubt causing a flurry of responses, ranging from the sympathetic replies of eager pedophiles to abusive notes from pull-the-wings-off-flies cynics) until eventually it was forwarded to a woman widely known as an advocate for children's rights. She sent it on to Alice, phoning her about it the next day. Alice had already sent **deadboy** her own equally brief reply:

You sound like you have a plate full of trouble.
Do you want help?
A., mother of two

When the woman called, Alice had yet to receive an answer. If none came in four or five days, she told her friend, she would try again, using another address and taking a different tack from the maternal, which they both knew might only have served to frighten the boy off.

However, three days later an answer came:

you cant do anything. Its my problem.
db

Allen, reading Alice's reply, couldn't fault it. Give the woman her due: Prickly as she might be with adults, particularly adult males, she was great with kids. She sent a matter-of-fact paragraph, the bottom line of which was that despite what the boy knew about life, there were adults who were in a position to help kids, and although she did not expect **deadboy** to trust her, he seemed bright enough to be able to use her. Eventually she would need to ask his name, but for now, maybe he could just tell her what was going on?

A week went by before the boy responded. Allen could imagine Alice's growing anxiety, her imaginary images of the correspondence discovered, of a violent episode that left him unable to get to the library, of the thousand things an angry adult could do to a child. But he did answer.

why should I trust you?
db

She wrote:

You shouldn't, not yet. I could be a 40-year-old man just getting kicks. Tell me whatever you're comfortable with.
A.

He shot back:

what the hell, *I* could be a 40 yr old pervret. tell me about yr kids
db

Allen, reading this nearly a month after it had appeared on Alice's screen, laughed aloud. The kid was quick, all right—plus, he had a sense of humor, a rarity among the abused. And to top it off, the first thing he'd done was turn the conversation around on Alice. Smiling with admiration, Allen read on.

My daughter teaches history in Oregon. My son was killed by his father fifteen years ago. This may explain my interest in your email.
A.
whats your daugther's name?
db
Sorry, can't tell you that.
A.
I think yr bullshiting me. you never had a son
db

(Actually, Allen knew, this was true: Alice's dead child had been a girl, twin to the surviving daughter whose injuries had not only left her well qualified for her job teaching in a school for the blind, but had also plunged her mother into the peculiar life of a professional kidnapper. A certain amount of obfuscation was necessary.)

I'm glad you're skeptical about what people tell you over the Internet [Alice wrote back] **and you're right, there's no way I can prove anything this way. But that's not the point. I thought you had a problem you wanted some help with?**
A.
I never said that
db

**No you didn't. So, DO you have a problem you want help with, or were you
just bullshitting me about your father hurting you and your mother being
dead?
A.**

Allen winced when he read this, and wondered where Alice was going
with this. It didn't do to get confrontational with a kid, not when it was
so easy for him to just vanish. But somehow she'd known this would
not drive him off. After a delay of four days (two of which were a weekend, on which days the boy never wrote), an answer from **deadboy**
came.

**I told you, nodoby can help me, its my problem
db**

Alice shot back:

**You wouldn't try to build a house without a hammer and saw, would you?
You wouldn't get on a plane without a trained pilot, would you? I help people
who need help. It's what I do. Use me.
A.**

At this point in his reading, Allen got up from the terminal and went to
make himself some coffee, more as a means of defusing his apprehension than because he needed any more caffeine. Was Alice losing it?
Alice the cool, Alice the analytical, putting down there on an email for
the world to read (her computer email might be securely encrypted,
but the boy's in the library was most certainly not) the stark fact that
she helped people, such as young boys who needed to disappear. His
immediate impulse was to pack his things and leave town before she
slipped so badly that she slipped him straight into a jail cell.

He'd glimpsed this vulnerability in her once or twice before, whenever mention of suicide came up. This, he imagined, was because her
dead daughter had only indirectly been killed by Alice's ex-husband;
the girl had, in the end, finished the man's job herself.

Apprehension not in the least assuaged by his actions in the kitchen,
he went back to the study. There he found that, indeed, Alice's risk of
exposure had done the trick, that the boy seemed to relax under the
idea that he was in control of his fate, that Alice was nothing more
than a tool for him to use. Over the course of the next two weeks, their

dialogue slowly spiraled in on the facts, the kid's town (on the outskirts of San Jose) and what he liked in school (math mostly, and he secretly enjoyed chess club although it was only for geeks), that his mother's parents lived in Chicago although he hadn't been allowed to talk to them since his mother had died when he was seven, and that he was only allowed to bike to the library because it was on his way home, and the housekeeper thought he was doing research for a school project.

It was here that Alice had turned the file over to Allen. Allen slept on it, and the next morning picked up the phone to book a seat on the next available flight to San Jose.

He arrived in San Jose shortly after noon on the first Friday in May. He hired a car at the airport and drove west a few miles on the freeway; the exit he took set him down in a sprawl of suburban development, cheap houses from the Sixties alternating with clots of Eighties apartments and brand-new condominiums. He had maps, a lot of good maps, and found the library without difficulty. Pulling the rental car into the back of the parking lot, he put on a respectable but well-used mechanic's jacket with the name "Bill" embroidered over the pocket, massaged a thin layer of grime under and around his nails, ran his hands through his hair to rumple it, slid on the heavy glasses he'd brought, and touched his bushy moustache to make sure the glue was holding. He then locked the car and went inside.

He found the auto repair section and pulled out a couple of technical manuals, setting them down on a table with a clear view of the main door and the computer lab, then began making notes with a chewed pencil stub on some creased pieces of paper he took from his jeans pocket. He looked like a mechanic with an engine problem knotty enough to send him to the library, and he did work his way through the electrical section of the first book with some attention: A person never knew when he'd have to disable a 1995 Honda.

At two-thirty the first kids started to appear, high-school students with a short day and young children accompanied by the parents who had picked them up from school. The middle-school students didn't start coming until after three. Allen leaned back in his chair, crooked glasses propped on the end of his nose, and continued reading until he spotted his first solitary boy at three-twenty.

Color in the kid's cheeks hinted that he'd come on his bike rather than a car, and the way he walked straight past all the tables showed that he wasn't here to meet someone.

But even without these slim clues, even if Allen hadn't been looking for him, even if he hadn't arrived just at the time during **deadboy** was usually online, Allen would have known at a glance that this was a kid who knew what fists felt like. He couldn't always tell—some kids had such powerful repression mechanisms, they managed to forget the abuse themselves between episodes. But **deadboy**—and Allen was pretty sure this was him—was one of those who tried to make himself small.

He wasn't very large to begin with. In one of his emails, he'd claimed he was twelve, and although at first glance the boy looked more like ten, a closer look revealed the first gawky signs of approaching adolescence. His dark hair had needed cutting a week ago, his thin cheeks and surprisingly full lips had been reddened by the wind, providing contrast to the nearly black eyes framed with long lashes. The boy's narrow shoulders were inside a jacket that was a bit too light for the weather and a bit too short in the sleeves, but which when new had cost someone a few dollars. He was unexpectedly beautiful, in the way boys are before the muscle- and hair-building hormones of puberty shape them into men. The beauty would be a problem, Allen thought. It was easier when a kid had a chunky body and a face like the hind end of a pig: Nobody seeing the photograph of such a child would automatically think, *Pedophile,* and call to mind the middle-aged man they'd noticed hanging around. Hell, watching this boy made Allen *feel* like a pedophile, eyeing his target over the top of a car repair manual.

The boy eased his heavy backpack onto one of the tables and walked over to the nearest shelf. He made a show of choosing a book from the American History section, leaning up against the shelves to survey the room out from under his eyelids, in much the same way that Allen was watching him. Then on the dot of three-thirty he walked back to the table, dropped the book next to his pack, and went to the glassed-in room with its bank of computers. There he nodded in response to the greeting of a gray-haired woman who was tidying up and setting out stacks of scrap paper. He signed in to the book on the desk near the door, and sat down at a monitor. In moments, the boy was blind to the world.

Allen figured that the library allotted its computers in one-hour time slots, which gave him plenty of time to check out the kid. Ten minutes into the hour, Allen closed his manual, folded the notes into his back pocket, and returned the two repair manuals to the shelf. The magazine stacks were on the opposite side of the room, so he walked in that direction. As he passed the table, he glanced down at the book the kid had taken as decoy, then stopped dead, peered around as if hoping to spot the patron whose volume this was, then shrugged and pulled the book over. He thumbed through the index, paged back through it to page 279 and read a paragraph about the New Deal before abandoning the book, taking care to shove it back more or less where he'd found it. Over in the magazine stacks, he pulled out his scraps of paper to write down what he'd read on the ID tag hanging from the kid's backpack—no name, but something almost as informative: a phone number.

He wandered over to the New Fiction display, picking out a thick volume to cover his surveillance through the lab windows. The boy seemed to be writing a paper, his fingers moving rapidly over the keys, but slowing laboriously when time came to squint at the screen and make corrections on what he'd written. It took him half an hour to write his two pages, and when he'd retrieved his assignment from the printer and his disk from the machine, he settled down with evident relief, and logged on. His fingers flew, now that spelling and punctuation didn't matter; Allen wished he had some way of tracing what the kid was saying and who he was saying it to, but short of taking up a position behind his back or staring through the crowded library with a pair of binoculars, he didn't see how he'd manage.

Before the hour was up, Allen retreated into the gardening and cooking section, sampling a number of cookbooks before he spotted the kid coming out of the computer center. He moved straight for his backpack to swing it over his shoulder before heading rapidly for the exit, solitary all the way. Allen let him go. Better to risk losing the kid than to show himself too early.

When the boy was safely out the door, Allen gathered his papers, rambling over to give the computer room a once-over, just happening to glance at the sign-in sheet. The signature began with the letter J, but after that, it could have been anything. Back at the main desk, he asked for a library card application and said to the gray-haired librarian he'd seen laying out scratch paper in the computer room, "Was that by any chance Mike Flannery's son? That skinny kid who just left?"

The trusting woman followed the direction of his eyes toward the automatic doors, then smiled at him. "You mean James? No, his name isn't Flannery, it's O'Connor—no, O'Connell, that's right."

"That's funny, the kid's a spitting image of a guy I used to know when I worked for a software company, three, four years ago. After it went belly-up, we sort of lost touch. Maybe fate's telling me it's time to look Mike up again. You need a letter, as ID, you say?" he asked, diverting her attention back to library business.

"Anything that's been delivered by the post office within the past

KEEPING WATCH 169

thirty days, as proof of address," she repeated patiently. He thanked her and went out, frowning over the application card as if it were his SAT exam.

To be granted not only a phone number but a name as well made for a jump start on the case, and when he'd found himself a place to stay, Allen logged on. In no time at all, he had the kid's identity pinned down, found the address that was connected with the backpack's phone number, and printed off a map of the neighborhood. That evening he did his preliminary reconnaissance, driving past the front wall of the gated community in which the address was located. O'Connell had money, that was for sure. And in Allen's experience, people with money guarded their possessions closely—and people who abused their kids generally thought of them as possessions. Setting up a surveillance inside those gates was not going to be easy.

But with the thought of those dark, hooded eyes with the feminine lashes, he figured he'd manage somehow.

Chapter 19

AFTERWARD, JAMIE COULD SEE THAT IT WAS THE DEATH OF THE COMPUTER that had done it. Before the computer's murder (or, to give the fuller truth that his mind tended to shy away from, before his participation in that murder), he would never have dared to carry on such a conversation with the woman who called herself **A**. Before that ivory-and-brass poker nestled into his palm, he would never have considered open rebellion against the man who had placed it there. Only after the killing had anger been born, and he hugged the heat of it to his thin chest. Afterward, he found himself thinking more and more about the small white-and-brown dog he'd seen on the TV program, the terrier who *Couldn't be trusted* not to snap at its unfaithful owners.

Everything I love dies, had been his last thought before sleep. *Everything, except Father.*

*   *   *

ON FEBRUARY TWENTY-SIXTH, THE MORNING AFTER THE COMPUTER'S violent dismemberment, Jamie had woken to a sore shoulder and the knowledge that something had changed. He sat up hastily in a confusion of nerves, thinking that Father must be standing at the foot of the bed, but the room was empty. More empty than it had ever been. Jamie blinked at the debris strewn from desk to blanket, and felt himself flush all over. Shame was a familiar companion of his childhood, but not like this. He'd have felt shame if he'd merely watched Father smash the computer and made no objection; this was something hotter than shame, this memory of Father's manipulation. He'd continued raining down blows even after Father's hand came off his own; he'd *wanted* to. Jamie wished he could vomit up the memory of last night, not only the strange, perverse satisfaction, almost pleasure (*yes!*) he had taken in crunching and smashing the computer as if he was smashing Father—not (his mind hastened to add) that he'd really want to do that. But the truly mortifying thing, the knowledge that was already eating at his guts like some sour parasite and making it hard to think about getting out of bed and facing the day, was the haunting humiliation of his collapse into Father's arms.

He did get up, of course, when he heard Mrs. Mendez call up the stairs. He even remembered to fish his slippers out from under the bed before venturing across the carpet. However, there were so many tiny pieces strewn over the entire room that a sliver of glass had made it inside the slippers, and with his first step it jabbed deep into the bottom of his foot. He got it out, but its ache stayed with him throughout the day, reminding him with every step he took. As if he needed a reminder; he hadn't felt so completely . . . empty since his mother had died. While he dressed, he avoided looking at the pieces of the clever mechanical brain with which he had spent so many hours. He'd killed it himself, that he knew; not only with the poker but by making the fatal slip that had triggered a phone call from the teacher. He played various scenarios of revenge through his mind, but after a while, he had to admit to himself that the stupid bitch (he thought the term in his father's voice) was only trying to help. She didn't understand. And since he'd known she wouldn't understand, what had happened was entirely his own fault. Not hers, not even Father's. He'd known the consequences; he'd slipped anyway.

But what was he going to do now? Not only was he now completely cut off from the chat rooms and the games communities, but from a purely practical point of view, how was he supposed to do his schoolwork? Handwritten papers were a joke—only losers handed those in—and without the computer's spell check, he didn't think he could avoid discovery for long. Of course, it was entirely possible that when he got home from school this afternoon, the bedroom table would be polished, and sitting on it would be a newer, faster model, after which nothing more would be said. But it was every bit as likely that he'd get home to find that his father had forbidden Mrs. Mendez to clean, that the glass would still be in the carpet, and even after he'd cleaned that up, Father would make him do without for weeks, until he was satisfied that Jamie had paid hard enough for every scrap of an inadequate replacement. Jamie never knew what Father would decide. Never.

But before he left for school, Jamie had stood for a minute in the door of his room, looking in, and it was somewhere during that time that he became aware of the tiny burn of rebellion, lit deep inside. It wasn't right that a harmless, sweet-running computer that hurt no one should be made to pay with its existence. And it was even less right that Jamie himself had been forced to participate in its destruction. Since he'd gotten it the previous summer, the computer had become very nearly a living thing to him, the pet he could never have, the confidant he dared not take on, more a friend than any other person he knew. It had been a beautiful machine, and seeing its parts strewn around brought to mind a picture he'd seen somewhere, when the Nazis in Germany had assembled great piles of books in the streets and set them alight.

He bent down to retrieve a shard of the machine that had landed near the door. The "A" key, he saw it was. He slid it into his pocket and left for school.

When he came home, the room was spotless, but the desk was naked.

Had his father been around during the days that followed—and certainly if the man had chosen that time to take the boy camping or fishing, or even to a movie—Jamie's tiny spark might have smothered under the weight of his father's affection, and open rebellion never come about. But his father was off again, for a week this time, and because Jamie could convince the softhearted Mrs. Mendez that he absolutely had to spend time in the library after school, the spark was nurtured, and glowed stronger. Under the impetus of that rebellion, with the happy coincidence of his afternoons of freedom in the library, Jamie's first inchoate plan settled and grew within his clever mind, and eventually culminated in the **deadboy** email that ended up in front of Allen Carmichael.

**my mother's dead. my father hurts me
soemtimes I want to die too**

Jamie didn't know why he wrote it that way. In truth, he had no intention of dying. Not if things worked out.

WHEN ALLEN HAD SEEN THE SORT OF NEIGHBORHOOD HE WAS DEALING with, he drove to a twenty-four-hour print shop, where he used their computer to design flyers and business cards for a hastily invented gardening service that charged five dollars an hour less than any of the other services he'd found in the paper. The bright, professional-looking flyer he mailed out to all the households in the community explained that Victoria's Garden was a husband-and-wife operation that could undercut the competition because it made use of each household's own equipment. It had the added bonus (although this was nowhere directly stated) of being run by a man whose primary language was English. (Not that they were being racist or anything, the half-dozen callers from the gated community reassured themselves as they dialed the number on the flyer the following week; it was just more practical to be able to communicate clearly with the help.) He spent half the night addressing and stamping them to the residents of the community, caught a few hours' sleep, and went out in the morning to mail the flyers and find the local electronics store for middle-class families paranoid about their nannies. There he bought an assortment of tiny cameras and microphones—paying cash, which surprised the shop owners not in the least.

On his way back to the motel, Allen took his rental car back to the airport and went shopping for a pickup truck. At the third lot he found a seven-year-old Ford with some dents but a clean history. He paid cash. At a huge hardware store he stocked up on the sorts of tan pants and cotton shirts a high-class gardener might wear, along with rubber boots, a hat with a brim, and an assortment of hand tools and gardener's whatnot. Early Sunday morning, he drove to the woods and rubbed dirt into everything, using 120 grit sandpaper on the wooden handles and running over the work pants a couple of times with the truck. Then he went to a Laundromat and pounded everything to softness in the industrial machines.

Allen's first client hired him on the Monday, just three days after he'd seen **deadboy** in the library. The woman was pleased when Allen told her there'd been a cancellation the following day, and he could come then if she liked. At nine o'clock Tuesday morning, he gave his name to the gate guard (along with a flyer and a twenty-dollar thanks) and was waved into the estate, where he spent the morning trimming hedges, weeding flower beds, and mowing the woman's ankle-high lawn. After his sandwich lunch, taken with ibuprofen to alleviate the aches of unaccustomed muscles, he spent an hour walking up and down the manicured streets, delivering more of his distinctive flyers to the residents as a follow-up to his earlier mailing. Whenever he found someone at home, he made sure to tell them which of their neighbors he was already working for, thanked them politely (tipping his hat in mild flirtation to the women, which went down well), and left them his card as well. One time he spotted a team of real gardeners, and went down the next street instead.

The O'Connell address was in the literal and figurative upper end of the estate, where the lawns of the suburban houses lower down spread out to become meadows, and where the only way you could hear the neighbors was if they were standing at an open window shouting at the top of their voices. "Privacy," Allen muttered to himself. There were no doubt a lot of perfectly innocent individuals in the world who valued privacy for itself, but they were not the people he met in the course of his job. His householders sought distance from other ears, not a sense of spaciousness.

The woman who answered the bell was clearly a housekeeper. He gave her his card, told her which houses he was already working at, tipped the baseball cap he was wearing that day, and left her before the kid could appear. He did not expect to receive a call from O'Connell, and indeed, he did not. But he did ascertain that there was no dog, and that the man of the house was away for the day. He also took careful note of the house layout, its relationship to the perimeter wall and neighboring houses, the trees behind the wall, the color of its dark shingle siding, and where the phone wires came into the building.

He spent the afternoon and evening building his devices and testing the transmitters and receivers. Late that night, wearing black clothing and smears of camouflage makeup, Allen hiked in from the back reaches of the estate and went over the perimeter wall behind the O'Connell house.

Most of the time, what he did required no special skills. Ninety-five percent of the hours spent on the job involved sitting in front of a screen or monitor. But for the five percent that required him to venture out to retrieve information or the person, Allen put in a lot of practice. Sometimes, deep in his lessons with Dave the burglar or Yoshi the black belt, he would be struck by how silly it was for a grown man to play secret agent; he'd have to bite back giggles. But he kept at it, refreshing his skills in jungles natural and man-made, keeping up with the technology, teaching himself to use, mount, and disassemble his spy equipment blindfolded. He had even built, or adapted, some of it for his own particular purposes. Most of what he did required nothing more cutting-edge than common sense and a screwdriver, but for those times when high tech was called for, he was prepared.

Tonight he was there to set some fairly sophisticated bugs onto the O'Connell home. He crouched at the foot of the wall, allowing the sixth sense of patrol to unfurl, waiting for the internal reassurance that he was alone. At three A.M. on a weeknight, the neighborhood seemed to be asleep. Lights shone here and there behind drawn curtains, but none that Allen could see had movement or sound to accompany them. Certainly not in the house ahead of him, where the only light burned in the kitchen, its gleaming surfaces visible from his position under some young native oaks. The air was fresh with odors of new-mown, well-watered lawns (thanks to the other gardening service), orange blossoms, and crushed wisteria from the neighboring arbor.

In twenty minutes, nothing moved but a silent-winged owl overhead.

Allen got to his feet and followed the meadowy lawn down to the freestanding three-car garage. A touch pad glowed next to the side door, armed against intruders, and a glance inside the garage (only two cars at the moment, a black Lexus and an SUV whose make Allen couldn't tell) showed the master alarm control, its green eye glowing in baleful warning. He found another armed pad on the wall outside the kitchen door. So O'Connell was serious about his household security, but not paranoid, and the placement of the security lights told Allen that the man was less concerned with a secure perimeter than he was that the lights not shine into the eyes of people inside.

Allen wouldn't attempt to overcome the alarm system, not tonight, particularly without knowing if the house was inhabited or not. Instead, he circled the house, studying what he could see from the outside, which wasn't a great deal. Cameras might not be of much use here, just microphones.

He set his bugs on the phone box and on three likely ground-floor windows, one of which was some kind of den in which he could see a bar, black leather sofa, and gigantic sound system. The room's single window was high and vegetation grew up around it, so he mounted a tiny camera there as well. He took care concealing the transmitters and the waterproof, long-life batteries he buried under the soil, along with the automatic half-hour cutoff devices he'd begun to build in after one of his paranoid fathers had tried out a new counterspy bug detector and nearly brought down the entire operation. Everything Allen mounted on the O'Connell house was the same dark brown as the shingles, and all of it was concealed either by the shingles themselves or by the shrubs that grew near the walls. It took him the better part of an hour, avoiding the two motion-sensitive spotlights at the back corner and making sure he touched nothing with his bare hands, before he was satisfied. If nothing came of these particular eyes and ears, he would have to figure a way to get inside the house, or at least gain access to the upper-floor windows.

For now, he would begin with these. He concealed the receiver and recorder with their big batteries in a tree well outside the wall, and was back in his apartment before dawn.

From that point, the case went much as usual. The audio bugs proved clear, and from time to time, the back curtain was left open when the room was occupied, so Allen had many hours of the housekeeper or the boy staring straight ahead at the television that was just under the lens, and occasional glimpses of O'Connell or another man walking into the room, pouring a drink, or picking up the remote—usually on the way to shut the curtains. A variety of the household's activities were captured for Allen's records—and, if it worked out that way, for the police to receive anonymously.

He spent his days gardening, his nights retrieving and watching the surveillance recordings, and his spare hours compiling a dossier of information on father and son. The online records of newspapers and some amateurish hacking gave him O'Connell's business history, while a couple of well-placed bribes got him some of Jamie's school records. He napped when he could.

It didn't take long to confirm that **deadboy** had not been making up his oppression. Some of Allen's cases had dragged on through the surveillance stage for months until the evidence of abuse was sufficient to justify their intervention. The shortest surveillance he'd ever run was a case involving a bank president with a serious cocaine problem, when after a mere nine days it had become terrifyingly clear that holding off even another forty-eight hours might easily leave them with nothing but the videotape of a murder. The O'Connell bugs ran for twelve days; the phone tap gave him nothing whatsoever, two of the room bugs and the back-room camera were satisfactory, but the microphone he'd stuck near the dining room kept going dead. This could have been some fault in its transmitter, or could mean that O'Connell had a bug sensor in the upstairs room, which he turned on occasionally to sweep for illicit ears. It didn't matter all that much; the camera alone gave Allen all he needed.

Seventeen days after he had been given the **deadboy** email, he sat down and watched the father's appalling game with the shotgun. The boy's expression, a twelve-year-old child ripped in two between his longing for his father and his terror of the man, hit Allen harder than some of the rapes he'd witnessed. In minutes, he was on the phone with Alice.

"You want to come down and look?" was his opening greeting.

"Already?" she asked, surprised.

"I've seen enough. The man's a brute, the kid's in danger. Besides which, he was talking about taking the kid off somewhere for the summer. Vacation starts in a week and a half."

"I'll be down tomorrow. Let me just check when."

He held on for a couple of minutes, then she came back on to tell him her flight number. "It gets in at eight-forty. Can you pick me up?"

"I'll be there."

He met her at the airport and drove her back through the Monday morning commute to his nondescript apartment. He had been up most of the night, first returning to the house to remove his devices, then editing the recordings on his laptop to delete all the hours of Mrs. Mendez vacuuming and O'Connell sleeping in front of the television, so he showed her where the fridge was and told her to wake him when she was finished. It took her five hours, three of the audio and a little over ninety minutes of images, before she stood outside the door to his bedroom and pronounced his name.

He came awake instantly. "Yeah," he said into the pillow. "Be right with you." He showered to shed his grogginess; when he came into the kitchen he found Alice fixing sandwiches.

He reached into the fridge and took out a beer and one of the flavored teas he'd bought for her, pouring hers into a glass with ice. "What did you think?"

"That last tape."

"Ugly." The faint tremble of the two shotgun shells on the smoky glass table as the boy braced himself against the weight of the gun. Allen twisted open the beer and poured half of it down his throat.

"I have seen a great deal over the years, but that . . ." She paused for a moment, and continued with great precision. "I do not know that I've ever seen anything quite so inherently evil as that performance with the gun. And yet it didn't seem to surprise the boy."

"I thought that, too. But he was still scared."

The boy's back rigid with terror, the man's face alive with laughter as he rested the barrel of the heavy shotgun against his son's chest. And that expression on **deadboy**'s face as he left the room, rich with self-loathing and yearning.

"The father's a psychopath. The boy's bright, but confused."

"Who wouldn't be confused, a father like that?"

"You know what I'm talking about," she told him curtly. So she had picked it up, too, the boy's expression, torn between his need for his father and his fear of him. Angry clients were far easier than the conflicted ones, particularly when there was no mother around to act as client and make the decisions. He thought about it while he was eating one of the sandwiches.

"Want to wait?" he asked her. "Only, that conversation last week between O'Connell and the housekeeper, it sounded like they're leaving as soon as school lets out."

"It looked and sounded to me as if things may be escalating," she suggested.

He nodded. "The boy's beginning to show signs of adolescence. Not much physically yet, but the attitude is there. Dad can't handle being stood up to. It's only going to get worse, and fast. I'll go with your decision, but I have to say that the idea of letting it go for three months makes me nervous."

"Is the boy old enough?"

Rarely—four times in the decade they'd worked together—had they performed a rescue on a young child, and then only if they had a member of the family waiting in the wings. Generally, it was better to take their illicit tapes and turn them over anonymously to Child Protective Services, and let bureaucracy do its thing. A young child lacked the self-awareness to assist in his or her own decisions. Twelve was borderline.

"Like you said, he's bright, you can see that even in the emails. He can't spell worth a damn, but that doesn't mean anything."

Alice retreated into thought, her eyes on the laptop's screensaver pattern but her mind clearly far away. Allen left her, to go make coffee and wash the dishes. A few minutes later, she followed him into the narrow kitchen.

"I think you're right. He needs to be away from that man before vacation starts."

"Any family?"

"None so far. I'm afraid the boy's story about having grandparents in Chicago was either a lie or a fantasy."

"So where does he go?"

"What do you think of Rachel and Pete?"

"Aren't they kind of stretched?"

"The girl we placed with them is in college now. Rachel herself contacted me to say she'd be willing to foster another."

"They'd be ideal."

"How do you want to contact the boy?"

"I think you should do it, at the library. If I'm remembered talking to him, all hell will break loose." A woman talking to a boy, on the other hand, would be forgotten in a week.

"You can't take him from his home?"

"No way, there's a housekeeper and a man, I don't know what his job is but he always seems to be there whenever the father's home. Plus alarms, and the entrance gate. Far better when the boy's out in public."

She nodded, and went to fetch the wig and costume she'd brought from Seattle.

Two hours later, when Jamie got to the library's computer room, he found an older lady at the next terminal, looking a little confused. After a minute, she asked him a question about doing a search, and while he was showing her what to do, she said quietly in his ear, "Try not to show any reaction, Jamie, but my name is Alice. I'm your friend 'A' from the Internet."

When their hour was up, Jamie climbed on his bike and Alice went back to her car. They met again the next day, and the day following that. On the fifth day, the last Friday afternoon in May, Jameson Patrick O'Connell disappeared. He was last seen in the library, conversing with the same white-haired woman he'd been talking to every day that week. He was wearing a red T-shirt, jeans, and scuffed white sneakers, and carried a green backpack. Both the boy and the woman had left the library around the same time, separately. No one saw the boy, wearing his helmet, steer his bike into a side road half a mile from the library and stop next to a parked car. A woman got out and lifted the bike into the trunk while he climbed into the backseat. Once the car was under way, the boy sank down beneath a blanket. Half an hour

later and fifteen miles away, in a parking lot between a busy pizza parlor and a nine-screen movie house, a woman with brown curls and a
blond kid with a bright orange backpack and black T-shirt got out of a
car and went to talk with the driver of a dented but clean tan Ford
pickup truck fitted with a well-used camper shell that wrapped over
the cabin. The driver, who greeted the woman with a hug and the boy
with a handshake, was a tall, stooped grandfather of a man with longish
gray hair gathered into a stubby ponytail, a full moustache, and a faded
Marine Corps tattoo showing on his left forearm beneath the rolled-up
sleeve of his chambray work shirt. After a few minutes, the boy got into
the truck and waved a small good-bye to the woman. The camper drove
onto the freeway and joined the surge of traffic pouring out of the Bay
Area for the long Memorial Day weekend.

Smooth as can be. They had a piece of luck that Allen had not
counted on, when Jamie told him that his father had left that morning
for a few days, and he thought it extremely unlikely that the housekeeper would call the police on her own initiative. By the time the
woman located O'Connell and he had called the police, the trail would
be cold. Near Tahoe, Allen had Jamie crawl up into the camper space
overhead, and pulled the truck into a campground that was wall-to-
wall with vehicles. During the night, the boy's blond hair and orange
backpack found their way into the campground trash cans; the tattoo
on Allen's arm had been scrubbed away, the moustache vanished, his
hair gone short and white; and a thicket of fishing stickers had
sprouted on the camper shell.

The truck left the campground before the sun was up, and crossed
the Nevada border. Half the country was on the road this weekend,
and unless Allen began driving up the wrong side of the road or otherwise behaving erratically, there was little danger that any cop would
have enough time on his hands to pull over a camper driven by a white-
haired man with his grandson. They took a fairly direct route, a luxury
Allen didn't always have, and he spent the time educating the boy to
the new rules of his life, getting him used to being called a nice anonymous "Jim" instead of the more ear-catching "Jamie," all the while
making small, surreptitious probes into the boy's history, problems,
and sensitivities.

They stopped Saturday night just south of Twin Falls, at a motel located at a confluence of roads. The tall man who booked a pair of adjoining rooms shook his head as he told the desk man about his
daughter who'd been so eager to shop, he had to go back and pick her
up when the discount mall shut, can you believe it? No one noticed

that when the camper drove back into the parking lot that night, there was no daughter with the old man and the boy.

Sunday morning, they circled west around Twin Falls to a small town on the main road. One of Alice's clients lived here, now happy and safe in her second marriage, this one to the town doctor. The camper drove around past the clinic's front door with its CLOSED sign and pulled up at the back entry. The door opened, and Allen ushered Jamie in.

He and Alice had both discussed with the boy the necessity of a physical exam. Jamie hadn't liked it, but he was resigned. Once inside, Allen asked him if he'd rather be alone with the doctor and nurse.

Jamie hesitated. "I guess you can stay here."

"If you change your mind, just say so, I'll step out in the hall and wait for you."

The checkup was as thorough as it could be without making the boy feel too invaded. Which meant they could draw blood and take X rays, but evidence of sexual trauma was limited to questions alone. The exam brought to light two broken fingers on the boy's left hand, an old greenstick fracture of the left radius, a slight hearing loss in the right ear, and the suggestion of trauma to the skull, bad enough that the boy had probably been knocked unconscious. At least the blood work showed no signs of infection, drug abuse, or sexually transmitted disease.

Then the nurse handed Jamie his T-shirt and asked him to remove his trousers. "You can leave your underwear on," she added.

As soon as the jeans were off, all three adults stared at the enormous black bruise on the pale thigh. The doctor cleared his throat and explored the area gingerly with his gloved hands. "Was this a kick?"

Jamie looked down at his leg. "I think so."

"Does it hurt?"

"Not really."

"Son, this must have been very painful."

"I don't remember it hurting," Jamie told him.

The doctor looked skeptical, but his wife and Allen exchanged a knowing glance: It was not bravado speaking, but the simple truth: Jamie had excised the pain from his awareness. It took a lot of experience with pain to be able to do that.

"Any headaches, stomachaches, problems with urination?" the doctor rattled off in a disapproving voice. He clearly thought the boy was lying about the pain, and Jamie did not like that. He sat on the examining table, increasingly stony-faced, answering with grunts and monosyllables.

At last it was over. The X rays and blood work would be sent to Alice, to join the boy's evidence file of tapes and email and Allen's anonymous statement, bulwark against the ever-present possibility that the case would go bad on them and they would need to piece together a legal defense for kidnapping.

The adults looked at each other, relieved that it hadn't been any worse than it was, and plied the indignant, embarrassed youngster with the picnic meal the woman had brought to the clinic. No twelve-year-old kid likes strangers asking intrusive questions and poking his unclothed body, no matter how professional they are; the meal was not a comfortable one. When they left, with most of the food crammed into the camper's small fridge, Allen listened without comment as his passenger concocted an elaborate explanation of the broken bones, looping through an ever-more-detailed story of an accident when he was learning to ride a bicycle. Who knew? It might even be the truth, and it was not Allen's business to question him. He was just relieved that he could hand over to Rachel Johnson a boy with no severe physical problems.

He was also relieved that the trip was nearly at an end. This part of a rescue was always tricky, the time when a client fell in love with the rescuer. Woman with kids, woman alone, kids alone, it didn't matter— Allen took care to stay as remote as he humanely could. His job was to get them out and get them safe, not to lay the groundwork for a long-term relationship. Fortunately, Jamie slept a lot, and he seemed easily entertained by the handheld electronic games Allen had brought along. Theirs was a temporary relationship, and allowing bonds to form between them would only cause more of a wrench when they reached the boy's foster home in Montana and Allen drove away.

Jamie showed little inclination to talk, anyway. Their conversations were concerned mostly with the mechanics of the escape, getting the boy used to his new name and history, telling him all about the town in Texas he was supposed to have come from, the specifics of his fictional family. When they stopped on Sunday night, Allen asked Jamie to empty out the green backpack, so he could check that there were no pieces of incriminating evidence that he'd overlooked. He removed a printed receipt and a scribbled phone number, and with apologies cut out the front page from a paperback novel with Jamie's name on it, but he stopped at the picture of a young woman smiling down at the baby on her lap, both of them with dark eyes and pale skin. He could have guessed who the woman was, but he asked Jamie anyway.

"That's my mother. She's dead."

Committed suicide when the boy was seven—and no doubt the kid blamed himself. Abused kids always blamed themselves, for everything. "Do you remember her?"

"Not really," the boy said with a studied indifference, and took up his electronic game.

"Not at all?"

"She was stupid, and weak."

"That doesn't mean she didn't love you."

"She didn't. And I didn't care when she died. She was stupid."

Allen knew he should confiscate the photograph, but he didn't have the heart to. He merely checked to be sure that there were no identifying marks on the back, and laid it on the table in front of the boy with a warning to keep it to himself. Jamie continued with his game for a few minutes, then shut it off impatiently and turned to shove his clothes, CDs, and comics back into the green pack. He snatched the photograph up and stuffed it inside the outer pocket, but Allen noticed the fingers smooth its corners out carefully before pulling the zipper shut.

Monday morning, working their way through Idaho and southern Montana, Jamie grew talkative, almost in spite of himself, the words pushed out by the growing tension of journey's end. He put aside the game unit, and began to comment on things they drove past. Most of his remarks were negative, even sullen, and when Allen tried to extend them, the boy would draw back into himself for a while, then venture another remark. Their conversations went something like this:

"The kids here sure dress stupid," Jamie said, staring at a group of half a dozen boys in ordinary jeans and T-shirts coming out of a drugstore. "They look like hicks. I bet they don't even play computer games."

"Probably a lot of them do. Not in the library, though."

Allen felt a glance hit the side of his face. "I used to play at home. I had a great system."

"What happened to it?"

"My father broke it." The answer came just a bit too quickly. Allen raised a mental eyebrow.

"By accident?"

"No. Yeah. No. I mean, yeah, he meant to break it, but he could just as well have broken it by accident. He's not really very good with computers."

"So you used one in the library."

"Yeah."

"When did your computer break?"

"Month ago maybe. Not long. He was going to buy me a new one, a lot better, only I couldn't decide what I wanted."

This was such a blatant lie, Allen took his eyes off the road for a moment to look at the boy's face. The delicate features were taut, jaws clenched and eyes focused on something at once far away and deeply internal. For an instant, Allen was seeing a soldier riding a Huey out toward a hot zone, the ghost of an M16 barrel rising up alongside the boy's face . . .

The boy picked up the handheld game, and retreated into silence.

At midday on Monday, Allen pulled into a dirt road leading toward the rambling farmhouse in which lived a family of what Alice called "easygoing Mormons" (which Allen had considered an oxymoron until he met the Johnsons), the mother of whom owed a large debt to Alice's organization.

Smooth, the whole operation.

It was only later that things began to get interesting.

Chapter 20

MONTANA WAS EVERYTHING ALLEN REMEMBERED; RACHEL JOHNSON WAS even more. Rachel and he were sitting on the wide porch of the house she and her husband had built when they moved here two dozen years before. It was in a marginally fertile valley surrounded by high hills, more farm than ranch, halfway between Bozeman and Billings. At first glance it appeared an ideal setup for a survivalist militia, but Pete and Rachel Johnson were only farmers. At least, they were farmers on the surface.

Pete had a degree in history, but after teaching high school for several years, he had grown dissatisfied with a life away from the earth. Rachel had gone on to a Ph.D. in child psychology, and worked for five years in a Chicago mental health clinic before deciding that the inner city was not where she wanted to raise her own children. They had left the city and come here, to farm, and to raise a family, and to help those who needed it.

When Allen had first met them, six years before, they had struck him as somehow Quaker, but both had actually been raised Mormons, moving away from that tight-knit community during their college years. Although the habits of the Latter-day Saints were in their blood, they now simply worshiped at the nearest church, which happened to be Presbyterian. They even drank coffee, enjoying, Allen thought, the secret sin of it. At the moment, Rachel was pouring out two glasses of homemade lemonade and offering Allen a plate of spiced applesauce cookies. The youngest Johnson child, four-year-old Sally, had been overjoyed at having a newfound cousin all to herself, since her siblings wouldn't be home from their long-weekend church outing until evening, and had dragged "Jim" away immediately to admire her chief responsibility, the chickens. The child had allowed her cousin to hold the egg basket, and "Jim" was trying not to look too apprehensive about the flock of dirty, noisy, weirdly aggressive hens that squawked and pecked at their feet. With the two children out of earshot, Allen was taking the opportunity to fill Rachel in, giving her the information he'd dug out, a synopsis of his surveillance, and his impressions gathered from the drive up. Knowing what she would be dealing with in the years ahead was every bit as essential as the forged documents that Alice had provided for the boy.

"Jim's an only child," Allen told her. "No family at all apart from the father, although he's given to inventing grandparents far away. His mother committed suicide five years ago, one day before his seventh birthday. Jim found her. She'd used a shotgun—her husband's favorite one, according to the newspaper reports—while he was away on business. Pretty emphatic statement there, as someone commented: husband's pet gun and in a place the kid was sure to discover her when he came home from school.

"The father traveled a lot, he's an investment counselor, whatever that is. A very successful one, it would appear—big house, full-time housekeeper, a new Lexus, a nice little Cessna he's licensed for. Jim was a difficult kid, acting out at school, smart-mouthing the teachers, accusations of bullying from the younger children. One of his teachers thought he might have a learning disability, but his father took him out of there before they could test him, and stuck him in a private school with a reputation for discipline. That worked for a while, even though it involved an hour-long bus trip each way, but then there was a rapid succession of catastrophes: One of his school friends drowned, the school had a fairly serious fire. This was about six months before his mother killed herself. With the fire on top of the drowning, the entire

school community was in chaos, half the classes working out of portables, trauma counselors wandering the halls with their stuffed dogs,
the whole nine yards. By the time the repairs were done and the teachers a little more settled, Jim was beyond the reach of any counselors.
The principal had to suspend him after a graffiti incident in the boy's
bathrooms, and said he'd let him back in only if he was in the care of a
psychiatrist. It was the principal's opinion that Jamie had an attention
deficit disorder, needed to be on Ritalin at the very least. The father
flat-out refused, which as far as the Ritalin goes I'd have agreed, but
the boy would have really benefited by a lot of hours with a counselor.
But no—one of those macho things, you know? 'No kid of mine needs
a shrink.' "

Rachel nodded; she'd worked with children a long time, had come
across all the parents, and if she tended to avoid using labels such as
"conduct disorder" and "flat affect," that did not mean she was unfamiliar with the diagnosis. Or the reality.

"The next school was a very expensive academy, not quite military,
but big on structure. Decent curriculum," he admitted, "and only
three miles away, but it wouldn't have been my choice for a kid who'd
just lost his mother. Jim seems to have settled down somewhat, but I
have a feeling that as soon as the tight restrictions are off, he's going to
test the boundaries pretty aggressively. I'm afraid you're going to have
your hands full for a while."

Rachel merely smiled; hands full of problem kids she was also
used to.

"When the father's away, he leaves the boy with the housekeeper,
Mrs. Mendez. That's another odd relationship: You'd expect an older
woman in a house with a more or less parentless child would bond
with him, become a surrogate grandmother, but she seems remarkably
uninterested in the boy. Does her job, cleans and cooks, then retreats
to her room and leaves him watching television."

"The father encouraged her aloofness, you think?"

"Almost a sure thing, I'd say. Both to keep the boy isolated and because it was less of a danger that the details of his relationship with the
boy come to light."

"How much abuse was there?"

"Physically, it seems to have been sporadic, although from something Jim said, there's been more recently than there usually is during
the school year."

"It's a controlled abuse, then? Not a drunken rage?"

"As far as I saw, the father only drinks heavily on occasion, so yes, it's a deliberate and controlled cruelty." He described the scene with the shotgun, an act of pure psychological torture. Rachel listened without comment. He went on. "It could be escalating because of the perceived threat of the boy's increased height and maturity. And as far as I know, there's been no overt sexual abuse, although you'll watch for the signs." Incest was always the most deeply buried secret of all, the last violation the victims would admit. Allen would not discount the possibility that Jamie's father had included rape in his litany of domination, but the bugs he had planted on the house's ground floor had not recorded any, and Allen had not picked up on the markers during the drive up here. Jamie had certainly been victimized, but perhaps not sexually.

"He wet the bed on our first night out, not since then. I have seen him with his thumb in his mouth, though he tends to chew the nail rather than suck on it. He doesn't trust women any more than men, I'm afraid, so make sure Pete spends plenty of time with him. But no hunting. In fact, I'd lock away the guns completely for the summer while he's around. It might just be the circumstances of his mother's death, or the gun game his father plays, but I noticed on the drive up here, there's something about hunting that sets all the boy's nerves to twanging."

"You think maybe dear old Daddy used to take his boy out in the woods to slaughter a pile of bunnies?" Rachel asked shrewdly. Her husband Pete and the boys all hunted for the table, as rural folk often do, and Allen knew that their big freezer depended on killing a deer during the season, but she had no illusions about the motivations of some hunters. "That old macho thing again?"

"Blooding his son," Allen commented bitterly, and the phrase reached in and startled up a tangle of memory from the back of his mind: the shattering BANG! and a spew of water across his face, his fingertips with a faint smear of blood on them—his first bloodshed—and the M16 kicking in his arms as it flung death at small men in black pajamas. He blinked, and was back in Montana again, with this war-hardened farmwife in a calico blouse and blue jeans.

"Deer season's a long way off, so it won't be a problem for a while. I'll just have him and Pete Junior keep the guns locked up. And watch their tongues about it."

"Jim's a bright boy, and once you get through that hard shell of his, I think you'll find his mother treated him well." And Rachel would get through to the boy, of that Allen was certain, rubbing at Jamie's protective shell with easy conversation, hard work, and the strong bonds of community, until one morning the boy would wake up and find the shell crumbled around his feet. If Allen was right, if in Jamie's early childhood his mother had surrounded him with affection and respect, then freedom would come early: Trust was far easier to regain than to build from scratch.

And speaking of trust: "Don't tell him we were watching his house, will you? I'd rather he didn't know that Alice and I saw what his father did to him."

"I won't mention it," she assured him. "So, how long will you stay?"

"Until he feels comfortable with me leaving. I imagine three or four days ought to do it."

"It's too bad I couldn't have been there when you first picked him up. A boy like this, it's hard to be passed from one adult to another. Not getting trust off to a good start."

"You make it sound like geese hatching, imprinting on the nearest living thing," Allen said.

Rachel laughed with delight. "My lord, Allen, a person would think you were a farm boy. How'd you pick up on that bit of lore?"

"Read it in a psych textbook ten thousand years ago. Look, Rachel, you really don't want to be exposed any more than necessary. The very worst thing would be for Jim to bond with you, and then have you arrested. I'll stay around until he gets used to being here, and then slip away."

"Like shifting a sleeping baby from one lap to another," she commented. "Come on, you conspirator, you; time I was getting dinner on the stove."

In the end, in spite of his yearning to be away, it took until the end of the week before Allen could ease himself out from under Jamie's weight and drive off, although by Thursday, he had begun to suspect that the hesitation he felt was not entirely for Jamie's sake. Over the years he'd helped a lot of kids, but never had he met one who intrigued him like this boy. Although Jamie allowed himself to be taken into the family with more ease than Allen had anticipated, there remained about the boy a sense of reserve, a feeling that those dark eyes were watching his own interaction with his new family, standing back with a heavy dose of scorn at his own willingness to be drawn in. This deliberate distancing made Allen itch to do something to bring the boy out of his hermit's cave, but in the end, he had to admit that his continued presence was on the verge of causing more confusion than assistance. Time to leave the family to get on with it; time to turn toward his own retirement.

On the morning of the sixth day, he announced at breakfast that he would be leaving after lunch. When the dishes were cleared, he and Jamie took a walk through the pasture in the general direction of the stream that divided the Johnsons' land from their neighbor's. Pete was out on the farm tractor, pulling out the stumps of some trees he had cut down the year before. Allen and Jamie paused to watch the contest.

"Wonder why he doesn't just blow them up?" the boy asked.

"Maybe he finds this safer than dynamite."

"Dynamite's safe, if you're careful."

"Maybe it's just more satisfying to yank them out. And I suppose it makes for a cleaner hole than blowing the tree to a million hunks."

"I guess." Jamie's gaze indicated that he'd much rather have been watching pyrotechnics than a straining engine.

"You think you're going to be okay here?" Allen asked him.

The thin shoulders shrugged.

"I mean it," Allen persisted. "If this place isn't going to be comfortable for you, it's my job to find you a place more to your liking. You're going to be spending several years here, before we can count on a judge declaring you an emancipated minor." This was one of the things they'd talked about on the long drive north, and in the end, Allen had felt even more certain that he and Alice had been right, that Jamie was mature enough to have a voice in his own future.

The boy shrugged again. "Yeah, I guess it'll be fine. It's just weird, you know? Cows and people and chores and all. I mean, I didn't exactly see myself growing up on a farm."

"One thing those chores will do," Allen said mildly, "is put muscle on a man. You see the shoulders on Pete and Pete Junior?"

"Yeah," the boy said, sounding more interested. He was just old enough to be starting to take an interest in his body, Allen thought; farm work, fresh air, and Rachel's cooking would build up the slight frame and put steel in the stooped backbone.

"Okay, if you're sure this will do, then I need you to write a letter to your father, telling him that you've run away and found a new home, and that you're happy. I'll help you with the wording, and I'll arrange to have it mailed far from here, so no one will be able to trace it. It's better if the police think you're a runaway rather than the victim of a kidnapping. They won't look so hard, if they know you left under your own steam."

"That makes sense," said the veteran of a thousand police television dramas.

"And Jim, you're going to have to watch yourself, every minute of every day. We've talked about this, I know, but you're going to need to remember it in the same way you'll remember to introduce yourself as 'Jim.' Every time you make a friend, you'll want to tell them your secret so you won't feel like an absolute fraud." Allen could feel the boy give a little grimace of disbelief, not at the thought of betraying his secrets, but at the idea that he might make friends. "You're going to make friends here, even though they're just a bunch of farmers, and you're going to feel like a liar every minute, for not telling your friends and your new cousins who you really are."

Rachel, Pete, and their seventeen-year-old son Pete Junior knew Jamie's story; it had been decided that the others were better off knowing just Jim's public face, until they were older.

"And from time to time you'll make enemies, and you're going to be pissed off and you'll want to show them up by telling them how much better you are than hicks like them. But you aren't going to do that. Because if you do, word will travel, upwards to their parents and sideways through other kids and their friends, and sooner or later, someone at school or church will catch wind of it, and one day the local sheriff will knock on the door and ask Rachel for the phone number of that sister of hers in Texas whose illness meant she couldn't take care of you for a while. And you really don't want to see Rachel and Pete arrested for conspiracy to kidnap." Then, in case the boy had failed to grasp it, Allen drove this last point home, hard. "Rachel and Pete are putting the future of their family in your hands—their children, the farm, everything. They are trusting you with their lives. If you talk, they could go to jail and lose it all."

Jamie's head jerked up, and he stared at Allen. "Why the hell would they do that? They don't even know me!"

"If you asked Pete, he'd say it's his Christian duty and leave it at that. Rachel would tell you that a person who doesn't stand up to the wickedness of the world might as well be one of the wicked, which I suppose amounts to the same thing. And if you're asking me, I'd tell you that the reason those two good people are offering you refuge and not working as missionaries in the Amazon or running a soup kitchen for the homeless in Harlem is because one of Rachel's family found herself in a similar situation to yours, years ago, and someone helped her out. Lending you a hand, like they did one or two others before, is their way of paying back that help."

Allen glanced down at the boy's face, and nearly laughed aloud at the disbelief. "Jim, I don't expect you to know what I'm talking about now. But if you tell me you still don't understand after you've lived here a year, then I'll begin to worry. You want to turn back yet?"

"Can we go down to the creek?" This was not permitted to unaccompanied children, Allen knew. Jamie hadn't yet noticed that the other boys his age were not, for this purpose, considered children. Or if he had, so far he had chosen to accept the restriction.

"Sure."

They continued walking, Jamie concentrating on the ground so as to avoid the cow pats, Allen wondering—as a solitary man will, walking next to a child who is not his—what kind of father he would have made. When he caught himself starting down that pointless path, he wrenched his thoughts back to what the boy would do in the next few minutes. The boy was about to lose the person who had rescued him from an abusive father, a man who had spent five days in the car at his side, who had gentled his dreams, who had fed and clothed him and given him a new name and history, and who was now turning him over to that strange entity, a family. This was the point at which a sexually abused child would reach out—literally—to cling to an authority figure in the only way the child knew.

But Jamie made no attempt to take Allen's hand, gave him no desperate and coquettish glance from under those dark lashes; for that, Allen was profoundly grateful, and immensely encouraged. Then the boy asked him a question.

"Do you think my father misses me?"

It hit Allen like a blow to the ribs, the question and the way it was asked, with neither hope nor expectation. Allen took a breath, blew it out between pursed lips, and for the first time since they'd left California, deliberately spoke the boy's true name. "Jamie, I wish I could tell you that as soon as you left, your father realized how much he loved you and is making all kinds of promises to himself that if only you were to come back, he'd never mistreat you again. But my friend, I'm afraid your father has some pieces missing from his heart. No normal man would do what he's done to you."

"I deserved it," the boy cut in. "He was only trying to make me stronger."

"Jamie, no; you didn't deserve any of it. You don't make a person stronger by beating them. Believe me, I know." *Don't criticize the father too much*, he reminded himself, *the boy will only defend him.* He modified it to, "It may not even be entirely his fault—he may have been treated the same way by his father as he's treated you—but I have to tell you that as far as I could see, your father will be missing you in the same way he'd miss his car if someone stole it, or his favorite jacket. Personally, I think your father's main reaction will be primarily one of rage. I think he's probably feeling very, very angry that you're gone."

The boy shuddered; Allen couldn't miss the reaction—not of grief that his father did not love him enough to miss him, but of visceral terror at the idea of a very angry father. Yes, he thought; Rachel and Pete had their work cut out for them this summer. Before he could stop himself, he reached out and smoothed the boy's hair, then snatched back his hand as if he'd been burned. He'd learned early on to be cautious with physical contact, after the time he'd patted a six-year-old girl between the shoulder blades and had her dissolve into hysterics: Turned out the girl's uncle had been in the habit of doing that after he'd raped her.

But the boy did not wince or duck away, and Allen breathed a sigh of relief, that the father hadn't been accustomed to caressing his son's hair.

"I guess you're right," Jamie said after a while. Then he added a peculiar thing: "My father's really strong."

"Jim, if you're under the impression that strength and not needing anyone are the same thing, you really ought to think about that."

"It's just, my father is big on not showing weakness."

Allen opened his mouth to pursue all the implications behind that idea, and then shut his jaws so tightly his back teeth protested. This was a cry for help if ever he'd heard one, but if he responded here and now, he'd never leave, and this dark, vivid child would never shift his allegiances to the good Rachel and Pete. *Yes,* he thought, *it really is time for me to go,* and merely said, "Again, I'm not sure that I'd agree that grief is a weakness where anger is not."

The boy puzzled over the words as if they'd been in a foreign language, and then shook his head. "I don't know how I'm going to do this."

"What's that?"

"Everything. Keep my mouth shut about who I am, live on a farm, pretend to be part of a family. Jeez, I'm not even used to having a door on my room."

This last wry revelation was followed by an abrupt silence and a momentary jerk in the boy's step, as if the words had surprised him by just slipping out. It was obvious that this was something he hadn't intended to mention.

"You want to tell me about that?" Allen asked mildly. He didn't need to see the boy's face to know that he was blushing: The bend to his neck was indication enough.

"It's nothing," the boy said. "Just one of his punishments."

"Your father."

"Yeah. I wasn't supposed to be reading one night and he saw the light around the door, so he took the door off. And, you know, the one to the bathroom, too. In case I decided to read in there." He hesitated, but then the words came in a hurry as the boy tried to cover the revelation of his humiliation with distraction. " 'Course, I never had much privacy to begin with, there wasn't a lock or anything, and Mrs. Mendez always used to come in and move things around when I was at school, which I didn't like but when I asked Father if maybe I could clean up the room myself so she didn't mess up the computer he . . . well, he didn't like that."

Further humiliation, Allen gathered, and nodded. Oppressors never allowed their victims privacy, or the opportunity for making friends; when combined with random acts of violence and making food, warmth, and affection into rewards, the oppressor was set up as the center of his victim's universe.

He asked merely, "How long ago was that?"

Jamie's head rose a fraction at the reassuringly ordinary question. "That I complained about Mrs. Mendez?"

"No, that the door came down."

"October."

"I hope the book was worth it."

The boy's head came up all the way at that, and he grinned up at Allen; for a moment just a handsome kid without a care in the world. "Yeah. You ever read *Lord of the Rings*?"

"Long time ago. It was great."

"Awesome. I was just at the end of the second book, where Sam is going to rescue Frodo from the giant spider Shelob? And I knew I was supposed to turn the light out but I just had to see what happened."

"And he caught you."

"Yeah." The boy's voice went dead again.

"Did he do anything other than taking down the door?"

"I don't think I want to talk about it."

"That's fine. I just hope you got to finish the trilogy."

"I did. It took forever, because I had to make sure to read only at school or when he was away. I wanted to bring those books with me here, but I couldn't."

"I wouldn't be surprised if one of your cousins has a set you could read."

"I guess."

The patent lack of enthusiasm in his voice made Allen wonder. "Is your set a special one?"

"Nah, just those big paperbacks that slide into a box. But my teacher at school gave them to me for my birthday, so I kinda wanted to keep them. And then Alice told me to bring just the things that would fit into my backpack and, well, they'd have taken up most of it."

"They'll be waiting for you," Allen told him.

"I don't think so," the boy said in a bleak voice. Allen glanced down at his troubled young-old face, saw the faraway look, and wondered what memory of paternal brutality the boy was dredging up now. Or maybe he was picturing the father happily packing up all his son's possessions and giving them away, to embrace his newly unburdened life. More likely, the boy was visualizing a bonfire of all the beloved childhood possessions he'd been forced to abandon, heaped in the backyard and drenched with gasoline by a vengeful father. Allen could have kicked himself: Surely he should know by now that platitudes did nothing for kids who had grown up knowing what an angry parent could do. And Mark O'Connell sounded to him like a man who would not take easily to being thwarted.

"You could be right," he admitted to the boy. "But then again, possessions have a way of getting away from a person eventually anyway. Books fall apart, or a house burns down. What's important is the words and the story that you've read and loved; those are a part of you now."

"And I like that Ms. Rao gave them to me."

"She sounds like a good teacher."

"I guess. Yeah, she was. She tried hard, and it wasn't her fault that . . . She told my father something that made him so mad—jeez," he said with an uncomfortable laugh, "I thought it was about all over. Anyway, I was pissed at her for a while, but it really wasn't her fault. She was just doing her job. And she was nice to give me the books." He sighed, and straightened his shoulders. "Yeah, I guess I'll see if someone has a set I can borrow. And I'll get used to having a door again and I'll learn to get the eggs out from under the hens without getting grossed out and I'll remember to call them Aunt Rachel and Uncle Pete. Wouldn't it be great if they could just take your brain and erase your memories, and plant a new set? Like in the movies?"

"Some memories," Allen admitted. "Some of them we could do without. But I promise you, take it one step at a time, and every day it'll become a little easier."

"I guess."

"It will. Look, Jim—I've been there. Maybe not where you are, but right next door. When I was twenty, I came home from Vietnam just a basket case, so completely screwed up I felt like an alien. It wouldn't have surprised me to look in the mirror and see one of those gray *X-Files* creatures with no hair and giant eyes looking back at me." He was startled, and gratified, to hear the boy snort with appreciation. "I didn't have any help, mostly because I was too stupid and too messed up to ask for it, so it took me forever to get my head straight. But when you talk about feeling like a stranger in a strange land, I do know how that feels, Jim, I really do."

The boy's head was down, so what he muttered next was inaudible.

"Sorry?" Allen asked.

Jamie threw back his head to shoot Allen a look that was both challenge and something darker: resentment, perhaps, or an accusation of betrayal. "I said, so why aren't you sticking around?"

"I wish I could." The boy took it as yet another dismissal by an uncaring adult, and turned his back. Allen reached out, then drew back his hand before it landed on the boy's shoulder and instead said firmly, "Jim, look at me." The boy came to a halt, staring at the ground. Allen wanted to drop to his knees so he was on a level with Jamie, but he knew the boy would take the gesture as patronizing. Instead, he bent his shoulders and waited for the boy's eyes to meet his before saying, "I swear to you, Jameson Patrick O'Connell, that in all my years, I've never, ever wanted to stick around a kid as badly as I do at this moment. It's going to hurt like hell to get in the car today and drive off."

Allen saw his brutal honesty hit home, and thought, *Good.* What the boy needed more than anything else in the world—more than a bedroom door under his control, more than adults who raised neither hands nor voices, more even than the freedom to be a boy—was to know that he mattered to someone, that the presence of Jamie O'Connell on the earth changed the very landscape. Under his father's reign, in his father's presence, Jamie had been nothing but an insignificant blot. Rachel and Pete would spend months—years—building up in their new foster son a sense that the world was a place that cared, but Allen

himself had no time at all. If he wanted to impress this, his last rescued child, with a sense of worth, he needed Jamie to know from the
beginning that in this, his new life, he mattered.

"Jim, I would like nothing better than to stay with you, even take
you with me, but if I stayed here or you came there, we wouldn't last a
month before all kinds of alarm flags went up. As the son of Rachel's
sick sister from Houston, you're safe here. If a grown man suddenly
appears with a boy who looks nothing like him, people ask questions.
Neither of us can afford that. And I think you can see why."

He saw in Jamie's eyes that the boy did indeed see, the wistful regret and the acceptance.

"Can we at least—" the boy started to say, and then he broke off,
startled, to crane his neck upward, searching the sky.

A small plane circled lazily back and forth on the horizon, the distant drone of its engines rising and falling through the still morning
air. It was too far away to see its details, but Allen assumed it was a
crop duster, surveying the country before it dropped down to spray a
field. Jamie, however, seemed about to bolt for cover, or faint dead
away. Allen was seized by a weird double vision of himself, both back in
Vietnam, and yanking Lisa to safety from the beat of a chopper's blades.

"What's the matter?" Allen grabbed the shoulder of the white-faced,
trembling creature cowering against his legs. "Whoa, Jamie, what is
it? That's just a crop duster. They use them around here to spray the
fields. What's wrong with it?"

Jamie couldn't tear his eyes from the distant object, buzzing in the
full blue sky. "It looks . . . it's the same color as Father's plane."

"How do you know? I can barely tell it's a plane."

The boy's eyes slitted in concentration, every muscle taut; then as
abruptly as it had come, the tension dropped out of him. "No, it's different. The wings, they're, like, stubby." He stepped away from Allen
and shot him a look of embarrassment. "Sorry. I guess talking about
him, and then hearing the plane made me think . . . It was one of the
last things we did, him and me, the night before Alice picked me up.
We went out to the airport to get something he'd forgotten, and he let
me go on board and sit behind the wheel while he was talking to some
friends. It's a really nice little Cessna. He lets me . . . he used to let me
take the controls sometimes, when we were up high. I really wanted to
go up that afternoon—I mean, I thought we were going to, since there
we were at the airport and all, but Father said he was really busy and
that we couldn't. Pissed me off. But anyway, that up there's not his
plane."

"What were you about to say to me?" Allen asked, offering a distraction. " 'Can we at least,' you were saying."

"Oh, nothing. I was just wondering if maybe I could write you a letter sometimes. You know, paper, pen."

Allen hesitated, torn between the potential for exposure and the boy's obvious need to cling to him, trying to leave his own desires out of the equation. Finally he said, "I'd like that a lot. I think that if Rachel agrees, maybe once or twice a year we could risk your sending me a card." A boy could never have too many male mentors, Allen told himself, and refused to hear his mind adding, *And a man can never have too many adopted sons.*

BACK AT THE FARMHOUSE, RACHEL WAS PUTTING LUNCH ON THE TABLE. Jamie responded little to the family's conversation, but Allen thought it was more his habitual shyness than because his rescuer was abandoning him. When the table was cleared, Allen got out the cheap paper and pen he'd brought for the purpose, both bought in Miami, and had Jamie write his runaway letter to his father. Not that the man would be appeased by it—indeed, Allen thought it would make him angrier than the outright theft of the child would—but it was a means of distracting the police, who were sure to be closely involved.

Allen went upstairs to fetch his things, followed by Rachel. While he packed, he told her what Jamie had said on their walk, the boy's startling reaction to the crop duster, his conviction of his father's omnipotence, and his doubts about the summer ahead. Rachel nodded at each piece of information. Allen went on.

"Two more things, and then I'll stop telling you your business. First is, Jim wants to correspond with me. I should have asked you first, I know, but it seemed important to him, so I told him that a card once or twice a year wouldn't be too much of a risk. You'll have to read them to make sure he's not accidentally giving anything away, and then send them through Alice."

"I shouldn't think that's a problem," Rachel said. "He's young enough, you'll probably soon fade into the role of some mythic being. A knight errant."

"In a dented Ford pickup."

"Of course, when he gets older, he may want to see you, so he can see how much was real and how much he imagined."

"When he gets older, we won't have to worry so much about his father."

"What was the other thing?"

"The other . . . ? Oh yeah. I remembered something else that happened on our drive here. Jim spotted a man walking one of those Jack Russell terriers, you know, little white shorthair with brown spots, and he talked about it solidly for the next ten miles. I know you already have a dog, but if you and Pete are ever thinking about getting another, you might look around for one like that."

"Allen, you're the most softhearted scoundrel I've ever met," Rachel told him.

"He's a good kid," he retorted, then undermined it by adding, "basically. Although some of the things he says make me nervous. The glorification of violence has already started, and the equation of power with right. And it concerns me, how quickly he's able to shift off one emotion and seize on another that might be more useful at the moment. Another year of that man's regimen, the boy would've been lost for good."

"Instead of which, he's been found for good."

He looked at her placid face and felt a twinge of concern. "Rachel, this is a boy with more problems than three solid meals a day are going to solve."

"Allen, give me a little credit. We'll give him three solid meals, and along with that, the solid concern of a loving family. He needs to learn trust. After that, self-respect."

"Just be careful. He's . . ." Allen found that he'd been on the edge of telling her, *He's like a loaded weapon,* and was not sure where that image came from. "He's shut down emotionally, but there's a lot of resentment stored in there. He's had a shitload of trauma and he's in a precarious state. Don't let yourself forget that a kid on the edge can strike out."

"Allen, remember who you're talking to? I've worked with multiple personalities, written papers on dissociation. I may look like Betty Crocker, but I know what I'm doing."

"I know. I'm just not sure that what he needs isn't a bit more intensive than you're set up for, here."

Rachel sat down in the window seat. "Allen, have you ever read Stephen King?"

He was startled into a laugh by the question. "My lord, Rachel, don't tell me that you have?"

"I read everything my kids bring into the house. How else do I know what's going on with them? Well, a couple of years ago Pete Junior had one of King's books, a story about a disease that wipes out most of the population and polarizes the remainder into good and evil. There's this one scene that has stayed with me. I forget the details— something about, the hero has joined up with a woman and an emotionally damaged boy, and they have to siphon some gasoline from an underground tank. The man has the tubing, but he needs one of the others to hold up the heavy lid for him. And he chooses the boy, who to that point has shown not only a general instability but a specific dislike for the hero. The man inserts his fingers under the heavy metal lid, the boy holds it open, and then all three of them become intensely aware that if the boy lets go, the man loses his fingers. The man doesn't snatch his hands back, doesn't ask the woman to come and help, he just looks into the boy's eyes and gets on with the job. It's a wonderful scene, which could only have been written by a parent who knows what it is like to put yourself every day at the whim of a child. Yes, there are kids out there who are beyond the reach of trust; I've met some of them, they're terribly sad and quite terrifying and I wouldn't allow them within shouting distance of my family. Jim isn't one of them, Allen. You got him to us in time."

Allen gave an involuntary glance at the woman's ten vulnerable fingers, folded together in the lap of her cotton apron. "Just so you keep your eyes open, especially at first," he said.

"Stop worrying and go live your life, you wonderful man. Give your lady friend my respects."

Allen jerked around from the bag he was zipping shut. "I never said anything about . . ."

"You didn't need to. We girls can tell."

"I didn't know Mormons encouraged psychics," he said, then picked up his bag and hugged her, hard.

At the farmhouse door, Jamie shook Allen's hand in a good-bye, his face calm, his dark eyes unreadable.

Those eyes followed Allen across portions of five states as he meandered his indirect way across the northern part of the country to Seattle, and home.

Chapter 21

On the first Saturday of June, Allen left the camper truck in the airport parking garage, crossed over to the terminal, and caught a shuttle into Seattle. He walked up to the docks a scant five minutes before the boat left for the islands, and found that Ed not only had received Allen's message but was waiting for him in Friday Harbor. Jimmy and Jimi—Buffett and Hendrix—accompanied the *Orca Queen* over the water. Rae must have heard the racket when they were a mile away, because she was on the beach with her hands shading her eyes from the afternoon sun when they rounded the point into the cove; when she saw who was on deck, she flung out her hand to wave, then ran down the path to meet him.

Neither she nor Allen invited Ed to stay for dinner.

That evening, they sat at the end of the point to watch the sun set. Rae leaned her back against Allen; he rested his chin on her shoulder, breathing in her fragrances of lemon, sweat, and sawdust.

"What have you been working on?" he asked her.

"It's a surprise."

He tightened his arms around her, nipping at her neck with his teeth. "We have ways of making you talk," he warned.

"A bed," she told him.

"What, no more mattress on the floor? How can I call myself a hippie if I sleep in a bed?"

"When did you ever call yourself a hippie?"

"You have a point."

"Are you really finished?" she asked, so abruptly that he knew it had been riding her mind.

"I am. I told Alice that I would think about coming back on what you might call the board of directors, if they had either a board or directors. But I didn't even promise that. I'm afraid you're stuck with me underfoot. How about you? Don't you have to be away this summer?"

"A couple of weeks in July when the book comes out, I'm holding workshops in Pennsylvania and Santa Fe. And then there's Japan the end of August. Have you thought any more about coming with me?"

"I might. I was there in sixty-eight, but I never got out of Tokyo."

"You'd like it. Of course, you're welcome to come along to the July workshops as well."

"Massage your aching shoulders at night and comb the glue out of your hair?"

She laughed. "Or you and Ed could do your Baja trip. Would July be too awful there?"

"Hot but not unbearable."

With the unspoken agreements, Rae nestled her back more fully into his embrace, and his body responded with an amiable discomfort. He nudged his hips forward against her, and she laughed, deep down in her throat, a sound like the purr of a big cat. His arms pulled her to him. *Think of it,* he told himself, not for the first time, *a man has to reach retirement age before he falls in love.*

Not the least part of his pleasure was knowing the happiness it brought to Rae as well. The real reason, he suspected, that Rae Newborn, world-renowned woodworker and three-times would-be suicide, was flying around the world so much was to prove to herself that she could. She originally had come to these islands to rebuild her life, following great loss and a catastrophic mental breakdown. She seemed, at last, to be succeeding.

Which was—although Allen would do nothing that might make her suspect it—another reason that he had to get out of the kidnap business. Maybe the most valid reason of all. As Allen saw it, if a man became involved with an emotionally fragile woman, if he allowed her to lean on him even a little, then he had no right to threaten her tenuous stability by putting his own freedom and safety at risk. Rae had lost a husband and child already; losing Allen to a prison sentence might sink her for good. For the present, she needed him more than the children did. He had spent twenty-six years helping others; now, he was here.

They sat wrapped up in each other as the sky flared through its spectrum from fluorescent orange to indigo blue. When the light was nothing but a blue glow in the west, they rose and went back to the house.

For the next two months, Allen set about the creation of a new life. The island, Sanctuary—Folly—was the last piece of solid land before the international border, with neither neighbor nor electricity. In the past, the house that Rae's hands built had hidden Allen from the world's view. Now, there was no longer a reason for him to be invisible.

The week after he came home, Allen made an overnight trip to Seattle to fetch the pickup from the airport parking lot. He cleaned it out, ran it through a car wash, and sold the camper top to one place and the truck itself to a used car dealer. Back at his apartment, he sorted out some clothes and drove out of town a ways to fetch an order of woodworking supplies for Rae. Then he spent the afternoon putting together the documents of Jamie O'Connell's case, making printouts of the boy's original emails and burning CDs of the recordings, ending with a photocopy of the boy's letter to his father and Allen's own report on Jamie's state of mind. He went out to the local mail service and sent one set to Alice, stashing the other in his own storage locker. Back in the quiet apartment that evening, he gloated at the empty fax machine and the dark computer, then picked up the phone.

The number hadn't changed since they were kids, when the prefix had been an abbreviated word instead of three numbers. It rang twice, and then his brother's voice said, "Hello." It was a man's voice, filled with years and authority. Allen had forgotten; for a moment, he couldn't think of anything to say.

"Who is it?" Jerry asked, half-irritated, half-suspicious: He was, after all, a cop. Allen felt a sudden urge to hang up, lest his brother find out everything he'd been doing all these years, and be faced with the necessity of arresting him. Jerry would do it, too.

"Hi, Jer," he forced himself to say. "It's Allen."

Now it was Jerry who went silent. Allen couldn't even imagine what was going through his brother's mind; the last time he'd called home had been four years before, when he'd been in a desolate state after hearing that one of his rescues had gone back to her husband, and that within the week, she and her child were dead. Allen of course had been unable to tell his brother why his mood was so grim, and he knew Jerry suspected he was back on drugs or booze; the conversation had not been a success.

"You probably thought I was dead," he told the silent receiver.

"I wondered."

Well, at least Jerry hadn't hung up on him. "No, I'm fine. Really well, in fact. Jerry, I'm thinking of moving back to the islands." Not, he was careful to say, "coming home"—he couldn't see living with Jerry again, even if he could bear to live under the same roof as their father, and he didn't want to give Jerry the impression that the threat existed.

"When?"

"Soon," he said. He didn't quite know how to tell Jerry that he had already moved back, that he was, in fact, living with a woman whom Jerry had at one time shown considerable interest in. Take it slowly, give him one idea at a time to chew on. Some things, like Allen's work and the fact that he'd been using the Sanctuary cave under Jerry's nose for years, might have to be passed over entirely. "I have a place in Seattle right now. Any chance you might be coming to the mainland, we could have a beer, or dinner?"

The offer of neutral ground went down well. "I don't have a lot of free time," Jerry's voice told him. "You know how crazy summer is— but I do have a meeting there on Tuesday. That any good?"

The relief of his brother's acceptance was so huge, it kept him from responding.

Jerry took his silence as something other than relief. "Doesn't have to be then, why don't you give me a call when—"

"Tuesday'd be great. Will you have time for dinner?"

"So long as I catch the last ferry out. Where and when?"

Allen started to say the name of his favorite place, then choked back the words. Better to go somewhere they didn't know him than to risk troubling his brother with the fact that he'd been in the area for years. "How about I ask around, let you know?"

"Fine. Call me back and leave me a message, here or at the office."

"I'll do that," Allen said, although something in Jerry's voice told him that his younger brother suspected he wouldn't call. "How's Dad?"

"He's Dad. What can I say?" Long ago, Jerry had gone through a period of resenting mightily the chronic adolescence of their unreconstructed hippie father, his multiple wives (each one younger and blonder than the last), and his benign neglect of his two sons. The old man still went his blithe way, certain that the world loved him, knowing that his many sisters would stand in and do parental duty for him. *John's just hopeless* was the family's oft-repeated verdict, but now Jerry seemed more willing to accept the affection with which the rest of the clan said the phrase, and leave behind the condemnation. In fact, that was what he did now: "He's just hopeless. You want to know where he and Number Six are?"

"Six? What happened to Five?" The woman whom the whole family called Five had been a thirty-year-old barefoot but extremely successful pot grower from northern California, who the last time Allen had heard was supporting Hopeless John in the style, and in the high-grade cannabis, to which he was accustomed.

"Well, she sort of got herself arrested. And before you ask, no, I didn't have anything to do with it. She divorced him so the lawyers couldn't get ahold of what money he has left, and he's now living in a solar-powered underground house in New Mexico. You know, where the cactus grow?"

Ah, thought Allen. *Cactus; as in Carlos Castaneda; cactus as in peyote buttons.* "He is truly hopeless," he told his brother. Shared knowledge of the eighty-year-old hippie they called Dad broke the ice, and they exchanged inconsequentials for a while before Jerry said he had to go. Allen hung up, content with the beginning.

There was one more piece of business to take care of before he could leave the city. He booted up his computer and sent a short encrypted email, and later that night went to one of their meeting places for a talk with Alice. She nodded once at his brief explanation of why he could not continue to stick his neck out for her, then nodded again when he told her that *if* he was satisfied that he could be thoroughly insulated legally, he *might* be willing to talk about becoming a scout for the organization, with an eye to expanding their havens overseas. All the ifs and caveats he attached to his agreement seemed to trouble her not at all—assuming that she even heard them—and she merely nodded a third time when he told her that she would have to wait until October to talk further. An outsider would have thought her unconcerned about whether he took the job on or not, but Allen knew her well enough to suspect that she was, very secretly, pleased.

He retreated home to Folly the next day, his own man for the first time in his life.

Dinner with Jerry the following Tuesday was surprisingly warm and easy, and afterward, Allen came back to the islands publicly. His first time out was an effort; walking openly and undisguised down the streets of Friday Harbor after twenty years of avoiding just that, he felt like some underground creature violently jerked into the light of day. He kept wanting to obscure his face with one hand, or buy a hat with a wide brim. The first half-dozen times old friends and schoolmates did a double take, followed by exclamations of astonishment and the inevitable "Where on earth have you *been*?" questions, he had to stifle the urge to break and run. By July, the urge was still there, but was fueled less by panic than by the agonizing boredom of answering the same questions over and over again. Allen Carmichael could be a person again; retirement had a lot going for it.

Before Rae went away for her July workshops, Ed took the *Orca Queen* down to Baja; Allen caught a plane an hour after Rae's left and flew down to meet him, for ten days of warm water, Mexican beer, philosophical musings, abstention from razor blades, and old-time rock and roll. The two men reluctantly pulled anchor and turned north, working their way up a thousand miles of coastline to Seattle, leaving just enough time before Rae's plane got in for Allen to shave his beard, get a haircut, and change his clothes for those that didn't stink of fish and good times.

Life was good. So good, Allen found himself bracing against the return of the dreams: In the past, letting down his guard had opened him up to the green eyes of Flores, the dripping fingers of deRosa, the shiny black visage of the lieutenant from hell. But July merged into August, and the nightmares stayed away. And when he went down one day to the cave under the island, the hideaway where he had stashed maybe a dozen families over the years, the cots and equipment were only mildly reproachful, and the stones held nothing but the sound of water.

The only thing to haunt him was the dark gaze of a twelve-year-old boy in Montana. It was difficult, walking past a phone booth in Friday, not to stop and punch in Rachel Johnson's number, a persistent urge that had never happened to him before. He was even tempted to call Alice and ask if she'd heard anything about the boy. He did not, because she would be alarmed at the sign of attachment, and rightly so: Countertransference was a dangerous thing in the business he had just left.

So he did not call Rachel, and he did not contact Alice; he did not even go onto the Internet to follow San Jose's search for the missing boy. He would cut the cord here as he had all the others, and if the cord did not wish to be cut, well, he would pretend it had been. He had a life to live; with a bit of luck, and no interference from errant knights on Fordback, Jamie would be doing the same.

For two months, Allen worked at constructing his new life. It was an unfamiliar position he found himself in, retooling his mind so that the first thought each morning was of Rae, or fishing, and not new techniques of spiriting an abused woman from her husband, or how to arrange a safe house in one of the many places across the country where they had none.

He was not one of "them" anymore. He might be, peripherally, in the future, but not for the next few months. The next months belonged to him, and to Rae. And so throughout that summer he lived on the island called Folly with his beloved madwoman, and he saw his brother from time to time and once even their father, and he had long talks with Ed, and he tried to tell himself he really wasn't bored and he was not in the least worried about a slim, dark-haired boy in Montana.

But when the letter came the third week of August, Allen knew that he had only been waiting for the other shoe to hit the boards above his head.

Chapter 22

JAMIE TRIED, HE REALLY DID. HE WOULDN'T EXACTLY SAY THAT HE'D GOT used to the smell of animal shit, and the sound of the cows and roosters jolted him out of sleep when it was still night outside, and the constant press of people and talk made him jumpy—even the milk the family drank was weird, tasting too . . . alive for him to swallow except if it was icy cold. But he felt he had honestly made an effort. And the endless work on the farm was a revelation, just how much labor went into putting a meal on the table and a roof over a family's head when you had to do it yourself. If the country's industries went under tomorrow—if the oil wells ran dry or a bomb froze all the world's machines at once—by the next day about ninety-nine percent of the population would be starving or freezing or both. Except for people like his new family.

Were the rest of the world to vanish, the only thing these people would notice would be that *Jeopardy* disappeared from the television and the sugar bowl would go empty. And no doubt Pete would soon have sugar cane planted and Rachel would construct a board and invent topics for family *Jeopardy* games around the kitchen table. The pantry looked like some kind of health-food supermarket, they had their own gas pump and electrical generator, and shopping once a week was more for entertainment and luxuries (corn flakes, bananas, and the Sara Lee cheesecake Pete adored) than from anything resembling necessity.

Rachel even made a lot of the family's clothes—not jeans or underwear, not that he'd seen so far, but all kinds of shirts and dresses and things. He didn't know anybody did that, but there she'd sit, bent over the whirring engine of the shiny black sewing machine stitching together unlikely shapes cut out from the cloth she'd bought in town (at least she bought *that!*) and somehow making them come together in a shirt that fit his cousin's shoulders as if they'd been born together, or a wodge of multicolored scraps that turned inside out and made a puffy pillow. Once she'd embarked on a series of long, long seams on some patterned cloth that Jamie had told her he didn't mind too much, and produced a set of curtains for his new room. Sometimes when he woke up in the morning, up in the white-walled room at the very top of the house, the light was just coming through those curtains, and he just stared and stared at them, like they were the most wonderful thing in the world, magic or something. If he hadn't been there when they were made, he wouldn't even have noticed them, or if he had, he'd have thought, how hard could they be to make, really, just curtains?

The day she'd made them, Rachel had known he was standing in the doorway watching her—not that she said anything, just did that little humming thing she did under her breath like she was singing with the whirring machine. But when she got to the end of one of those seams that seemed to go on for ten minutes, she lifted the cloth, clipped the threads, and asked over her shoulder if he wanted to try. Of course he said no, but somehow she'd talked him into it, maybe because they were alone in her sewing room, and so he sat down at the machine and held the cloth down in front of his chest like she had, then eased his sneaker down onto the foot pedal. The machine leapt into life and whirred madly, biting furiously at the fabric and jerking it around so much that in an instant the flat metal foot was sewing air. He dropped the cloth and snatched his foot from the pedal, and he would have abandoned the attempt except that Rachel was already standing close behind him, her cheek resting against the side of his head and her arms pushed through his, and she was telling him to put his hands in front of hers on the seam and press down his foot. He didn't want to, really, felt so nervous he thought his throat would close up, but he didn't want to look like a jerk or a coward, so he'd gripped the edge of the cloth like she did, and pressed down gingerly with his shoe. The little machine jerked to life alarmingly, but with her hands in control, the cloth stayed in a straight line. After a minute he began to relax, and then it was kind of fun, seeing the needle blur up and down, and the thread feed through the guides in a series of continuous jerks, and the cloth steer itself through like magic. The flowered cloth of the dress that Rachel wore had brushed his arms, and she smelled warm, more like one of the cows (although he'd never tell her that) than any woman he'd ever met, because she didn't use perfume and deodorant and stuff, just soap. And the long seam came out a little wavy, but smooth enough by the end, even after she let her fingers go and he was guiding the cloth through all by himself.

So that was why he looked at the curtains in his bedroom up high in the house as if they were magical or something, not because he liked them that much.

There were, he had to admit, things he did like about being here. Rachel's cooking was great—not as fancy as the food Mrs. Mendez made when his father was around, but satisfying, kind of . . . motherly. And really, he got along okay with his new "cousins," even the littlest kid Sally, who was kind of a pain, but secretly, only to himself, he'd admit that he sort of liked the experience of being looked up to. He was somewhat nervous around Pete Junior, the seventeen-year-old, who had, as Allen had said, a grown man's shoulders but also the potential for devastating scorn, if he decided to turn it on Jamie. Not that he had, he seemed pretty nice in fact, but Jamie didn't know enough people that age to be sure. And the other two kids were okay, thirteen-year-old Eli, who'd been away at a band summer camp for the last week, and bossy eleven-year-old Vera, who tried to be as grown up as her old-lady name was, helping Rachel in the kitchen a lot.

Then there was Terry. He still didn't know what to make of that, still woke up barely able to believe that the heavy lump on top of his feet wasn't his imagination. When Pete had driven off, two days after Allen left, Jamie'd had no idea, none at all. Sometimes, in fact, he replayed the whole morning in his mind, making a kind of movie out of it: Pete driving away in the dusty pickup with his elbow resting on the door, Rachel sitting the kids down at the kitchen table with enormous bowls of cherries in front of them and handing each a weird gadget that turned out to be what you used to remove the pits. Only she called them "pips." They could eat as many of the huge, black, tart-sweet

cherries as they wanted, but she wanted each bowl empty before its
owner was free for the rest of the morning. Eli and Vera whipped
through theirs at warp speed, and even Sally seemed to pit two to his
one. It was humiliating, but Rachel just hummed away and pretended
he was nice to go slow and keep her company. Anyway, he finally got
through his bowl and took his purple fingers outside, where he didn't
have anything to do but stare at the stupid chickens and wish that he
was allowed to watch TV during the day. Not that there'd be anything
on the three channels they got but farm shows and soap operas. How
could you live without cable? And the computer—he was allowed half
an hour a day, like everyone else, on the same line the house telephone
worked on.

   If you'd told him six months ago that he'd be living on a farm with
no online games, he'd have said you were nuts.

   So he went upstairs and got the well-thumbed paperback of *The
Fellowship of the Ring* that he'd borrowed from Pete Junior. He started
to lie on his bed to read, where it was quiet and there was a chance nobody would notice him, but it was already hot upstairs (no air condi-
tioning, either!) and Rachel had promised that they were free for the
morning. He knew what adult promises were worth, and the relative
security of his bedroom made even the sweating seem attractive, but
then he heard Eli's voice from the barn, and he felt a small surge of defiance. He went down the stairs and marched openly through the living room to the porch, where he settled down in the wide, two-person
porch swing, just waiting for the adult recall to work. The first few
pages were distracting, but when no one came to claim him, or to be-
rate him for wasting his time, the treacherous words began to settle on
the page. In a while the screen door screaked open and he braced himself (*I knew she wouldn't go through with it!*), but without a word,
Rachel just set a tall glass of lemonade down on the wobbly wicker table next to the swing and went back inside, leaving him in perfect
peace.

   After lunch he helped her make labels for the cooling jars of cherries, lined up on the sideboard and looking like a magazine illustration.
One of them gave a loud *ping,* and he looked over to see if the glass
had broken, but Rachel explained that the noise was the metal tops
locking down over the fruit, when the hot contents had cooled into a
vacuum. Pretty neat, he had to admit.

   With the jars labeled he was free to go back and read for a couple
of hours, and he had just reached the part where the Dancing Pony
was being invaded by the black riders when he heard Pete's truck drive

in and around the back of the house. His body's automatic response to the arrival of a vehicle was dry mouth and racing heart, but having been here for a week now he was able to tell himself that it was only Pete, and try to settle down again into the swing. Still, Pete's return might not bring threat, but he wouldn't be surprised if it heralded the next round of chores, no matter what Rachel had promised. And sure enough, in a couple of minutes the screen door screaked again. He dog-eared the page (it was only a paperback) before looking to see what Pete wanted, and was startled to find the whole family in the doorway, staring at him. He jerked upright, wondering what the hell he'd done now.

Then Pete stepped forward, big, silent Pete with his arms even thicker than Howard's, both enormous hands held out in front of him. Jamie instinctively scrambled backward to get out of the man's reach, but before he could get free from the porch swing, Pete's hands were an inch from his stomach, and Jamie could see that he held some object, which he settled gently onto Jamie's lap.

It was white and brown and warm, waking up in confusion, shiny black beads of eyes settled into a wide forehead beneath ears almost too soft to prick to attention, wet nose snuffling Jamie's shirt for clues.

"It's a terrier, a Jack Russell terrier," Pete told him gruffly. "Had to drive halfway to Butte to find one. If it makes a puddle in the house, your aunt won't be happy."

Jamie stared at the man for a moment, utterly speechless, before tucking his chin down to peer at the puppy. It was trying to stand on the uneven surface of his lap and get its unbelievably delicate paws onto Jamie's chest. It stumbled; without thinking, Jamie reached out to steady the animal as its tongue found his chin and its cold nose traced the line of his jaw to his hairline. He squirmed at the sensation of the creature snuffling into his ear, its wriggling warm body pressed itself against him as if trying to get inside his shirt, or his skin. Jamie's eyes sought out Pete. "You mean, it's for me?"

"Allen said you'd talked about that kind of dog one time, seemed to me we could use another dog around here anyway. If you don't like it, I can take it back, look around for another kind, a Lab or something."

Jamie's arms hunched forward, as if Pete had moved to take it away, and he shook his head fiercely. "No, I like it fine. I don't . . . I haven't had a dog in a long time. It's so small. What if I hurt it?"

"They're tough little guys," Pete reassured him.

The puppy abandoned the assault on Jamie's ear and half tumbled onto the swing seat. Gingerly, Jamie closed his hands around the creature's round belly and lifted it down onto the porch before it fell there, and the family watched their newest member explore his home, stump of a tail in the air, every hair bristling with fascination. Rachel laughed aloud, and Jamie glanced up at her, his wary disbelief giving way to wonder.

"What's his name?" Sally asked her father.

"He doesn't have one yet. That's up to Jim."

It's a boy, Jamie thought. At least they hadn't made him ask.

"Call it Jack," Vera suggested prosaically.

"Its name is Terry," Jamie told them. And that was that.

So yeah, there were some good things about living here, in spite of always seeming to have cow shit on his sneakers. He managed to keep Rachel and Pete happy most of the time, and so far he hadn't kicked anything but chickens (which seemed not to mind) and his hands hadn't done one of those weird compulsion things where they just reached out to hurt something—the puppy, or even worse, the little kid—and the chores were manageable and he was getting used to the quiet and all in all he thought he could get used to pretty much everything, if only he could only have a little more time on the computer. He just couldn't get used to going to bed when it was still light outside, for God's sake, and lying there playing with Terry's ears while the rest of the house snored and the computer just sat there, with nobody on it, nobody even needing the phone line because in all the time he'd been here, five weeks now, they'd never had one single call after nine o'clock at night. The games and the chat rooms were going on in the absence of RageDaemon and Masterman, as if he'd never existed. It had been months since Father had made him smash the computer, weeks since he'd even had the limited but unsupervised freedom of the library terminals. Here, the computer was in a corner of the living room, and anybody was likely to walk by and comment on the goriness of the game you were playing or look to see what your conversation was about.

So he tried, he really did, but that keyboard downstairs in the sleeping house just called to him, and the more he tried to ignore it, the more his fingers craved it. Rachel just couldn't understand that he didn't need all that much sleep, not like he needed the computer. If she really understood, he knew she wouldn't mind. What would it hurt? And anyway, he wouldn't have to tell them—he knew where all the creaking steps were. And if he carried Terry down, the dog would just curl up and go to sleep on his lap, and provide a ready excuse for being there if anyone came downstairs—puppies always needed to go out and pee. He could eject the game and be offline and on the porch in seconds if he heard someone on the stairs. Nobody in this family would think to check and see if the computer was warm.

And indeed, in that family, nobody thought to check, not until it was too late.

Chapter 23

THE LETTER CAME LATE IN THE AFTERNOON ON THE THIRD MONDAY OF August. They had spent most of the afternoon hanging some cabinets Rae had built—Allen was becoming a halfway competent woodworker's assistant—and Rae decided it was time to think about dinner. She moved around the kitchen, chopping onions and bacon and dumping them into a heavy pan, accepting a beer from her assistant. Allen leaned against the door frame, looking out, savoring the day.

The house Rae had spent the past two years rebuilding was the "folly" that her great-uncle had originally built here eighty years ago. Uncle Desmond might have had some odd ideas about architecture, Allen reflected, but the man knew how to choose a site. The house rested on stone foundations between a pair of impressive stone towers, halfway up the side of a hill overlooking the island's small wooded cove; from the upstairs window, a person could look straight south along the Straits of Juan de Fuca to the Olympic Peninsula. On a summer's afternoon like this one, sailboats were a common decoration.

Allen set his beer bottle down on the porch and walked back inside to wrap his arms around his woman. She answered his embrace with a rhythmic sway as she stirred the wooden spoon through the browning onions.

"Steer it up," Allen sang in a vaguely Jamaican accent, his chin hooked over her shoulder. "Leettle darlin'."

"I take it Ed's on a Bob Marley kick?" The two men had been out on Ed's boat the day before, picking up supplies in Friday Harbor.

"Rasta rules, mon. God, that smells great," Allen murmured into the side of her neck.

"It does, doesn't it?"

"Oh, the food smells okay, too."

He felt her chuckle under his arms, felt her shoulder blades press back into his chest. He nibbled his way down beneath the collar of her shirt, tasting salt and the faint flavor of sawdust that always permeated her clothing, waiting for the little shiver that she would give when her attention was well and truly caught. It came when his lips were a half inch from her spine; she let the spoon fall against the side of the pan and turned around to meet his mouth.

After a minute or two, Allen reached past her to shut off the stove. No point in wasting propane, after all.

But in another minute, Rae pulled away from him. "Did you hear something?"

"A bomb going off?" he said, unwilling to be distracted, but she stepped free and walked over to the open front door.

"Damn!" she exclaimed, and hurriedly stuffed her shirt back into her jeans as she moved to turn the gas back on under the onions.

Before Allen could get to the doorway himself, the top of a well-known head appeared, coming up the steps. Ed De la Torre paused on the narrow porch, shuffling his feet against the mat and squinting into the darkened interior.

"Anybody home?"

"Hello, Ed. Watch the bottle." Allen walked over to pick up the abandoned beer. It was still cool. "Want a beer?"

"No thanks, I've got a date on Orcas, just wanted to drop off this stuff from the post office, thought it might be important."

He came into the house to lay the mail on the table, Rae's over-sized express mail envelope on top. He took one look at the side of Rae's face, shot Allen a glance that took in his rumpled shirt and his ill-concealed irritation, and a grin spread over his leathery features.

"I won't interrupt you kids any further," he told them. "See you in a couple days."

He tromped down the steps, whistling, and halfway down the hill started singing one of Jimmy Buffett's ruder songs. Rae, blushing like a schoolgirl, turned to the mail. She opened the envelope that had looked so important, found in it just a copy of an already signed contract, and dropped it on the table to sort through the other things. One of those she held out to Allen.

Surprised, he took it from her hand. One glance at the printed address and his heart stuttered: Alice's writing. He ripped the envelope open and glanced at the tidy script that covered both sides of three sheets of paper, which was not Alice's but that of a stranger. He flipped over the last page to read the signature: Rachel.

A letter from Rachel Johnson, forwarded by Alice, omitting Rachel's last name with her usual care for anonymity. He had, he realized the moment he saw that precise hand, been expecting something from her.

Without pausing to read the words, Allen took the few strides onto the porch and shouted out Ed's name. The man was nearly to the little dock, but he turned around in inquiry.

"Can you stop in on your way home?" Allen called.

"You need a ride?" Ed shouted back.

"I might."

"I could take you now," the boatman offered.

"Morning's fine." Ed's dates were rarely confined to dinner and a movie.

Ed waved his understanding and continued on his way.

"Allen?" came Rae's question from inside. "Are you going somewhere?"

Dear God, he thought, *I hope not,* but he said only, "Let me read this first, and I'll tell you." He sat on the top step of the porch and, with mounting apprehension, began to read about the state of Jamie O'Connell.

MY DEAR FRIEND,

I know that you had not expected to hear from me again, and trust that, knowing your concern for our young friend J, my letter does not trouble you. I write because I am having problems that I find myself uncomfortable about facing alone, and wish to consult the only other person who knows the child well.

I will not lie to you—we had some initial difficulties in getting J settled here. As you yourself indicated, terrible experiences teach terrible behavior, and although I persist in believing that love conquers all, I will admit that there is in our young friend a great deal to conquer. However, as the summer holidays came on and the others were home more hours, J began to emerge from the distant state and make tentative forays into the unfamiliar business of becoming a family member. There is, as you suspected, a great turbulence in there, and much testing of boundaries must take place before J feels safe to let the anger surface. But as you know, behavior such as that is a thing we are well used to, and it does at least indicate that J begins to trust that there are rules to test, and not just the random dictates of an abuser. J has succumbed to the charms of my youngest, whom you will remember as the official gatherer of eggs in the henhouse.

I should perhaps note here that I have so far seen no signs pointing at a history of sexual abuse, although I believe that J is somewhat dyslexic (a vigorously concealed problem that I shall take notice of before school begins) and also, as you told me, slightly deaf in the right ear. J tells me that the father was right-handed, so if the deafness comes from blows, they were delivered from behind. As I think about this, I find that much as I detest a man who will strike a child to its face, it is even more unsettling to envision the man in the habit of giving a hard slap when his child is unawares.

These, however, are concerns for the longer term. I first noticed a change in J a couple of weeks ago, when the child began to appear at the breakfast table looking tired, and was occasionally short-tempered. I would have assumed the latter at any rate a positive sign—that J had become comfortable enough in this new setting to feel able to express emotions and be mildly self-assertive (and truly, thus far the ill temper has been very mild, nowhere near that of the average two-year-old)—except that it was joined with a certain secretiveness and a habit of meeting my questions with that wide-eyed innocence which children imagine conceals all wrongdoing.

Again, hiding things from authority is not in itself either unexpected or even undesirable at this point. However, before I could sort out what was happening, two events occurred which together seem to have precipitated a crisis in J's mind. The first was when my elder son decided to go out and shoot some rabbits and, without thinking, brought them home uncleaned. J walked in on him at the very goriest part of the operation, when my boy was up to his arms in blood and the shotgun was propped against the table in the summerhouse. J was shocked into near immobility, so much so that I thought I would have to call the doctor, but a night's rest, with me and my husband reading aloud from one book after another, seemed to calm the child, and after sleeping half the day away, J was quiet, and slightly wary around my son, but more nearly normal.

Then on Monday—the twelfth—my youngest disappeared for half a day. I know that to you, the place appears a bedlam of people and children, but I assure you, my children do not wander off—there are too many dangers on a place like this, mechanical and natural, to allow a casual attitude toward that. J was the one to discover her missing, and came running into the kitchen where I was working, white of face and trembling too hard to get out words. I finally understood that J had seen my daughter at the edge of the far field, talking with a stranger, yet when J ran out to be sure all was well, child and stranger were gone. J was convinced that my daughter had been kidnapped.

My immediate impulse—to call in the police—would, I knew, inevitably bring about questions about J's history. I was also aware, even in the concerns of the moment, that considering J's own history, the idea of kidnapping could be a more automatic assumption than it would be for the general population of children that age. Nonetheless, if my girl had actually been abducted, even if she merely had met with accident, there would be no time to waste. So instead of phoning for the police, I sent out my family and called our neighbors. Within ten minutes we had more men and women than the police could have brought to bear, all of us beating the bushes for her.

We found her in less than an hour, unharmed but for some scratches on her arms from the blackberries she had been picking when the man appeared. For there was a man, that much was clear; however, a four-year-old's powers of description and communication are inadequate for much more than that. He had light hair, wore a necktie and sunglasses, was maybe as tall as my husband, and told her he had found some kittens and needed her to help rescue them. She assures me he did not touch her, except once to help her over a ditch, and I could see no sign that her clothing was disturbed, nor her state of mind—and I assure you, had some strange man tried to do more than walk with her through a field in order to show her kittens, I have no doubt that I would see the result in my daughter. Her greatest distress is that the man had left her before he could show her where the kittens were, so that she thinks the poor things are now out there alone.

But the most peculiar element, and the one that J seems to find ominous, is that before the man left her, he told her to say hello to "her new cousin J." If she was even a year older and told me this, I would believe that the man actually knew J's name, and would indeed worry. But she is so young, she doesn't know the difference between what the man said and how she interpreted it. He might easily have said something along the lines of, "Say hello to your brothers and sisters," and when she added that she also lived with a new cousin, J, he could have repeated the name, and that was what lodged in her mind.

You see my dilemma? There was a man, someone my daughter did not recognize, who led her away and then turned her loose unharmed. Everything else is uncertain (except the necktie—that foreign object I am sure she could not have invented!) and I would hate to introduce another disruption in J's life on the merest suggestion that a threat has appeared. I would almost be tempted to resort to nothing but a regimen of extreme watchfulness on the part of the adults here, were it not for J's extreme state of mind.

J is frightened—no, *terrified* to the point of incapacity, and although I cannot get any details from the child, it is clear that it is not so much for J's own safety that the fear lies, but for ours. In fact, J's immediate response to my daughter's story was to offer to pack and leave, lest trouble plague our door. It is a most generous and responsible reaction, but of course, we cannot have it. I have told J I would write to you immediately, and ask for your advice.

I believe what troubles J is the possibility that the father may have discovered where his child went, and be out to exact revenge—a fear, I would say, akin to that raised by the airplane you two saw that last day. My friend, I know it is asking a great deal of you in your current state, having moved on from us and our problems, but if you could simply check on the father's whereabouts—or arrange to have someone reliable check for you—and make certain that he has remained in place during the past week, it would go far to soothe J's worries. And, frankly, my own—fear has a terrible contagion to it, does it not?

Until we hear from you, my husband and older son will remain doubly vigilant, and J will not be allowed out of our sight. (J, in the meantime, refuses to go very far from my young daughter, and seems to take her safety as a personal responsibility.)

Again, I regret having to ask this of you. And in case you think I
am asking to be relieved of J, I say vehemently that I will not permit
you to remove the child unless it becomes a clear and immediate
necessity.

With respects and well wishes,

RACHEL

Yes, he thought, Rachel had omitted her surname through concern for
security; why else never give Jamie's name, or even his sex? She was
taking as few chances as possible, revealing nothing that might lead
back to her family were the letter to be intercepted. He read the letter
a second time, folded it away, and stood. His bones ached, he thought.

And Rae wasn't going to be happy.

HE HANDED RAE THE LETTER, AND WENT BACK OUTSIDE SO AS NOT TO
watch her while she read it. The pages rustled, a passing boat trailed
happy voices in its wake. It seemed to take her a long time; Allen spent
most of it thinking about fingers, and trust, and vulnerability: the insane lengths adults will go to in teaching their children self-respect.

When Rae came out, she laid the letter on the rustic table under
the window and sat in the other chair.

"You'll have to go away for a while." It was not a question.

"I'm afraid so."

"We leave Sunday." For Japan, in six days: Allen already had his ticket.

"I might only need a day or two. If it turns out, as I expect, that the
father has a clear alibi for last Monday, then that will be the end of it.
There'd certainly be no reason for me to go to Montana—that would
only disturb the boy further. All I need to do is reassure him, and
Rachel, that they've just got a potential neighborhood problem, not
one imported from California."

"But it could be longer."

"It could," he admitted.

"And there isn't anyone else who can do it."

"I won't know until I get down there. But I promise you, if I can get
free of this, I will. And if I can't by Sunday, I'll take a later plane."

She smiled, finally, and moved over to sit on his lap. The chair,
which looked as ramshackle as the small table, creaked slightly under
their combined weight, but Rae had built it, and he knew that even a
pair of Sumo wrestlers wouldn't end up on the ground.

"You like this boy," she said.

"I guess I do, yes. He isn't what you'd call likable, but he's intense, and has a lot of inner strength."

"He needs you." It was a flat statement and difficult to argue with, although Allen made the effort, simply because he didn't want her to think that this was going to be a common occurrence, his past life perpetually threatening to reach out and drag him back in. He didn't want to think that himself.

But she cut short his protest. "Allen, it's okay. It's disappointing, but I'm not going to break into pieces. Sometimes things come up. Just come when you can. But can you let me know if you're not going to make it back by Sunday?"

"I'll try, sweetheart."

SO MUCH FOR RETIREMENT, ALLEN MUSED, WATCHING THE SUMMER TOURist playground go past from Ed De la Torre's boat. Good thing I haven't cleaned out those storage lockers yet. Good thing I didn't return my working cash to the bank.

Tools were basic, since it was no longer possible to travel with sophisticated electronic equipment on a plane. His most important tool was the money belt he wore around his waist, a strip of shiny brown leather that concealed ten thousand dollars inside its length, enough cash to buy him out of almost any emergency. But just what sort of disguise should he wear with that belt? Surely he could leave behind his smelly biker's jacket—he would be making inquiries about a rich man's whereabouts, not hanging around noisy bars. The other end of the spectrum, more like it, the Armani jacket a grateful client had thrust on him, and the silk shirt that looked like really expensive cotton.

He could only hope they hadn't absorbed the smell of cat piss from the jacket they'd been stored with.

Back at the apartment, he arranged an assortment of plain and costly clothes in a leather garment bag (since a man in an Armani with luggage is less noticeable than one without) and put his laptop and various odds and ends into an equally showy carry-on. He even managed to snag a first-class ticket on the last flight to San Francisco, an hour's drive from San Jose. He went by his club for a workout, then found a place that would cut his hair into the latest Harrison Ford style for older men, and had the gray touched up just enough to be deceptive. In downtown Seattle, he found a place that sold no-contract cell phones, and paid cash, adding a snug leather case to dress it up. He then ate dinner in a restaurant filled with men like himself, executives on expense accounts, studying their mannerisms, getting into the role.

The late flight was uneventful, the car reserved for him had no obvious rental company marks on it, and he stayed the night in a hotel halfway down the peninsula. In the morning, shaving the face under Harrison Ford's hair in the mirror, he drank his tepid room service coffee and listened with one ear to the state of the world as presented by one of the San Francisco television stations. Wars and would-be wars, a juicy political scandal, a drive-by shooting in Oakland, a missing light plane, a fire in the Tenderloin, and to top it all off, the traffic was awful. Welcome to the twenty-first century. He rinsed off his shaving cream, splashed on a small amount of an aftershave that smelled of power, checked that his new haircut still presented the proper amount of tousle and that he hadn't forgotten how to tie a necktie, and zipped up his garment bag. *San Jose, here we come.*

Chapter 24

JAMIE'S FATHER, MARK DAVID O'CONNELL, WORKED FOR A COMPANY called Revista. When Allen had first heard the name it sounded to him like software, but it turned out to be investment strategy. Back in May, his inquiries had told him that the company was small, with seventeen employees, and that O'Connell was one of three partners.

Their offices were in one of the big new buildings along Highway 280. Allen had phoned the day before and demanded to speak with "Mark," gave his name to the secretary as "Tony" (no surname), and grew highly indignant when the woman informed him with polite regret that "Mr. O'Connell" would be out of the office all week. By the time he'd hung up, he was satisfied that he had left her with the impression of yet another self-important dot.com asshole. So that today, when he showed up with that air of inborn good manners that could only come from someone who actually is important, she wouldn't connect him with the rude upstart Tony. He parked in the newly resurfaced parking lot where the air already shimmered with heat, reached under his shirt to activate the wire he wore, and walked briskly up the steps of the glass-and-steel building.

The entrance foyer was air-conditioned down to frigidity, and Allen was glad he'd worn his jacket. He glanced down the directory board, saw that Revista was on the top floor, and joined a pair of women dressed in three inches of heel and the severe skirts made necessary by the belief that it was a man's world, or at least a man's firm. They got out at the sixth floor, a place as grim-looking as their expressions. Four floors up, Revista's secretary was wearing a stark white shirt and an oatmeal-colored jacket, but, he noticed, she wore pants, and comfortable shoes. Mrs. Phillips (as the nameplate on her desk revealed) looked older than her voice on the phone had indicated, and somewhat softer around the eyes than Allen would have predicted. His distracted charm softened her further, to the point that it was actually she who apologized for any misunderstanding, telling him that the missing PDA he so eloquently bemoaned must have recorded his appointment not for tomorrow, but for the following Thursday, because Mr. O'Connell had taken the week off, and was not due in until Monday.

Allen patted his coat pocket for the third time, caught himself, and gave her a rueful smile. "It's terrible, being dependent on these things. I mean, I downloaded all my appointments about a week ago, but the thing went missing between the time I made the appointment and that night when I went to plug in my laptop. I'll have to buy a replacement, but I keep hoping that someone's going to call and say they've found it. I can't even remember the restaurant I met your boss in, that should tell you what kind of shape my head is in."

"Do you remember what day it was?"

"Not exactly, just the first part of last week. Nice place, I do remember that, Chinese or Japanese, something Asian. I wasn't paying much attention, tell you the truth. Someone else was taking me there, and introduced us."

"Could it have been a Korean restaurant?"

"It was spicy," Allen said helpfully.

"Try Kim's," she said. "He eats there a lot. He used to anyway, before . . . well, I don't suppose there's any reason not to tell you. Mr. O'Connell's son was kidnapped three months ago." Allen made the requisite noises of distress and disbelief; Mrs. Phillips went on to say that the boy was twelve and no ransom had ever been asked. "Mark— Mr. O'Connell—was absolutely devastated. He's just beginning to get back to normal. So he may have started having lunch at Kim's again."

"I don't suppose you know if he was there a week ago?"

"I wouldn't have any way of knowing."

Allen looked at her. "Sorry, I thought you were his secretary."

"More a receptionist and answering service," she told him. "Actually, I work for half a dozen small companies and individuals, people who don't need a full-time phone service. They stop in or call for messages, come here when they need to meet clients."

"You mean, there's not really such a thing as Revista?"

"Sure there is. It's just not the kind of business where Mr. O'Connell needs to spend a lot of time in the office. He's mostly on the road. Or in the air—he has his own plane."

"But he does have an office here?"

"Oh yes. I suppose I shouldn't be telling you this, you being a potential client and all, but really, there's no point in keeping up a lot of show, is there? I mean, if you think about it, it's better to have a higher return for the client than a set of offices with expensive furniture and an art collection."

"Makes sense to me." Allen gave her an amiable grin, wondering what the hell had happened to the other sixteen employees who were on the records—and the other two partners. "Well, thanks for your help. I'll phone Kim's and see if they found a PDA. A week ago Monday?" he said, as if he'd suddenly thought of something. "Could it have been Monday, I think that was the twelfth, that I met him?"

"I don't work Mondays, so I wouldn't know if Mr. O'Connell was here or not. Would you like to leave a message for him, when he comes in?"

"Why don't I just leave you my card, and I'll try to reach him next week? I'm going to be out of communication for a while, myself."

The slip of heavy card stock he gave her held an imaginary name and the address of an abandoned warehouse in Santa Monica. He thanked her and went back to his car, where he retrieved the miniature tape and labeled it, his mind working furiously.

Back in May, running his searches on O'Connell and his son, he'd never thought to look further than the man's financial statements and the business description that was on the public records. O'Connell had appeared so clean, Allen never suspected that Revista was a front, its most substantial asset the secretary, a sixth of whose services the company hired each month along with meaningless conference rooms. And an office, although Allen would have bet one of Rae's tables that a search of the office would reveal about as much as a search of a furniture-store window display.

So what the hell was Mark O'Connell selling, if not investment strategies?

And if he'd told his semi-secretary that his son had been kidnapped, why hadn't he also told her that the boy was actually a runaway? Surely Jamie's letter had reached him?

Not for the first time, Allen wished he was a cop, to whom many investigative doors would open at the flip of a badge. Alice's group did have one or two pet police officers, but none around here, and they had to be used sparingly. He had no way of knowing if the local police department was already investigating O'Connell for some kind of fraud, or if they remained in blissful ignorance, and he could think of no immediate means of finding out. He did remember that Alice knew someone on one of the newspapers in the Bay Area; that might give him an in.

He passed the afternoon (his Armani-and-silk exchanged for more workaday Levis-and-cotton) in a public library very like that in which he had first watched **deadboy**, alternating between the computer lab and back issues of the local papers. He learned from the latter that Mark O'Connell was a partner in the investment firm Revista, that his son Jameson was a difficult student whose fellow students and teachers spoke of him primarily as keeping to himself, and that this was the third adolescent boy who had vanished on his way home in the past fourteen months. That scanty information was for Saturday, the day after Jamie vanished; Sunday's paper had another article, this one with a snapshot of Jamie in jeans and sneakers, standing in front of a rock, with no discernible expression on his face. There was also a sidebar article concerning the other two boys who had disappeared, with photographs that bore only the most superficial resemblance to each other. Mark O'Connell had read a statement to the press, saying simply that he was too distraught to answer questions, but that he was praying that whoever had taken his son would turn him free unharmed, as the boy was all he had left in life.

Allen scrutinized the picture of the self-described distraught father, seeing a handsome blond man in an expensive suit, who was also the man in a silk shirt who had swallowed four double whiskeys and propped a shotgun against his son's chest just for laughs. True, the man in the grainy photograph looked both exhausted and deeply troubled. But come to think of it, if O'Connell's business was fraudulent, or even just shaky, having the police nosing around after his son's disappearance would create its own world of immediate concerns. Maybe he looked tired because he'd been up half the night shredding papers.

The thought cheered Allen, and he went back to the papers and the Internet with renewed interest. He found little. Ten days after Jamie's disappearance, the paper ran a brief follow-up article, two paragraphs in length, to inform readers that nothing had been heard from the boy or his abductor, and that the police were still treating it as foul play, since the boy was on the young side for being a runaway.

Nothing about having received a letter from Jamie himself, freely admitting to being just that.

Allen sat at the library table, drumming his fingers on the fake wood surface, oblivious to the hum and buzz of the busy patrons as he struggled to come to grips with the possibility that he'd screwed up. He had, without a doubt, allowed himself to be rushed—wham, bam, three weeks from contact to snatch. And although sometimes fast proved best, why hadn't he dug a little more deeply before he and Alice had opened the door and taken Jamie away?

Back to square one.

Sorry, Rae.

THE SECOND-FLOOR MOTEL ROOM HE RENTED GAVE HIM A REFRIGERATOR, microwave, and once-a-week cleaning, and allowed him an open phone line in exchange for a hefty cash deposit. Even more important, the front door was sturdier than it looked, and the back window gave him an emergency exit that wouldn't break his neck. Normally, that kind of security was a minor consideration, more habitual than necessary, but the possibility that he'd missed O'Connell's shady business had made him concerned. The man might be guilty of nothing worse than making himself appear more successful than he actually was, but if he did turn out to be immersed in criminal enterprise—or even in organized crime—he might well have a greater capacity for violent response than the usual abusing parent. Allen had taken children from crooks before, but those offenses had generally been along the lines of turning back odometers or peddling kiddie porn. Only rarely had he come across the darker underworld—but if O'Connell was a part of it, Allen did not wish to be taken unawares.

He hung his clothes in the chipboard closet, then went out again to the grocery and hardware stores. When the motel had gone quiet, he took out his hardware store purchases and screwed locks onto both window tracks, then replaced the door's dead bolt with one that looked nearly identical, but for which he had the only key.

He spent most of that night lying beneath the sheets staring at the ceiling, pondering Jamie O'Connell. In the morning, he made some phone calls and checked his email; nothing there.

He was aware of an odd feeling in the day, as if the dingy air of the city had a mild electrical current tingling through it. His nerves were jumpy, his body felt as if he hadn't worked out in too long, even though he'd both run and lifted less than forty-eight hours before. Lack of sleep and a day bent over the library records, he decided; better look around for a club hereabouts, work off the scholar's stoop.

But this morning, he would remain a scholar, or at least, he'd surround himself with them. He drove through the sprawl of San Jose to the school Jamie had last attended, private and semimilitary, to make inquiries about enrolling his own troublesome son. Back in May, he'd confined his contact with the school to the phone, so he didn't have to worry about being recognized, and that morning he'd been pleased to find that, although the full school term had not begun yet, the school was running its two-week preliminary course for those needing to catch up, and that most of the staff was on board.

The principal, named Kluger, was exactly the sort of person Allen would have asked for, so self-absorbed it was easy to lie to him, so self-important it was a pleasure. Kruger glanced at the Armani, and became less interested in young Eddie's problems (fictional young Ed was a thirteen-year-old with tattoos, a marijuana habit, and a peculiar interest in Nietzsche; Allen thought Ed De la Torre would like his godson) than he was in Allen's bankbook. By dropping a few references to exotic vacation spots and Hollywood first names, Allen had the principal eating out of his hand, and it was a simple thing to establish a few peculiarities of his own. Such as ethnic preferences.

"Do you have any Indian teachers?" Allen inquired, squinting over at the yearly school photographs on the wall as if he couldn't be bothered to get up and study them.

"Indian?" Kruger's caution was no doubt due more to lack of understanding of the reason for the question than any incomprehension of the question itself. Should he admit to the presence of a minority on the staff? Or trumpet one?

"Yes, you know, from the subcontinent. A Hindu, a Sikh would be good, Parsi if you can get one. Not a Jain, they're not disciplinarians."

"Ah, Indian. Yes, we have two. Mr. Ram— er, Ramaswami I think it is, he's just joined our computer lab, and Ms. Rao in the middle school English program. She has a degree from London University," he added.

"Good, can't do better than an Indian for teaching boys," Allen declared, as emphatic as a Raj colonel. "Let me talk to the Rao woman."

"I, er, I think she's probably in class at the moment."

"Of course she is, that's where she should be. But surely you give the poor woman a break sometime?"

The hint of outrage in Allen's accusation of overwork put the cap on the principal's state of confusion. "Yes, of course. I mean, her break, let me see." He leaned forward over his wide, empty desk and pressed the switch on the speaker phone. "Ms. Gillespie, can you tell me when Ms. Rao has her prep time?"

"Third period, Mr. Kluger."

He cut the connection without thanking his secretary, and said to Allen, "Third period."

"And what time would that be?"

The confusion returned, and Allen decided that Mr. Kluger was not exactly a hands-on kind of a principal, if he didn't know for certain when the periods began and ended. "After ten. Ten-thirty, might be a good time to catch her."

It was only eight-forty now, and Allen was not about to sit around chatting with this pompous ass for two hours. He stood. "How about I come back then, if that's okay with you? So as not to waste your time. Say I meet you back here at ten-thirty, you can introduce me to Ms.—Rao, was it?"

The blithe assumption that the school principal had nothing better to do than show a potential student's father around at the drop of a hat might be slightly insulting, but was almost certainly true. Allen shook Kluger's hand and was out the door before the man could open it, and disappeared through the outer office in a flash. He stood in the hallway, patting his pockets as if he'd forgotten something; as soon as he heard the principal's door close, he stuck his head back inside the office to smile at the woman sitting behind the desk. "Ms. Gillespie?"

"Yes," she said expectantly.

"I'm Mike Ellis, I'm thinking of bringing my son here. Can you tell me, when does third period begin?"

The woman hid her amusement, but Allen could see that she knew quite well that he had asked her boss just that and Kluger hadn't had a clue. "Second period ends at nine-fifty, there's a twenty-minute break, and the bell for third period rings at ten after ten."

"Thanks a lot," he told her, and left the school with a spring in his step.

He was back in the building well before ten, asking for Ms. Rao's room when the students came pouring from their rooms at ten to. A series of students directed him to an empty classroom just as the teacher was leaving. One glance, and Allen could only wonder that Jamie's praises hadn't been more effusive. The woman was gorgeous, small, slim, brown-skinned, and sloe-eyed, and he knew without thinking about it that every one of her students who didn't embrace neo-Nazi principles would be madly in love with her.

"Ms. Rao?"

"Yes," she said. In dress she was pure Californian, khaki pants and a linen shirt with a thin sweater over it against the school's air-conditioning. Her accent seemed to be English, with a faint brush of Indian music that raised the end of her single word.

"I'm Mike Ellis. Mr. Kluger said I could come and talk with you for a minute about your class."

He could see her thinking that if Kluger gave permission, it had to involve money in some way. "Would you like to talk here, or in the staff room?"

"Actually, it's kind of nice outside, if you have the time for a stroll."

She dropped the sweater over the back of her chair, and locked the classroom door after her.

When they were well clear of the school, and safe from the threat of having Kluger scurry up behind them, Allen drew his breath, and took the very risky plunge he had decided on. "Ms. Rao, I told your principal that I was here to look at your school with an eye to enrolling my son."

"Yes?"

"I don't have a son. I came to see you. I had some questions about Jamie O'Connell."

The young woman stopped dead, her face going taut with dismay. "Has he been found?"

"Not that I know of."

"Are you with the police?"

"No."

"I think you had better explain yourself, Mr. Ellis," she said with an edge to her voice. "If that is your name."

"It's one of them." He watched her think about this, and he continued. "I am trusting you, Ms. Rao. Rather more than I had intended before I saw you. I want to ask you about *The Lord of the Rings*."

She waited for more; when it did not come, she nodded to urge him on. "*The Lord of the Rings*. J. R. R. Tolkien. Yes, many of the children are reading it. When I was growing up, we all read Roald Dahl."

"Would you tell me please, why did you give Jamie a copy of the trilogy?"

Her face closed; she took a step back. "Mr. Ellis, do you work for James's father?"

"No, I most certainly do not. Although," he said carefully, "I'd like to know more about him."

"Why?"

"Ms. Rao, I don't think I can go into that right now. Let's just say it involves Jamie."

"Then the boy's not dead?"

"As far as I know, he's fine. Safe," he added, to see what she did with the word. Her face didn't alter, but after a minute her body relaxed minutely. "Did you have reason to believe him dead?"

"The newspapers seemed to think it likely."

"Why did you give him the books?"

"It was his birthday."

"Do you give all your students expensive sets of books for their birthdays?"

"Just those who need it."

"Jamie's father is a wealthy man."

"Most of the students here come from homes with money," she agreed evenly, evading the unstated question as smoothly as she had all the direct ones. And then she seemed to relent. "Mr. Ellis, are you doing anything for dinner tonight?"

"It sounds as if I may be. Would you like me to pick you up?"

"There is a bookstore on the corner of St. Helena and Main. Park in the lot out in the back of the store, and we can walk to the restaurant. I shall be out in front at seven o'clock."

"White tie or none?" he asked, smiling.

"What you have on will be fine. And if the dinner goes well, you can take me dancing."

He grinned. "Isn't that just what we've been doing for the past few minutes?"

Her black eyes sparked to life with mischief, but she merely repeated demurely, "Seven o'clock, Mr. Ellis," and her slim body swept back the way they had come.

Oh yes, all her students would certainly be in love with her, Allen thought happily.

As he bent to unlock the door of his rental car, his spine exposed to all the world beneath its thin layer of expensive wool, Allen suddenly understood why his shoulders seemed to crave a strenuous workout, what the electrical feeling to the air all morning had been. The hot, dry San Jose air had the same smell as the tropical jungle across the ocean or the rainy night under a Portland overpass, lifetimes ago. It was not the air itself, but the smell of setting out on patrol, stepping into the green, knowing that Charlie waited there.

Pure, unadulterated adrenaline. How could he ever imagine giving this up?

BACK AT HIS MOTEL ROOM, ALLEN TURNED HIS NEW DEAD BOLT, HUNG his jacket and tie on hangers, and checked for email. He had one message, cleansed into anonymity by Alice's remailing service, and even then it was in the woman's own version of code: a string of nine digits, the final 2 and 5 separated by a slash. This gave the seven-digit phone number where he could reach her, between the hours of two and five. No area code meant simply the Seattle area.

Satisfied, he checked to make sure neither window had been tampered with, then cranked up the air conditioner to full rattle. He arranged his three-hundred-dollar shoes and his silk-looking-like-cotton shirt in the closet with the jacket, and turned on the bathroom tap to splash his face with water as cold as it would give, which wasn't very. He was feeling his pair of sleepless nights, and knew he wouldn't get much rest later, so he stretched out on the slippery flowered chintz of the bedcover. He was asleep in ninety seconds.

His internal clock prodded him after three hours. His eyes opened to the strange room, sun bright around the skimpy curtains; he blinked, and turned quickly over to look at the bedside radio alarm. Just after two. He used the toilet and stuck his head under the cold-water tap again (finding it even warmer than before) before pulling on a pair of shorts, worn sandals, and a T-shirt declaring him an alumnus of Hanover College, Indiana. The car was an oven, its seat scorching the backs of his legs. Half a mile away he spotted a pay phone that wasn't directly on a freeway or ten feet from a noisy gas station; digging a roll of quarters from the glove compartment, Allen stepped up to the booth.

Alice answered on the first ring.

"We may have a problem here," he told her. "The father looks like he might be involved in an illegal business."

"You're not talking about a meth lab," she stated.

"More like a scam, or money laundering," Allen told her.

Her silence was eloquent.

"I'm not sure how we missed it, and I could be wrong now, but I like to keep you in the picture."

"We missed it because we were hasty. I rushed you. I should have—"

"Alice," he interrupted, "it was my decision, too. We missed it. The question is what to do now."

"What do you need?" she asked, and Allen found himself smiling, just a little. One of the things he'd always liked, working with this otherwise difficult woman, was that she knew how to get over it, and get on with it.

"Information." Better late than never. "I think you know somebody on one of the papers down here. If they could get me an ID, I'd have an excuse to ask questions." Bluffing only went so far; sooner or later, you ran up against someone who demanded to see identification. If that someone was a cop, things would go to hell in a hurry. Call it smarts, or short-timer's jitters, but Allen had no wish to spend his retirement in prison.

Alice said, "I think I can get something better than that. You need it immediately?"

"I'm okay tonight, I have a date with the kid's teacher." No reaction from Alice, not that he expected one. "Business, in case you're concerned. And later . . . well, I thought of some other things." Illegal things, and he wasn't about to go into details on a phone line.

"I'll have something for you by this evening. And, take care," Alice said, which didn't sound like her. Then she added sternly, "It would be very difficult to bail you out," which did.

Chapter 25

ALLEN WENT INTO A MEN'S STORE THAT HE HAD SPOTTED WHILE DRIVING to the telephone, and bought two new shirts and a pair of slightly more extreme trousers than he usually wore. When he came around the corner of the assigned bookstore that evening, he saw Ms. Rao's eyes sweep over him and return to his face with approval. He came to a stop before her and bowed slightly.

"My lady."

"Sushi or pizza?" she greeted him.

"I like anything. You choose."

Somewhat to his surprise, she chose the pizza.

It was no chain pizza joint, though. The men in the kitchen greeted her as a friend, and the waitress showed them to a table at the back, next to a window. He ordered beer, she ordered red wine, and when they had their drinks, he raised his and said, "Mike."

"Sorry?"

"You can't keep calling me Mr. Ellis. I'm Mike."

"And I'm Karin, with an 'i.' Cheers."

"Kluger said you were at the University of London," Allen opened, and the conversation was launched, back and forth with history and interests. Little flirtation, he was relieved to see: a complication he could do without. Karin seemed to feel the same way. The pizza was excellent, the talk easy, and he waited for a sign that she was willing to move on to the next stage, the reason she'd asked him out for dinner. When no sign came, he gave the conversation a nudge.

"Tell me about Jamie O'Connell."

"I call him James. 'Jameson' seemed too big for him."

"He's a nice kid."

"Bright, quiet," she said, not quite an agreement.

"Many friends?"

"Almost none. There are a couple of other outsiders he talks to from time to time, but it's always a problem, kids who move schools a lot. It's hard to work your way into a group that's been together for some time."

Outsiders, Allen noted. "Is he bullied?"

"We don't permit bullying at the school," Karin said quickly.

"But at a different school, he would be?"

"At a different school, different conditions would apply. Who knows?"

"I'll take that as a yes."

"Not necessarily. Bullying depends on a lot of factors. As far as I can see, it's as much a matter of chemistry as anything else. Someone becomes a victim with as much random chance as falling in love. All I can say is, here, no one person or group picked on the boy. If anything," she added, almost reluctantly, "James picked on some of them. He tripped one of the kindergartners and broke his wrist—although that may have been an accident. I saw him pinch a second-grade girl."

The chemistry of bullying, Allen thought, and wrenched his mind away from the image of shiny black glasses. "Did you talk to the boy's father about it?"

But instead of answering, she asked, "You don't need any dessert, do you? What do you think about dancing?"

"In the abstract, or the particular?"

"Would you like to go dancing with me? Not here," she explained. "There's a place a few doors down that has ballroom dancing on Thursday nights. My husband and I go sometimes, but he's on the East Coast just now."

"If you don't mind my size tens landing regularly on your toes, I'd be willing to make an effort."

Ballroom dancing was a skill Allen had left behind with his high school graduation, but he managed not to step on her feet too seriously. Because he was so rusty, it took him a while to realize that in the process of guiding him around the floor, the woman's hands were covering rather more ground than was really necessary: By the end of the first song, she had managed to feel her way around most of his belt line and up both armpits. When the song ended, he leaned close to her ear to murmur, "How about we sit this one out, and you tell me why you're patting me down?"

Her blush was delectable, but she did not protest the accusation. Back at the table, he took the chair beside her, so they could talk without raising their voices.

"So, Ms. Karin Rao, why do you imagine I might be wearing a gun?"

"You said you weren't working for Mark O'Connell. I wasn't sure if I believed you, and if I did, I wanted to know if maybe you were like him, just not with him."

He reared back in surprise. "Are you telling me that Jamie's father wears a gun?"

"My stepfather's a police detective. American. I know what a gun worn under clothes looks like."

Oh shit, Allen thought as the first half of her statement sank in. *A cop's daughter, just what I need, oh shit.*

"Why are you asking questions about the boy?" she was saying.

"I'm asking questions about the father." *Did she set me up? She had hours to do it.*

"Is that because you already know where the boy is?"

Allen sat back sharply. *Get up and go, now, before her reinforcements storm in.* She must have seen something of the apprehension in his face, because suddenly she smiled, and moved in so close that an onlooker might have thought they were about to kiss. She said to him in a low, firm voice, "He's a troubled boy, is James, but it's hardly surprising, with a father like that. Anything I can do to help you keep that man away from his son, just let me know."

Allen laughed in relief and delight, and her smile deepened.

"You can begin," he suggested, "by telling me what you know of the man."

"Have you met him?"

"No." Just spent a week and a half listening to his voice and watching him torment his son.

"I only met him once," Karin told him. "At Back-to-School night in October. Really nice man, enthusiastic about the boy, good questions, sympathetic. And very attractive—he has these sparkling blue eyes and a little dimple in his chin. But then there was the gun—this was before our metal detectors went in. A gun seemed a little extreme for an investment counselor. And when I talked with him on the phone a month or so later, I began to wonder. It was . . . It's hard to explain. It was almost as if, on the phone, without the physical charm, I was talking to a different person. As if he wasn't working so hard to be a great guy, when I wasn't there in front of him. Face-to-face, he seemed to hang on my every word; on the phone, he didn't seem at all interested in what I had to say. He seemed, in fact, on the point of hanging up in boredom. I'm sure that doesn't make much sense to you, especially since you've never met him, but the result was that although after our parent-teacher conference I'd been thinking of Mark O'Connell as a great guy who'd been through a lot—lost his wife, trying to do his best by his problem kid—after talking with him on the phone, I started to reevaluate. Anyway, that was our first phone conversation."

"And the second?" Allen asked.

"The second one was, frankly, scary." She shot him a glance to see how he was taking the statement, and seemed reassured at his reaction. "I even told Kluger about it, but he just climbed on his sexist high horse and all but patted me on the head. It wasn't my imagination," she insisted.

"I'm not arguing with you," Allen told her. "Why'd you call him in the first place, if I may ask? Do you call all the parents?"

"I try to contact each parent every two or three months, not only when there's a problem, but when their child has done a particularly good job, or if something happened I think they should know about. The classes are small enough, it's not difficult to do. And it helps a lot, to keep the parents involved."

"But not Mark O'Connell?"

"I know, I'm driveling. It was so awkward, it makes me uncomfortable to talk about it. But what happened, the second call I mean, came out of something James had written in one of his essays that rather alarmed me. The assignment was to describe a scene in a kitchen, using all one's senses, and employing metaphor and simile to explore nuances without making obvious parallels—although of course I didn't put the assignment in those words for the class. In his story, James was describing a woman dropping a plate of food onto the floor, and he wrote something along the lines of, 'The meat hit the linoleum dead flat, with a crack like a wide leather belt hitting naked skin.' You can see why it caught my attention."

"I sure can."

"Anyway, I might have thought it was just some flight of imagination, or something he'd picked up somewhere, but for the way he reacted when I asked him if he'd ever been hit like that."

"He denied it."

"Absolutely and strenuously. And laid me a nice side trail to lead me away from a phone call. Which I probably should have followed."

"What happened?"

"I have no idea. I mean, I called the father, and found him home even though James had said he was out of town. I asked him—very gently, I thought—if he was having any difficulties with James at home. You know, not accusing him or anything, just suggesting that boys of that age, particularly those who had lost a mother, often acted out and went through a period of misbehavior. I suppose it was too ham-fisted, because instead of admitting that yes, he did find James a handful sometimes and needed to discipline him strongly, in about two minutes flat he somehow managed to turn the conversation around and was soon quizzing me in this quiet voice about the boy's misbehavior at school, saying that he'd hoped all would go well here, that James had seemed to respond so well to the sterner structure—his words—and how disappointed he was that James had given me problems. It took me aback, how smoothly the man turned things completely over on me, and then before I could do more than protest that it wasn't at all what I'd meant, he thanked me and hung up. When I tried to ring him back, the line was busy, and stayed that way until after ten o'clock. I didn't know what to do. My husband even offered to go with me to James's house and check that things were okay, but I couldn't help thinking that was a bit extreme. And I couldn't very well call the police over a creepy conversation with a parent—a wealthy, upstanding, involved parent who would then yank his kid out of school and probably threaten to sue over being accused of beating his kid."

"And did he?"

"Beat James? That's why I said I had no idea what happened that night. James came to school the next morning, and he was fine physically—no bruises I could see, no limp, no indication of soreness or distress, but I have to say, he certainly acted like a beaten child—the startled eyes, the jumpiness . . . He even raised an arm as if to fend me off when I appeared beside him without warning."

"Abuse isn't always physical," Allen noted; she was on it in a flash. "You *do* have James hidden away!"

"Me? Nope. Like I told you, I'm interested in the father. But I have seen men like him before. You say he carried a gun? Even to a parent-teacher conference?"

"I also saw him one time with a group of other men, maybe three or four, coming out of a restaurant when I happened to be driving by. One of them, I'm quite sure, was armed. They all looked like crooks. And I overheard James talking about guns one time, he seemed remarkably knowledgeable."

To an Englishwoman, he reflected, any knowledge about guns might appear extreme. "When you say the men looked like crooks, what do you mean?"

She thought for a moment, her eyes slowly coming to focus on a clot of high-spirited young professionals near the busy bar. "You see those three men in the suits over there? When you have a group like that, they're interacting—even if they're all business, they bounce off each other. Each of them is always aware of himself through the eyes of the others. Well, men like those I saw with Mark O'Connell don't do that. They're only aware of others as either people they can take advantage of, or people to watch out for. Victims or threat. You can see it in their body language," she elaborated, and the precision of her pronunciation made Allen wonder if his companion was accustomed to the amount of wine she'd put away.

"You're talking about sharks," he told her.

"Yeah, human sharks." She nodded, and Allen hid his disappointment. To Karin Rao, the word "crook" described any sort of ruthless businessman. She hadn't been all that much help, after all.

"Well, Karin," he said, "you've got to be up in the morning, and I have to go see someone tonight. The pizza was great, and I'm sorry I'm not a better dancer."

Obediently, she stood up and gathered her coat around her, swaying slightly as if to the music. He handed her the purse she'd left on the back of the chair and followed her out of the dance hall, a solicitous hand hovering near one elbow.

Outside on the street, she blinked owlishly around her. Allen asked, "Did you drive?" There was no way he was letting this woman behind a wheel, but she shook her head.

"No, I live just around the corner. The walk will do me good."

"I'll go with you, I could use some air, too."

It was four blocks, into the world of condos and duplexes that lay behind the main road. The Rao home was in a ten-year-old condo, through a courtyard with a fountain and security gate and up a set of external stairs. He shook her hand formally, and thanked her again.

"I hope you can help James," she told him, sober again.

"Look, I know you like Jamie, but really I have nothing to do—"

"Did I say I liked him?" she interrupted. "I don't remember saying that."

He gaped at her. "Well, surely . . . I mean, you gave him the books for his birthday, you seem very concerned as to his welfare—"

"I'm a teacher, he is one of my students. Or he was, until he disappeared. Certainly I felt sorry for the boy, since there was obviously something terribly dysfunctional about his relationship with his father, and I felt—still feel, clearly—some degree of responsibility to intervene if I can, but no, I wouldn't say I liked the boy. He struck me as secretive and manipulative, and I tried never to take my eyes off him."

Allen was speechless, as if he'd just been fluently cursed to perdition by a parakeet. She saw it, but this time her smile was a wintry thing that belonged on a face decades older.

"Mr. Ellis, despite what the press would have us believe, bad kids are created, not born. When a teenager murders a child or shoots up a school, it isn't because he's innately wicked, it's because his parents are. I believe this in my bones. I even have the optimism to trust that James O'Connell is not too old to be saved from his father's influence. But that doesn't mean that I have to close my eyes to wickedness, or to pretend that I like a child I feel sorry and responsible for."

"What . . . what didn't you like about the boy?" he demanded, but that was too strong for the teacher in Karin Rao, who hastened to correct him.

"I should say less 'dislike' than 'mistrust.' And even with that, it would be very difficult to explain why I do not. James simply made me uneasy. And when I had talked to his father, I began to understand why. Please, Mr. Ellis, if you are in any position to do so, get the boy some help. Before he hurts someone.

"And before you ask, no, he has not done so yet, not that I know."

"But you think he could?" Allen asked, but she was turning away.

"I hope I'm wrong," she said firmly. "Good night, Mr. Ellis."

There was nothing he could do but say good night to the closed door. And, as he reached to shut off the pen-shaped tape recorder in his shirt pocket, to add under his breath, "But I would have sworn that Jamie liked you."

HE DROVE BACK TO THE MOTEL WITHOUT PAYING MUCH ATTENTION TO THE streets. Twenty-four hours earlier, he'd arrived with the simple intention of pinning down O'Connell's location on August the twelfth, but since then he'd uncovered an unsuspected side to the man. He'd known O'Connell was a sadistic abuser, but now it was as if Allen had caught a glimpse of some creature in the undergrowth. A tiger—or a two-legged killer in black pajamas. He shook off the image and speeded up: too much imagination.

Back at the motel, an email from Alice gave him seven numbers, with no time restrictions or area code. He glanced at his watch, saw that it was barely ten-fifteen, and punched the digits into his cell phone. He got the notes and recording of a wrong number, so he hung up and tried it beginning with the local San Jose code. This time a woman said hello into his ear, with music and voices in the background.

"I'm sorry to call so late, but I was given this number by a friend—" he began.

The woman interrupted. "Is now good for you?"

"I . . . sure."

"Fourth and Pine, there's a phone booth."

"Sorry?" he said, but he was talking to a dead line. He sighed; too many years of this damned cloak-and-dagger stuff. He looked at the screen of his laptop, wondering if he was expected to memorize the number and consign the email to electronic oblivion, the modern equivalent of eating a secret message. But in the end he just shut down the connection before changing his dancing clothes for the dark jeans, navy sweatshirt, and soft-soled shoes he'd need later.

At Fourth and Pine there was indeed a phone booth, tacked up to the side wall of a huge furniture retailer. The phone was ringing as he pulled up, a lonesome tremor in the night. Yanking hard on his brake, he jumped out of the car and sprinted to the booth before it could stop.

He snatched the receiver up and said, "Have you been calling all this time, or did you see me drive up?"

"I knew how long it would take you to get there," the mystery woman replied. She had a very nice voice—businesslike, but low enough to be sexy.

"So where am I going now?"

"Are you armed?"

"Why does everyone ask that?" Allen complained. "Do I look like someone who goes around with a gun in his belt?"

"Are you?"

"No, I'm not armed. So if you want me to shoot someone for you, you're out of luck. All I could do is rip off this damned receiver and beat them with it."

"Don't do that, this is one of the few pay phones in the valley that still takes incoming calls. You see the sign for the liquor store?"

Allen looked down the street, then reversed to look the other way. "Yes."

"Drive in that direction. Halfway between you and it, there's an alley with a white mailbox on the right. Come down that and park in the garage."

The phone went dead again. Clearly, this woman had learned her social skills from Alice.

He got back in his car, found the alleyway, and drove down it to an open ground-floor parking area that held five other cars. He got out of his rental car, locked it, and waited for further instructions. On the other side of the garage, a rumbling started up, then stopped. Elevator doors parted.

Looking at the small, enclosed, brushed-steel cubicle, Allen began to wish he actually was armed. *That was Alice's email,* he told himself. *There's no reason to think this is some kind of a trap. Get in the elevator.*

He did, in the end, step into the elevator, but it took an effort to allow the doors to slide shut without leaping forward to thrust his hands between them; he was sweating when they opened again at four, the top floor. He swallowed, and put his head out.

The high, featureless corridor could have been anything from legal offices to the service entrances of retail shops, completely institutional except for a peculiar five-foot-wide wrought-iron chandelier overhead, its ornate black vines and leaves studded with a dozen or so pointy bulbs. Two doors on this side of the corridor, the elevator and one with a knob; five metal doors on the other, all painted the same pale yellow as the walls and nothing to distinguish them, not even numbers. He straightened, stepped out, and allowed the elevator to close behind him, expecting one of the yellow doors to draw itself open as dramatically as the elevator had. They remained shut. With a mental shrug, he walked down the corridor to the one at the far right and grasped the knob; to his surprise, it turned unhindered.

He stepped into a dim, air-conditioned room the size of the first-floor parking garage, a combination of living space and high-tech dream. Two of the walls resembled a NASA control center: a mosaic of screens, printers, long metal desks with multiple hard drive towers, and assorted machines whose purposes he couldn't immediately identify. Half of them were on a raised platform, either to incorporate an original difference in the floor level or to provide electricity and ventilation for the machines. The platform had three ramps, one at either end and one in the center. The third wall seemed to be where the inhabitants ate and slept, with the only screened-off space in the entire area behind a full-length maroon leather sofa. Above the kitchen table was an enormous flat-screen television on which a network drama was playing—the source, he decided, of the noise he'd heard behind the woman's voice. The center of the giant room was an open expanse of polished wood, clear of furniture. As Allen stepped away from the door, he saw that all five entrances opened directly into the space. He also noticed that the doors were extremely solid-looking, and that the wall into which they were set, which from the other side had seemed to be everyday Sheetrock, was nearly as substantial as its doors. The locks on the doors themselves would have occupied a locksmith for hours.

"I don't like unwanted visitors," said the low voice from behind him. He turned, and saw that it was low in more ways than pitch: Its owner, a slim, pale, blond woman in black jeans, orange turtleneck sweater, and bright yellow shoes, was seated in a wheeled chair more like a lunar landing module than a wheelchair. Allen wasn't even certain the woman was paraplegic—it could have been some mad techie's idea of a desk chair. "You're Allen?"

"I am." He went forward and shook her hand, which was strong and cool. His eyes glanced across her legs, but he couldn't tell if they were useless or not.

"I'm Gina."

"I can see why you're a little concerned about armed invaders," Allen told her. There must have been nearly a million dollars' worth of hardware on display, to say nothing of the wheeled chair.

"It's also that the alarm system gets upset if it sees a gun. Takes me a while to calm it down again."

"I didn't see a metal detector."

"Built in to the elevator. It tells me you have a small multibladed work knife in your jeans and a metal pen in your T-shirt pocket."

"Which means I can either fix your chair or write you a note," he said, glad that he'd left the tape recorder in the car.

"Neither of which is necessary at the moment, but thanks for the offer. Alice said you need some information."

"You're an information specialist." Allen was feeling two steps behind the woman.

"Isn't that why you're here?" She sounded a little impatient.

"Maybe you could tell me why I'm here. Last I know, I asked Alice to get a newspaper friend of hers to fake me up an ID so I could ask questions. I take it you're not the *Mercury News* crime reporter?"

"I could be if you want," she answered. "But only online."

"You're a hacker?"

"Please, that's so passé," she said, offended. "I'm a player."

"And I've had a long day," he told her. "What do you know about Mark O'Connell, partner and very possibly only employee of a company called Revista?"

The chair pivoted and shot off to a nearby terminal, and Gina shifted programs, entered the name, and set to work, tossing information over her shoulder at him as it came up. "Juvenile record, sealed; one arrest at age nineteen for check forging, at age twenty-two he was investigated for a hit-and-run but it never went to trial. Parents died in a house fire when he was twenty-six, faulty wiring in some Christmas lights, left him a quarter of a million in property and life insurance. Police called out twice for domestic violence disputes, no charges. Wife committed suicide five years ago, shot herself with one of his guns while their kid was in the house."

"That's not right," Allen cut in. "The boy found her when he got home from school."

"Says here he was in his bedroom. I can check on it, if you want."

"If you don't mind."

"Have to be tomorrow."

"That's fine." He couldn't see that it made any difference, but disparities in stories always raised red flags.

Her fingers flew some more, and the display onscreen changed again. "Owns his house, refinanced last year when the rates went down, never declared bankruptcy, still—" The computer gave a small bleep; she leaned forward to read the contents of an inserted box, then swiveled her head to look at him. "Does your man own a plane?"

"Yes, he does. Why?"

In answer, she picked up a small remote control from the long desk, and pointed it toward the living quarters. The big screen's shot of a war zone gave way to a news desk and two polished people with the stock expression denoting Personal Tragedy. She thumbed up the volume.

"—on his first flight since his son disappeared last May. Workers at the airfield told Channel Forty-seven that O'Connell had seemed in good spirits this morning, telling them that he was looking forward to flying again after all these weeks, and mentioning during the pre-flight check that it was the first time he'd been in the air since his son disappeared. His son, we were told, often accompanied his father, and in fact had done so the day before the boy mysteriously vanished on the Friday before the Memorial Day weekend. According to the FAA, the plane gave no signs of difficulties until it disappeared from the traffic controllers' screens at six thirty-seven this morning. The Coast Guard is searching the area for wreckage, but a spokesman said that, if the plane did go down in the place where it was last recorded, there are several hundred feet of water there, making it possible that the wreckage, and O'Connell's body, may never be found."

The female anchor made some noises about how tragedy seemed to plague certain families, although it was obvious that she had her own stories pressing on her mind. Allen was thinking that it was a good thing he'd talked to Kluger and Karin Rao before the news got around, when Gina muted the television screen. They looked at each other in silence.

"Well," Allen said. "That puts a somewhat different light on the matter."

"Do you want me to continue digging around for O'Connell's history?"

"Oh yes, I certainly do. But I'm going to have to go. You don't need me, do you?" She gave him a look that said it all, and he nodded. "Can I call you on that same number tomorrow?"

"That number's gone. Just come by. Park where you did. Use the emergency phone in the other elevator to call up."

She went back to her terminals, and Allen turned to go. However, faced with the unnecessarily rich choice of doors, he spoke again to Gina's back.

"Why do you have four doors more than you need?"

"Mind games," she replied absently. "I like to see which one people choose."

He let himself out the nearest one, and as the elevator opened, he glanced up at the wrought-iron monstrosity. He had no doubt that it was bristling with pinhole cameras; he also knew that, without a ladder, he'd never spot them. Of course, he couldn't blame Gina for being a little phobic about her visitors. And it wouldn't surprise him to find that the snug little elevator had been wired with a killer voltage, as well.

One thing about this job he would miss: You sure met some interesting people.

It was now after eleven o'clock, and although there was still traffic, the side streets were all but deserted. When he reached the freeway, Allen turned the car west, coming off at the same exit he'd first used back in May, when **deadboy** had been just a name on a screen. Now, he was the dark-eyed center of a growing enigma.

Chapter 26

ALLEN DROVE PAST THE GUARDHOUSE AT THE ENTRANCE TO O'CONNELL'S development, relieved to see the guard sitting with his feet up reading a book, looking too relaxed for a man who'd had a stream of police investigators coming and going through his gates. The cops would come, of that Allen was certain, but it looked as though they had decided to wait to see what the Coast Guard turned up in the morning.

The hills behind the community were still undeveloped, although that would not last for long, given the history of Silicon Valley's transformation out of the vast plum and apricot orchards Allen remembered from his youth. He drove past the end of the development's ten-foot-tall cement-block walls, which aside from their height presented no great challenge to intruders, and pulled into the lesser road he'd discovered in May. It was a fire road originally, now used as access to a property higher up; by the accumulated dust on the gate's padlock, his visits back in May had been the last time anyone had driven through here. The padlock sprang open, and Allen got the gate closed and his car around the next turn before another vehicle passed by.

He stood outside the car, feeling the night. The engine ticked gently; the sing of crickets started up again. A dog barked, but it was a long way off, no threat. The air was still, and as he'd expected, the full moon along with the valley's light pollution gave resolution to the hillside. He checked to make sure his cell phone was off, then zipped it into the waist pack with the rest of his equipment. He daubed his cheeks and forehead with greasepaint, and when his eyes were adapted to the light, he started up the deer path that followed the high walls.

Half a mile along he came to the pair of innocent-looking branches he'd left at the base of the tree that had held his receiver. Wedged together against the concrete blocks, they made a step high enough to boost him to the wall's top. There he paused, resting on his elbows, until he was satisfied that he wasn't about to drop down on top of a roaming dog or a gathering of teenagers engaged in one or more illicit activities.

Lights burned in the O'Connell house, one in the television room (where the curtains were closed) and the other upstairs. Back in May, he'd found that those two lights were hooked up to clocks; if they went off soon—the ground floor at eleven-thirty, the upstairs room ten minutes later—he'd take it as an indication that the house was empty. He settled his back against a tree in the yard, breathing in the rich smells of cut grass (the other gardening service no doubt had been happy to see the end of the cheap intruder) and an evening barbecue that mingled with the dry chaparral odors spilling off the hill behind him. A bat worked the sky over the lawn; on the other side of the wall, coyotes yelped.

The lower light went off, and at eleven-forty, the upper. He got to his feet, slipped on a pair of gossamer latex gloves, and passed like a night animal over the well-watered lawn to the house.

In May, he'd been put off by the aggressive alarm system, and satisfied himself with planting his bugs on the outside of the windows. Tonight, he would see how far he could get. He badly wanted to do a reconnaissance of the inside of the beast's lair, needed a feel for exactly what the boy had been living with. He had no idea how he was going to get through the security alarm, could only hope that his mentor in the art of burglary could help guide him through it. Jamie would of course know the code, but the last thing Allen wanted was to ask the boy. Besides, O'Connell might well have changed it after his son disappeared. In any case, Allen had to try to bypass it.

But the alarm was not on.

Allen frowned at the box, searching for a trick. The alarm had to be on—in the two weeks in May that he'd had the house under surveillance, he had never seen O'Connell go any farther than the mailbox without locking the house up. And Mrs. Mendez did not have the code: Allen had seen her sheltering from the rain one morning until her boss came to let her in. When O'Connell was out of town, Mrs. Mendez stayed in the house with Jamie, having groceries delivered; when O'Connell was home, she slept at her own house ten miles away.

But the system's light was shining green for off, not red for armed.

Moving without a sound, his senses at high alert, Allen crept up to the house's back door. He felt for the knob, and was somewhat relieved to find it locked. He eased open the zip of his waist pack and bent to work.

The dead bolt was sturdy, but nowhere near as complicated as some he'd coaxed open. When he tried the knob again, the door obligingly opened into the mudroom and its kitchen beyond, with no sign of a hidden alarm having been triggered. Still, he left the bolt unlocked, and took a spoon from the sink to wedge between the door and its jamb, an impromptu alarm.

The house felt empty—certainly there were no sounds, no snores or distant television. Still, he would check all its rooms, just in case his instincts were wrong. The street lamp at the end of the drive gave sufficient light, even when the drapes were drawn, for him to make his way through the front rooms without a flashlight.

Next to the kitchen was a breakfast room, followed by a formal dining room with long, shiny wood table and a display of crystal and china behind glass doors. Then a hallway between the front door and a wooden staircase, across which Allen found a room with drapes heavy enough to cut off all outside light. His narrow flash played across a formal living room furnished with the sorts of tautly upholstered chairs that no one ever sat on, a shelf unit filled with leather-bound and probably never-read books, and a collection of small naked female figurines arranged across the fireplace mantel and on display shelves. He went back out into the hallway, then to the room at the back of the ground floor, at whose window he had placed his sole camera. The television room had comfortable-looking leather sofas and reclining chairs. Behind a rollaway screen was the television that he'd known was there, having spent hours watching people stare at a point just below his spying lens. The screen was nearly as big as Gina's, and next to it was a sleek sound system with enough controls to keep an engineer entertained, its speakers the size of small refrigerators. One end of the room was a wet bar, with a long mirror behind it, a dozen shapes of glasses, and a collection of alcohol more extensive than a lot of commercial bars Allen had been in. All the booze was top of the line. There was no shotgun under the bar.

Back in the hallway, the intruder silently opened the three remaining doors that clustered under the rising stairway. One room contained a toilet and hand basin, tiled in gilt and mirror; the next was a closet with vacuum cleaner, coats, and a tangle of shoes. The third opened onto the kitchen; just inside it was the room used by Mrs. Mendez on her nights here, small, furnished with a narrow bed and set of drawers, the closet holding little more than slippers, an elderly raincoat, and a few changes of clothing. The room was windowless, and had its own toilet and shower. Allen left the servant's quarters and went back down the hallway.

The oak stairway was solid and did not creak under his weight. To the left of the stairs was O'Connell's bedroom: king-sized four-poster bed with a cover of unbleached raw silk, a lot of expensive clothes in the closet, a lot of expensive marble in the bathroom, and an assortment of designer colognes by the sink. Allen stuck his head into the walk-in closet, but nobody leapt out at him from its cedar-scented interior. The next door opened onto an empty storage space, duplicating the shape of the servant's bedroom below it. It had been wallpapered at one time, but the paper looked as though shelves had once been mounted to the walls, since removed. The floor was dented and stained, but the only things in it were a carton of Christmas decorations and a massive cast-iron tree stand.

The next door stood open, or so Allen thought until he got close up to it and found the door missing altogether. This, then, must be Jamie's room. What had the boy said? That his father "took the door off" in October as punishment for illicit reading; looking at the jamb, Allen gave a silent whistle and revised his picture of a man with a Phillips head screwdriver. A crowbar, maybe, or a fireman's axe. Allen wouldn't have been surprised to hear that a bear had gone after it—the frame was gouged, split, still raw-looking ten months after the event: Absolute rage had ripped the door bodily from its hinges. Allen could only imagine what the eleven-year-old child cowering inside the room could have been thinking, hearing that storm of fury literally beating down the door as it came after him. As for what must have happened once the door was down—Allen drew back, to look at the next room.

The door to the bathroom was missing, too, although that had come down more gently, leaving only the screw holes. Walking back to stand at the entrance to the father's bedroom, Allen saw that from there, both toilet and shower were fully exposed, and the only part of Jamie's bedroom not immediately visible was the desk to the left of the door; four steps forward, and that came into view as well. The sole privacy Jamie would have had was if the steam built up on the clear glass shower doors. Allen had a mental image of a pale, skinny, self-conscious adolescent scurrying into the exposed shower, or standing at the toilet in an agony of humiliation lest the housekeeper or his father happen by. Allen pushed that image away.

The next room along was a guest room that looked as if it had been furnished from a display and never actually used. Then came the last room, sharing a wall with O'Connell's bedroom. The bug Allen had planted against the dining room window, directly beneath this room, had cut out regularly. He'd thought it was a glitch, something that happened with depressing regularity to complex electronics, but seeing the two inches of solid oak and electronic keypad on this upstairs room, he began to suspect that the cause had been the automatic cutout he'd wired into the bugs, triggered by the occasional sweep of an antisurveillance device. For this last room was, without a doubt, O'Connell's home study. Unlike the house alarm, the keypad on this room was armed and active. Allen sighed, and took the cell phone out of his waist pack.

Allen always found it amusing that, although most of the contacts provided by Alice were women (no surprise there), most of the assistance he had developed on his own came from men. It made sense, he just wasn't sure why. At any rate, this particular contact was someone he'd almost literally bumped into on a job, Allen going into a house one night to plant his devices, the other a dark shape on his way out. Fortunately, the dark shape didn't turn out to be a crackhead carrying a gun; more fortunate yet, the startling situation had, after a tense moment, tickled the man's sense of humor. He'd begun by whispering to Allen that if it was the contents of the safe he was after, there hadn't been that much to begin with. When Allen assured the burglar that he was welcome to the safe, Dave had become curious. He'd stuck around to watch Allen plant his miniature cameras in the living room, the study, and the hallway outside the bedrooms (the inhabitants of the house sleeping all the while). He'd even reset the alarm for Allen when he was finished. Afterward they'd retired to a nearby bar for a couple of beers, and—well, Allen had acquired a new mentor. If anyone could lead him through the intricacies of the O'Connell security system, it was Dave. And since he'd suspected he might need some help with the house, he'd taken the precaution of giving Dave the O'Connell name and address a couple of days before, so he could research the system.

Dave answered with a growl, although Allen knew he'd been awake. Dave was a nocturnal creature even when he wasn't on a job.

"Got an electronic keypad for you," was Allen's greeting, and he gave the man what details he could see of it. "Internal," he added.

"How'd you get through the outside one?" Dave asked.

"It wasn't set."

"Trusting citizens," he grunted. "God bless 'em."

Allen didn't think there was any point in distracting Dave with the fact that O'Connell might not be your everyday trusting citizen. It would only worry him.

"Try these," Dave told him, and began producing a list of four-digit numbers for Allen to try punching into the pad. Fortunately, the pad was not one of those that freeze up after a set number of unsuccessful tries, or Allen would not have had a chance. They tried the O'Connell Social Security number—last four numbers, first four, first and last pairs—and the birth dates of the man himself, his wife, and Jamie. They tried turning the numbers backwards, they tried elements of the man's driver's license number, they tried his wedding anniversary and the date of his mother's birth. Twenty minutes later, Dave was beginning to run out of ideas, and neither of them had to say that the longer they stayed on the air, the greater the risk of some idiot with a scanner tuning in.

"You sure you don't want to bash it down?" he asked hopefully.

"It's two inches of hardwood here, I'd need a jackhammer. You got any more?"

"A few, and after that I'll just have to talk you through surgery." This was a thing Dave hated, since his skills were closely linked with his own fingertips. He read off the address of the Revista office, the Revista phone number, and a number that appeared a lot on the O'Connell phone bills to George Howard, whom Allen had pegged as the bodybuilder assistant. Dave's voice was wearing thin when he gave Allen the suggestion "Try eleven-sixteen."

The light went green. "Christ, that did it. What the hell is eleven-sixteen?" Allen asked, straightening to ease his aching spine.

"That's the day his wife committed suicide," Dave told him flatly.

Allen's gloved hand froze on the doorknob. "His wife's death?"

"Weird, huh? But it's open?"

"It's open. Thanks. I'll be talking to you."

Allen turned off the phone and zipped it into his waist pack. What could it mean, to use the date your wife had shot her brains out as the security code on your private office?

Allen shook his head to clear it of unnecessary thoughts, eased the door open, and studied his surroundings. The room was ill-lit, with illumination from the street casting thin stripes through the slatted blinds onto the ceiling. If he kept his own light pointed downward and moved it little, no chance passerby would notice.

There was a safe on the wall, poorly hidden by a painting of a windswept beach, but Allen thought he'd leave it, just for the moment: Two tricky locks in one night was pressing his luck, and the kind of thing he was looking for might not be shut behind steel, anyway. He sat down behind Mark O'Connell's desk and got to work.

None of the desk drawers were locked, although they all could be, separately or together. Two of them were nearly empty, and to Allen's eyes appeared to have been cleaned down to the dust, although the other four side drawers and the long one in the center were untidy collections of office debris, files, and innocuous papers. In the center drawer he found an address book of leather stamped with gold and crimson patterns. He thumbed it open, not expecting to find anything of use, but at the very beginning something caught his eye, and he opened it more deliberately to the front page, where someone had written a number string: *06-23-14.* Allen's gaze rose to the painting of the beach; he shrugged, and went over to give it a try.

The safe opened.

He'd have been less astonished to find the number string trigger a trap that showered him with dye or fried him with a knockout jolt of electricity, but the steel door merely swung out to reveal several slim books leaning against the right-hand side of the twelve-by-twelve space, and three leather jewelry cases leaning to the left. The cases did hold jewelry, the first a woman's diamond necklace and earrings set into velvet, the second a gorgeous creation of gold and sapphires, the third a diamond tiara. Dave was going to shoot him for leaving these behind, Allen thought: Even a fence would give him six figures. But it was the books that interested him.

Five books, all of them ledgers that communicated little information to Allen other than telling him the man had a lot of money. In the inner flap of each had been taped an envelope containing a CD. He slid out the CD from the previous year's ledger, and saw the date written on its shiny surface with a felt pen. He was tempted; if he took them away, he could find someone to peel apart the man's finances and look for fraud, but on the whole, Allen thought it unlikely that a cautious crook, which O'Connell appeared to be, would leave his real records in a home office behind a bad painting, waiting for any cop with a warrant to find them. He slid last year's CD back into its envelope, and put all the ledgers back inside the safe.

Only when he was returning the ledgers did he discover the safe's last offering, propped in the dark recess behind everything else. He felt a very slight resistance as he was sliding the final ledger into place, so he reached back and drew the object out.

Another book, smaller than the others. DIARY, this one proclaimed; stamped below the word was the year of Jamie's birth. Inside, January 1 had a line drawn through it, but there the writing began: *My son was born today, nearly a month prematurely.* Jamie had been born in November, but other than using the appropriate year, O'Connell hadn't been much interested in following the dates. He had used the diary as a notebook, noting the day and month of the entries (which a quick glance showed spanned a number of years) without always bothering to cross out the printed dates.

Allen slipped the journal into the shirt pocket under his sweatshirt and closed the safe. He laid the address book back into its drawer, and continued searching the room, but he found nothing else of interest aside from another provocatively clean drawer and two ornate boxes similarly scrubbed.

Back in O'Connell's bedroom, his search revealed a drawer in the bedside table that was cleaner than when the piece had left the showroom. When he knelt and put his face directly into it, however, he caught a whiff of a familiar and distinctive chemical odor: There'd been a gun in the drawer, and recently. While he was on his knees, patting the area around O'Connell's bed, Allen noticed something else he wouldn't have seen in another position. He shone the penlight to the corner of the raw silk bedcover, and saw where the delicate fabric was frayed and crumpled. Just the very corner, where it brushed the carpet—the freshly vacuumed carpet.

Allen got to his feet and hurried down the stairs to the storage closet he'd seen, switched on the light and squatted down to pop the front off the upright vacuum. No bag. He thought about it for a while: He could picture Mrs. Mendez changing the bag after each use, given a particularly demanding view of housecleaning (hers or her employer's), but there was a fresh package of bags on the shelf; why would a responsible housekeeper fail to put a new one in then and there? Turning the machine over, he saw pale threads the color of raw unbleached silk caught at the corner of the beater, which confirmed his suspicions: The machine had sucked up the edge of that expensive bedcover and chewed away at it before the person running it had found the OFF switch. Not something an experienced housekeeper would do, although it had happened to Allen once or twice. Here it indicated that Mark O'Connell had done a thorough, if amateurish, job of cleaning the house.

Back upstairs, the rest of the bedroom gave him nothing. There were rather a lot of empty hangers in the closet, and he had yet to find any suitcases, but then, O'Connell might have been going for a while—except that his secretary expected him Monday. Allen stood in the brightly lit walk-in closet, thinking hard. What was he missing? Not a lot of jewelry, apart from the necklaces in the safe, but then maybe O'Connell didn't wear expensive watches and diamond signet rings. And the suits: what about . . . He began to go through the clothing on the hangers, and soon found that every one of the garments had a maker's label. Not one of the suits, shirts, or jackets here had been custom-made. Which was not what he'd have expected.

He glanced at his watch, saw that it was nearly three A.M., and turned off the closet light. The odd empty storage room drew him back, and he stood for a while pondering the holes in the walls on which something had hung, the stains and bashes in the floor. The light in that windowless room had burned out, but his flashlight gave him nothing but more questions. In the end, he peeled away one or two strips of stained wallpaper and put them into one of the sandwich bags from his waist pack. They looked like blood, but could as easily be wood stain from some home improvement project.

At the door to Jamie's room, Allen found himself curiously reluctant to go inside. The poor kid had been invaded enough; having another adult paw through his things seemed offensive. It was absurd, Allen knew that, but he disliked the sensation of following in Mark O'Connell's footsteps. And he was absolutely certain that the man had come in here regularly, keeping the boy under constant control. With a clench of his jaw, Allen made himself step through the mangled doorway.

Jamie's bedroom was almost as spartan as the downstairs quarters assigned to Mrs. Mendez. Narrow bed, its mattress zipped into a waterproof cover and the sheets and blankets folded at its feet; nearly bare bookshelves; a bedside table with a radio alarm on top; and a child's-size wooden desk with a lot of dramatic gouges and dents in the top. (Had that been done at the same time as the door? Allen wondered. Or was bashing up the boy's possessions a regular event?) It was hardly a child's room at all—no clutter of toys, no posters of rock groups or computer games, none of the collected treasures of a life, the beach pebbles and flattened coins, the sprung shoe boxes full of defunct games and pieces of string. Nothing but a few books (including the boxed set of *Lord of the Rings*) and a corkboard with five snapshots pinned in a neat line along its top border. Allen stepped closer to look.

The first photograph showed a pale young woman with fine bones and dark, long-lashed eyes. She was sitting on a bench under a tree, her hands crossed in her lap to show off a ring with a stone as large as the knuckle above it. She looked shyly happy. In stark contrast was the photograph beside it, showing a horribly wizened infant in a hospital nursery, tubes coming out of its old man's face, everything gone slightly yellow, as color photos do over the years: the month-premature baby referred to in the journal that was burning a hole in Allen's breast pocket. The third photo was of the young woman again, but with all her gentle beauty trodden down. She sat on a chair and her ring still hung (loosely) on her finger, but she had dark purple smudges under her dark eyes, a desperate expression on her thin face, and a squalling infant in her awkward arms. It could have been a textbook illustration of postpartum depression.

The fourth picture was of a dog, an unattractive animal with dirty white fur and nervous ears. Sitting beside it on the lawn, bony knees crossed between shorts and sandals, was a young Jamie O'Connell, recognizable even at that age (five? six?), a skinny kid with huge and compelling eyes. He'd obviously been ordered to smile for the camera, and he looked like he was trying to remember how to do it; behind the pasted grin he appeared every bit as nervous as the dog.

Last in the row was a more recent picture of Jamie with his father, dressed for the outdoors in jeans and heavy jackets. Both held guns, Jamie's rifle a diminutive version of his father's. O'Connell's right hand was resting across his son's shoulder, and the boy seemed more aware of the hand than he was of the gun, the snow around them, or the antlered buck bleeding at their feet.

Taken as a whole, the series presented a disquieting history of Jamie's family life; studying them, Allen grew more and more certain that Jamie was not responsible for the montage. Surely no sane child would have deliberately chosen those five photographs to gaze down at his desk every day. A tube-baby who had reduced his mother to a wreck, a sorry-looking dog who must have died, since he was nowhere in evidence now, and a father who killed things for pleasure—would a boy pick these? No—but a father wishing to underscore the boy's worthlessness (*Can't even keep a mangy old dog alive*) might well choose them as his constant representatives, to watch over his son.

Allen had a sudden urge to rip them down from the wall and set them alight; instead, he pulled open a drawer in Jamie's desk.

Pens and the heavily gnawed stubs of pencils, homework assignments, and a couple of school portraits of children Jamie's age, which Allen tucked into his pocket as possible future interviews. Two empty candy wrappers stuffed into the back corner and three CDs for violent games. In the back of the bottom drawer, a small stuffed monkey and a chewed rubber dog toy. Other than the discarded wrappers, everything was arranged with a mechanical precision unnatural for a twelve-year-old. Had the housekeeper or the father been through, tidying the desk and bookshelves along with the bed?

Two comic books under the mattress, no screw-off dowels in the posts where a boy might hide things, but when Allen tugged at the carpet in the back of the closet, it came up, revealing a small cache of photos, all of a young woman and baby, including a duplicate of the one he'd seen in the boy's pack. He left them where they were.

Finally, Allen removed each book from the shelf and rifled it to see if anything had been hidden in the pages. Nothing fluttered out but a bookmark. He picked up the boxed set of Tolkien, Karin Rao's complicated expression of discomfiture and professional responsibility that Jamie had mistaken for love. Without having intended to do so, Allen tucked the box under his arm. The hell with them all; nobody would notice that the books were missing. Even if they did, so what? It's not like he was taking the jewels from the safe.

The house had told him everything it could. He went through a last time to make sure the doors were as he had found them and that he had left no lights burning in the closets, then he let himself out, locking the door behind him.

Dawn was not far off. Allen crouch-trotted across the wide lawn to the wall, scrambled over awkwardly with the Tolkein stuffed into his shirt, and kicked the supporting logs back into the undergrowth. The car had not been disturbed. At the road he paused to listen for approaching cars before opening the padlocked gate; he drove through, snapped the lock shut, and was in gear before anyone came along. He stripped off the sweat-slick latex gloves and threw them on the seat beside him, wiping the paint from his face with a rag, then he leaned back in his seat, and laughed with the pleasure of release, just another innocent working stiff headed for the morning commute.

Safely back in his motel room before six o'clock, he kicked off his shoes and lay back on the bed to watch the morning drivel while he contemplated his next step: the Revista secretary, or Señora Mendez? However, in two minutes, a pair of cleaning women going past heard his snores, and giggled to each other in the morning sun.

Chapter 27

HE WOKE THREE HOURS LATER WITH A MOUTH THAT TASTED LIKE OLD ROAD-kill. He jerked upright on the sagging mattress, his brain trying desperately to reconstruct where he was and what he had been doing the night before. As it came back, he relaxed, scowled at the still-driveling television set until he uncovered the remote and silenced the talking heads, then staggered into the bathroom to stand beneath the cool shower, slowly warming it to comfort. He shaved and found a relatively clean shirt, noting that he'd have to drop into a Laundromat today, or a clothing store.

Before clean clothes, however, he required food, of the sort offered by the pancake house down the street. He bought a newspaper from the box at the door and read it with care, but found that they knew nothing more than they had the day before about O'Connell's missing plane. After three cups of what they called coffee and a large plate of greasy flour products drowned in syrup, he was ready for the day. He walked back across the parking lot to his room, and while he was stuffing clothes in a string bag, he booted up his laptop. There was one message:

G has what you asked for.
A

"Damn," Allen said in disappointment. He had hoped Gina might dig out a lot for him, even if what she found was mostly peripheral. To have reached an end after less than twelve hours was not a good sign. He hit REPLY, and typed in:

Need to talk. 4 okay?
A

By this afternoon, he might know enough to be able to tell her that it was safe to bring Jamie home.

He tossed the laundry bag into the backseat of the stifling car, kicked up the air conditioner, and drove the ten miles to Gina's information headquarters. The print shop in the front was open and a delivery truck was unloading into the back, but the garage under her building had the same five cars in it, and Allen parked in the same place he'd used the night before.

The elevator door did not magically draw open for him this time. He walked around the side of the shaft and thumbed the button to open the other set of doors. Inside the cubicle, he put his foot down to keep the doors from closing and unclipped the emergency phone from the wall. After a moment, Gina's voice said, "Hello, Allen."

"You want me to stay in this elevator?" he asked.

"The one you're in doesn't go to my floor," she said, and hung up.

When he had retraced his steps to the other elevator, it was standing open. He rode up, got out when it stopped, gave a glance to the snarl of wrought iron as he passed underneath it, and went to the door directly ahead of him. It opened smoothly.

Gina was in her living area, making coffee. The television was playing on CNN, but before the rattle of the coffee grinder took over, the big room was silent but for the perpetual low hum of machinery. Gina rolled over to the low sink to fill the pot; her hair was spiked, the right side of her face pink. She was wearing the same black jeans, yellow high-tops, and orange sweater she'd had on when he'd last seen her.

"Did I get you up?" he asked.

"Sleep is a waste of time," she said, which didn't answer his question—or maybe it did.

"Sorry," he said, but she merely nodded at the stack of paper on the low table, dumped the grounds into the filter, and switched on the machine.

The pile of paper was a good two inches thick—there must have been nearly three hundred pages. Allen thumbed through it, astonished. Back in May, he'd spent two weeks and come up with maybe a tenth of this. In less than twelve hours, some of which she'd spent asleep, the woman had assembled a dossier of everything that touched on the lives of the O'Connell family, from the wife's birth certificate to the husband's latest credit report.

"Damn, girl. Have you got a dozen elves living in those machines?"

He couldn't be sure, but he thought Gina looked pleased at his response. All she said was, "You want a bagel?"

"Thanks, I ate."

"Yeah, and I notice you brought me some." She began to saw away at what appeared to be a very firm object.

"I'm sorry, I didn't think you'd care much for cold pancakes."

"Makes for a change," she said. "Don't worry about it."

"Next time," he promised.

She shot him a look over her shoulder. "Why would there be a next time?"

She had a point, he thought, looking at the material in front of him; there couldn't be a whole lot more she could do for him. "In order to bring you cold pancakes?"

"That's really okay," she told him. "I'd rather have a stale bagel. Take your file and go, Allen. I've got work to do."

"Aren't you going to offer me some coffee?"

"Oh, right." The sarcasm grew ever thicker in her voice. "First you bring me none of your breakfast, then you guzzle my coffee."

He stood and went past her chair, opening cabinets and looking at their contents. Without a word, he began to take down packages and search for bowls and pans. She watched, saying nothing; after a minute, she picked up her mug and disappeared behind the room's sole partition. He heard water running, and looked in the sleek brushed-steel refrigerator, taking out a loaf of rather stale bread, some eggs, and an orange. The woman might not get out a lot, but someone kept her well provided.

She came back just as the French toast hit the table, her short hair wet against her scalp, wearing a blue T-shirt above the black jeans.

Because he was watching closely, he noticed the slight quirk of a smile as she saw the table, but that was her only reaction. The forgotten bagel sat where she had left it in the toaster, and she put away more food than Allen had that morning. At the end of it, she polished her plate with the last bite and said merely, "How'd you make the syrup?"

"You had sugar, so I caramelized it and watered it down. If you had any maple flavoring, it would've been easier."

"This was better."

He took that for a thanks, and carried her dishes over to the dishwasher.

"Tell me," he asked. "How do you get things off those high cabinets?" It had puzzled him, since he hadn't seen any kind of reaching stick.

In response, she wheeled out from behind the table, fiddled with one of the chair's controls, and the wheels rebuilt themselves, the body of the chair elongating until her head was at the same level as Allen's. She grinned at his reaction, and said, "Watch this."

She rolled across the floor to the raised platform on which the machinery sat, coming to rest in front of the step. More fiddling, and the chair reshaped itself again. The wheels tipped, rested on the edge of the step, and lifted her up. She pivoted to face him, and smiled at his pleasure.

"I've never seen one like that."

"It's experimental. I'm helping the designers get rid of the bugs before they put it on the market. At first, it tended to do a little hip-hop and dump you on the floor. Pain in the ass."

"A little more work, you could get it out on the dance floor."

At that she actually laughed aloud, and said, "I've already given them the modifications." She set her wheels at the platform's edge, and the chair felt its way down to the lower floor with the ungainly precision of a camel settling to its knees. She rolled over to the living area, raising the chair enough so she was more or less level with him as she handed him the thick file.

"Thank you for this," he told her.

"Your man's hiding something," she said abruptly, her smile vanishing. "I don't know what it is yet—nothing in that stuff gives him away—but I'm going to keep digging until I find it."

"What kind of something?"

"Don't know that yet. But it's got to be illegal—he's way too clean. It's a well-built façade, but I can smell something rotten behind it. And

I should also tell you, I got the feeling there's someone else out there interested, probably law enforcement. Nothing direct, but it's like seeing, I don't know, a broken twig or something. You need to watch your step so you don't walk into anything."

Allen smiled at her imagery, and mused, "Jungle instincts."

"What do you mean?"

"Oh, nothing. Just, you get to know the terrain, when you've lived there long enough. Hunted there for a while."

"Good analogy," she said. She fiddled with one of the controls on her chair, then said, "Look—it's none of my business, but that kid, O'Connell's son. Are you keeping an eye on him?"

"Somebody else is watching out for him just now, but yes, you could say I'm responsible for him."

"But is the other person watching *him*?" she demanded.

The urgency in her voice was clear, if the reason for it was not. "Why?"

She hesitated, then retreated with a shake of the head. "Like I said, it's none of my business. My job's to dig up information, which I've done. Take it. I suppose there'll be stuff coming in from this plane crash—if there's anything interesting, I'll send a message through Alice. But I expect that for the past history, you've got the bulk of it."

"It's an amazing amount of work you've done."

"It's all in the wrist," she replied. "And knowing the right people."

ALLEN LEFT THE PARKING GARAGE WITH LESS RELUCTANCE THAN IF HE hadn't had the pull of all that information drawing him away. He'd liked Gina, he'd wanted to stay and talk to her, hear her story and explore her mind. But more than that, he wanted to know what she'd seen in that stack of paper to make her ask, "Is the other person watching *him*?"

He drove down the wide, busy street, past car dealerships and Chinese restaurants until the sign WASH-O-MAT reached out to snag the corner of his eye. He circled the block and returned to the parking area behind the low cement-block building, taking with him both the bag of laundry and the thick packet of papers.

He fed quarters into the slot of the heavy-duty machine, and began stuffing his clothes into its maw, patting pockets as he went. The last shirt out, the first thing he'd stuffed into the bag that morning, was the one he'd worn the previous night. There was something in its pocket:

Allen's fingers reached in, coming out with a small leather volume stamped DIARY.

He held it, feeling an absolute fool. How could he have forgotten it, even for an instant? *You nearly tossed the thing into the machine,* he berated himself, but knew it was not true. *In fact,* he went on, closing the lid and sorting out change for a small carton of detergent, *the back of your brain remembered very well it was here; you just didn't want to read it.*

Allen grimaced, and transferred the diary to his current pocket. He shook the soap onto the clothes, pushed in the slot to feed the machine his quarters, and settled down onto one of the plastic chairs provided for the discomfort of the clients.

Gina's material first. She had arranged it in a more or less chronological fashion, starting with the birth certificates for Jamie's parents. His mother, born Paula Janine Whitefield, had won the school science fair prize in fifth grade, played flute in the high school orchestra, and spent two semesters at a small private college in the valley east of Los Angeles before meeting Mark O'Connell at a party. His history was a little more showy, with juvenile arrests for stealing a car and for threatening a neighbor (How had Gina pried that information from sealed juvenile records? Contacts, indeed.) and later for charges of check forgery, which were dropped, and for a bar fight, which had gotten him six months. No arrests after the age of twenty-six, which meant that either his hormones had settled down or he'd gotten smart.

Mark and Paula had married the October after she had left college, when she was nineteen and he thirty-one. Jamie was born three years later. They moved often, each time to a slightly more expensive house (Gina's information included the county tax records and a string of title companies—it is indeed all in the contacts) despite Mark's middle-of-the-road reported income on his tax returns.

It was like following a trail through elephant grass. Some of the papers Gina had given him were enigmatic, needing close attention to puzzle out their relevance to the case—such as the laconic, decade-old newspaper snippet noting that the investigation against someone named Thomas Church had been discontinued, and all charges against Church dropped. It took some shuffling before Allen discovered the name Thomas Church on the bottom of the O'Connell tax returns, as the accountant who had prepared them for the family. He nodded in appreciation: O'Connell's shady financial doings went back at least ten years.

He sat on the plastic chair, his legs going numb, completely unconscious of the heat and noise, traveling through time on the paper trail left by the O'Connell family. At some point he glanced up and saw that some other patron had dumped his wet laundry into one of the wheeled baskets, so he loaded it into a behemoth dryer, threw in all the quarters he had, and went back to his reading.

Twelve years earlier, Jamie's own bureaucratic trail began with his birth certificate. Not until four years later, when he was registered for preschool, did the papers with his name on them gain any detail, but after that, Gina's research had expanded to include the buildings and teachers connected with the boy's schools, even when the teachers were not his. A letter to the editor from one of the second-grade teachers about the benefits of teaching Spanish in schools, a three-year-old newspaper photograph of a sixth-grade class trip to Washington, D.C., a laconic article about a break-in to the school's computer lab—Gina's net had swept up anything and everything to do with Jamie's environment, and she had dumped it all on him.

After he'd been in the Laundromat for two and a half hours, Allen became aware of a presence just in front of his knees. He raised his eyes reluctantly from the pages, and saw a small brown-eyed urchin, sucking on a stick of candy and studying him with undisguised interest.

"Mister," the creature said, "my mama says someone's gonna steal your clothes if you don't take them."

Allen looked over at the dryer he'd been using, saw a bright flash of pink and orange tumbling around within, and finally located his own more drab possessions in a mound on one of the high folding tables. He slid the stack of papers back into their envelope and got to his feet, letting out an involuntary exclamation in the process. The chair had crippled him for life, he thought, stomping his feet to get the circulation going. "Thanks for the warning," he told the child, who to his surprise stuck out a hand. Allen obediently shook the sticky palm, but the kid rolled his eyes and left the hand where it was. Oh. Allen dug a dollar from his pocket and gave it to the clothes guardian. This earned him another roll of the eyes, but it wasn't as if the child had actually driven off a gang of furious trouser thieves. He folded up the clean clothes and put them into the string bag, carrying them, the papers, and the diary out to the tropical swelter of the car.

On the way back to the motel, he went through a hamburger drive-in for the day's second dose of grease and sugar, and carried clothes, information, and lunch into the cool room. He paused only to hang the shirts in the closet before settling barefoot onto the bed with the file and his food spread out around him, skimming briskly through the unbound sheets.

First grade had been a hard time for Jamie O'Connell. The school itself was located two blocks from the O'Connell home (Gina had sent a computer-generated map of the area, with the addresses highlighted in yellow). The year seemed to have started out well, and Jamie's name appeared (along with about thirty others) in the cast of the Christmas play. Then over the winter break, the wing of the school in which his classroom was located caught fire. Although the damage was not extensive, portable classrooms were brought in for the next weeks. Arson was suspected, aiming possibly at the computer lab that was in that wing, but no arrests were made.

Repairs were hurried along, and in March the classes were moved back into the building, the portables taken away, a picture appeared in the local paper of the principal cutting a ribbon across the door of her freshly painted, and planted, new wing. At the end of the month, the school had its spring recess, when many of the children joined Parks and Recreation programs designed to keep them busy while their parents were at work. Jamie, although his mother was at home and available, was registered for the day camp program. On the Thursday of that week his group spent the day at the park, playing baseball and being taken for rides in the rowboats. At the end of the day, when the parents arrived to pick up their exhausted children, one of the first-grade boys was missing. After a brief search, before the police had even arrived, two of the parents found young Able Shepherd, drowned in the weeds at the lake's edge.

The grainy newsprint photograph, taken by one of the Parks and Rec employees earlier that day, showed Able standing with some friends. The child's hair was so pale blond, it looked white, and the camera had caught him laughing aloud in gap-toothed high spirits.

At his side, a contrast in color and mood, was the thin, dark, subdued child who would become **deadboy**.

Memorial service, legal proceedings, charges and countercharges against school district and Parks department, until things faded with summer vacation. The O'Connell family moved again, and in September, Jamie entered a private school just half a mile from his new home. His teacher's written evaluation from October (*How on earth had Gina gotten that!*) suggested that the boy was bright enough, but did not try hard, that he was not as sociable as she would have liked, and that occasionally he was, in her word, "inclined to be moody."

On November sixteenth, Paula O'Connell had died in her second-floor bedroom. The flurry of official forms and newspaper articles generated to cover the event accounted for nearly half the stack of pages Gina had given him, from the initial police report to the coroner's verdict. Sifting methodically through them, Allen gradually formed a picture in his mind of how the case had progressed.

It began with a call to 911 from the O'Connell house, a child's panicky voice saying that his mother was shot and bleeding. The dispatcher tried to keep the child on the line, but the boy hung up before she could get his address from him. She identified the source of the caller's number and sent both police and ambulance to the scene. At the house, the police pounded for approximately two minutes before the door was opened, by a child with blood on his shirt and hands. The police ushered the boy out to their car, although he insisted that there was no one else in the house, and they went through the house for a possible shooter before they would allow the paramedics inside.

It was clear at a glance what had happened, equally clear that Paula O'Connell was beyond anything the paramedics could do for her. Crime-scene photographs (extremely indistinct—they'd been pixilated by a fax machine) showed a figure slumped into an overstuffed chair, a shotgun on the floor a few feet from her body. The father was in Las Vegas on business (he owned real estate there) and the housekeeper had the day off. The boy's mother usually met him at school to walk him home, but that day she had not come, so he had set off by himself, since he knew the route and there were crossing guards and lights all the way. He let himself in with the key he'd been given at the beginning of the year, went through the house looking for her, and found her. He'd gotten blood on him, he said, when he tried to shake her awake.

The medical examiner had taken some care with the investigation, since it is notoriously difficult to pull the trigger on the far end of a shotgun barrel, but the gun's position was consistent with having been placed on the floor at the victim's feet, and there was gunpowder residue all over Paula's legs and feet. They had even found a short stick that she could have used to depress the trigger; although there was no being certain, since it along with everything else was spattered with blood and it had been crushed under someone's shoe. And since the husband was away (this was confirmed by a speeding ticket he'd received, going through an infamous speed trap in Nevada at thirty over the limit) and

Paula had no enemies other than the depression that had plagued her life, her death was judged suicide.

The ME's main source of discomfort, reading between the lines, was timing: Why would a woman whom everyone described as a loving mother shoot herself in the head the day before her son's birthday, and knowing that the boy himself would find her? But in the end, the investigators had decided that her timing was of a piece with picking her husband's most valuable gun in order to do the deed. Paula O'Connell had committed suicide. The only powerful act of the woman's life was the way she had left it.

Allen skipped most of the material Gina had assembled on Jamie's disappearance, having seen it before. The police, he was interested to see, had looked at Mark O'Connell as a potential suspect, but the man's alibi for that day had held. Their most active lead was a gray-haired woman in her late fifties who had been seen talking with Jamie, but since Alice was only forty-seven and had naturally brown hair, Allen did not think he needed to warn her that the police were closing in.

The final pages in Gina's masterwork concerned the plane crash, and were frustratingly sparse. A statement from the airport employee who had helped O'Connell fuel the plane, another from a flight controller, and preliminary reports on the O'Connell finances and state of mind. Too early for the police to be thinking anything in particular, Allen knew. But they'd be looking.

He wondered if O'Connell had left everything to Jamie, or if someone else was now looking at a juicy inheritance. No doubt the police would be asking the same thing.

He turned over the last page, and looked at the leather diary.

Allen did not want to read Mark O'Connell's journal of his son's life. He knew it couldn't be any worse than some of the tapes he'd watched, but the words would be before his eyes the next time he looked at Jamie, and he did not want to give O'Connell that small triumph.

However, he had to read it.

Just not in the same place where he would later try to sleep.

IT WAS ONLY WHEN HE SAW THE LAKE THAT IT STRUCK ALLEN: THE PARK he'd chosen was the same site where Jamie's towheaded classmate Able Shepherd had drowned. He stood on the grass, the O'Connell journal in his hand, and thought about going elsewhere. However, the air was cooler here and smelled of lake instead of freeway, and the summer-worn lawn was a place of comforting normality, thick with beach umbrellas, Frisbee players, and toddlers. Stupid to get back in the car and fight the roads to somewhere less pleasant, just because of past associations. He found a bench in the shade, and opened the diary.

The writing was precise and controlled, changing little over the twelve years from first entry to last. Only a handful of words had been corrected or crossed out, two of those in a contrasting color of ink, which suggested that O'Connell had been in the habit of rereading his earlier entries and making small changes or clarifications.

Disappointment permeated the early pages, in O'Connell's sour assessment of his son's chances, first of mere survival, then of relative normality. He was unhappy with the boy and furious at the huge, ever-mounting bills, but he viewed his wife's part in the fiasco with a facile concern overlying a growing impatience. He couldn't understand her affection for the disgusting object in the ICU, and wanted her to get on with building up her health for another try. He'd clearly written Jamie off as a failed attempt.

But then Jamie was released to come home. O'Connell wrote:

December 19th

The hospital has decided to let us take the boy home, they think he'll live. It's hard to believe anything that feeble can even breathe on its own. Paula is dancing around in happiness, but I wouldn't be surprised if she fell apart before the baby did. She should be hospitalized herself. I don't know how I'm going to keep on working with the two of them on my hands. Great Christmas this will be.

On Jamie's third birthday, he wrote:

The boy cries all the time, and he never seems to settle to anything. His mother spoils him. She doesn't even see a problem that he's still in diapers.

When Jamie was five:

The boy is finally growing a little, so he looks less like a hairless monkey. He still clings to his mother more than is good for him, and cries when she leaves him at preschool. I take him now, whenever I can. He seems more in control of himself when she isn't around. He still wets the bed at night. At Paula's urging, I got him a dog, a dirty creature from the pound that I'm sure won't last a month before I have to take it back. But I do my best for him. He is, after all, my son.

At six:

As I expected, the dog died, although I don't suppose Jamie is to blame for anything but neglect. He let it out at night, a thing I expressly forbid, and something got to it. Paula is convinced it was one of those mountain lions they've been seeing in the hills in recent years, but I pointed out that a mountain lion would have eaten the thing whole, it was barely a mouthful. Personally, I think the mutt must have tangled with a real dog. Whatever it was, I made the boy bury it himself, to teach him what happens to a neglected animal.

And at the beginning of the new year:

I don't know what's up with the boy. Christmas vacation was one long round of crying and tantrums, and he disappeared three separate times, once for long enough that Paula wanted to call the police. I told her that we should go out driving and look for him, which was how we found him the last time, but as we were arguing about it we heard sirens. She was convinced that the boy had been hit by a car and took off running down the street, but it was only fire engines going to a fire at the school. Then she was absolutely certain that he'd somehow been inside his classroom and was burned to death, but just then I saw the boy watching the fire engines, and pointed him out to her. That was the end of his disappearing acts for that vacation.

In March:

James had a friend drown while they were on an outing today. He's terribly upset, it's hard to know what to do for him. It seems the other boy was allowed to wander off alone, and was playing at the edge of the lake when he must have slipped and hit his head, and drowned. James had been with him earlier that day, the teacher said, and seemed to have taken the death personally, as if he could have protected the boy. One of the parents who was around when they found the kid said James heard the news and kind of blurted out, "It's my fault, it's all my fault." Fortunately, no one has taken any notice.

August:

I decided James would be old enough for hunting this year. He's older than I was when I had my first gun, and I thought maybe having some time with me would counteract his mother's influence. Seven years old and I found them baking cookies in the kitchen the other day, for Christ sake. So I bought him a .22 like the one I grew up with, to see what he made of it, and I have to admit the kid's a natural. He hit the target his third try, and can't wait to go back to the range. He'll be ready, come pheasant season. And in a year or two, maybe he'll grow enough to handle a deer rifle.

December 1, shortly after Jamie's eighth birthday:

Paula killed herself two weeks ago. I still can't believe it, can't believe that she'd do it the way she did. Pills, even a razor in the bathtub, those wouldn't have surprised me. That sounds hard, but she's been threatening to kill herself for years. I'd never have thought she would put a shotgun to her mouth. And she chose a time when nobody would be home, so James found her. Poor kid, by the time I got back from Vegas he was practically catatonic, what with the shock and the drugs they gave him. Still, he seems to be taking it okay. He doesn't want to talk about it, but I can understand that. His teacher called yesterday and asked me if I wasn't concerned that the boy seemed so cheerful about his mother's death, like she wanted him to sit in class crying or something, and I told her it was none of her business. He isn't cheerful, not really. He's just getting on with his life. Although I'll admit I'm a little surprised he isn't more down about it, he and his mother spent so much time together. I'm staying in town a while longer, but I'll have to find a babysitter for when I have to be away. Maybe some kind of a full-time housekeeper who lives nearby.

Paula's death was followed in short order by a new house, another school, and the hiring of Mrs. Mendez. Entries were spotty, every six to ten months, and brief, usually a June review of "the boy's" progress in school that year or a winter description of one of their hunting trips.

The airplane was purchased eighteen months after Paula's death, when Jamie was nine and a half, and O'Connell found pleasure in his son's interest in the new toy:

> The kid's clever, give him that. I had to go to Vegas on Saturday, and took him along, and he spent the whole time asking questions and practicing at the controls. Then when I had to meet with my guys to sign some papers, he asked if he could stay behind with the plane. The mechanic's a good guy with kids of his own and he wasn't too busy that morning, so I left the boy there for a couple of hours, and came back to find him in a set of overalls with grease to his eyeballs. Looked funny, I have to admit. The mechanic said the boy could get a job with him any day. Nice to know the kid has a future, even if it is at union wage.

There was nothing at the time of Jamie's disappearance, although Allen supposed that could be a normal enough reaction on the part of a grieving parent. The final entry, the only one since May, was just four days old—written the same day Allen had received Rachel's letter, a scant thirty-six hours before O'Connell's plane had dropped off the radar. It read:

> My son has been gone nearly three months. Not knowing what happened to him is the worst, a torment day and night. I must force myself to carry on. I've decided to fly to Mexico to stay with friends, and when I get back, I will start anew. The boy's things are still in his room—maybe I will start by putting them in boxes, so they are not a constant reminder.
> This will be the first time I've had the plane up in months. In fact, the last time I saw the thing, my son went with me to the airport, and played happily around it while I had a meeting with some associates. He got greasy then, too, just like he did in Vegas that time, so I had to make him scrub off before getting into the car.
> At least my last memory of him is a happy one.

And that was it. When he reached the end, Allen flipped back and forth among the early pages for a minute, reflecting on what a peculiar document it was. The very fact of its existence had struck him as unlikely, given his impression of O'Connell. The journal's sole subject was Jamie, a child the man had consistently either neglected or actively tormented. Yet the entries seemed designed to present the other side of their relationship, that of a busy man who was yet very concerned about his son's well-being. It was almost as if O'Connell was aware of the criticisms the world would level against him, and he was writing for posterity. The words themselves seemed as stilted as the handwriting, highly self-conscious: Referring to business contacts as "associates" didn't strike Allen as the sort of thing a person would do in a journal meant for himself alone. And if he hadn't known what went on inside the O'Connell house, he would have thought that Mark O'Connell's protestations of affection were just a bit cautious. Almost, he thought, as if the man was nervous around his son.

It was an odd thought.

He stared unseeing at the busy lake, turning the implications over in his mind, while the park filled with its evening crowd. When the first smell of charcoal smoke hit the air, Allen looked at his watch, startled: nearly five, and he'd told Alice he'd call her at four.

He trotted toward the parking area and located a pay phone near the entrance kiosk.

"Alice?"

"I thought something had happened to you," her voice said in his ear, sounding more worried than he'd have expected.

"Did you hear the news?"

"About the plane crash? Yes."

"What do you want to do?"

"If the father's gone, the boy needs to come back."

"I agree, but there's a lot here I don't understand. Could we leave it a day or two, until we're sure?"

"What's not to understand? The man's plane went into the sea."

"And if he turns out to have miraculously escaped, we'd be in a hell of a place."

"You think that's likely?"

"I just want to be certain. Alice, the guy's a con man."

"You think the father faked his own death?"

When put as starkly as that, Allen had to admit that short-timer's jitters were a more likely explanation for his suspicions. "I know it's far-fetched. I'm probably seeing things."

"What sort of things?"

He was not about to go into the subtle overtones of the O'Connell diary over the phone. "It just occurred to me that maybe if a con man knew that the cops were closing in on his scam, he might . . . Oh, hell, I don't know, Alice. Except that you and I need to go over some of this stuff together."

"I can be down there tonight."

"No, I'll come back. I think I'm about finished here, anyway. Give me 'til Sunday."

"If you're sure?"

"I'm not sure of anything."

"What about calling our friends on the farm?" Rachel and Pete Johnson, and through them, Jamie. Yes, that was the question. Allen rubbed his face as if he could scrub away his confusion.

"You know, I really think we ought to wait to break the news until you and I have put our heads together. It's unlikely that there would be mention of his father's . . . presumed death on the national news."

"We can hope."

"Yeah. Okay, then. See you Sunday."

Allen got into the car and gravitated back to his motel room, where it was at least cool and relatively quiet, to brood over all the oddities piling up around the case of Jamie O'Connell. He had come to San Jose merely to look into O'Connell's whereabouts, either to reassure Jamie that the mystery figure who had briefly abducted little Sally Johnson could not have been his father, or else to find cause to remove him from the Johnson house immediately. Instead of that, all Allen had found was uncertainty and contradiction, even concerning things he'd taken for granted.

He couldn't get the reactions of Gina and Karin Rao out of his mind: two so different women, both of them all too ready to label Jamie as dangerous. How could Karin not like the boy in her care? Why would Gina assume that someone ought to be watching him closely? Allen found that he was pacing the worn motel carpet, four steps to the door, then back to the desk; he forced his legs to stop their restless movement and sat down in front of the desk, where the boxed *Rings* trilogy rested beside his laptop. Karin Rao's gift was as much of a conundrum as the boy she had given it to.

Absently, he picked up the case and let the three books slide out into his left hand, laying the box aside and opening volume one to its title page. Nothing there; no teacher's dedication inside the cover, just the books, a wordless gift that Jamie had interpreted as love. Damn the woman, anyway. Allen slid the first book back into its box and picked up the remaining two, but in the process of trying to thread the covers into their snug holder, he saw something sticking out from the upper edge of the third volume. He held the book's spine and gave it a sharp shake: A sheet of paper, folded into quarters, dropped onto his knees and then to the floor. He laid the books on the desk and picked up the piece of paper, unfolding it.

He wasn't sure what he expected to see. A woman's handwriting, perhaps—a long-treasured message from Paula O'Connell, hidden by her son in one place he might reasonably hope that his father would not find it. Or a secret letter packed with anger, or a childish last will and testament, or the instructions for a computer game, or a gynecological drawing, or—

Almost anything but what it was.

It looked to be a printout from an undisclosed Web site. At the top of the sheet, two partial sentences continued from some previous page, but an inch and a half down from the upper edge stood a phrase in bold, below which was a crude mechanical sketch and a list beginning with the number "1." Allen started to skim the list of terse instructions, smiling at this latest illustration of the gaming industry's ever more realistic plots and machinations. This story line seemed to involve sabotage, he decided, but as he read on, it dawned on him that this was no mere electronic fantasy. The smile began to flake off his face like dried paint, revealing an expression of disbelief shading into horror.

This looked like no game Allen had ever seen.

It looked like no game at all.

Hidden within one of Jamie O'Connell's meager possessions, in a book given him by one of the few adults who had ever shown him kindness, the boy had secreted a printout, a thing that appeared to have come from some sort of terrorist Web site. (*Christ*, a small part of Allen's mind said beneath the roaring sensation that was beginning to build in his ears; *is there* anything *you can't find online?*)

The heading in bold read:

TEN WAYS TO MAKE A SMALL PLANE
CRASH AFTER TAKEOFF.

BOOK FOUR

Man and Boy

Chapter 28

A SMALL WHITE PLANE, RIDING THE BLUE AIR ABOVE THE CALM PACIFIC Ocean, flashed and pattered down to the water; as if in echo, a flash and the sensation of shattering glass jolted through Allen's mind, and he was twenty years old again, skin crawling with prickly heat and leech bites, the beat of helicopters throbbing through his veins.

"I AM YOUR MAMA AND YOUR PAPA," CHANTED BRENNAN. "LET'S GO KILL US some gooks." The pounding syncopation of the approaching Hueys drowned out the actual words, but none of the platoon needed to hear Brenda, because the lieutenant used the same words at the outset of every patrol. They tossed their smokes and shouldered their packs, lining up to climb through the chopper doors. Allen wedged himself against his squad-mates and wrapped his arms around his rifle, sweltering in silence.

He didn't think about the heat, or the upcoming patrol, or anything much. He'd found it was much easier not to think, better just to keep on keeping on. He was, however, fully aware that Brennan was not in the Huey with him. The freedom from that blue-eyed gaze lifted his burden enough that his mind began to turn over, dully.

In the months since Woolf had died, the platoon had been reshaped into a fighting machine so self-contained, the rest of the world just bounced off its sides. Whenever new men came on board, they spent their first few days looking a bit stunned. Some of them requested a transfer out; those requests were always granted within twenty-four hours. Brenda's platoon was a reflection of its commander—hard, clean, violent, and more than a little deranged. The men polished their boots as if rubbing dirt into Charlie's face. The members of the Second Platoon had very little to do with the rest of the company. And every man there collected ears.

Except Allen.

Funny, his mind tossed out, how The Wolf as an officer was aloof and casual, yet had brought his men together like a band of brothers, whereas the ever-present paternalist Brenda took the same platoon, declared them his family, hammered them into a disciplined unit, and had somehow managed to turn them into a rabble of wolves, shaggy and sharp-toothed under the polish. Wolf—brothers; brother—wolves. There must be a lesson in that somewhere. He stirred, thinking of saying something to Mouse, but then the Huey lurched tail-up, and he didn't bother.

In moments the helicopter was high above the lush green landscape, and the air rushing through the tight-packed interior was delicious. As one, the young men raised their sweaty faces to the wind, and breathed deeply.

It was late June, a temporary break in the monsoon, and down there the heat was enormous. The post-Tet lull was but a memory, the Army wanted a victory to give the people at home, and men like Brennan were only too happy to go out there after it, chasing the enemy down in his lair, hunting him through his tunnels and hills, wielding the platoon like a bludgeon.

Brennan really was, Allen had begun to suspect, quite insane. The man glittered with a manic energy, first goading his platoon, then riding on their blood lust, a spiral that had brought him in front of the CO twice now for excessive use of force against civilians. He carried with him the smell of smoke, and of desperation, the need to stay on top, to be in control, to win his little section of war.

Then again, maybe it was all in Allen's imagination. He seemed to be the only man in the platoon aware of Brennan's edginess, the only one to question and object. Or, not object, but simply turn a deaf ear to certain orders. The kinds of orders that led to burning hooches and the taking of trophies.

He had thought for a while that this was why Brennan had begun to hassle him, but in truth, those black glasses had sought him out from the very beginning. The lieutenant had picked Allen out of the platoon that first morning, and hadn't let up since. Every time Allen turned around, it seemed, the lieutenant was already looking at him. Allen had developed a sixth sense about the man almost as sure as his sense for Charlie, a sensitivity that was weirdly akin to a schoolboy crush: He always knew where Brennan was, often felt the touch of Brennan's glance on the back of his neck. He'd tried once or twice to talk to Mouse or ThreeG about Brenda's peculiar attentions, but the others had scoffed, saying that every grunt in the Army thought his LT had it in for him. And invariably, the day following one of these conversations, Brenda seemed to look over at Allen with that infuriating smirk as if to say, *"I know what you were talking about, but this is between us."*

And it was a private war, with rules that took some figuring, but seemed to involve challenges. Not to talk to others about it, that was one of them. This extended to a general agreement not to involve the others: Brennan didn't try to make the rest of the platoon uncomfortable over Allen's holier-than-thou attitude, while Allen wouldn't try to undermine the platoon's leadership by pointing out Brennan's growing instability. Another rule was that Allen's refusal to burn innocent villages or commit violence on civilians would be permitted, as long as he never refused an order that merely put him in danger: crap jobs in exchange for moral purity; his ass on the line the price for his personal shield. So Allen shut up, even though he always seemed to be maneuvered into volunteering for recon and point duty, and he tried like hell to ignore those damned eyes on his back. It was making him more than a little crazy, too. He had recently found himself imitating Brenda's smile, both as a challenge and an assertion of victory. He had also begun to wonder of late if Brennan intended to allow the hostilities to remain at this level.

A private war, just him and Brenda out in the green, winner being the last man to break.

That Allen had already broken once, that he'd stood with the others at Truc Tho and raised his rifle at civilians, was both a danger and a protection: Like a broken bone, once healed it was stronger than the bones around it; like that broken bone, it would be vulnerable until it had healed. In the meantime, Allen held the knowledge of that act before him, forging his defenses from the raw material of weakness. *Never again,* he would chant to himself. *You won't get me to do it again, you bastard; not this time.*

The Huey made a sharp pull upward, sending the stomachs of all the passengers lurching and giving them all the brief thrill of knowing that someone had been shooting at them from the ground, and had missed. Allen hugged his rifle to him. The cooler air made him glad for the warmth of the men sandwiching him, and he thought back to the episode on the last patrol, puzzling over Brennan's apparent escalation of hostilities.

It had started when Brennan noticed Allen walking away from his squad as they were lining up the inhabitants of a tiny ville, softening them up for the interrogation to follow. The sequence of events was so standard by now—take the ville, then slap them around, while "Crazy" Carmichael found something else to do—that no one even thought about it, but this time, Brennan shouted Allen's name and ordered him to get back to his squad.

Allen glanced over his shoulder in time to see ThreeG lower his gun to the forehead of a man old enough to be his great-grandfather; he straightened out and told the lieutenant, "Sir, I didn't sign on to beat up civilians."

"They're VC, soldier."

"No guns, no food stores, and the kids half-starved. They're not VC."

"And I say they are."

"Yes, sir." Allen stood facing the distance, shutting his ears to the sounds behind him.

"Go back to your squad, Carmichael."

"All respect, sir, no. You can report me if you like, but I'll rejoin them when they're finished."

At that, Brenda came up to Allen, stopping inches from his chest, and pulled the lenses from those pale eyes. He stared up at Allen, that weird smile on his full lips, and murmured, "You turning into a communist, Carmichael? Maybe some kind of contentious objector hippie? Queer boy, maybe? I always wondered why you got so hot when pretty little deRosa went missing."

Allen's hands clenched white, wanting to strangle the bastard, pound those blue eyes with the butt of his M16, but he worked to keep it from his face. A reaction was just what Brenda wanted. When he thought he had his voice under control, he replied, "No sir, I'm here to kill the enemy. These people are just farmers."

"They're VC," the loot repeated, although by now Allen could hear in Brennan's voice that he didn't believe it himself.

Allen said nothing.

"I can shoot you if I like, for disobeying an order."

"Yes sir," Allen repeated, adding under his breath, *Not this time, you bastard; I will not give in this time.* He didn't actually think Brennan could shoot him, not without risking his career—or his neck—but he could almost believe that the man was crazy enough not to care. Allen stood as if he was back in boot camp with a drill sergeant cursing him out, gazing stony-faced over the top of the small man's head. After a long time, the glasses went back on.

"You're an interesting case, Carmichael," Brenda said, and walked away. It felt less like a reprieve than a declaration of open war.

Penroy had been standing within earshot; after watching Brennan stalk off toward the villagers, he said, "Christ, Carmichael, why don't you just do as you're told for once?"

"These people are not VC."

"What the fuck does it matter? He's your lieutenant, Crazy. You'd just be following orders."

"Yeah, that's what they said in Nazi Germany, too," Allen answered.

But the truth of the matter was, by now morality had little to do with his refusals. The game itself, the unacknowledged battle for superiority, was all. He wouldn't have admitted it to anyone, but he was having the time of his life. Every minute felt so intense, so alive, it was like being half-drunk all the time. He moved in an electric sea, tingling with awareness and with the sheer reality of things, his senses so finely tuned, they seemed near to clairvoyance. Colors vibrated, odors intoxicated, and even the more repulsive types of C-rations hit his palate like a blast.

In his own way, he knew he was as mad as his lieutenant, egging him on, carrying out their dialogue of death and domination, as if the whole war came down to him and Brenda in the green. Sure, sooner or later his luck would run out, and after one too many patrols on point he'd sit down on the mouth of a VC spider hole or walk into a trip wire and get himself shipped home in a box.

Didn't matter. Nothing mattered, except not letting Brennan win.

The Huey lurched and dropped down from the sky, going in fast in case the LZ was hot, rearing back when its runners were skimming the vegetation. The heavy-laden men jumped awkwardly, jogging through knee-high grass toward the bushes.

One by one the Hueys emptied, their door gunners giving the grunts a farewell wave, and the machines dipped their noses and rose, making for base like a line of dun-colored dragonflies. The thunder of their passing faded into the distance, and when the beating had passed, the jungle noises began tentatively to return.

Back in the green again.

It was to be a patrol of two, at the most three, days. Five days later, they were still out, high in the mountains, within shouting distance of the Laotian border. Radio contact had been spotty all that day, supplies were getting low, ammunition was down to one good firefight, and Brennan appeared to have given up sleeping. Eyes had begun to shift this morning, when the loot had folded his maps away and told them to prepare to move out.

Allen's squad leader had been the one to ask. "Sir, aren't we supposed to be lifting out from here?"

"Change of plans, Penroy," he replied. The grin on Brennan's face would have looked at home above a straitjacket—but then, by this time half the platoon wore that same grin. He raised his voice to shout, "Men, I am your mama and your papa. Let's go kill us some gooks."

"Sir, I thought—"

"The Army pays you to shoot, Penroy, not to think. Let's move out. That okay with you, Carmichael?"

"Oh yes sir," Allen answered, continuing their dance. He felt as if he hadn't slept in days. A small part of his mind warned him that he was going to crash sooner or later, that if he didn't attend to his body pretty soon he'd stroll blindly off a cliff, but he didn't listen, just bared his teeth at Brenda and kicked the remains of his breakfast into the dust.

The others glanced at Sergeant Keys to see what he thought about this unannounced change of plans, but they saw only his usual stoic expression as he stood to toss his C-rat cans into the bushes. So they followed his example, and set out due west, into the hills.

Four hours later they stopped for lunch, on the bald side of a hill with the wind whistling around them. The shade was cooler than their heat-thinned blood found comfortable, and a number of them huddled into the patches of sun, spooning down their cold rations and lighting up a quick cigarette. None of them were inclined to linger; they shouldered their packs without regret.

The ridge they had been following dipped into a sheltered valley, where they picked up the telltale odors of a village, shit and smoke and fish sauce. The men brought their rifles up across their chests, and walked quietly.

The platoon was practically inside the ville before being spotted. It was a scattered village, built around an outcrop of rock with jungle rising behind it and terraces of vegetables stepping down the hill. A shout went up from very close, sweeping like a breeze through the hooches and shelters, the cries of women, the hoarse calls of old men. An M16 sounded, down the line to Allen's right; a running man tumbled into the vegetables. Figures could be seen darting through the bamboo and trees into the rocky area; guns picked some of them off, and the platoon moved to secure the ville.

The villagers came out of their hooches with hands in the air and fear on their faces. Perhaps two dozen women and old men, and one young man missing his right leg and half his fingers. Most of them clutched papers in their upraised hands, and Allen felt his tension loose a notch. Brenda generally looked for some token resistance before committing his platoon to aggression; there was none here.

Then somebody said, "Why aren't there any kids?"

There were children, but only a handful, and none older than about three. Allen had never seen a farming village where the children didn't at least match the adults in number. Had there been some kind of childhood epidemic here?

Brenda called up his translator, an ill-tempered local named Lo Don, whom everyone called Lowdown. He translated Brenda's query about the village's children, and received only loud protestations and demonstrative fingers pointed at the babies.

"They say, these only children."

"I suppose the Cong are recruiting five-year-olds now?" Brenda said in a mild voice.

"You want I ask them that?"

"No, there's little point. I think we'll need to be a little more direct." Brenda looked around at his platoon of wolves, his eyes coming to rest, as always, on Allen. Then they shifted to the man standing next to Allen, and the amused smile came onto his lips.

"Tobin."

Mouse straightened. "Yessir?"

"How about you taking charge of this interrogation?"

Oh, shit, thought Allen. *The fucking bastard, here it comes.* Brenda must've decided that using Allen's squad-mates was the only way of levering up Allen's defenses. *Damn it all,* he thought, looking at Mouse's startled face. *How do I get us out of this one?*

"Me?" Mouse asked apprehensively.

"Yes, soldier. You bring your sixteen over here and shoot a couple of these kids, see if their mothers will tell us where the others are hiding."

Mouse stared down at the naked, round-bellied infants, appalled. "I can't do that, sir. They just babies."

"We're at war with the babies, too, Tobin. Shoot them."

He was talking to Mouse, but he was looking at Allen.

Allen felt as if the ground was falling out from under him. His private war had just moved to encompass the others, and he reached out to grab the only solution he could find. He cleared his throat and said, "I'll do it, sir."

The platoon turned as one to stare at him. Allen thumbed his safety on, handed the rifle to Mouse, and walked up to the villagers, gesturing to Lowdown to follow him.

At the cook-fire outside one of the hooches, Allen squatted on his boots. The people on the other side of the fire were a man and a woman, both looking about a hundred and twenty years old, toothless, terrified. He met their eyes, first hers, then his, before he spoke over his shoulder to the translator.

"You tell these people that we don't want to hurt their children. We just need to be sure they aren't hiding VC. Tell them that." He waited until Lowdown's voice had stopped, and he saw the disbelief on the old faces. "Now you tell them that the man with the dark glasses is crazy. *Dinky-dau,* you understand? Crazy as a rabid dog. That's right," he said when both wrinkled faces glanced with apprehension at the lieutenant's glasses. "That man will shoot everyone, including the children. Then he will find your other children and shoot them, unless they come out now. Do you understand what I'm saying?"

They understood, and they believed him. The villagers murmured among themselves for several minutes, the younger women protesting, one of them wailing in terror. The old man finally looked into Allen's eyes.

"They come out, you not hurt?" the ancient voice asked.

Allen swiveled his head to look at Brenda. "He wants to know, if their kids come out, you promise you won't hurt them?"

" 'Course not, unless they're VC."

"No VC," the old man declared.

"I have your word?" Allen persisted, holding the lieutenant's gaze. *I'm not giving in, not this time, you bastard.*

"Carmichael, get on with it."

Allen got to his feet and surveyed the platoon. "You heard Lieutenant Brennan. We've just promised that we're not going to shoot this ville's kids."

When he was sure, he looked down at the old man. He said, "We won't shoot your children."

The old man unfolded until he was on his feet and led the way, most of the ville trailing behind, the women's voices providing a chorus of apprehension as they went up the worn path. Two hundred yards away, the man stopped and pointed to some bushes. "There."

The bunker was a cave, its entrance hidden by vegetation and rocks. The old man rattled a singsong phrase, and in a moment two children came out, then three more. Soon ten kids were blinking in front of the cave, all under the age of nine.

Brenda nodded, satisfied, and walked over to examine the nearly invisible opening of the bunker. Allen let out the breath he didn't know he'd been holding, the other soldiers relaxed, and the villagers, reacting to the change in their stances, began to chatter. Then Brenda said casually, his voice echoing from the open space below him, "Tobin, shoot the old man."

As one, the platoon turned to look at their lieutenant, who chose that moment to step down into the cave. After a moment, Brennan's head reemerged, to fix Mouse with a look of mild surprise. "I gave you an order, soldier."

"Sir, the old guy—"

"You let them get away with this, next time they'll think it's okay to shoot at us. Waste him, Tobin. Hell, he's half-dead anyway."

With that, Brenda ducked back into the hole. Had he not demonstrated such a casual lack of interest in the whole matter, had he stayed to see his order carried out, things might have gone very differently. Mouse might have firmed up his resistance, while Brenda's authority teetered and began its downhill run. But with the order stated and left, in the vacuum of Brennan's absence the order took on its own authority. After a moment, Mouse brought his gun up and began to swivel to face the villagers.

With that motion, with the sharp rising wail of the women, Allen's world suddenly shifted. Silence came down over him. The faces of the people around him—white, black, and brown—became both achingly beautiful and ineffably strange. Certain things became transparently clear to him, above all the knowledge that if he did not act, then Mouse would live the rest of his days under an intolerable memory. Allen didn't even need to think about what he was going to do, because will and action were one, and the cool mountain air brushed his face, sweet as a kiss. It was time.

"No," he told Mouse quietly.

Four leisurely steps took Allen to the cave opening. A gentle tug and the grenade dropped into his palm like a ripe peach; a twitch and the constricting pin was freed. His ears registered the small *tink* of the spoon handle and his right arm curled smoothly down, back, and forward, the fingers relaxing at precisely the right point in the arc to allow the heavy metal handful to continue on its way like a miniature bowling ball, bouncing along Brenda's path through the entrance of the cave. The universe counted down the seconds before Allen would need to step to one side—all the time in the world for one final glance down into Brenda's face.

The lieutenant had taken off his sunglasses in the dim cave, and the pale eyes seemed to glitter with their own light. They widened slightly at the approaching grenade, and although Allen had a fleeting impression of something that might have been fear, it passed in an instant, replaced by the smile that already haunted Allen's dreams, amused and triumphant. The two men held each other's eyes, locked into an intimacy such as Allen had never known, as the grenade bumped and slowed and came to a rest at the toe of Brennan's polished boots. And then, an instant before Mouse tackled him, a heartbeat before the mouth of the cave vomited out fire and chunks of metal and rock, Allen knew the reason for the triumph and humor in the insane blue eyes.

There had been a noise from the cave in back of Brennan.

There were children in the cave.

Chapter 29

ALLEN DIDN'T KNOW HOW LONG HE STOOD IN THE MOTEL ROOM WITH THE twice-folded sheet of paper in his hand before the facts all came together in his mind with the impact of a grenade in a cave. He heard the spoon handle's tiny *tink*, registered the impact of Mouse's flying tackle, felt for the millionth time the exquisitely painful cut of the final irony: that the entire platoon had been looking toward the wailing villagers, leaving Mouse the only witness to the source of the grenade. In rescuing his last surviving squad-mate from one atrocity, Allen had delivered him to another. Brennan was ultimately granted a posthumous medal for venturing into a cavern full of armed VC children, and Mouse said not a word. He said nothing to Allen, either, and put in for a transfer soon after. Allen had saved Mouse and lost him in the same motion.

And now: instructions for bringing down a plane; the honed instincts of Karin Rao and Gina; the news anchor telling of Jamie's long-held interest in his father's Cessna; both Jamie and his father, describing an airport visit as the last thing they had done; the boy's weird reaction to the crop duster, and his unusually knowledgeable questions about blowing up trees; and his father's recent bout of rage after Ms. Rao's call from school at about the same time he "broke" the boy's computer— *Jeez, I thought it was about all over,* the boy had said, with a laugh to cover the tremor in his voice.

Any parent, any school administrator knew the lessons of Paducah and Jonesboro and Columbine: shame and social isolation to assemble the raw material for atrocity; a brutal upbringing coupled with a knowledge of weapons to shape the device; with a recent and intolerable event to trigger it. The facts had all been there, right in front of him, from his covert recordings of a solitary and abused boy to Jamie's casual remark about dynamite, but Allen hadn't seen the deadly mixture until it blew up in his face. The violence of revelation splintered his mind, leaving him standing with the paper in his hand; and then it hit him with the force of Mouse's tackle: *Move move MOVE!* and the thud of rotors seemed to fill his bones, making it hard to think of anything but sprinting for the car and jamming his foot on the accelerator until he reached Montana.

Only the decades of training kept his brain in charge. He was dimly aware of packing his clothes into garment bag and carry-on, couldn't have said later how he'd made his plane reservations, and nothing but the compulsive tidiness of patrol reminded him to change back the dead bolt—one loose end securely tied off. Another went with the mailing service on the way to the airport, where he bought a mailer big enough for all Gina's papers. He took the page he had found in Jamie's book, the instructions for crashing a plane, and photocopied it on the service's machine, then put the original into a smaller envelope, writing on the outside: *This should be checked for prints, and see if G can find out where it's from.* Into another envelope went the plastic bag with the tiny scraps of wallpaper from the bare room in the O'Connell house; on that one he wrote, *Have these stains tested.* He slid both small envelopes in front of the other pages, added the diary and the miniature tapes, and paid to overnight it all to Alice's service near Seattle.

But when he hurried into the terminal, hearing his flight number being announced over the speakers, his eye caught on the rank of phone booths, and the other, more problematic loose end dangled before him: Alice herself.

He should phone her. He owed it to her, to keep her abreast of everything that was happening. But what would he say? *Listen, Alice; you know that triad of psychopathy the psychologists toss around: bed-*

*wetting, fire-setting, and animal abuse? How would it feel to know we'd
got one of those, that you and I had taken the hand of a sixth-grader
whose bed still had a waterproof cover on it, whose school once burned
down, whose dog died mysteriously? A kid who had shown a particular
interest in the plane his father just crashed in? That we'd taken his hand
and led him to the arms of a family that was generous and loving and
horribly ill-equipped when it came to being suspicious of a child?*

No, he wouldn't call her. What did he actually know? What gain
would there be in alarming Alice? If the kid hadn't burned down the
Johnson farm in the last eleven weeks, he wasn't likely to do so in the
next eleven hours. Allen had said that he'd see her on Sunday, and
he would. Only, he'd have the boy with him.

But the urgent beat of helicopter rotors seemed to follow him, all
the way to Montana.

He made his tight Portland connection and touched down in
Helena late the same night, mildly aware that some self-congratulations
were in order: Had his instinctive side been given its way, had he just
gotten behind the wheel of his rental car and unthinkingly rushed
north, he'd only be halfway through Nevada. He strode to the taxi
ranks and told the driver he needed to go to the downtown bus station.
The man looked at him as if he was nuts, but he drove there, and left
him.

What Allen wanted was not a bus, but a person, of a type that
didn't tend to hang out in airports, not in this country. He walked up
and down until he found the man he wanted, in this case the driver of
an unmetered taxi, and told him what he needed.

"You wanna buy a car? At this hour?"

"If you can't think of anyone, just say so, I'll go on looking."

"Didn't say that. Just kinda surprisin', you know?"

"I'm in a hurry. There's fifty bucks in it for you."

"Couple of those would be better," the man noted, studying the
grimy ceiling.

"If I have the keys inside of an hour, we'll go to an ATM and there'll
be three of them."

"Then let's go."

With this sort of arrangement, there was always the danger that
the driver would turn on him and take what he could find, the misleading statement about the ATM notwithstanding. But Allen's luck
held, and he didn't find himself staring down the business end of a
gun, and the man's cousin-in-law hadn't actually gone to bed yet, and
he was happy to show Allen the cars in his lot.

There were two dozen vehicles under the glaring lights, and a Rottweiler bellowing its fury and biting madly at the doorknob inside the shack marked OFFICE. Allen ignored its threats while he walked up and down the rows, then asked for the keys to three of the vehicles. The cousin-in-law went inside the shack, shouting the animal into submission, and brought out the keys. One car Allen rejected on the basis of its reluctant starter, another by the dark stink of burning that rose up around him. The third car was a five-year-old, manual-shift Honda with the aroma of mildew and the beginnings of rust-lace along its wheel-wells. However, the engine started obediently, and a drive around the block betrayed no ominous noises, smells, or shimmies. It even had Washington plates, an added advantage once he crossed the state border.

"How much?" he asked the cousin.

"It's a sweet car, isn't it? And only twenty-seven thousand on the clock."

Allen hadn't even bothered glancing at the odometer, assuming it would show a fraction of the actual miles driven. "How much?"

"Night like this, nice guy like you, I'll let her go for six thou."

"I'll give you two. Cash."

The last word caught briefly at the salesman's attention, but he rallied fast. "Two! That's less than I paid for it."

"Then you were cheated."

"Might let you have it for five."

"Three."

They settled for thirty-seven fifty, and the man's eyes got wide when Allen took off the innocent-looking belt and started pulling the crisply folded hundred-dollar bills from its innards. Even pressed flat, the bills made a nice stack.

"I'll need the pink slip," Allen told him.

" 'Course you will," said his new best friend, and went to wrest the ownership papers from the guard dog. Allen traded the money for the papers and gave the taxi man his finder's fee. He was out of Helena not much after midnight.

He followed the main highway through Bozeman, past the last blandishments for Yellowstone, until finally he turned onto the lesser road that he and Jamie had passed over the final days of May. The gas station where they had filled up the tank and bought a sack of fresh, fragrant doughnuts was dark now. Ten miles later he caught the smell of the sleeping dairy farm that had made Jamie screw up his face in disgust, unaware of what Fate had in store for him just up the road. It was two-thirty in the morning when the Honda's headlights caught the Johnson mailbox. Allen bumped down the lane and pulled up to the dark house, leaving his high beams glaring on the front porch, and ran up the wooden steps to pound on the door. Dogs barked; a light went on, a man's voice came, sleep-thick and apprehensive, asking who it was.

"Pete, it's me, Allen."

The lock rattled, the door drew back. Allen was through it before it was all the way open, pushing aside Pete's questions as he went past the man's pajama-clad form. The farm's resident watch dog, an arthritic old retriever, grumbled its mistrust.

"I've come for the boy, Pete, I can't tell you why, I just have to take him."

Rachel was stopped on the stairs, her hair awry, dressed in a fuzzy bathrobe and out-at-the-toe slippers.

"Allen, what on earth has happened?"

"I have to take Jamie."

"You're taking Jim? Right now?"

That brought Allen up short. The family was fine, no smoke was curling from the eaves; did he really need to turn the entire household upside down at three A.M. in order to remove his cuckoo child from their midst? Nothing was going to happen before morning.

He passed a hand over his hair. "No. Jeez, I'm really sorry. Go back to bed. I'll have a snooze on the sofa." Not that he intended to sleep.

Rachel came the rest of the way downstairs. "As if I could get back to sleep wondering what is going on. Pete, why don't you try to get another couple of hours?"

Pete looked from his wife to the madman intruder, and shrugged. He locked the door, patted Rachel on the shoulder in passing, and retreated up the stairs. The bedroom door shut behind him. Rachel tightened the belt of her robe around her, and led Allen into the kitchen. The old dog came along, settling back onto its bed behind the stove with a sigh.

"We can talk in here," she said. "Just keep it low."

"I'm really sorry," he told her again. "Why don't you go back to bed, too? We'll talk in the morning."

"Oh, sure, while Jim is sitting there with his big ears. You want cocoa, or tea?"

Allen wanted a lot of strong coffee, but he settled for tea.

"What has happened?" she asked, moving from stove to refrigerator. She was such a sensible woman, and Allen was desperately tired;

he craved the relief of telling her all of it, of dumping his entire shit-load of suspicions and fears onto someone else and letting her tell him what to do. But the very length of the story itself saved him, made him hesitate long enough to realize that he could not tell her, not until he knew the whole of it. In the end he just told her, "The boy's father died."

Rachel set his tea down on the oilcloth and settled across the table from him with her cocoa. She had switched on a wall heater; the growing warmth combined with the fragrance of hot milk made him want to curl up next to the old dog.

"Why does the father's death bring you up here at this hour?"

Allen cupped his hands around the mug, seeing the reflection of the overhead light dancing on the surface. "I've discovered that the man was involved in illegal activities. There may be a lot of money involved. It appears that he was murdered."

All true, however misleading.

Rachel frowned. "Are you saying the people who killed the father may come after the son as well? But why?"

"Rachel, I honestly can't go into it here and now. You'll just have to believe me when I say, I have to take the boy away."

"You can't, Allen, you just can't. Last week we had his first night without horrible dreams. He denies he has them, but he sleeps with the light full on. He hurts himself, or puts himself at risk to be hurt. He's been here for three months and he's only now on the edge of putting out lines of communication. He's just beginning to trust us."

Trust: the hardest lesson of all for abused children to learn. Most never did.

"It may not be for long. I'll try my best. But if the father's dead, circumstances have changed. We can't simply leave him here."

"Why not?"

Because he may have killed the man, was the response on the tip of Allen's tongue. *Because his father's systematic emotional torture may have been more successful than he could have imagined, and he's built himself a killer for a son. Because I know how it feels to hate an abusive authority figure so much that in the end you become him. I know how it feels to murder. And I have to take Jamie aside to a quiet place where I can look into his eyes, and know if there's a killer looking back at me.*

But he could say none of that here. Merely, "I'll make sure he understands that I'm the one to blame, not you and Pete. It's possible that I'll be able to bring him back here, and if so, it would be better if you appeared to be victims, too."

"But why would anyone want to harm Jim?"

Why indeed, if the father was out of the picture? "I don't know that they do. But I need to be sure, before I can let him stay here." That much was true.

"And if they come here, and find him missing? What will they do?"

He was so tired he wasn't thinking straight. Of course his night-mare scenario led straight to this question, which would be a valid concern if any of the rest of it was true. He needed to reassure her that there wasn't some band of murderous thugs on the boy's trail, about to burst in some night and murder her family, but he couldn't very well do that without telling her that the only potential murderous thug was an adolescent boy already sheltering under her roof. "Rachel, look. No one is after him. His father's plane went down, apparently with him on board. They haven't recovered the body yet, but surely you can see that it changes everything. The father's not there, and the boy will probably inherit a lot of money. I have to take him back."

Rachel thought about this, then sat back in her chair. "Allen, I don't think you understand. You and Alice asked us to take Jim in, and that's what we did. We took him in, to our family, to our hearts. You can't just rip him out again. It doesn't work that way, not with us."

"It's going to have to, Rachel."

"That sounds pretty final. You talk about returning him to us, then you say something like that. You're not going to bring him back, are you?"

"I honestly don't know," he said, but she heard the answer in his voice: No.

She stood up. "Oh, Allen. This is going to cause so much pain, all around. I'll go get dressed, and put some of his things together. Will you be taking the dog?"

"Oh, God. Did you get him one, then?"

"You told me to, Allen," she said, suddenly angry, biting off each word. "You stood in my home and you told me to get Jim a dog, and so I called over half the state until I found someone with a puppy like you said he wanted and Pete drove to the other side of Helena and paid two hundred dollars for the animal, and Jim fell in love with it the minute he saw it. And now you're going to break that up too."

Before he could protest, she stalked out of the room. In a minute, he heard water running. He unlatched the back door and went to sit on the dark porch, watching the stars fade.

He ached to be home, with Rae. She would leave for Japan in thirty hours; at the rate things were going, he did not think he would be in the seat beside her.

It was after four when Allen heard sounds in the kitchen behind him. He cast a final look up at the lightening sky, and let himself back inside. Rachel was making Pete's once-a-day coffee. Pete sat at the table, fully dressed; he looked up at Allen, his face grim.

"So you're taking our boy." In spite of his gruff farmer's exterior, Pete sounded nearly as devastated as if Allen had been taking one of his own children. (*So there, Ms. Rao,* the back of his mind retorted, *other people love this boy.*)

"I don't have any choice, Pete. If I saw any other way, I'd do it."

"I believe you."

To his astonishment, Allen found himself not far from tears. *Good, good people,* he thought, and opened his mouth to offer yet more hollow reassurances. But what came out was, "What do you make of him?"

Pete looked taken aback and Rachel turned from what she was doing to listen to his answer. "Well, he's not an easy boy to get to know. I guess that's what makes him interesting."

"What about you, Rachel?"

"What do you mean, what do I make of him? He's a child who needs a lot of love, and as far as I can see, won't be getting it for a while longer."

"I mean . . ." Allen began, and then stopped. What did he mean? She loved Jamie, that much was abundantly clear, but for a person like Rachel, love was what one gave a child who needed it. Wasn't that why he and Alice had brought Jamie to her in the first place? But he also needed to know how the other side of Rachel Johnson responded to the boy, the canny side of the woman who had seen abused kids and knew enough about them not to fall for their manipulations, even while she was lavishing on them all the love they could handle. "I guess what I'm asking is, do you like him?"

Perhaps it was the intensity with which he asked the question that made her come to the table and sit down next to her husband, absently letting Pete thread his massive fingers through hers.

"Jim keeps the world at a distance," she said. "He's polite, even thoughtful, but he rarely allows you to draw him in to family activities. He watches. The reluctance with which he lets himself get interested in something could just break your heart. But you get the feeling that, once he does, that bond is there for life. Like with Terry, the dog. I thought at first that when Pete put the animal on Jim's lap, Jim was going to have nothing to do with it. He looked like he'd been slapped, he was so shocked. Of course, as soon as the puppy started licking his face, his hands seemed to take over. Now, he and Terry are inseparable, but at first, I didn't think he was even going to let us give it to him."

"I thought he was going to throw the thing against the wall," Pete commented, and then looked horrified at what he'd said. "Not really. It was just for a second. I surprised the kid is all, and someone who's been through what Jim has, well, he's not going to be used to good surprises."

"Personally, I think he was afraid of it—or, not of the dog itself, but of his reaction to it. It was the same with Sally. He was kind to her, but standoffish, up until the day she disappeared. Since then he's become her fiercest protector. So if you're asking if he is capable of forming relationships, I'd say yes. At least, he *was*," she added grimly.

Allen had to look away from her accusing eyes. He understood all too well what Jamie had been afraid of: Once you learn the names of the new guys, they're inside your defenses. *Jesus,* Allen thought, *what the hell am I doing?* If he was wrong, this could well be the final blow to the poor kid. Jamie would never let himself bond with anyone, ever again.

Rachel continued. "But you asked if I liked Jim. I'll be honest: I didn't at first. But when I understood how hard it is for him, how much he's missing, I began to see that you can't relate to a boy like Jim the way you do other kids. In two months, he's started to get an idea of where he could be, if he let himself. He's a lot like that little dog: not much muscle, but when he sees something he wants, he throws his whole being into it. I respect that. And you have to respect someone before you can like them, don't you?"

In other words, yes, she liked him. It was a relief, hearing that. Allen felt as if he'd just let out the breath he'd been holding since he'd walked away from Ms. Rao's apartment door.

The kid wasn't a monster; he hadn't caused his father's plane to fall out of the sky. His dad was a crook and the boy's future was uncertain, but in a few days, or weeks, Allen would drive up that long dirt road one last time and push this kid back into the arms of this family for good.

God, he hoped.

But in the meanwhile, it was time to get things moving.

He laid his hands on the table and pushed himself up. "You want to get him, or should I?"

"I'll get him," Rachel said. "Let me put breakfast on first."

But once she had laid the sausages in the pan and taken a loaf of

grits from the refrigerator, Allen took the knife from her hand. "I'll finish up here, I'm sure Pete can eat my cooking as well as yours. But,
Rachel? Don't tell the boy about his father yet, okay?"

Reluctant to relinquish her kitchen to a mere man, Rachel hovered
until she had seen that he knew how thick to slice the loaf, then gave
Pete a worried glance and walked away upstairs. Allen finished slicing,
turned down the flame under the spattering pork links, and lit the fire
under the other griddle.

"You want to tell me what's really happened?" the gruff voice behind him asked.

Allen, paying close attention to the empty cast-iron surface,
thought about it. "Pete, I don't know. The kid's father disappeared on
his plane, I went down to see about it, and what I found confused the
hell out of me. Pardon the language."

"Allen."

Allen forced himself to meet the eyes of this good Christian man.

"Allen, I been in the Marines, and what I saw there drove me to
God. Since then I've seen just what one of these abusing . . . *bastards*
can do to a child." The obscenity was deliberate. "Now, I won't pretend
that I'm much a part of the modern world, but I haven't spent my life
in Neverland either. I'm asking you, if Jim's father is a criminal, and
he's somehow tracked the boy here, is my family in danger?"

"Pete, I wish I could say, absolutely not. Like I told Rachel, I honestly don't think there's any threat to you. But the whole picture's so
fuzzy, all I can say is, I'm ninety-five, maybe ninety-eight percent sure
there's not so much as a whiff of danger to any of you."

The big farmer nodded, his face thoughtful. Allen wished the man
would rise up and attack him with the iron skillet, but he didn't even
give Allen a reproachful look. He merely accepted the information,
that his family's adoptive son might somehow be in danger, and by contagion, his whole family. Allen again felt the inexplicable urge to weep;
turning, he began laying the slices of cornmeal grits into the heating
pan. It was light outside before Rachel reappeared with the boy in tow.

Jamie had grown during the summer, taking on the gangly appearance of early adolescence. Right now, awakened from a sound sleep,
he looked rumpled and apprehensive; Allen, looking up from his empty
plate at the boy, was oddly reassured by the normality of his reactions.

The third person entering the room was canine, a young white and
brown dog with almost no tail. It gave a brief *whuff* under its breath at
the presence of a stranger and trotted across the linoleum on clicking

claws, to plant its wet nose under the cuff of Allen's pants. Allen reached down to offer his extended hand, felt the animal's tongue dart across his fingertips, and then Jamie was opening the back door and sharply ordering the dog outside. The puppy paused to greet the old dog with a respectful sniff, then raced gaily out past his owner's legs. The boy closed the door and returned to his chair, having said not a word to the newcomer. Allen hoped this silence wouldn't last all the way to Seattle.

Allen cleared his dishes, letting Rachel serve the boy a final breakfast. Pete swallowed the dregs of his coffee and went out the back door, where he stepped into his work boots as if this morning was no different from any other. Jamie bent over the food on his plate and inserted each bite into his mouth, chewing as if it was a school assignment, taking large swallows of milk after each mouthful to force it down his throat. Seeing the heavy weather the boy was making of it, Allen went back outside, leaning against the post that held up the porch roof.

The cows mooed in the milking shed, a rooster was crowing, birds flitted overhead in the sweet blue sky, and Allen wanted nothing more than to drive away and leave them to it. He was paranoid, he was nuts. This kid hadn't followed the instructions on that sheet of paper, he wasn't some juvenile psychopath ready to succumb to a fit of pique and burn down the Johnson house with everyone inside. *You've been in this business too long,* he berated himself. *Short-timer's jitters got to you, and now you're about to undo all the good these people have done for this poor kid in the last two and a half months, and for what? A sheet of paper. A sheet of fantasy hidden inside a box of stories.*

But he couldn't chance it. His head told him to go home, but his gut told him that Jamie was just the kind of prepubescent boy who snapped, who took a rifle to school one sunny morning to get even with the bullies, who bashed in the skull of the neighbor's kid to see what happened.

Who cold-bloodedly rigged a booby trap in the controls of his abusive father's plane.

Had Jamie intended to be on the plane, when he'd set the trap? Was the device another form of the self-destructive play that Rachel had mentioned, typical of the disturbed adolescent—suicide as ultimate control, linked in Jamie's case with a means of ensuring his father's love, plunging together into the deep blue sea? Had the boy intended a murder-suicide, only to have it thwarted by the chance timing of Alice's appearance in the library?

But the question that really tormented Allen's inner vision was this: Five years ago, with his mother's blood drying on his clothes, had anyone thought to test the bereft child's hands for gunshot residue?

And eight months before that, had there been a search for a rock—not a big rock, fit for an adult hand, but small enough for a slight seven-year-old to lift—with a stain and perhaps a few blond hairs attached, discarded in the lake?

It was too much. Allen left the porch and took a slow circuit around the barn. Pete was muttering to his cows. When Allen neared the house again, he could see Rachel talking to the boy. Her face was serious, but not tragic. The boy's face was not visible.

Allen took two steps up and crossed the back porch. When he opened the kitchen door, the small dog shot out of nowhere, skittering across the linoleum, coming to rest with his paws on the boy's knees. Jamie reached down to ease the dog back to the floor, a gesture that appeared habitual. He followed it by a caress of the puppy's ears, then, for the first time, looked at Allen.

"You're sure we can't take Terry with us?"

"We need to leave him here for now. But I promise, I'll do everything I can to get you two back together as soon as possible."

The look Jamie gave him held no belief in it at all.

At the front door, Jamie stood stiffly while Rachel hugged him, then shook hands with Pete and turned for the steps. Rachel stayed on the threshold, but Pete went with the boy, his hand resting on Jamie's shoulder. The dog fretted around their feet, knowing something was up and not wanting to be left out. Jamie took one step and the puppy got in his way, bouncing eagerly around his legs and nearly tripping the boy. Jamie took another step, again hindered by the animal, and then the third time the dog got underfoot, he drew back his leg and aimed a vicious kick straight at the small animal's rib cage. Pete felt it coming; either that, or he happened to bend down at just the right instant, because his hand on the thin shoulder unbalanced the boy just enough that his kick landed a glancing blow, spinning Terry around and off the porch steps, but saving him from real injury. The dog yelped in surprise and pain, and then Pete scooped the creature up and handed him to Rachel. She set the dog down on the floor inside, and shut the door in the animal's face. Nobody said anything, least of all Jamie, who continued down the steps and got into the car, taking with him only the backpack he'd arrived with.

In the rearview mirror, Allen saw Rachel drop her head and turn to

Pete, the farmer's powerful arms wrapping around his wife. The house receded in the back window; the road rose and dipped, and the last thing Allen saw in his mirror was the small head of a dog, stuck out from between the bright curtains of a room on the top floor, barking furiously.

Jamie did not look back.

Chapter 30

TEN MILES DOWN THE ROAD, ALLEN SPOKE FOR THE FIRST TIME. "I'M sorry, Jamie." *Sorry you had to get a father like yours, sorry we adults weren't there sooner, sorry I can't close the door yet.* When there was no answer, Allen took his tired eyes from the road and leaned slightly forward so he could see his passenger's face. The dark lashes were lowered, the young head nodding with the movements of the car.

The boy slept for two hours, waking when Allen stopped at a busy gas station to fill the tank and use the john. At Allen's suggestion, the boy followed him into the rest room, going into one of the stalls to pee.

"You want anything to drink? Maybe a snack for later?" he asked, but Jamie just returned to the car, fastened his seat belt, and closed his eyes. Allen went into the small store to pay, picking out some cans of fruit juice and snack food for the boy, and a large coffee and packet of No-Doz for himself. He paid cash for the lot.

By one in the afternoon the car had left Montana and was in the narrow strip of northern Idaho, and its driver was beyond the resuscitating powers of No-Doz. Coeur d'Alene was enough of a tourist center to offer an anonymous motel room even at this early hour. He picked a place at random, bringing the car to a halt under some trees a distance from the office.

He rested his hands on the wheel, wanting desperately to let his forehead follow suit. "Jamie, I haven't slept much in the last few days." *Since Tuesday,* he realized. *And Rae leaves in twenty-one hours.* "Can I trust you not to run away?"

"Where would I go?"

It was their first exchange since leaving the Johnson farm, and Allen might have wished it was something positive, or at least personal, but he was too weary to do anything more than take note of how dead the boy's voice sounded. He half fell out of the car and trudged across the sweltering parking lot to register.

He chose a room with two beds, upstairs at the back, and told the woman he'd only need one of her plastic key-cards. As he walked back through the sun, he would not have been too surprised to find the passenger seat empty, but Jamie was there, staring straight ahead. Allen moved the car around to the back of the motel, taking a space immediately next to the open-air stairway.

He turned off the engine and said, "We need to follow the same routine we did before, going in so people don't notice a man in his fifties traveling with someone your age. The room is up that flight of stairs and to the left, should be the second door along. You remember how to use one of these things?" He held out the key-card.

Jamie nodded and took the plastic strip, gathered up his backpack, and climbed the stairs. Allen watched the boy disappear around the corner. He'd put on a few pounds over the summer, and some height, but he still looked young for his age, and was still unreadable. *What was going on inside that head?* Allen asked himself.

Allen shook off his reverie, reached back to grab his carry-on and the bag of junk food from the backseat, and followed Jamie up the stairs. The second door was ajar; once inside, Allen turned the dead bolt and fixed the chain.

The boy was sitting on one of the chairs across from the television, staring down at his hands. Allen dropped both bags onto the fake-wood desk next to the phone, reached past the sitting figure to close the drapes against the afternoon sun, then lowered himself to the edge of the second chair.

"Jamie, we have a whole lot of talking to do, you and I. I don't want you to worry about it, because I'm still on your side." As he said it, he realized that, God help him, it was nothing short of the truth. Even if he was eventually forced to turn the kid in for murdering his father, he would fight for him every step of the way. And he'd thought the Johnsons were hopeless ... "But an awful lot has happened. Did Rachel tell you anything?"

"She said my father had disappeared and that you'd have to take me away for a while, until you figured out what happened."

"I'm taking you to Alice. She and I will help you. Jamie, we're not going to abandon you." *Betray you, maybe, but not abandon you.*

The boy's eyes came up, and Allen was interested to see the apprehension in the slim body ease a fraction. Had he been afraid Allen might be returning him to a still-living father? Or was his relief because Allen did not appear to know what he'd done to the plane? The brown eyes gave away nothing.

"Where are we going?" he asked.

"Seattle. We'll meet Alice there tomorrow. But we'll stick to the smaller highways once we get into Washington, and I need to be rested for that. I've got to get some sleep. Will you be okay? I have to ask you not to leave the room."

"Can I watch the TV?"

"Sure, if you keep the sound down. Or there's this." Allen went to his carry-on and retrieved the *Rings* trilogy he'd stowed there. He tucked it into his arm, keeping it concealed until he was standing directly in front of the boy, then presented it to him, watching intently for any sign of fear or guilt. But all he saw was surprise followed by curiosity, as Jamie reached out to take the books.

"They're the ones from your room," Allen explained, in case the boy thought they were a replacement.

Jamie looked up quickly. "You've been in my house?"

"I was looking for some indication of where your father might have gone," Allen said, with a meaningful raised eyebrow. This, too, made no impression on the boy.

"My father wasn't home? Did Mrs. Mendez let you in?"

"I got in myself."

"You broke in? What are you, some kind of spy or something?"

Allen laughed aloud. "Nothing like that. Just lucky."

"But my father wasn't there."

Allen looked at the boy's clever young face. He sat down again. "Jamie, I believe your father is dead."

The boy's pupils darkened. "No. He can't be."

"Jamie, it's been on the news, but I asked Rachel not to let you know. His plane went down over the sea. As far as I know, they're still looking for the wreckage." There was some reaction to the detail of the plane going down, but hardly anything that looked like a start of guilt. Maybe now was best, to push for it. "Jamie, I found the piece of paper in the back of the third book."

The boy looked confused for a moment, and then it hit him, what Allen's words meant, and his face flushed with enough guilt to make any prosecutor grin with joy. The expression made Allen, reluctant prosecutor that he was, feel queasy.

Still, he pressed on. "It had to do with how to make a plane crash," he said, but he was talking to boy's bent head. "What do you know about it, Jamie?"

"I found it, in my father's office. I thought, I don't know, maybe he was going to do some kind of insurance thing. He'd been talking about it the day before, how the plane would be worth more crashed than it was on the ground. And he must've asked Howard to research it, because it was some kind of printout from the Internet, it looked like. My father . . . he really doesn't know anything about computers." He glanced up at that, as if to see how Allen took this revelation of weakness in the All-powerful. Seeing no reaction, he ducked his head again, waiting for Allen's response.

So what did you expect, a tearful confession? Allen rubbed at his second-day stubble and went to use the toilet. He splashed the road film from his face and drank some cold water, thinking that his mouth was going to taste monstrously foul when he woke up if he didn't brush his teeth, but the effort of digging through his carry-on was too great. He went back into the main room and tossed Jamie the remote for the TV.

"No X-rated films, you hear?" he said, dredging up a grin to make it a joke. "Your aunt Rachel would never forgive me."

Jamie gave him an uncertain smile back, and Allen was overwhelmed with the pathos of the whole situation. Before he could think about it, he squatted down and put a hand around the back of the boy's neck, giving it a soft squeeze. "We'll get through this together, Jamie. I promise you."

Before Allen could rise, Jamie whirled in the chair and threw his arms around Allen, hanging on for all he was worth. Allen's immediate impulse was to pull away fast—with abused kids, you had to watch out for their own assumptions about adult behavior. But he caught himself; the boy was vibrating with tension, but there was no eroticism in the contact, so Allen stayed where he was, allowing the boy to cling to him until the tremors began to fade. Only then did he stand up, slowly. He patted the boy's shoulder and walked to the bed near the door. His boots came off reluctantly, unlaced for the first time in thirty hours, and he gave his body over to the embrace of the blessedly firm mattress. Paradise.

The TV came on behind him, immediately dialed down to a whisper. Allen said into the pillow, "You can put it a little louder than that." The sound came up one increment, and then a second. "Oh, and if you get hungry, there's some snacks in the paper bag."

Allen's watchful brain, fading fast, did a final perimeter check of the room and the situation, making sure he'd covered everything. He thought he had; if not, he'd done his best. Now if only the kid didn't try to crawl into bed with him and send him straight through the roof. If only he could be absolutely positive that the boy's fervent embrace had not been the gesture of a clever manipulator. If only he didn't keep seeing the open, smiling brown face of a boy in a ragged Eiffel Tower T-shirt, leading his new GI friends into an ambush.

Allen lay, motionless and beyond the reach of any dreams, for four hours. The room was dim when his eyes came open. He lay for a minute, to be certain that nothing nearby had caused him to wake, but his ears held no fading memory of a disturbance; merely his internal clock telling him that it was time to be on their way.

He turned over in the bed, obscurely pleased by the awareness that despite his mind's doubts, his jungle reflexes had trusted Jamie enough to turn his back on him while he slept. Jamie heard his motion and looked across the room, a chocolate smear in one corner of his mouth and a half-empty bottle of apple juice in his hand.

Allen sat up, scrubbed at the remnants of his Harrison Ford haircut, and asked the boy what he was watching.

"A Jackie Chan movie. I've seen it before."

"You hungry?"

"Yeah. I ate the chips and most of the cookies."

"That's fine. I saw a burger place coming in, I'll go and get us dinner. What kind of burgers you like?"

"The big ones. With bacon?"

"Fries? Milk shake?"

"Can I have a Coke?" He made it sound like a rare treat.

"Sure."

Allen shaved and showered and put on a clean shirt, then his jacket, since it seemed to be cooling off. At the door he told Jamie, "Lock the door and do up the chain behind me, and don't let anyone in."

He waited until he heard both locks slide shut, and went to buy their dinner. In the end, he bought enough for four, including the dinner salad and iced tea that a woman might order.

He knocked on the room door, and saw with approval the peephole go dark before the locks opened. They ate most of the food watching the end of the Jackie Chan movie, and Allen packed away the remaining burger in case one of them got hungry later. The iced tea went down the toilet, the salad he emptied into one of the bags to leave in the next garbage can he happened across. The ghostly family of four packed their bags and left Coeur d'Alene. By nightfall, they had crossed into Washington State.

As a native of western Washington, Allen had never really felt that the dry, flat farmland east of the mountains was part of the same state. Still, it was comforting to see the familiar colors of the highway signs, and to know that by morning, he would be closing in on home ground.

Not that he intended to be home. Twenty-six years of painfully constructed habit died hard, and he could no more have pointed the car's nose straight west along I90 than he could have strolled into the Coeur d'Alene police station with Jamie and asked one of the cops if the kid looked familiar. He had no reason to think anyone was looking for them; on the other hand, he'd not reached his current ripe old age with no felonies tacked to his name by flirting with carelessness. That was one of the reasons he'd bought the Honda back in Helena, because here its Washington State plates would blend in. And why he would now follow the roads less traveled, not only as the less obvious way from there to here, but because any pursuing car would have a harder time to hide, to say nothing of avoiding the risk of looking up to find a bored Highway Patrol car riding his back bumper. The southern routes were longer and more tiring, which made it unlikely they would reach Seattle that day, but the back of his scalp was happier if he didn't zero in on the target.

Besides, it would give him more time to talk with Jamie. If the kid ever woke up.

The curly dark head was resting against the passenger window, using one of Allen's sweatshirts as a pillow. From time to time, when oncoming headlights lit up the front seat, Allen would glance over at his companion, wondering. It was such a straightforward job, the one he'd done all these years—complicated in its details, sure, but basically it had boiled down to taking endangered innocents from a threat and hiding them until the threat could be rendered null, either by distance or steel bars.

He'd never before faced the question of whether or not he was helping an actual innocent. Sure, some of the mothers had taken out their own pain on their children, but once the main tormenter had been removed from the picture and counseling begun, they had generally settled down to a guilt-ridden but affectionate maternal role.

As he'd thought back in May: If Jamie was even a year older, Allen might have been more willing to consider the boy lost, already formed into his adult role as a perpetuator of abuse. A year younger, and he'd have been more confident of the child's malleability, more secure in the knowledge that surrounding the boy with Rachel's family would wither the root cause of violent behavior. Violent adults are created, and the chief element in their makeup is shame: shame at being pushed around, shame at being too weak to protect themselves (and often their mothers and siblings) from Dad's fists, shame at passing on the only form of self-respect they had ever learned—beating up someone smaller. A childhood of humiliation rides up on the tumult of adolescence: It was at Jamie's age that kids joined gangs, that kids shot up schools full of tormentors. That kids hauled off and brutally kicked the dog that loved them.

The boys who brought guns to their middle school were often as soft and unformed-looking as Jamie. They probably looked every bit as innocent when they were asleep with their head against the side window of a car, traveling an unlit road in the middle of the night. They probably showed just as little grief at the news that a father was dead. Allen opened his mouth to ask the kid about explosives, to ask him if he'd ever researched bombs or looked at one of the school-shooter Web sites on his computer, but then he made himself shut his mouth, unwilling to bring it all out into the open here and now.

Alice, Allen said to the road ahead, *I hope to God you can sort this mess out.*

Chapter 31

JAMIE WATCHED BETWEEN SLITTED EYELIDS AS THE ROAD SCROLLED PAST the headlights of the car. This was turning into one of Father's hunting trips, endless back roads at all hours, the warm feeling of having Father all to himself alongside the growing knot of what was to come, until it would feel like when he had the flu, shivery on one level but safe in bed on the other. He often pretended to be asleep when Father was driving, too. But he'd never really thought that Father was fooled by the act.

Allen, though, seemed to be buying it, which made Jamie both happy at the man's innocence and frightened for him. Because Father wasn't dead, whether his plane went down or not. Jamie didn't know how he could be so sure about it, but in his bones he just couldn't imagine that the world was now without Father. Which meant that Father was not dead. And if Father was alive, sooner or later he would come for him, that too was beyond question. If Allen was standing between them when it happened, the big man wouldn't stand a chance.

He just wished he could get his thoughts straight. Allen was a good person who wanted only to help him, and Father was . . . well, he was Father, and about as helpful as a coiled cobra. So why didn't he side with Allen? Why couldn't he just shift his loyalties? He did understand why Allen had to take him away from Montana—he didn't like leaving, even though Montana bored him to tears, but he understood it. One thing he did have straight in his head: The Johnson farm was no place for Father. Jamie had been living in a state of huge frustration and cold terror ever since Sally had gone missing, and (other than leaving Terry behind, which really sucked) he'd have been willing to run through fire to get into Allen's car and drive away. He felt like one of those mother birds that fakes a hurt wing to lead a predator away from the nest. In spite of his intentions, first Rachel and then Sally had got in under his skin, and although he'd do his best in the future to make sure nobody ever did that again, he still had to say, he didn't want Father anywhere near them, not in the sort of mood he was sure to be in when he finally laid eyes on Jamie.

That was why he'd gone into a panic when Sally had disappeared. The idea of Father's hands on that little girl was more than Jamie could bear. He'd wanted to run off then and there, to give Father what he really wanted, so he'd leave the Johnsons alone.

But he'd allowed Pete and Rachel to keep him there, partly because he wasn't absolutely positive that it was Father—or Howard—who'd led Sally away, but also because he figured that if he wasn't there when Father came, it would make it even worse for the Johnsons. He'd stayed, in truth, because he couldn't convince the whole family that they had to leave, and he figured that he, at least, knew what they would be in for, and he would be on the lookout. He'd not gotten much sleep, the last week. And no computer time either, since he'd spent most of every night watching the dark driveway and the access road beyond, praying that he wouldn't see a set of approaching headlights that slowed and then went dark.

At least Pete had a gun. And although Jamie wasn't supposed to know how to get at it, he'd figured out where the key was before dawn the day after the stranger had appeared. He didn't think he could shoot Father face-to-face, but maybe he could have made Father think he would, and buy time for the Johnsons to escape.

He'd pictured the scene a hundred times during those long nights just past: Father looming up in the front door; Jamie standing his ground with Pete's bird gun; Rachel and Sally and the others creeping down the stairs at his back and fleeing out the kitchen door; Terry standing by his leg, teeth bared; and the look on Father's face. Jamie's guts would go into a cold twist at the thought of that look, the rage that turned Father's eyes to ice chips and made his mouth turn up into an expression only a crazy person would imagine was a smile. But Jamie's cinematic imagination persisted in adding to Father's expression just a trace of respect, when Jamie stood up to him at last. Late on the fourth or fifth night of his watch, the strange thought had come to him that Father might even like to be killed by his son, that it would make him proud, as he bled to death on Rachel's braided carpet, to know that his son had the guts to pull the trigger.

But it was nonsense, and that particular part of the fantasy had burst faster than a soap bubble. Gun or no, Father would have taken him apart. And then he would have gone after the Johnsons, for protecting him. And then he would have come after Allen, and Alice, and anyone else linked to Jamie's helpers.

But then Allen arrived so openly that anyone for miles around could see, and led Jamie away from the Johnson house in broad daylight, which was about as much safety as Jamie could give the family. And so here he was, sitting in a car with a man who figured he was rescuing Jamie, while all the time Jamie knew that he himself held the man's life in his own skinny hands. He would allow Allen to carry him far away from Montana, since it was just possible that everyone was right, that Sally's abductor was some stranger and that the family hadn't come onto Father's radar, and nobody was watching to see him get into the car and drive off. But in any case the question was the same: How long would he let Allen keep him? He kind of liked Allen, more than he'd thought possible, but he had to stop doing that; he might have to give Allen to Father in order to save his own hide, before this was over.

It was so confusing, and he was really tired. It was no wonder that he'd turned to the laptop, its black case so comfortingly real, the on-line conversations so unconnected with murderous parents and the stench of cow shit. Last night, spotting the familiar shape in Allen's leather carry-on while he was looking for something to eat, it had been like settling into a mother's lap. *Allen's laptop's like a lap,* he thought, sleep rising up until his thoughts began to run together. And Allen never even suspected. He was as clueless as Rachel, Rachel who'd thought Jamie generous and good for wanting to get away from the farm. None of them knew what Jamie was inside; none of them realized that Father was the only one who really knew him.

As Jamie's eyelids closed for real, his last confused image was not of the road, but of his shoe kicking hard at the warm, eager, loyal dog at his feet.

Why had he done that, anyway?

ALLEN DROVE THROUGH THE NIGHT, STOPPING ONCE FOR GAS AND COFFEE; Jamie did not stir. The hills rose up and the vegetation in the headlights greened. They went over White Pass, and on the other side, for the first time, Allen began to feel safe. Home ground now, he told himself. Just a matter of hours until he could meet Alice and begin to unlock the conundrum.

There was a diner open in Morton, and he went in and bought some dry-looking sandwiches. Jamie was sitting up when he got back into the car.

"You hungry?" he asked the boy, putting the sandwiches on the dash.

Jamie hesitated. "I need to pee." He shot a glance at Allen to see his reaction, but the admission—which Father would have twisted around, made into a sure sign of weakness, and then used to torment him—had little or no impression on this driver.

"The toilet's just inside the door," Allen said, starting in on his sandwich. When the boy got back, Allen put the car back into gear. "We'll get to the freeway in a little while, check into a motel for a couple of hours before we turn north for Seattle."

"Wish I was old enough to help drive," Jamie offered.

God, don't we all, Allen thought fervently. If the boy had been eighteen, none of these problems would have come up—others, no doubt, but not these, and they sure as hell wouldn't have been Allen's. He would have spent the last week putting up bookshelves with Rae then packed his bags and gone to the airport with her. That was another reason he wanted to stop when they got to the freeway instead of pressing on to Seattle, barely two hours north: Rae's flight was at ten o'clock. If he reached Seattle in plenty of time, he did not think he could bear it, knowing she was so close.

"Too bad it's not daylight," he told his passenger, to take his thoughts off of Rae and airplanes. "You'd see that we're driving straight between two mountains. One of them's a volcano."

"Really?"

"Mount Saint Helens. Used to be the most beautiful mountain, had a gorgeous lake right at the top. I went there when I was your age, we used to find these rocks that would float on water. Of course, that's because it was a volcano, but nobody thought about it then."

"Is that the one that erupted a while ago?"

"She sure did. Covered three states with ash, killed fifty-two people, knocked down millions of trees, and blew off half the mountain."

Jamie was craning to look out of the driver's side window, as if gouts of red lava might shoot up through the darkness.

"Maybe you'll see it in the morning. For sure you'll see Mount Rainier, which is on the other side. That's a volcano, too, but so far it's stayed dormant."

"Man," Jamie commented, impressed despite its invisibility. A real volcano.

By eleven P.M. they were off the busy freeway, at a motel, locked securely in a room that smelled of cigarettes and room freshener. Again, Allen bolted the door, pulled the drapes, and dropped onto the bed near the door. And again, once the big man's breathing had slowed, the boy crept over to the leather carry-on and eased the laptop from its interior. The television played on, just loud enough to cover his sounds; Allen didn't hear a thing.

AT LAST! JAMIE THOUGHT. FOR THE FIRST TIME IN TWO WEEKS HE COULD log on at a time when the good players were on board. Between keeping watch over the Johnson house and being on the road, he hadn't had a good game session since Sally had met the man. And he could probably count on at least two or three hours of uninterrupted play time, by just keeping an ear out for any change in Allen's breathing. God knew he'd had plenty of practice listening for oncoming adults.

There were a couple of familiar names, one of whom greeted the appearance of Jamie's player with a rude message that Jamie took as it was meant, as an electronic high-five. Jamie sent him a similar message, and slipped into the game's progress as if he'd never been away.

Online games were a community venture, with players you got to know and either liked or didn't, just like real life. Some of them were diabolically clever, others so clueless, Jamie didn't know how they managed to boot up their computers in the first place, but that, too, was how things went. Every so often, usually really late at night, when just the right combination of good players were on at the same time, the game took on a life of its own, and became considerably more real than the flesh and blood creatures whose fingers manipulated the keyboards. Hours would flash by, alliances made and broken, electronic creatures blown away, experience points accumulated, and riches hoarded or spent, and Jamie would come out of it bleary-eyed but content with the world.

No danger of that happening tonight. Lord Bane was there, a guy Jamie visualized as six-four, stoop-shouldered, and covered in zits—he was such a perma-newbie, thought with that name was the coolest thing, but a ten-year-old girl could outplay him. His name was probably Seymour or something. And Skidgirl, who wasn't a bad player but she had a habit of stabbing you in the back after you'd made a covenant, which had gotten her shunned for a while but maybe she'd learned her lesson.

The action wasn't too bad. The zone had a new player called King Barney who was pretty good, and there was a kind of interesting development between two of the alliances. Then after half an hour one of his favorite rivals logged on.

Silverfish was a hard-core brain. Once when Jamie had asked him why he'd called himself after a bug, the guy had told him, "It's because they're ubiquitous." Jamie'd gone on, left it like he knew what the guy meant, but he copied down the word with care, and later he looked it up. It meant that they were everywhere, and Silverfish sure was. Nothing seemed to get by him, he always spotted the best loot, always slipped in and snatched it up, always managed to outsmart the other players. Ubiquitous.

Of course, the guy practically lived online. It was rare for Jamie to play for very long before Silverfish slid onto the screen—maybe the maniac played two games at once, shifting between one and another. Like yesterday, when Jamie'd logged on in Coeur d'Alene (which he'd spelled Cor dalene) and within five minutes the guy'd been there, asking him where the hell he'd been and then telling Jamie some cool things to do when he got to Seattle on Sunday.

After twenty minutes and a couple of clever moves, Silverfish began to exchange messages with Jamie, whose character for that game was RageDaemon. In between moves, Silverfish went right to the point.

S: you hear anything about a new game coming up, combo of Tolkein and Lovecraft?
RD: gotta name?
S: Death Head, somethin like that. Heard it had some killer graphix. Didn't wanna put it out to those losers, mite be nice ta have a game only players can get into.

RD: I no what u mean, but sory, never heard of it

S: You been outta touch today, man.

RD: yeah, still on the road

S: hope you're someplace cool

RD: Holiday Inn, god watta dump.

S: Fer a minnit I thought you meant you had a satellite link in your car, that'd be killer.

RD: I wish. we're talkin laptop and phon line here, the download time sux.

S: They make video players for cars, why not wire in modems?

RD: why not

S: Seriously, they even have those Onstar things, why not just upgrade the link so you can use it for somethin more than asking where the hell you are when you wake up with a killer hangover on a deserted road. Not like I'd know, ya unnerstand, haha. Fords have em I think, the Onstar things.

RD: hondas don't, not this one anyway. but u gotta great futur ahed of u man, as an invetnor.

S: Yeh right. You seein anything good on your trip, or just drivin to gramma's with the folks?

RD: screw that, man, no gramma here. ever seen a voclano? they should put one on the game

S: Mt Doom, throw in that ring, Frodo.

RD: that's what it looks like, steamin and everthing.

S: You serious?

RD: nah, not when we went by. but it does, they say. blew up a few years ago, wiped out a bunch a people.

S: Hey, killer. Yr right, I can just see a nice juicy volcano in the middle of the game, blowin up and everythin.

RD: gotta go, man. lemme know if you hear any more about that Deth Head game.

S: Will do. I'm gonna go crash for a while. Too wired, cant see straight.

RD: see ya

The game after that wasn't as much fun without Silverfish, but Jamie played anyway for another three and a half hours, until Allen's breathing changed, ending in a snort. Snatching the phone and power connections from the laptop, Jamie pushed its lid down, shoved it under a pillow, and stared fixedly at the television screen. He waited, eyes glued on the screen, until Allen's breathing resumed, slow and regular.

However, there didn't seem to be much happening online, so he shut down the game properly, then went back in to the control panel to wipe out his footprints, resetting the dial-up to get rid of his phone card numbers, wiping out all traces of the game itself. He slid the laptop back into the carry-on, drawing the top shut as Allen had left it. He plopped down again in front of the television, and started scrolling through with the remote.

There was even less happening on that.

Allen woke for real a while later, having slept for five hours. He stretched, and turned over to see what Jamie was watching at four in the morning. It appeared to be a hot-dog-eating contest. Allen shook his head at the antics.

"You hungry?"

"Not for hot dogs," the boy told him, making Allen laugh aloud.

"It's a deal."

Again, Allen went out for the food, bringing back two hamburgers and an order of French toast from the twenty-four-hour restaurant down the road. He'd bought the breakfast for himself, but he offered it to the boy, who shook his head and reached for one of the burgers.

"Thought you might be getting tired of hamburgers," Allen said.

"I haven't had hamburgers all summer," the boy answered around a mouthful.

"Doesn't Rachel make them?"

"Oh yeah, I mean this kind of burger. Hers are more like steaks, with these big fat slices of red tomatoes and buns she makes herself. She even makes the catsup and pickles!"

"They're interesting people, aren't they?"

"I guess. I remember thinking one time, if the world got wiped out, they probably wouldn't even know it for a month."

"You'd tell Pete, and he'd nod and go milk the cows," Allen said with a smile.

"They'd have to eat an awful lot of eggs, though, to make up for not selling them in town."

"Do you want to go back there, Jamie? I mean, if you could choose any place in the world to live, would it be with them?"

Jamie hunched over his half-eaten burger as if this was a trick question concealing a threat of punishment.

"You don't have to decide now," Allen hastened to say. "Let's see what turns up, in the next few days."

"When will we see Alice?"

"We're only a few hours from Seattle. I want to stick to the back roads, but even then we'll be there by mid-morning."

"Okay." Jamie finished his meal and, at Allen's suggestion, brushed his teeth. Showers could wait until Seattle. They went down to the

Honda together, and Allen pulled onto the northbound 15, but in a few miles he got off again, to join the smaller road that ran more or less parallel to the freeway.

A low-slung rental car pulled out of the motel complex behind him. A car that had been hired by its driver at the Seattle-Tacoma airport late the night before, following his arrival on a flight from Las Vegas, a flight that was booked four minutes after Silverfish left RageDaemon sitting alone in the Coeur d'Alene motel.

In the darkness, Allen did not notice the car.

Chapter 32

SOME MILES UP THE DARK TWO-LANE ROAD, WITH THE SWEET SCENT OF hay coming through the half-open window beside him, Allen glanced in the rearview mirror. Since leaving the freeway, two or three pairs of headlights had ridden there for a while before turning off into a side road or a farm drive. Two cars were back there now, but the drivers did not seem to be in a hurry

Allen was, but he could not allow his impatience to influence the weight of his foot on the accelerator, any more than it had the choice of highway over back roads. Rae would be having her coffee and checking her passport . . . But tickets could be changed, and with luck, Alice would soon take over responsibility for this child sitting beside him. However, until he had Jamie off his hands, he would continue at his pace of three miles over the speed limit, on roads where no Highway Patrol lurked, where a dusty five-year-old Honda was an un-remarkable thing.

The boy sat motionless, facing the windshield, radiating patience and innocence. Allen might not be anyone's father, but he was enough of a parent-by-proxy to sense when a kid was hiding something. There was something the kid didn't want him to ask about. What that might be, Allen hadn't a clue. Well, he thought, no time like the present.

"Jamie, I was wondering: Why were you so sure it was your father who took Sally away from the farm?"

After a minute, Jamie gave a sigh. "I guess I never really believed I could get away from him. He always knows everything. You can't hide anything from him. So when I heard there was a strange man around the place, I just figured it was him, coming to take me back."

"You don't think that he's dead?"

"No." No hesitation, none at all.

"Why?"

That was more difficult. "Because . . . I think I'd know. Like, I'd feel it. And besides, if he did die, it wouldn't be because of some dumb plane accident."

"How would he die?"

"Somebody would kill him. I mean, like shoot him or run him over or something. Not an accident."

This was getting them nowhere, Allen thought, this glorification of the all-powerful father. "Okay, then tell me something else. Why did it panic you so, when you walked in on Pete Junior cleaning the rabbits?"

That got a reaction: Jamie hunched up as if Allen had jabbed his belly.

"Jamie, I'm just trying to figure out what's going on. I can't help you unless you tell me. You can wait and tell Alice if you'd rather, but you're going to have—"

"No!" Jamie said, his voice quiet but sure. "Not her. I can't tell her that. She'd never understand."

"I doubt that. But why don't you give it to me, and if I think she needs to know, I'll give her the parts of it I judge that she can handle." Absurd, of course: What Alice had seen by way of atrocity left him in the dust.

"I don't know. It's . . ."

"Was it the blood?"

As Allen anticipated, the word set off a response. "I don't like blood. I mean, even before . . . My mom, she died . . ."

"I know how she died," Allen said gently. He didn't intend the child to relive that particular horror—but it was too late.

"There was . . . God, there was so much blood. At first I figured it was a joke, you know? Or an accident, like somebody'd dropped a can of paint or something, it was just all over the room. I remember thinking, Mom's going to be so mad, it's got on Father's favorite chair." Allen translated this: Father's going to be so mad. "I was just a little kid, you know? I guess that's why I thought it was paint. And then I saw that she was sitting there and it wasn't just *on* her . . ."

"And the rabbits reminded you of that?" Allen interrupted.

"I wish," the boy exclaimed, to Allen's astonishment. "No. About a month later my father took me hunting. I think it was out of season or he didn't have a deer license, something like that, I don't know, but it was the first time I'd gone and he really wanted to take me out. Anyway, we went out to this place a friend of his owns up in the hills, and went shooting. The friend has a salt lick—deer like salt, you know?—and he puts out corn in the winter to bring the deer around, but it still took all weekend for us to get one. Father saw it first, and told me to shoot it, but I couldn't. You know, like its eyes reminded me of Mom or something. Like I said, I was just a kid. So he shot it instead, and made me go up with him and help him bleed it, and clean it." His voice wavered and climbed, but he went on. "I was sort of crying, you know, like kids do, and that's when he got mad."

Allen braced himself.

Jamie drew a breath, and on the exhale he said, "He made me wear the skin."

"The fresh skin?" Allen said, appalled.

"Yeah. It was gross. He kind of, well, he sort of tied it around me and made me walk back to the cabin in it."

"Ah, Jamie," Allen groaned, but the boy wasn't quite finished.

"And that's when he started the hunting game. Like I was the deer, you know?"

Ice tingled through Allen, and he took his eyes from the road, looking with horror at the boy. But Jamie's face was calm, now that he'd told it.

"You mean, he'd pretend to be stalking you?"

"Yeah. And sometimes I'd hear his rifle behind me, you know the noise when you slide a bullet in?"

"But he didn't . . . ?"

"You mean, did he actually shoot at me? Oh, no. Well, once or twice, but only as a joke."

"Fuck, Jamie."

The boy laughed, at the unexpected adult obscenity as much as Allen's reaction. "Kinda creepy, isn't it?"

"You could say that."

"So I guess," Jamie mused, going back to Allen's original question with remarkable equanimity, "Pete Junior's rabbits kind of took me by surprise. It was like, the farm was this whole different world, then to walk in on all that blood. It just was sort of a shock. Stupid of me, I know. I wouldn't do it now."

Shock's the word, thought Allen, stunned to momentary silence by the response to his first question. There was a lot more he needed to ask; would all his questions lead them to searing images such as the boy wrapped in a bloody deerskin? He tried to choose his next one. What about, *Tell me about the death of your first-grade friend, smiling blond Able Shepherd?* Or, *How did that scruffy-looking white dog you used to have actually die?* And, *How did you feel about your mother, before her death? Did you know how to use a shotgun, when you were seven?* And, *You say your father was an ignoramus when it came to computers, yet it was his muscle-bound assistant who printed the page from an obscure Web site?* And, a big one, the answer to which Allen already shied away from: *What went on in that small, windowless room next to your father's bedroom?*

While Allen's thoughts roiled and Jamie congratulated himself on getting away without revealing the most shameful part of Father's hunting game, a quarter of a mile back a blinker signaled and the squarish headlights of the Volvo that had been following them slowed to turn. Allen nursed the Honda around a tight S-bend in the road, then picked up speed again as his lights showed a straight way ahead. The smell of manure came strongly through the windows, causing Jamie to stir and comment, "It stinks just like the farm."

"Cows everywhere—" Allen was starting to say, when high beams filled the back window and a lot happened all at once.

The car riding behind the Volvo had reacted to the open road like a loosed arrow. It shot toward them, a low, fast shape that took the bend at high speed and was now barreling up on the Honda as if it was parked. Allen's foot jammed onto the accelerator, with no discernible change in the rate the following car was gaining on them.

"Get your head down between your knees," he ordered the boy. He heard the seat belt catch at the sudden movement, and then unreel as the thin chest curled more slowly down behind the dash. *I should've put him in the back,* passed through Allen's mind, and then there was no time for thinking.

The low-slung lights came so close to the Honda's back bumper, they vanished, then emerged in the side mirror as the car moved out over the center line. Allen, too, veered over the yellow line, and then the window in front of him made a slapping noise and cracked into a thousand fine lines that spread with the force of the wind. Two more shots came, Allen cursing and struggling to maintain control of the car, aware that one of the shots had hit him somewhere in the meat of his left arm—but it hadn't killed him and he would worry about the damage when the battle was over. He let the Honda sway over the center line while its engine climbed to full push, then in a movement that rational thought had nothing to do with, the hand-brake jerked up, the wheel slammed around, the other car swerved around them and into a white picket fence while in a furious squeal of reversing energies the Honda's smoking tires bit down and catapulted them down the road in the direction they'd come.

Back around the S-bend, Allen spotted the road the Volvo had sedately entered on the left. On the right side its continuation, though paved, was nearly invisible between fences. Allen yanked the wheel and sent the car on two wheels into it, slapped off his headlights (thanking the gods that not all cars were fixed with full-time running lights). He kept his foot down and the wheel rock-steady, blinded by darkness and by the wind funneling through the holes in his windshield, praying that the road stayed straight beyond the last glimpse his headlights had given him.

"Better sit up," he told Jamie. If they went head-on into a parked tractor, the kid had more of a chance if he wasn't already pressed up against the dash.

He felt the boy move upright. A pair of low headlights swept around the bend in back of them; when the lights were past, Allen flicked his own beams on for a fraction of a second, just enough to imprint the road ahead onto his retinas. All clear. He let the car slow, cursing his middle-aged eyes, but he'd made out a fence on his left with a vague shape looming behind it. When the fence broke off, he dove in after it, taking the dirt track slowly so as not to raise any dust. The looming shape was an old barn, plenty big enough to hide a Honda.

He pulled in, turned off the engine, reached up to switch the inside lights to the off position, and jumped out of the car.

"What—" Jamie started to ask.

"Quiet."

Half a mile away, headlights raced back up the main road before turning in to the road that the Volvo had entered. He'd bought them a few minutes.

He patted around the back floor until he found the sweatshirt that Jamie had been using as a pillow. The left sleeve of his shirt was soaked with blood, although he wouldn't know just how bad the damage was until he had a chance to peel away his clothes—the bone and muscle were intact enough to have gripped the wheel, but he'd had to crank it around one-handed. The most immediate danger was leaving a bloody trail, so he bound the sweatshirt around his shirt, pinning its sleeves under his upper arm. Still working by feel, he retrieved the leather carry-on holding his jacket and laptop, slinging it over his good shoulder and transferring the flashlight to his pocket. The rest he would have to abandon: The car would take time to trace, and although he didn't have time to wipe down everything for fingerprints, he assumed that whoever was after them wasn't on the side of law enforcement's records computers.

"Come on," he told Jamie. "Don't shut your door all the way."

"Can I bring my backpack?" came the whisper.

It wasn't heavy, and it was all the boy had. "Okay."

The boy moved with caution across the uneven ground, and Allen rested his hand on the thin shoulder, straining to see. He knew the full moon was up there—if only they'd been in the desert instead of the cloudy Pacific Northwest, they might be able to keep from walking into a ditch, or a string of barbed wire.

His eyes picked out shapes to suggest that the derelict barn had collected a wide assortment of vehicles, but he didn't hold out much hope that any of them would start on first try. Instead, the overgrown once-graveled track continued on, in the same direction as the paved side road but concealed from it by fences and high weeds. They stumbled at first, then found their night feet and were walking with quiet efficiency when the headlights went past on the road, fifty yards away, moving slowly. Allen's hand tightened on the boy's shoulder; they stood still until it was out of hearing. A few minutes later it cruised by again; it wouldn't be long before the car started nosing its way into driveways. He urged Jamie on; in half an hour, it would be growing light, and Charlie would—he caught himself: He was light-headed; there was no Charlie here to fade into the jungle. Fifty-four years old, and he was still walking his first nighttime patrol with the smell of blood in his nostrils.

The house that belonged to the old barn was half a mile down the lane, and apart from the porch light, it was dark enough to suggest that the inhabitants did not attend to predawn milking chores. A dog barked inside, and Allen froze, but it sounded to him like a bark of boredom, not of alarm. That no one hushed it meant either that the inhabitants were heavy sleepers, or that they were away. He urged Jamie up the grass next to the driveway, making for the buildings in back of the house.

There was a garage, but a brief shine from the flashlight revealed a lot of garden furniture, three wheelbarrows in various states of disrepair, and a workshop for refinishing wooden chairs. On the flat graveled ground behind the one-time garage was where Allen found his riches: a two-year-old Ford, next to a Dodge pickup so old it was probably made of cast iron, with drips and tire tracks marking where a third car habitually stood. Allen skipped the securely locked sedan in favor of the pickup. He popped open the door; the overhead light stayed dark, but the interior smelled of cigars, an encouraging sign. He began to search for a key: Just as no farmer would lock up an old truck, neither would he leave its key inside the house, where he'd have to strip off his muddy boots whenever he had to shift a bale of hay or a load of wood. He used his right hand to feel under the seat, cursing under his breath: The left arm was no longer numb. The first metal object his startled fingertips encountered was no key, but an old revolver. He pulled it onto the floor of the truck, and continued his search. No luck there, or in the pocket of the overhead visor. He climbed in and flipped open the glove compartment; when the pale light went on, there it was.

He grabbed the key and closed the flap against the spill of light, then slid out again and whispered to his companion, "Get in."

When the boy was inside, Allen climbed up behind him and eased the heavy door shut, tugging it only until it clicked. He put the key into the ignition, then paused, trying to think against the pain that was now grinding seriously into his left shoulder. The hat—he'd found a baseball cap wedged into the visor. He pulled it on, then reached back into the glove compartment for the glasses he'd glimpsed there—not sunglasses, maybe the farmer's reading specs, but the shape of them would change his face. Next to the glasses lay a half-empty pack of six-inch panatelas. He stuck one between his teeth and slid the box of kitchen matches from their niche inside the cellophane wrapper.

"You better curl up on the floor," he told Jamie.

As the boy sank down, Allen lit the cigar, blew out the match, then turned the key. The truck started, and he found reverse on the second try. Allen backed around, and with no hesitation he switched on the headlights, put it in first gear, and rattled down the driveway, singing clench-toothed into the cigar at the pain shooting up his arm. Without slowing, as if this was a trip he made every morning of his life and he knew there would be no traffic on his road, he swung the wheel to the right, past the big rural mailbox marked THE REIENBACH'S, heading back the way they had come, straight toward the low lights of a slow-moving sports car.

For a moment, he was afraid that the car was going to stop in the middle of the narrow lane and force him either to mow it down or to reverse madly down the narrow road, bullets flying; however, the old truck was so patently not the Honda the gunman was seeking, Allen was allowed to rumble over the weed-covered shoulder and go on his way, puffing his cigar and squinting under his hat through the smoke and the distorting lenses of an astigmatic: old Farmer Joe Reienbach on his way to town. Again with the merest pause, he rolled the truck out onto the main road, turning south, and slowly brought the truck up to speed. No lights followed. As soon as the crossroads was out of sight, he accelerated, tossed the cigar out the window and glasses onto the dash, and watched for some kind of paved surface leading off to the left.

He was lost in no time, which was just fine with him. The road he'd chosen was too well maintained to be a dead-end, and he was bound to come across something going north soon enough. He'd have to do something about the arm before too long, but although it felt as if a pit bull was ripping into it, the bleeding seemed to be slowing; for the moment, they were safe. Time to find out what was going on.

"You can sit up now," he told Jamie.

The boy climbed up from the roomy well, saying with the first excitement he'd ever shown, "Man, that was really amazing, that spin-around turn. How'd you do that?"

"Practice," Allen said, although in truth, he'd been wondering the same thing himself. "How about telling me who that guy was?"

Silence.

"It was someone I saw at your house back in May, big guy with real short blond hair." O'Connell's right-hand man; Allen had recognized him despite the distorting lenses.

Jamie turned to gape at him in the thin dawn light. "Howard? You got away from *Howard*?"

The sheer disbelief in the boy's voice made Allen glance at him and immediately wish there was more light. The kid looked flabbergasted and terrified, and was staring at Allen as if he'd never seen him before.

"Who's Howard?" Allen did know that "Howard" was George Howard, weight lifter and odd-job man, but he made for one of the few gaps in Gina's dossier; Allen knew little more about him than he had in May.

"My father's . . . associate, he calls him. Howard works for my father."

"Doing what?" Hauling garbage; fetching boys for torture.

"Everything. You sure it was him?"

"Either that or his twin brother."

"Was he alone?"

Allen had been puzzling about that, himself. "Is Howard left-handed?"

"He's ambi— You know, when a person can write with both hands?"

"Ambidextrous."

"Yeah, that. He does some things with his right hand, but he writes with his left."

So it hadn't been mere luck that had enabled the driver to shoot at him out of the side window. Allen hadn't seen any passenger, and the sports car did not appear to have a sunroof. Which meant this man Howard had been driving and shooting at the same time. A formidable assailant.

"But was he alone?" the boy persisted. "You didn't see my father with him?"

"Jamie, your father went down in a plane crash."

Silence answered him.

"Why does Howard want to kill me?" Allen asked.

"If he'd wanted to kill you, you'd be dead." The boy said it flatly.

"Not yet, although he did manage to wing me."

"Howard *shot* at us?"

It occurred to Allen that Jamie, curled up below the Honda's dash and later kept literally in the dark, could not have followed much of what happened; all he knew was Allen's dramatic high-speed movie turn, and later that Allen had rummaged around in the back of the car before they'd abandoned it behind the barn. "He sure did."

"And he *missed*?"

This, by Jamie's reaction, was more extraordinary than that the man had been shooting in the first place, on a par with the sun rising in the west.

"Not entirely, no," Allen said with heavy sarcasm.

Jamie leaned forward, taking in Allen's injury for the first time. Allen told him, "It went through the upper part of my arm, and it may have chipped the bone, but it doesn't seem to have hit any major arteries. It's bloody and it's painful, but the hand still works and I'm not going to pass out while I'm driving." He hoped.

But Jamie seemed less concerned with the state of Allen's arm than with how it had come about. "That means he couldn't have missed killing you by much."

The words could have been the dregs of belated terror, but they did not sound that way, not at all. The boy sounded pleased, as if some anomaly of the universe had been explained.

"Does this happen a lot, Jamie?" Allen asked, struggling to keep his voice mild. "I mean, if your friend Howard is in the habit of riding up and down shooting at people for kicks, maybe you could have mentioned it to me?"

Silence.

Allen couldn't decide if the boy realized that he had been an intended victim as well—Howard may not have been actively gunning for the boy, but if they'd crashed at that speed, the boy could have been killed. "Jamie, talk to me." And after no response: "Jamie, how do you think he found us?"

At last, he had hit a weak spot. Jamie winced, and then let loose with a torrent of words. "I'm sorry, God, Allen, I'm so sorry, I didn't think you'd mind. I saw your laptop at the motel and there wasn't anything on the TV that I wanted to watch and I just thought I'd check in with the game. I didn't tell anyone where we were, I swear I didn't" (*except Silverfish,* Jamie's mind whispered), "but I used my phone card so it wouldn't go on the motel bill and maybe he tracked that. I don't know how he could find me through the card—I mean, not him, not Father, he doesn't know anything, but he has people working for him who maybe could do it, but the card, it's just one of those you buy in the store. Maybe you can trace a user through the phone line, but I didn't tell anyone—" *except Silverfish the Ubiquitous* "—I swear it."

Allen looked out of the corner of his eyes at the boy, sweating with earnest denial. It was within the realm of probability, he thought, that someone with the know-how and resources of a Gina could trace the uses of a specific phone card. However, there remained another possibility: Maybe it was time to jettison the boy's backpack, just to be safe. "Are those new clothes you're wearing, or things you brought with you from California?"

In confusion, the boy looked down at his legs. "I think, yes, it's all stuff Rachel bought me."

"Even the shoes?"

"Yeah." They weren't as cool as his old ones, but they didn't hurt his toes.

"Jamie, we'll have to leave your pack behind, in case it has some kind of tracking device in it." Which sounded so melodramatic, Allen couldn't believe he'd even thought it, but stranger things had happened than a parent planting a location bug on a child. And it was easier to believe than the alternative, which would be that a gun-wielding maniac happened to be driving country roads shooting at perfect strangers.

Before the boy could protest, Allen spotted a road sign that said "SPEED LIMIT 45." Someone had neatly plinked half a dozen holes through the two numbers, leaving them rusted but legible. The sign stood in front of an enormous chestnut tree: probably the most distinctive spot they'd passed in miles. He slowed and pulled onto the shoulder. "Empty your pockets and put everything in your pack," he told Jamie, and when the pack's zipper was shut, he said, "You take a good look at this sign, okay? So when we come back for your pack, we can find it again."

He reached across himself to work the door handle with his right hand, and eased down from the truck. The pain took his arm in its teeth and shook it, so that the thin dawn flared and sparkled for a few moments before his eyes. Allen undid one of the buttons on his shirt and gingerly took his left hand over to rest it inside, just above the belt, as an impromptu sling. That was better. He reached back for the boy's drab green backpack and carried it under the wide branches of the chestnut. At the bottom of the tree, he looked up: The sky between the branches was noticeably lighter than it had been. Taking a breath, he swung the pack hard by its straps and let go; it dropped directly down in the tree's fork. Two steps away, it was invisible. Unless some child decided to go tree-climbing, nobody would spot it until winter.

It was work getting back into the high truck one-handed. Allen reached up for the steering wheel, and froze.

There was a gun in his face, inches from his eyes, the round hole of the pistol he'd dislodged under the seat. A hush dropped over the truck's cab, no sound of breath or rustle of clothing.

Then: "Jamie," Allen whispered, and forced his gaze upward to the boy's face.

The handsome features were a mask, rigid and betraying nothing of whatever it was the boy was seeing.

"Jamie," Allen said more firmly, his body motionless. "I'm not your father, Jamie, not Howard. I'm just a friend. You and I are going to figure this out, Jamie. I'm going to help you."

The dark eyes slowly focused, and in a moment the boy's finger uncurled slightly from the trigger guard, his hand pushing slightly forward in an offer. "I thought, if Howard is after us, you might want this."

Allen swallowed, finished pulling himself up, and then reached to remove the gun from the boy's thin hand. He had to brace it between his knees under the truck's steering wheel in order to work the cylinder open: three bullets. One of them ready in the chamber. He spun the cylinder around to place an empty chamber in front of the hammer, then after a brief hesitation, returned the gun to the glove compartment a hand's breadth from the boy's knees.

"Let's leave it there for the moment," he said hoarsely, and started the truck's engine.

IT TOOK THEM A COUPLE OF HOURS TO REGAIN THE FREEWAY, WITH Allen keeping to the back roads and navigating by the compass in his head. They came to the I5 a bare fifty miles south of Seattle, but Allen resolutely turned away, following the signs toward Olympia.

Jamie stirred. "I thought we were going to Seattle."

"I can't endanger Alice," was Allen's terse answer.

On a Sunday morning, even gas stations on the interstate were not busy. Allen drove around until he found one with a freestanding phone booth, one of the old-time glass-walled booths with a folding door. He pulled in close beside it and turned off the key; the heavy old engine shut off smoothly. His arm burned and thudded, his head spun dangerously.

In the ticking silence, he and Jamie stared at the vacant booth.

"I've got to make a couple of phone calls," Allen told him. "Are you going to run off as soon as I get out of the truck?"

"No!" Jamie said, sounding surprised. "Why would I do that?"

"Jamie, I don't know what's going on with you, and I don't have the strength to find out right now. If you've made some kind of arrangements with your father's 'associate' Howard, let me just give you some change so you can make your phone call, and I'll leave you here."

"I don't want you to go." The young voice was so urgent, Allen had to believe him, although there might be any number of reasons for the boy's desperation.

"Okay. I'll make my phone calls, and then we'll go to another place and buy gas." Allen reached for the heavy jacket, draping it across his upper body to hide the bloody sleeve. He'd look like a hunchback, but it couldn't be helped.

"Okay, I'll stay here. Unless . . . Look, shouldn't I go buy some bandages or something? I mean, you're bleeding all over the place."

Allen looked at the boy. He could find no trace of deception in the young face, no blatant innocence or lurking secrecy, only a concern for an injured companion. Still, he had to be sure.

"Jamie, do you *want* to go back to your father?"

The boy twitched, a physical shudder accompanied by an unmistakable look of fear and revulsion, and although there was longing in the expression as well, Allen reached for his wallet. Surely no twelve-year-old could school himself to react like that.

Handing over two twenty-dollar bills, he said to Jamie, "Don't buy bandages, that would be too obvious." The logical alternative was women's menstrual pads, sterile and absorbent, but he could hardly ask a boy Jamie's age to casually pick up a package of those. "If they have any cotton T-shirts, get a big one, or another sweatshirt. And a couple of candy bars—not a whole bunch, we'll stop down the road and buy more."

Jamie took the money and hurried across the parking lot. Allen fastened the jacket's top button under his chin and got out of the car. While he was standing and waiting for the fresh nerve-endings to settle, jaws clenched against a moan, he distracted himself by watching the boy enter the bright shop and wander the aisles. Rachel's image came back to him, the Stephen King character trusting his vulnerable fingers to a disturbed child. He dug some quarters out of his pocket, and went to the phone.

The first call was to Alice's emergency number. The line picked up and without waiting for any answer, Allen said, "Somebody's tracked the boy and taken a shot at us. Better call Pete and have him send the family on a holiday, just in case. I'll let you know when we've set down somewhere." He broke the connection, let the toggle rise, and dialed for information. When the voice came on, he asked for "Reienbach, I'm not sure of the town, but it's a little ways north of Centralia."

As he had hoped, after giving him the number, the recording offered to connect him. He fed the required coins into the slot. After the fourth ring, another recording came on, the voice of a middle-aged woman making an effort to be cheerful as she recited the name and her suggestion that the caller leave a message.

"Mr. and Mrs. Reienbach, you may have noticed that your truck is missing. You may also find that you've got a five-year-old Honda out behind your old barn, that is, if the guy who's after me didn't get to it first. The pink slip's in the glove box, you're welcome to fake my signature and keep the car. I'd really appreciate it if you didn't tell the police about it, not for a while anyway. I know you'd have no reason to believe me, but I'm trying to help some people, and it's not proving easy. That's why I had to borrow your truck. And I swear it's only borrowed—I'll get it back to you as soon as I possibly can. And . . . thank you." He hung up, grateful that he hadn't had to deal with a live voice.

Now for the third call. He sagged against the glass side of the booth, wanting only to sink to the filthy floor and go to sleep, wanting desperately to think of some way to do this without making the call. But there was no other way, and here was the boy, standing at the folding door to the booth with a bag in his hand, looking worried.

"You'd better get back in the truck," Allen told him; when the boy was out of hearing, he let the quarters drop into the phone slot and punched in the number he'd known since before he could read. Jerry was home; nearly every word of the two-minute conversation was Allen's.

It was a hellish drive, up the western side of Puget Sound and Hood Canal, and it took longer than Allen had reckoned. Jamie had managed to fill the gas tank, with instructions called from inside the truck's cab, and he added a roll of gauze to his purchases at the service station shop. Behind a deserted fruit stand up the road, Allen eased his shirt off and peeled away the blood-soaked sweatshirt, looking at the injury for the first time.

It was ugly and clean and he was very lucky. His left fingers worked, under protest, and the bleeding had slowed. He reached for the gauze.

"Wouldn't it be easier if I did it?" Jamie asked. Allen had kept the arm turned away from the boy.

"You don't need to see this," Allen told him.

"It's only blood," Jamie said, sounding remarkably calm. "I've seen blood before. I mean, I dressed out my own deer. Which is a whole lot messier than your arm."

Allen met his eyes for a long moment, then handed over the gauze. Jamie got out of the truck and came around to the driver's-side door, to have room to work. Allen shifted over to let him in behind the wheel, and lifted his arm away from his side.

The kid did indeed seem little troubled by the gore. He wrapped the sterile bandage around Allen's arm, covering the entrance and the larger exit wounds firmly. Next, Allen handed him the T-shirt he'd bought, proclaiming the virtues of Tumwater, Washington, and watched the boy's concentration as he covered the gauze with gray knit cotton. He wrapped the whole with another glove-box find, duct tape, then helped Allen thread the arm through his jacket. He still looked like a hunchback, but less like the sole survivor of a massacre. The boy got down and came back around the truck, and when in his seat, he reached back into the bag of purchases and pried open the bottle of Tylenol.

"You want two?" he asked.

"Better make it three, and I'll have some more in a while." That many aspirin and he'd be leaking down to his boots, but Tylenol didn't thin blood the same way. He swallowed the pills and put his right arm through its jacket sleeve.

"Thank you," he said. The boy merely nodded, and snapped the top back on the bottle.

Allen's left arm was useless, which meant that he could either shift gears or steer, not both. There were several exciting moments on the tourist-clotted roads, but eventually the road veered west. Another twenty minutes, and he turned laboriously down a narrow drive leading toward the water.

That last mile nearly killed him. The bumps and jolts seemed to be ripping his arm right off his body, and the sounds he was making behind his gritted teeth had to be frightening the boy, but he couldn't keep them back, couldn't open his mouth to tell Jamie he would be okay, couldn't do anything but endure and try not to pass out or drive off the track.

They came out from the trees and rounded a ramshackle building, and there was the water, sweet open water graced with the most beautiful boat in all the world, an old converted fishing boat in need of paint, the *Orca Queen*. Ed was already on his way up the dock, as near to a run as Allen had ever seen him, even the time when the goons belonging to the husband of Streak Rychenkow's widow had been shooting at them. Allen applied the brakes without taking the truck out of gear, and the engine jerked and coughed itself into a stall. The silence was so profound, so perfect, Allen longed to sink into it like a warm bed.

Ed's face, creased and brown, was at the truck window, then somehow the door was open. "Jesus, Allen, are you dead? You sure as shit look it."

"Not quite," Allen croaked.

"Can you walk?"

"Guess we'll find out." The old man reached in as if he was about to lift him out bodily, but before he could do that, Allen told him, "This is Jamie. If I bleed out on the way over, take him to Jerry."

"You sure about that?"

Allen had never been less sure about anything in his life, but in the end, Jerry was all he had. Anyway, it was out of his hands now. "He's expecting us," he told Ed, but when the old boatman eased Allen from the cab, the world quivered and receded. He did not quite black out, but clung to Ed's broad shoulders as they wavered down the strange dock onto the boat. Once on board, Ed hauled him belowdecks and draped him across a padded bench.

Allen heard Ed's gravelly voice alternate with Jamie's piping tones of childhood, but he couldn't quite follow the conversation. It was all he could do not to roll onto the floor with the gentle pitch of the boat.

Ed swung up the stairs, and Jamie came over to Allen and propped several pillows against his free side, wedging him from falling. The boy even managed to work one under Allen's head.

"Thanks," he said.

"Your friend told me to keep you from passing out."

"Old wives' tale," Allen muttered. Passing out would feel good about now.

"He said I should talk to you, keep you awake." Allen felt Jamie's gaze on him, and made an effort to open his eyes. "What do you want me to talk about?"

"Tell me a story." Allen's mother had read him stories, when he was sick one winter. He'd done the same for Jerry a few years later, after she had died. *Wonder if Jer remembers me reading to him?* Allen thought.

"I could tell you *The Lord of the Rings*," Jamie offered.

"That'd be great."

The sheer number of names made it impossible for Allen's fuzzy mind to follow the story, but after Gandalf and Frodo and Sam, he didn't try. It was pleasant, lying like a wet rag in Ed's boat with a nervous juvenile reciting a long and confusing story. So much nicer than the last time he'd been shot, when the VC bullet had smashed into his leg and landed him in a knee-deep paddy. Buddies were great, but none of the guys had told him stories while they were waiting for the medevac. None of the nurses, either.

"You'd make a great nurse, Jamie," he muttered.

The boy's narrative faltered and died away. After a minute, Allen felt a presence above him and he opened his eyes again.

"It's okay, Jamie. I'm not going to die on you."

"I thought you were going to leave me."

"I'll be fine."

"No. I mean, back there, when I told you about Howard."

"Jamie, Howard's not your fault. And I don't walk out on my responsibilities."

A long pause followed, with Allen drifting far and wee. Then, in a voice so small the engines nearly drowned it out, Jamie told him, "My father used to drive away and leave me in the woods. In the cabin. It was so scary. Sometimes I cried—when I didn't think he was coming back, and I thought I was going to die out there."

Somehow Allen's hand found Jamie's, although whether he reached out or the boy had, he neither knew nor cared. He left his hand over Jamie's all the way across. And he kept his eyes open.

Chapter 33

ALLEN'S EYES REMAINED OPEN, BUT HIS MIND DRIFTED IN AND OUT OF awareness. What seemed like a couple of weeks later, he came fully awake with the sound of the boat's engines backing and the sway of a maneuvering hull. It was still bright outside, but the light was that of late afternoon. He then realized that the small hand was no longer in his, and he battled a moment of panicky confusion—Jamie: gone. But no, the boy had been there minutes before, of that he was certain, and Ed would not have lost him during the crossing. It took a while for these thoughts to expand into a full awareness of his surroundings, but by then he had heard voices, and his mind was again occupying its place in the world.

He considered trying to sit up, but before he could do more than contemplate how difficult it was going to be, a sudden dip of the boat told him that someone had stepped on board, and in a few seconds the cabin darkened with a person coming down the steps. Two people, as it turned out: first Jerry, then an old man he helped steady down the stairs, a bent man who must have been in his eighties, carrying a black doctor's bag. He set the bag down and pulled a pair of latex gloves from his coat pocket, and with that gesture Allen recognized the neighbor, the surgeon who'd patched him together some twenty-five years before. The man had been retired then, for God's sake.

"Christ, Weintraub, are you still alive?" he blurted out.

The old doctor wheezed a chuckle. "Seems to me I should say the same thing to you, young man. Let's see what we've got here, before we try to move you."

He took out a pair of scissors and briskly cut away clothes, duct tape, and bandages, pursing his lips at what lay beneath. With the help of Ed and Jerry, he got Allen onto his side so the entire shoulder was in sight. It hurt like holy hell; Allen wished he could just faint and get out of it, but it didn't work that way.

"I admit I'm no expert, Sheriff, but that looks like a gunshot wound to me," the old surgeon said, although he did not sound terribly worried at the fact. Allen opened one eye to see his brother's reaction; incredibly, he too seemed more concerned at the injury than the source of it.

"You can't report it," Allen wheezed. "I'll explain, but you can't."

"Yes, your brother rather figured that would be the case," the doctor said, and began digging quantities of gauze from his bag.

It was still full daylight outside, and the weather was good enough for people to be around. Moving Allen down the dock and into the house on a stretcher would draw some beachgoer's attention. He could stay where he was until dark, or they could try to get him more or less upright. Everyone there wanted the latter, if possible. Allen thought it might be.

"If I can lean on you," he said to his brother, "anyone who sees will just think I'm drunk." And if they knew Allen well enough to recognize him, they'd know his history well enough not to be astonished at his condition. "But you can't risk having Jamie spotted."

"The boy can stay on board until nightfall," Ed offered. "We'll go find us an Orca pod, come back when it's full dark."

"That okay with you, Jamie?" Allen asked.

The boy shrugged. The doctor's gentle hands wrapped up Allen's shoulder, and once he was sitting upright, the doctor taped his arm securely against his chest. Then Jerry draped one of Ed's old shirts over the bandages, and he and Ed lifted Allen to his feet. With his right arm around his brother's shoulders, Allen managed to negotiate the steps and the side of the boat onto the dock. Jamie remained in the cabin while Ed followed the staggering Carmichaels; halfway up the dock, Allen stopped him.

"Ed, you better go back with the kid. And look, keep an eye on him. Make sure he doesn't go anywhere near your radio."

That was all he said, but Ed immediately turned back, casting off and hopping back on board with the ease of a young man. The *Orca Queen*'s engines growled to life, and the boat pulled away into the privacy of open water.

RATHER THAN TRY TO CARRY ALLEN UP THE STAIRS, JERRY EASED HIS brother onto the TV room sofa. Then the arguments commenced. Doctor Weintraub insisted that Allen had lost so much blood he had to be transfused, in a hospital, and only backed down when Allen told him that if he went into a hospital, that kid on the boat might die. The doctor looked his disbelief at Allen, but he did not speak it, merely then speculating aloud on how he might arrange a transfusion on his own. Jerry offered his own blood (which was, in fact, the same type as Allen's) but Allen put an end to it all by pointing out that if the good doctor would just do something to stop the bleeding now, before the last of his blood leaked out on the floor, his own body would soon enough make up the difference. "Jerry can feed me steaks three times a day," he said.

"Not on a sheriff's salary," Jerry objected, but at any rate, the doctor turned from argument to treatment. He continued to object, saying that Allen needed an X ray, but when Allen asked him what he would do if the bone proved to be cracked, he admitted that unless it was actually broken, which it didn't seem to be, all medical science would do was give him a sling and wrap it firmly, which he would do anyway.

At the end of it, stitched and strapped and woozy from blood loss and painkillers, Allen stretched out on the scruffy old sofa and listened to his brother, thanking old Weintraub and shutting the door. Jerry's footsteps went past the television room to the kitchen; he rattled around for a while, then made a phone call. He seemed to be checking in with his colleagues, because Allen heard him say that he'd be at home that night if Bobby needed him. There followed some more rattling, accompanied by the odor of frying onions. In a while, his head poked around the door; seeing Allen awake, he came in all the way, carrying a pair of plates.

Jerry had produced the traditional Carmichael bachelor's meal of Joe's Special: fried onions and hamburger with spinach added, then a couple of eggs broken over the whole mess to glue it together. Allen gulped the food like a starving dog. Jerry took his empty plate out to the kitchen and brought it back with the dried-up dregs from the pan, and Allen polished that off as well.

"Iron, you know," Jerry said, amused. "It's supposed to build up the blood."

"I love you, Jerry," Allen said, intending a jest, although it didn't quite come out that way. Must be the painkillers, he thought.

Jerry cleared the plates away, came back with coffee, arranged a couple of pillows to support Allen's head, then shifted one of the armchairs until it faced the sofa and sat down in it.

"So, what kind of a mess have you gotten yourself into?"

"This is going to take a long time, Jer."

"Took you long enough to get into it," Jerry said over his cup. "Thirty years or so? Let's see how far you get explaining before you pass out."

It had to be done sequentially, and thoroughly, or else not at all. So he had to begin with Vietnam, and a good man with a white streak in his dark hair and a penchant for privacy when it came to his life back in The World. He talked about The Wolf and the squad and friendly fire in a muddy river—but not Brennan. He didn't want to tell Jerry about Brennan, ever. But the rest of it, yes, because only within the context of Vietnam could what Allen had done seven years later for Streak's widow even begin to make sense, and only when that adventure was explained did the rest of it follow: the letter that had reached him a year later from the Rychenkow widow, concerning a woman she'd met in the shelter whose husband had framed her in order to gain custody of their three children. And after that, a similar problem, and eventually his association with a group that existed solely to help women and their children when the law could not. He was careful to use no identifying names or places—Jerry might well turn him in when this was all over, and he'd be damned if he was going to give up Alice and the others as well—but Jerry didn't push, didn't even ask many questions, only those necessary for clarity. And if he noticed the number of times his brother failed to mention the name of his coconspirator with a boat, he did not ask about that, either, he just nodded and grunted and made more coffee.

It took over an hour to lay the groundwork, to bring Jerry up to the time when **deadboy** had first appeared on Alice's screen. Allen stopped, eyes shut, exhausted by the effort of speech and, more, of guarding his speech.

"Let's take a break," Jerry said. "I need to make a run down and pick up some more bread and milk before the market shuts. You need to take a trip to the can?"

"Not now, but I think I'll be able to do it myself." If Jerry intended to make a phone call summoning deputies with handcuffs, he could do it from his own kitchen: Allen was in no condition to make a break for it, and they both knew it.

Jerry drove off, and Allen fell into a deep sleep, broken only when the rattle of grocery bags came through the door. Allen inched himself upright and off the sofa. The pain pills were wearing thin, leaving him with a fire in his shoulder but an adequate sense of balance. He managed a trip to the toilet, although refastening the button on the top of his jeans defeated him. Allen got himself a glass of water and sat at the kitchen table. Darkness was gathering, the Carmichael dock nearly invisible.

"You need me to open the pills?" Jerry asked over his shoulder.

"I'll leave them for a while. Maybe some Advil?" They'd help with the inflammation, anyway, and leave his brain unclouded.

Jerry put the open bottle on the table.

"How you feeling?"

"Like an old banana peel with a blowtorch on one side. I'll mend."

"Weintraub's a good man."

"I hope this doesn't get him in trouble."

"He'd like nothing better. You've probably made his week—hell, his year. He gets bored."

"Glad to oblige."

"Rae left this morning," Jerry said abruptly, his back to Allen. This was the first time he'd mentioned her aloud to his brother, since he had discovered their relationship.

"I know," Allen said. "I'd hoped to see her off last night, but things got . . . complicated."

"I asked Nikki to marry me."

"Finally! Hey, that's great. Well, it is if she said she would."

"She did. She wants to wait 'til after Christmas, for the sake of the boy."

Red-haired, ethereal Nikki Walls, the younger sister of Allen's ex-wife Lisa, had been married to a wife-beater, and had come out of that marriage with a red-haired son and a distinct wariness toward men in general.

"I'm happy for you, Jerry."

"Yeah, me too. You want a steak or a hamburger for your second dinner?"

"Hamburger." Not just because it was less of a strain on the law-man's budget, but it would be easier to eat one-handed. Jerry tore open a parcel of butcher's paper and used a spatula to carve off a lump of red meat, smashing it flat in a cast-iron skillet and adding a second lump beside it. He turned on the gas to high, and went back to the bags for buns.

"If you're not going to have any painkillers, you want a beer?"

"Sure."

Jerry popped open the bottle and set it on the table in front of Allen, then went back to his sizzling pan. "I remember reading about this character a few years ago, used to help women get away from their husbands. She'd sit in a doughnut shop, I think it was, down in Dallas or something, and wait for women to drive up."

"Atlanta. That was Faye Yager, and yeah, she was something else. The people I work with are a lot lower-key, and they're pretty careful about who they take on. A big part of my job is—was—to make sure the clients weren't trying to pull one over on us."

"So what went wrong with this kid?"

"I don't know that anything did."

Jerry turned to give him a look. "Allen, you're sitting at the table with a bleeding arm while Ed keeps some kid under wraps. I can't imagine that happens every day."

Allen concentrated on the drips gathering on the green bottle before him. He drew a deep breath, and began. "Jameson Patrick O'Connell, prefers to be called Jamie. Twelve years old, mother died when he was seven. I first came across him back in May, an email that had been for-warded through several people." He drank the beer and talked, telling his brother about his last abused kid in a lifetime of them. The surveil-lance, the somewhat rushed rescue, stashing the boy with a family across the country (no names there, either), and returning to Seattle in June a free man, to phone his brother for the first time in years. Relaxing into a summer with Rae on the islands. Finished.

And then Rachel's letter.

Back to San Jose and what he'd found there (leave Gina out of it), things that he should have discovered in May. Mark O'Connell's ques-tionable job and his plane going off the radar. Breaking and entering the O'Connell house (and again, let Jerry think he'd gotten into the study on his own, not mentioning the phone call to Dave). The father's diary, the number of losses in the boy's immediate vicinity—pet, fire, suicide, drowning—and the slow accumulation of suspicion, then finally the printout that had fallen out of the book, giving details of how to sabotage a plane.

The hamburgers were ready. Jerry put them on the table, along with catsup, Aunt Midge's homemade relish, and two more bottles of beer; the two brothers ate wordlessly.

When his plate was bare, Allen looked up. "Do you understand why I was concerned?"

"Every law enforcement officer in the country receives regular briefings on the cause and avoidance of school shootings. I've been on three courses about it. I'm no expert, but even I've heard of the three danger signs of enuresis, arson, and animal abuse. Not that I put much stock in them," he added. "It's always struck me as a pretty simplistic judgment."

Allen started to nod, cut the motion short at the objection of his mangled muscles, and changed his response. "Sure. If every kid who lights a fire or wets his bed had to go into therapy, every parent in the country would need to take on a second job. But in Jamie's case, we also had the history of chronic paternal abuse, the almost complete lack of peer support, and an early familiarity with firearms and explosives. Again, none of those are a sure prescription of a dangerous kid, but the accumulation of things gave me a really bad feeling in my gut. Basically, I didn't want to take a chance. The family we'd placed him with had children."

Allen described in general terms his rushed cross-country trip, the removal of the boy from his foster family, and the drive toward Seattle.

"I had decided that I needed to consult with my . . . I guess you'd call her my partner, on the boy's stability. So even though it was disruptive to everyone, most of all the kid himself, I simply took him. We were on a back road south of Olympia at five this morning when a car pulled up next to us and started shooting."

"Could it have just been something random?"

"Single occupant, middle-aged male, a guy capable of driving a car at high speed while shooting with some accuracy out the driver's side window at a car in the right-hand lane. He kept after us, too, until I shook him off."

"How'd you do that?"

"I, er, borrowed somebody's pickup."

Jerry stood up abruptly to dump the plates into the dishwasher and pour coffee into a pair of mugs. Allen could just imagine what was going through his brother's mind: kidnapping across state lines, illegal surveillance, breaking and entering, car theft. The unreported bullet wound was the least of Sheriff Carmichael's problems.

"I called the truck's owner to let him know we'd be returning it." If Ed could get some of the blood out of the upholstery.

Jerry didn't say anything, just sat down with his cup and propped his head in his hands. Allen could only wait and see which way things would fall. He didn't think Jerry would turn him in, but it was very possible he would throw Allen out. Just because some cops might be sympathetic to the plight of a trapped victim didn't mean that a man whose law enforcement problems were predominantly summer drunks on boats would be one of them.

"Tell me more about the kid," Jerry said eventually through his fingers.

"To begin with, there is no doubt in my mind that Jamie was brutalized by his father. Not sexually, as far as I can tell, or if so it was only indirectly, but he was clearly chronically abused, even tortured, both physically and mentally. His father used to take him out hunting and play these horrifying games with him, pretending to hunt him down, driving away and leaving him for hours at a time—this is a child of eight or nine. If you need convincing, there's one tape I can show you, although I wouldn't recommend it. The boy walks into the room where his father is drinking and watching the television, and the father calls him over, picks up the shotgun that's lying on the sofa next to him, rests it against the boy's chest, and pulls the trigger. Empty of course, but how can the kid know that for sure? Father laughs, big joke. Creepiest damn thing I've ever seen. And Jerry? I've seen a whole lot."

At that, Jerry looked at him. "Jesus," he said, and in a while, "But why not call the cops on him?"

"Cases like that, sometimes we do. If we can make sure that the abuser goes away for a long time, and can't get back at the victims, it's always best to let the family return to its home, see what life is like in familiar surroundings without the abuser. If Jamie's mother was still alive, we might have tried it. But O'Connell's a manipulator, and rich. More than once he convinced schools that his boy was a liar and a troublemaker. No saying he wouldn't do it again, and then life would really be hell for the kid. And I didn't know about it then, but I suspect that O'Connell had some well-oiled strategies for disappearing once he caught a whiff of the law. Anyway, as soon as I saw that perverse little game with the gun, I knew we had to get the kid away from him."

"But now you think this kid may be dangerous, too?"

"Violent men are made, not born. Abuse permeates their image of what it is to be an authority figure—what other role model do they have? And at a certain point in a young victim's life—not always, but often—he will turn, and either begin to abuse those he perceives as weaker—animals, younger children—or else strike back at his own abuser. I'm sure you've seen it. And as you know, if the reaction is open, immediate, and reactive to a specific event, there's a feeling that the violence is justified—that's when you see failures to indict, or verdicts of justifiable homicide. But if the abuse victim takes an indirect route, if there's any planning or entrapment involved, well, juries don't like that."

"And you honestly think that this kid—"

"Jerry, I don't know. Like I told you on the phone, all I heard is that the father's plane went down. Last I knew, the Coast Guard hadn't even decided if the father actually went down in that plane. I heard the news, saw a lot of uncomfortable evidence against the kid, and felt I was running out of time. Before Al—" He caught himself, changed it to, "Before my partner and I could take the boy aside for a closer look, find out how he was ticking, all hell broke loose. I'm working blind here, Jer. And I need help."

"From me."

"I didn't have anywhere else to turn."

"Do you think the boy killed his father?"

Allen heard a faint *tink* in the back of his mind, saw a grenade bouncing down a cave floor, looked into a pair of mad, triumphant blue eyes. Then he blinked, and his brother's calm brown eyes were waiting.

"I hope to God he didn't, for his own sake. But like I said, we don't even know if the bastard is dead."

"Okay. Let me make some phone calls."

"Jer—"

"Don't worry. I won't give you away, or the kid. Not until we both know more."

"Thank you."

Jerry studied his older brother, pale and hurting as he had been the last time desperation drove him to the door, in the spring of 1975. "You've spent your whole life doing this? Kidnapping children?"

"Rescuing them. Usually with their mother. Almost always."

"Why?"

Jerry wasn't asking why it needed doing: He'd seen enough cases where abused kids were not taken from their parents to know why it needed doing. Rather, Jerry was asking, *Why you?* And it all came down to that, Allen knew. Not just whether or not Jerry would help him now, but whether Jerry would have anything to do with him when this episode was over. Allen wished he wasn't so nearly out of words.

"When I got to Vietnam, early on, I had a conversation with this guy who did long-range recon. He'd been in the bush for years, knew everything there was to know, all the ways to survive. I'd been in-country for about two minutes, so I asked him for advice, anything he could tell me that would help me make it out alive. What he said was, *Don't trust the children.* He was right, of course; in a vicious war like that, even small kids carry grenades or can sell you a Coke with ground glass in it. But I listened to what he said, and I believed him, until one day I killed a whole cave full of children."

Something moved in the back of Jerry's eyes, and Allen waited, dreading the growth of revulsion, the final wedge that would split his brother from him forever. He waited, and saw Jerry review both the statement and the way in which he had said it. He saw Jerry deliberately put aside immediate judgment. He saw his brother choose to trust him.

Shaken, it took Allen a minute before he could start again.

"It took me seven years to get around to how I might make up for that act. And even then I didn't know what I was doing, just that I had to do it. Eventually it came to me, that what it boiled down to was, *Trust the children.* Since then, I've spent my life trusting children. Listening to them and having faith in them. I owe them that. Even this one. Jer, I don't know if Jamie's a killer or not. I do know he's a boy who's had the most appalling things done to him, and he needs my help. I promised I'd give it to him. I'm not asking you to make phone calls or to help me with this. All I need is shelter until I'm strong enough to take him away."

In the end, it was Jerry who turned away. "Let me think about it," he said.

ALLEN RETURNED TO THE SOFA FOR A COUPLE OF HOURS AND WOKE TO voices in the kitchen, Jerry and Ed talking about food. He rubbed his face and craned to see the clock on the front of the VCR. Nearly midnight.

Getting up was damnably awkward, and he still couldn't get the button on his jeans done with one hand, but he felt more like a three-dimensional man and less like a flattened carcass along a road. Jamie looked up when he came into the kitchen, his face open with pleasure.

"Hi, Allen, how's your arm? Ed and I saw some killer whales and a bunch of dolphins, and we went swimming and made a campfire on a beach and cooked s'mores, and he let me pick the music. Ed's got some way cool music, for old stuff."

"Hey, boy," Ed protested, "who're you calling old stuff?" He winked at Allen, who suddenly felt shaky with relief over a worry he'd not known he had: Ed liked the boy. Yet another person on the kid's side— and Jamie knew it, too; Allen had never known him so effusive.

Either that, or he'd inherited his father's ability to con.

"I mean your music. That guy without the teeth, and the song about something that came out of the sky."

"Creedence," Ed explained, although Allen had been out with the man often enough to identify the musicians.

While Allen had slept, Jerry was cooking, and now produced a large pot of meaty spaghetti. Jamie ate two servings, and suddenly looked as if he'd been clubbed. Allen glanced at Jerry.

"I think we'd better continue this in the morning," he suggested. Jerry started to object, then looked more closely at the state of his two houseguests, and backed down.

"You're welcome to tie up overnight, Ed," he told the boatman.

"I'll do that, thanks. Give me a whistle when breakfast is on."

"I should have done more shopping," Jerry muttered, and led Jamie away to the guest room.

That night, the boy made no excursions to the computer downstairs.

DAWN CAME EARLY IN THE ISLANDS, FINDING JERRY ALREADY GONE. HE RE-turned before the sun had chased the mist from the water, dressed in his uniform and wearing his gun—which only meant that he'd had a meeting with one of his deputies and wanted to make it official. Weintraub came not much after Jerry got back, to loose Allen's arm from its sling and poke around with what seemed to Allen an unnecessary degree of curiosity before pronouncing himself satisfied that the foolish decision to avoid the hospital wasn't going to mean the loss of the arm. He changed the dressings, replaced the strapping with an adjustable sling, and left, saying that his wife was expecting him back for breakfast.

Allen shaved, using Jerry's electric razor so as not to leave his face looking as if it had been drawn through a blackberry patch, and came downstairs to the rich scent of browning sausages.

"Jerry, you're going to make a fine wife for Nikki."

The younger Carmichael glanced down at the frilly apron that one of their aunts had left behind after a Thanksgiving dinner. The sprigged cotton barely reached his thighs. "Cute, huh? I thought I'd make some chocolate chip pancakes. You think Jamie'd like them? Nikki's kid can eat more of them than I can."

"Twelve-year-old boys will eat anything," Allen said, helping himself to coffee. The sun was pouring through the east window overlooking the sound, and after glancing down at the dock to see if Ed was on his deck, he settled with his back to it. The smells, the warmth, the sense of safety and comfort washed over him: home. "Mom used to make chocolate chip pancakes," he told Jerry, surprised by a sudden memory.

Jerry turned with the spatula in his hand. "Really? I don't remember that. Aunt Midge mentioned them one time, I thought they sounded like a good idea. She didn't say Mom made them."

She had, though; on a late summer's morning just like this, thin already with the cancer that would kill her before Christmas. She'd been standing at the same place as Jerry, using an earlier stove but probably the same cast-iron griddle that Jerry was watching so closely, filling the sun-bright kitchen with just the same odors of hot butter and spicy sausages. Allen had been thirteen and Jerry six; later, Allen went to California with their father, and that had been the end of home. This man bending over the griddle, his brother, was both the closest person to him and a relative stranger. He couldn't even tell which way Jerry was going to go when it came to helping Jamie.

Jerry put a laden plate down in front of Allen, poured four more circles of batter into the pan, and then shed the apron to stride down to the dock and tell Ed that there was food when he wanted it. Allen's eyes followed his brother, as they used to do when he watched from the trees on Sanctuary, when Jerry would come to visit Rae the year she moved here. Jerry gave no more sign of knowing he was watched than he had on the island, and Allen reminded himself, as he had ten thousand times before, that normal men did not twitch with jungle sense.

At the end of the dock, Jerry leaned over the side of the *Orca Queen* for a moment, then turned and came back, not waiting for Ed. Nor would Ed hurry to respond to his summons: He had spent eight months in jail thanks to Jerry, and Sheriff Carmichael had no doubt that Ed continued to break pretty much any law he could get away with. Not, Allen reflected as he returned to his plate, a match made in heaven.

But Jerry cooked Ed pancakes and talked easily about the most recent proposal to expand one or another of the yacht harbors and about the *Elwa*'s latest exploit and why it always seemed to be that particular Washington State ferry that plowed into its dock or tried to circle the wrong way around an island or . . .

All very relaxed and friendly, with the serious issues placed on the back burner. Ed pushed back his plate and his chair, Jerry moved the griddle off the flame and was carrying his own plate to the table when Jamie appeared in the doorway, hair rumpled, the mark of a sheet pink along one cheek, and an expression of blossoming horror in his eyes.

Before any of the men could react, the boy turned and bolted. Jerry, already on his feet and the resident expert on apprehending fleeing suspects, was after him in a shot, followed rapidly by Ed and, trapped by infirmity on the far side of the table, Allen. When Allen got to the front door, his brother was holding Jamie by the back collar of his shirt, bemusedly trying to avoid the flailing fists and kicking feet. He looked like a veterinarian with a furious kitten.

"Jamie!" Allen shouted. "Jamie, what the hell is wrong with you? Stop it! Jerry, let him go."

Jerry glanced to make sure that Ed was blocking the boy's retreat, and let go the collar, planting his boot at the bottom edge of the door. Jamie leapt away, his back to the wall and his head down, fists clenched, eyes blazing.

"Jamie," Allen repeated, over and over until the angry black eyes flicked over to him for a moment. "Jamie, what the hell's wrong? You met Jerry last night. He's my brother. This is his house. What's the matter?"

"You didn't tell me he was a cop!" the boy spit out.

"Well, yeah, he is. Jerry's the sheriff up here. What's that got to do with it?"

The boy stared at Allen, too flabbergasted to answer. Jerry stepped forward, and the black eyes flew back to him, but the man was only moving clear of Allen in order to squat down to Jamie's level—incidentally laying himself open to attack from the boy's fists and feet.

"Jamie, the four of us have a lot of talking to do, but let me begin by saying that I'm not about to arrest anyone in my own house. My brother trusted me enough to come here with you. Can you just trust him enough to have some breakfast first?"

The dark gaze continued to blaze, then wavered and went to consult Allen; after a moment, the boy gave a sullen nod.

"You give me your word you won't try to run off?"

"Yeah."

Jerry stood up and led the way to the kitchen. Jamie's eyes went to the unguarded door, then again to Allen, before he followed his host and jailer into the fragrant kitchen, where the sheriff began by slipping the silly apron over his uniform. He turned, the spatula cocked in one hand, and Allen nearly laughed aloud: Jerry couldn't have been more instantly disarming to the boy if he'd lain down on the floor and barked.

"How many pancakes can you eat?" he inquired, sounding eerily like their chronically cheerful Aunt Midge.

It turned out the boy could eat more than Ed, winning the informal contest hands down. While he poured and flipped and stirred up more batter, Jerry led the conversation into harmless channels, mostly about the orca that had interested the boy. The import of his uniform faded under the influence of homey food and chatter, and Jerry used an exaggerated quantity of soapsuds in the washing-up bowl to complete the domestic image.

When the last utensil was dried and in its drawer, Jerry untied his frilly apron and slipped it over his head, folded it with deliberation, and sat down, taking a chair across the table from his brother and the boy. Wariness returned, but not the fear and resentment. We are four men sitting in a kitchen discussing a problem, Jerry's attitude said, and Allen again suppressed a smile.

"All right, Jamie," Jerry began, "we've got some serious thinking to do here. My brother has told me a bit about what's gone on, but I'd like to hear the details from you." The mouth clamped down, and Jamie studied the table. Jerry sighed. "Okay, look. Two days ago, it was just you and Allen, and his partner in Seattle whose name he won't tell me. Then he got shot, and he had to come here for help. Now we've got ourselves a situation where, like it or not, we've got to depend on each other. Allen is trusting me not to turn him in, and trusting Ed not to sell him out. Ed's trusting us not to land him in prison for whatever he's got himself involved in, and they're asking me to ignore this uniform I'm wearing and not report a gunshot wound and a kidnapping. I trust my brother enough to know that he wouldn't ask me this without a damned good reason, so I've gone along with it so far. But, kid, in the end everything comes down to you. Whatever it is you're holding back, it's an axe over all our necks. I think you need us to protect you. We can't do that if we don't know the full extent of the problem."

Jamie's gaze had risen, brought up by Jerry's calm and serious de-
meanor, half-hypnotized by the repetition and rhythm of his words. He
was now staring in fascination at the skilled interrogator before him, as
unable to pull away from Jerry's eyes as he had been unable to free
himself from the man's hands. He seemed to be wrestling with some
inner demon, torn between the absolute necessity of keeping it to himself and the terrible compulsion to let it out. His mouth tightened, his
teeth clamped down on his lower lip as if to keep the words inside, and
then the dark eyes suddenly filled. One tear freed itself to run down his
cheek, then Jamie tore himself away from Jerry's gaze and flung his
thin body into his rescuer's arms. Allen grunted with pain and tried to
ease the clinging child over to his right side. When he could breathe
again, he pressed the heaving shoulders against his chest and waited
for the storm to pass.

It took a long time.

Eventually, when Jamie's gulps had abated and his shudders died
down, Allen pushed him gently away, grasping one bony shoulder with
his good hand and looking into the boy's eyes. Now was the time, he
thought; now I'll hear him say that he's murdered his father, and we'll
all be in the shit.

"Jamie, what have you done?"

"Not me," the boy gulped, and swiped a fist across his nose. "My . . .
my father." The tears rose again; Jamie took a tremulous breath, and
gave to Allen his final betrayal (*Couldn't be trusted. Not to bite.*) "I think
my father . . . he kills people."

BOOK FIVE

Trip Wires

Chapter 34

ALLEN HAD ALWAYS LIKED IT BEST WHEN PATROLS WERE KEPT TO A BARE minimum: a night-ambush party stripped down to three men and their rifles, slipping into the green.

And he'd always hated the waiting, standing around the LZ in the fresh dawn, cooling his heels while the Hueys took their time, all pumped up and nowhere to go.

The three weeks between Jamie's tearful confession and the afternoon when Mark O'Connell came for his son were the worst of both worlds for a man who for twenty-six years had operated on his own: a staff of thousands, nothing to do but wait. He thought he'd go insane.

It couldn't be helped, any more than Saigon or HQ could be helped. He'd pulled Jerry into this, knowing what that would entail, knowing that there was no chance in hell that Jerry would agree to being one of a night-ambush party of three—he was an elected official, for Christ sake, picking up drunks before they drowned and filling out paperwork; what else could he do but bring in the brass?

But three weeks of it was about twenty days too much, even for Jerry. And so when Allen had told his brother that if Jerry didn't get him out from under this . . . bureaucratic bullshit, he'd just take Jamie and disappear, Jerry had believed him. Maybe not completely—he wouldn't think that Allen would up and abandon Rae—but the press of manpower and paper was getting to him, too, and so he'd allowed himself to take Allen at his word.

And now they were here, eased quietly away from the mob of badges, a night-ambush party of only a little more than three, all handchosen by Jerry, all taking personal leave for however long it took.

The house lay quiescent, hushed but for the eternal susurration of the rain and the similar patter of quick fingers on the keyboard upstairs. Allen was in the kitchen, working a painful set of reps on the fivepound dumbbell his arm had recently graduated to, wondering if it was too soon to make another pot of coffee, while upstairs, RageDaemon battled the enemy in splashes of electronic gore and the agonized if repetitive cries of the victims.

The borrowed safe house was a modern two-story wood cabin at the end of an ill-paved road on the western coast of the Washington mainland, the very definition of back of beyond. And since the Olympic Peninsula was a rain forest and it was now the last week of September, it had been raining when they drove up, it had rained every one of the seventy hours since, and it would probably rain every day for the next seven or eight months. Even in the so-called summer, a person would be hard-pressed to tell if the sun was actually shining, unless he was standing on the roof—between the drooping tree branches, the waisthigh ferns, and the swaths of epiphytic moss connecting them, there didn't seem to be any room for air, much less sunshine. It was a frigid jungle: Vietnam with Gore-Tex.

He put the dumbbell down and went to rummage through the kitchen drawers, hoping he might come across a few more of the stale low-tar cigarettes he'd discovered the day before. No luck, and he was down to three. Maybe Jerry'd think to bring him some. Tomorrow was Allen's fifty-fifth birthday. If he had been home, Rae might have baked him a cake. If Jerry showed up with one from a bakery, he'd find it hard not to shove the thing into his brother's face.

The shack at the rainy end of nowhere had been Jerry's bright idea, located through the friend of a friend. Its owner was an Arizona native who had driven through the peninsula on an eerily sun-filled weekend two years before, seen the FOR SALE sign without stopping to consider what the thick layer of lichen on the sign's top edge meant, and bought the place on a whim as a summer vacation home for his family. The family had spent exactly sixteen days here, frantically slopping brilliant yellow and white paint on every surface, before his wife gave up on the transformative possibilities of cheerful curtains and threatened to divorce him, saying that the children's games had begun to take on macabre twists. The friend's friend had kept the place, no doubt aware that finding a second innocent to buy it would be on the thin side of impossible. He claimed to enjoy the peace and quiet; Allen suspected the man came here to drink himself into a stupor. God knew, if it weren't for the computer player upstairs, Allen would have been doing just that.

Once, Allen had been good at ambushes. Now, his mind seemed unable to settle down to it, to shut out the boredom and the incessant internal chatter of possibilities. Trying to concentrate in the presence of cops—federal and local from five states so far—had been like trying to sleep under an outgoing mortar launcher. And it was not much better out here, wondering what was going on in their absence.

Gina had been right when she'd smelled the presence of law enforcement around Mark O'Connell—the feds had been looking at him since almost exactly the same time Jamie's first email had reached Alice. When Allen snatched Jamie, it had acted like a stick thrust into the federal anthill; as soon as he and the boy surfaced, the badges had swarmed over them. They would have eaten Allen alive if it hadn't been for his connection with Jamie, a boy whose father did indeed kill people for a living—seven at least, they thought, by bullet and bomb— and on the side embezzle a shitload of money, all funneled offshore. Jamie O'Connell: a boy with sharp eyes and a quick brain, a child who'd had the good sense to keep quiet around his father, a kid whose testimony could bring the whole thing down. Jamie, whose only human bonds were with his father, Allen Carmichael, and Rachel Johnson—and Rachel wasn't playing.

The investigators had spent a lot of taxpayer dollars pulling the plane up from the sea bottom to determine that its pilot was not inside. They were spending a lot more trying to find some loose end left in O'Connell's tying-up process. The only one they'd found so far was Jamie.

The feds thought that if O'Connell came for his son, it would be because the man was afraid of what Jamie might tell them. That if he came, it would be with a car bomb—this hitman's preferred method— or by a sniper's scope from the top of a building, as he'd done twice in his career. But Allen had witnessed the pleasure on O'Connell's face when he'd pulled the shotgun's trigger, and he knew that testimony had nothing to do with it: O'Connell could no more allow Jamie his freedom than a cat could let the mouse between its paws run free. O'Connell would come, because he couldn't help himself.

However, Allen was half wishing that Jerry hadn't agreed, that the feds had just thrown Allen's ass in jail and taken over the whole situation. At least in jail a man's shoes didn't take on a greasy film of mildew overnight. And they gave you nice orange suits to wear instead of the drab green and brown flannel shirt he'd put on that morning. Maybe he'd ask Jerry to bring him something fluorescent to wear, or at least Hawaiian.

They'd decided that three weeks here ought to do it, but it was only three days in and Allen was already taking the cabinet drawers off their tracks in hopes of uncovering a pack of year-old cigarettes fallen down behind. *Three weeks,* he mused. *Jesus.* He remounted one drawer and reached for the next, doing the calculations: twenty-one days, minus the three they'd been here made eighteen, times twenty-four hours was (carry the three) four hundred thirty-two, plus the hour and a half short of precisely three days came to four hundred thirty-three and a half hours, times sixty made—

It happened faster and harder than any of them could have anticipated. Both doors, kitchen and front, smashed open within half a second of the other, locks shattering as two men stormed inside, guns in their hands as they cleared the door frames. Allen dropped the drawer and was reaching around for the Glock in his belt when the bullets hit him, spinning him around and throwing him against the sink as if he'd been kicked by an ox. The Glock fell from his lifeless hand, landing with a crack on the white enamel sink; as Allen sank down, his eyes registered the gun going past them, followed by the tiled edge of the sink, then the cabinet doors, and finally the cheerful green and white linoleum with the new red spatters.

Long before Allen hit the floor, the man with the weight lifter's build was hammering up the stairs on the heels of the slimmer man who'd broken through the front door. They knew where they were headed, and did not pause before the door on the right was down and the handsome blue-eyed man's gun was coming down on the figure at the computer. One moment of hesitation, words strangling in his throat as he stared in confusion at the slim, dark-haired figure rising from the monitor, a figure that was not his son but a small woman with a sleek Smith & Wesson in her hand. The man fired as he threw himself to the side, but the brief pause had allowed the weight lifter to reach the doorway, and when the woman's gun boomed, Allen's shooter went down. Two more shots, overlaid with shouts and the pounding of feet and shattering glass, then a volley of shots ripped through the rain-forest hush and all was chaos.

After ninety seconds, a single man emerged from the shouts and turmoil, flying down the stairs as he shouted into his cell phone. At the bottom he leapt for the kitchen and skidded to a halt, and a great deal of the urgency left him.

"Are you hit?" he asked the man on the floor.

Allen glared up at him from where he'd propped himself against the cabinet. "Stupid question," he croaked. "Did you get him?"

"Got one of them, big guy with muscles, don't think he's going to make it. Here, let me help you up."

Allen put out a hand, cursing. "Jesus, I think that bastard broke every rib in my body. You lost O'Connell?"

"Went out the window. I called for reinforcements—he won't get far." Jerry seemed less interested in the failure of their trap than he was in Allen's injuries. The only blood appeared to be from where Allen's forehead had smacked into the edge of the sink, but his face was screwed up in pain. Jerry brushed his brother's fumbling fingers aside and ripped open the buttons on the plaid shirt to peer at the Kevlar vest beneath. It had trapped two rounds: One would have gone through Allen's stomach, the other his heart. Thank God for good aim, Allen thought, and had to firmly stifle the impulse to laugh. He reached for the vest straps, allowing Jerry to help him.

"Everyone okay?" Allen asked. He could smell the sweat and the gunpowder on his brother, and it seemed to him that Jerry's hands were almost as uncertain as his own.

"Annie was nicked in the leg, she'll be fine. Marty took one in the side, but it doesn't look too bad. I don't think O'Connell was hit, but the other guy, shit, he just wouldn't stop shooting. I don't know which one of us got him in the end. Christ," he said, trying to make light of it. "My hands are shaking. I never had to shoot at anyone before."

"Must be Howard. If you hadn't got him, we'd all be dead meat. He blew through here and shot me almost casually, like you'd kick a chair out of the way. Ow!"

"Here, let me get that."

Gently, Jerry lifted the vest away from his brother's body. He tossed it on the counter and eased up the army-green T-shirt Allen wore underneath it. The skin was angry, and it wouldn't have surprised Jerry if he was right about the ribs. Jerry handed Allen an ice tray from the freezer.

"Get some cold onto that," he suggested. "You going to be okay for a while?"

"Sure," Allen assured him. Jerry left, to go upstairs and see to the injured. Allen put down the ice, retrieved the Glock from the sink, and took his waterproof jacket from its hook next to the door. Silently, he let himself out into the rain.

Ten paces, and the rain forest took over. Another ten, and the sounds of voices and equipment became distant, muted. In less than a minute, Allen was all by himself in the green. Just him and a man with blue eyes.

At first, the rain was an irritant. He kept feeling that if only someone would shut the damn hiss off for a minute, he could hear his quarry moving through the undergrowth. But then the instincts crept back in, and reminded him that acuteness of hearing was only necessary for the prey. Deer and rabbits had big ears; their hunters did not. And in this jungle, Allen would be the hunter.

O'Connell had gone out the upstairs window and sprinted straight across the cleared space for the trees, shoving in among them at full speed, wanting only to put distance between himself and the guns that had so suddenly erupted from the corners of an apparently empty house. He'd spent time in the woods, hunting deer (and mock-hunting his son, Allen reminded himself grimly), but he'd never been a target himself, as far as Allen knew. That was about to change.

Allen, following the man's northbound trail, saw the point at which O'Connell's mind clicked out of panic mode—far too soon for Allen's taste, since it was easier to follow a man who wasn't thinking clearly. Allen paused to shrug off his rustling jacket, and moved on through the wet, his eyes picking out the disturbed moss and the places where the fern fronds had shed their drops, his ears alert for any sound that wasn't a steady pat and hiss, his nose—or was he imagining this?—following the expensive cologne that he'd smelled in the marble bathroom and on the silken bed covering. Glock against his thigh, Allen slipped through the gloom between the ferns and the moss-thick trees, a shadow in the green.

Sudden motion at three o'clock: big, fast-moving—but two of them, and not men: elk. *What startled them?* Allen crouched a little more, setting aside the pain in his chest, trying to ignore the once-familiar chafe and bind of soaked clothing. The elk had been trotting off to the right, which meant O'Connell was dead ahead, maybe half a mile north.

But going where? The man had paused briefly, a quarter of a mile back, his footprints pressing into the moss with the delay. When he'd resumed, his path had angled slightly to the east. But he hadn't scuffed the ground with indecision, merely stood for a moment, then started up again.

Shit, Allen thought abruptly; *the bastard stopped to look at a compass. He's making for his car.*

No time to waste. Allen started up again, but hadn't gone a dozen paces before he halted; predator or not, he was making too much noise. He laid the gun on a log thick with moss, whipped his folding knife from his pocket, sliced through the sodden laces on his boots, and dropped the knife into his T-shirt pocket. He stepped out of the boots, did the same with his sodden jeans and socks, and went on, dressed in nothing but olive-green shorts and T-shirt.

The freedom was extraordinary. His skin seemed to drink in the forest. Why hadn't the Snakeman gone naked in the jungle? he wondered. Maybe he had.

Allen could trot now on the soft forest floor, and he set a path curving out around to the left. He figured he had at least a mile or two before O'Connell reached his car, since the next road was that far away. Of course, if O'Connell was traveling on foot, he could set off due east, and Allen would be screwed. But he believed the man would have a car.

Allen moved faster, dodging the trees, barely touching the thick growth, slipping through the green like a wild thing as his hair and clothing plastered against his body and his feet patted the mossy earth. Suddenly he stopped, his head coming up as if to taste the breeze. Somewhere, deep inside, a switch had been thrown, and its current began to wake an entire set of long-buried instincts. He *knew* where O'Connell was, he could feel him like the blip on an internal radar. The man was moving swiftly, though not as fast as Allen was, and his path would intersect the trajectory of Allen's curve in less than ten minutes.

Two minutes later, Allen became aware of O'Connell's growing assurance, knew when the man paused to sweep his gaze over the woods behind him, felt the man's glee that he had escaped and fury that Howard had not. The man's thoughts touched on his son then, and the flare of his anger came across the forest like the heat from a fire.

At five minutes the forest stopped abruptly and Allen was stumbling into an unnatural clear place, a confusing bare strip, harsh gravel digging into his bare feet: the access road. It ran arrow-straight to the west, disappearing around a corner a few hundred yards to Allen's right. He stood in the center of the foreign thing, listening in his mind for O'Connell's progress. He could run down this road and hope to reach the car before its owner did, or he could set up an ambush.

The green was ready for him. Sometime earlier that year, the forest had given up a tree. Not a terribly large tree, and not so long ago that it had become a sodden and immovable mass along the edge of the road. Sparsely branched, with no root ball to speak of, it seemed set there for his purpose: perfect. He laid the Glock on the ground, and braced himself under the curve of its trunk.

The weight of it was almost too much, particularly the first wrenching motions needed to loose it from the soil's embrace. His ribs shrieked at him, his shoulder groaned, but the tree came, an inch and then a foot, and he staggered across the bruising rock surface with the dead branches wrapping his face, letting go only when his feet hit the softness again on the other side of the road.

He retrieved the gun and sat against a tree trunk, hugging his ribs and whining with pain, trying not to pant any more than he had to. The dead tree now lying across the road was not big enough to block a determined driver, particularly in a four-wheel-drive vehicle, but it would force him to slow to a crawl, and that was all Allen needed. After a minute he checked the gun, then sat with it sheltering under his bent-up legs. His thumb began to play with the safety: on and off, on and off.

He felt (imagined? Did it matter which?) when O'Connell reached the car, knew the man's surge of satisfaction when he found it undiscovered. Allen's ears picked out the whine of its starter from the rain noises, and then the thing was coming down the track. He got to his feet, taking up a position clear of the trees so he would have an open line of fire, and so O'Connell would see him. He dashed the hair and dead leaves from his face, and he waited.

Had Mark O'Connell spent less time as hunter and more as prey, he might not have made the mistakes he did. Had he remained cautious once he gained the car, been capable of thinking of its two tons as a liability instead of weight to throw around, he would not have gone down the road at such a speed. He might have listened to the voice of the hunted, telling him that there was no safety in steel, that a man with a handgun could be equal to a heavily armed killer in a tank of an SUV, given the right circumstances. But he did not listen to any

voice but the gloating tones of the habitual victor, and he came around
the curve moving too fast to stop.

The dead tree and its mud-covered guardian froze him for one crucial half second, allowing his arm to make a brief automatic jerk away
from the standing wild man before he caught himself and yanked his
juggernaut back toward Allen. But the moment of indecision cost the
heavy car its momentum, and the wet soil under the gravel gave beneath its skidding tires.

The big black vehicle with the smoked-glass windows crunched
one wheel up onto the tree while its back passenger side slammed into
one of the tree's standing brothers, stunning the forest and sending
buckets of collected raindrops splashing to the ground. The driver,
however self-assured, had prudently fastened his belt and did not go
through the windshield. Instead, he kicked open the front passenger-
side door and dropped to the earth, protected now by all that steel. He
edged his head over the hood; in his hand he carried a small automatic
machine gun.

But the naked maniac was no longer in front of his tree. O'Connell
lifted the gun and sent a brief spray into its trunk, hoping to drive the
man out from behind it, but there was no response. He went around
the back of the car, his shoes slipping on the wet moss at the side of
the road, but he could see nothing from there either.

Allen was not behind the tree. When he'd seen the big car waver
and come at him, he'd flung himself behind the moss-green trunk, but
he had continued on, plunging deeper into the woods. He could no
longer see the vehicle or its driver, but the shots told him all he needed
to know: O'Connell was sticking with the car.

Allen worked his way up the road until he reached the curve. Checking to be sure the roadway was clear, he trotted across, then turned
back. O'Connell might expect him to try an approach from behind, but
he couldn't be sure, and he couldn't look in all directions at once. Gun
down but ready, Allen let his feet choose their path between the trees.
The hanging mosses brushed his shoulders, the ferns parted for his
knees, and green surrounded him, the multiplicity of green that cloaked
all his dreams.

Thirty yards from the car, he stopped. The shift and murmur of the
rain forest were unbroken, no sound of bird or beast. There had been
no shots after that one brief burst, and although Allen was certain that
O'Connell was still there, he couldn't tell what the man was doing.

Setting up an ambush of his own, Allen's mind whispered. The man
was after all a hunter. But he was the kind of hunter who valued results

over challenge, who put out grain to lead the deer in. The car was the bait; O'Connell would wait within view of it.

Of course, the only deadline in a deer hunt was the man's wish to regain the comfort of his hearth before darkness fell. Here, both sides knew it wouldn't be long before that houseful of guns followed the would-be assassin's track. Both men knew that time was on Allen's side. He moved with infinite caution across the forest floor, tasting the air, his instincts probing to find the other.

O'Connell was, he finally decided, back inside the car, hiding behind the dark reflective windows of the SUV. He trusted his urban protection more than the wilds, and valued his comfort. The naked man with the gun was sure to come; he would be met by death. Except that Allen had no intention of sticking his head into that vehicle. He was happy to wait in the rain. O'Connell wouldn't be able to stand it, not knowing. In a few minutes he'd begin to think he had imagined that mud-smeared, leaf-clotted creature pointing a shiny gun at him, think that maybe the tree'd just fallen there. Think that all he had to do was put the vehicle into low and set it to crawling over the trunk.

Give the bastard ten minutes, Allen thought.

It took seven. The black sides of the car shifted slightly. A dark shape ventured up close to the windows, disappeared again. Another shift, and Allen slid the Glock's safety off. The shape of a body slithering over the seatbacks, keeping well down from the clearer glass of the front windows, settling into the driver's seat. Allen prepared to sprint up to the side of the car.

Then abruptly the silence was broken by a well-known voice, shouting, "Hold it right there!" and a lot happened fast. The ignition caught, the car jerked and died again as O'Connell snatched up the gun with one hand and held down the electric window control with the other, jamming the gun's barrel into the gap and pulling the trigger. *He'll be completely deaf,* Allen's brain registered in passing, and then he was ripping open the front passenger door and pointing the Glock at the back of Jamie O'Connell's father.

"Put it down," Allen told him. The man turned his head just enough to catch a glimpse of Allen's weapon; O'Connell's hold on the machine pistol loosed, its barrel tipped to the sky before it fell to the gravel. "Now, reach out the window and put both hands on top of the car."

Jerry's head reappeared around the tree he'd dived behind, and he squinted, trying to make sense of the sight. He came out, moving cautiously and with his gun ready, approaching the car.

"It's me, Jer," Allen called.

Jerry's pace picked up and he reached for the door handle. It took some wrenching to get it open, and then O'Connell was stepping out, two guns on him.

He was a smaller man than he appeared in photographs or on Allen's television screen, and his eyes were more intensely blue. The eyes glittered with fury, and with something else. Amusement, perhaps? Certainly with a strong conviction of his own superiority to these two hicks who had somehow managed to turn the tables on him. The man's meandering gaze rested briefly on the badge clipped to Jerry's shirt, then he dismissed both it and the man wearing it and turned to Allen, clad only in T-shirt, shorts, and mud. The corner of his mouth twitched in disdain, and he tipped his head to look into Allen's face, holding his gaze. Now the smirk was unmistakable.

"You must be the pervert who kidnapped my son," he said to Allen. His voice was conversational. "I hope you got your pleasure out of the boy, because by the time I finish with you, you're going to wish you'd been castrated at birth."

And then Jerry hit him; Jerry the staunch upholder of order, Jerry the paragon of self-control, Sheriff Carmichael, who had never once in all his career treated a prisoner with anything but firm good manners, succumbing to a rush of brutality at the brief phrase of a man he'd never met, never seen except on tape; he reached out with the flat of his gun and smacked O'Connell in the head.

Then he looked down at his hand in surprise, as if it had nothing to do with the man on the ground. *Even Jerry,* Allen thought, and reached to tug the handcuffs from his brother's belt.

When the first wrist snapped on, O'Connell began to laugh through the blood on his face. Jerry gave a shudder. The murder died from his eyes, and only then did he holster his gun and reach for the radio.

Chapter 35

JAMIE O'CONNELL SAT ON THE HARD BENCH AND TRIED NOT TO THINK. IT would be so much easier if he could just go empty, turn into a brainless moron, become a smiling vegetable. Then maybe they'd all leave him alone. Let him go back to the Johnson farm and sit on the porch swing with Terry on his lap, talk to the chickens. Montana had been a dream, even though he'd seen Rachel and talked to Pete on the phone since then; it had been something he'd made up, like his arms had made up their memory of a wriggling Jack Russell terrier, like his feet had invented the feel of a warm weight during the night.

It was all so confusing. They all wanted something from him, and he didn't know how to give it to them. The men in the suits wanted him to tell about his father, and Rachel wanted him to come back with her, and Allen . . . He didn't know how to put what Allen wanted, he just knew it was the hardest thing of all. Because Allen wouldn't say what it was, just, "Do what you think is right."

What you think is right. Shit—how could he know what was right? If even the grown-ups couldn't agree what to do, how could he be expected to? Sometimes he just hated Allen. Just purely hated the big man with the hole in his arm that he didn't even blame Jamie for, like he didn't blame Jamie for fucking up his life, even though Jamie could see it there in his face, that kind of haunted look that Allen wore sometimes when the FBI was threatening to lock him up or something. Not that he'd ever tell Jamie just what it was that made him look haunted, but Jamie figured that was it. And it was Jamie's fault, for dragging him into all this in the first place with that stupid **deadboy** email, instead of figuring out how to deal with his problems on his own. Jamie's fault Allen got shot and Alice was in trouble and Howard was dead and that strange woman Rae looked so nervous and *everything*, but Allen just sat there and told him to do what was right. And he *hated* Allen when that happened, wanted to gouge his eyes out and take his old deer rifle and aim it right at the man's chest and pull the trigger so he'd be *gone* and leave Jamie alone with Father like he belonged, just him and Father.

But the strange thing was, even when he was most pissed off with Allen and just wanted Allen to LEAVE HIM ALONE, for some reason the endless conversations with the men in suits went more easily when Allen was there. Not that Allen stopped them from pushing at him, or that he helped Jamie figure out what to say. It was less definite than that. More like, when Allen was there, it was easier to breathe. It wasn't that he'd tell Jamie when to breathe, or what to say with the air that came out; he was just there, and it was easier.

And when Allen wasn't there? Well, those were usually the times when he'd imagine Father looking on. He'd almost convinced himself that Father really was there, behind the mirror that had to be a one-way window, until Allen found out what he was thinking and took him behind it to see. But when the men with the suits started in on him, asking him about dates and when his father had been home and when he hadn't, and who they had seen when they were in Vegas one time, and the places they'd flown last summer, and a hundred other things he knew the answers to deep down, he couldn't tell them because he'd look over the shoulder of Father's lawyer and see Father's ghost through the glass—or after they moved to the room with the stupid bright kiddie prints on the wall, he'd see someone in the hall or walking down the street and think it was Father, even though he knew that Father was in jail.

Yes, when Allen was in the room, there was more air to breathe, and he could think better, and Father's ghostly figure wasn't as sub-stantial.

But sometimes he hated it when Allen was there. Sometimes he'd be sitting in his chair with a clean man in a suit going at him—really polite, they always were, and Father's lawyers were always ready when-ever they got too pushy, but he could tell they wanted to pry him open like a clam. And he'd start to feel Father there, looking on, approving of his son's silence, like it was strength under fire. Then Jamie would feel a little smile begin to grow on his face, like he and Father had a se-cret. And it was true, Father always *knew*, he knew what Jamie was thinking and what he was going to do—he'd have known what Jamie was up to back in May if he'd been around and not off in one of those places the suit men kept asking about. And Jamie was absolutely gut-certain that Father knew now, even locked in jail, exactly what Jamie was doing and saying, and those times when Jamie just stared at the clean men and thought, *Oh, go fuck yourself*—that was when Father would stir in the back of his mind, and nod his approval, and Jamie would smile to himself, an echo of that scary smile of Father's.

But then Allen would come in and Father would fade in Jamie's mind just a little, and he'd just hate Allen, *hate* him for a few minutes until the extra air kicked in, and he'd remember Allen was his friend, and get confused again.

Yes, all in all, Jamie wished he could just cut out his brain and stop thinking.

But maybe not today. Today, at last—weeks and weeks after Allen and his brother had set the trap in the woods that Father had walked into, where Howard had died—Jamie was *finally* going to see Father. He'd been aware for some time that lawyers were maneuvering and people were fighting over this, and he'd tried not even to think about it, knowing it might never happen, and not knowing how he'd feel about it if it did.

Because Father was sure to be really mad. With good reason— Jamie had brought this all down on him, Jamie's unwillingness to be raised as Father saw fit, Jamie's sissy-weakness that Father had worked so long to cure. And Father was sure to be mad in other ways, too: One thing Jamie had learned since May was, normal people didn't live like that. Normal fathers didn't do things to their sons like his did; when they went hunting, they hunted the deer; when they needed to be gone for a day or two, they got a baby-sitter, they didn't lock their kid in a dark room or leave him in a cabin in the woods.

Of course, Father would say that "normal" is another word for "stupid." Ordinary people played baseball with their kids and helped them with their homework because they wanted their kids to be as stupid as they were, as dull and boring and spineless and weak. Herd animals. Father was something else, and his son would be something else, too. Stronger, more independent, with sharp teeth.

Funny thing was, it was Allen who'd been the soldier, tough and trained—and you could see it, if you looked, see that there was something hard as rocks inside him. Yet it was Allen who now went along with the herd, who allowed the FBI and everyone to do things their way even though he very obviously thought they were clueless; Allen who'd walked freely into confinement, who stuck around when he clearly hated it, who could so easily walk away to freedom but let himself be dragged down by Jamie, and Rae, and even Jerry. Stupid. Weak to hang around, to put himself through hours of interviews where no one wanted him—not the suit men, not the lawyers, not Jamie. Stupid not to have dealt with Father when he had the chance, like a soldier (wasn't this a war?). If he'd just shot Father—not that Jamie wanted that to have happened, but if he had—then it all could have ended and Jamie would be free of all this confusion and crap and he could get on with life, even though he'd hate Allen forever for killing Father, and probably never want to look at him again. But instead Allen and his brother had busted Father (and Jamie still couldn't understand how that had happened, still held a strong suspicion that Father had arranged his own arrest as part of some incomprehensible scheme) and there was Father behind bars, more like a spider behind his web, tugging at them all through the lawyers, waiting there in jail until it was time for his lawyers to get him out.

And they would, Jamie could feel that. The pressure was on, the men in suits seeming to sweat as they pressed him for information, giving Jamie the impression that they'd just love to take him by the throat and shake it out of him, even when they looked cool and unconcerned on the outside. Allen was there at most of the interviews now, never telling Jamie what to say, just being there and looking on, keeping the suits and lawyers in line and giving him room to breathe.

Like he was going to be inside the room today, when Jamie and his father would meet for the first time since May.

Jamie remembered thinking, during that strange drive away from Montana when he'd imagined he was leading Father away from the Johnsons, that if Allen tried to get between him and Father, Allen wouldn't stand a chance. And it was weird that, even though Allen seemed to be ordinary and weak, Jamie was no longer quite so certain that Father's capture had been a fluke, or part of a clever plan. He'd even thought, lying awake the night before, that with the three of them in a room together, he himself might be the one who got torn apart.

But again, he couldn't decide how he would feel, if Allen turned out to be a match for Father. He did honestly hate Allen for putting Father behind bars. If he and Alice had just left Jamie the hell alone back in May, it would be all right, instead of this. Well, maybe not all right, because even before **deadboy,** Father'd had sharp teeth, like a tiger, a man-eating tiger. But wasn't Jamie his son? Wasn't Jamie strong and independent as well, with teeth and claws and brains?

Love and hate went round and round and it was all so confusing. He was nearly thirteen now, but some days he just wished someone would pick him up and hold him and tell him in a calm voice what to do.

Oh, Jamie really wished he could just stop thinking.

ALLEN CARMICHAEL SAT ON THE HARD DECK CHAIR, A BEER ON HIS KNEE and the lights playing across the water in front of him, but he paid no attention to either, because he was thinking about tomorrow's meeting with Jamie and Mark O'Connell. He was dreading it, had hated the very thought of it ever since it was proposed—his every instinct shouted, *Keep the boy away from his father.* But he was the one who'd proposed it, he'd fought for it, he'd wheedled and maneuvered and made vows he probably wouldn't be able to keep, because Jamie had asked him for it.

Don't let him see the man, don't let the bastard get his screws back into the boy.

Allen Carmichael had been an advocate for children half his life, allying himself to their needs and wishes as he worked out the burden laid on him by the blue-eyed cave demon. He had thought he was accustomed to laying his trust at the feet of the children he served, thought he knew what it was to take risks. But never like this.

Keep Jamie away from him, lock the bastard away and lose the key.

And therein lay the problem. A man downing his own plane might be fined for littering, or pollution, but O'Connell hadn't even made an insurance claim. And there were no laws against taking skydiving classes, or buying a pristine twelve-year-old diary from an antiquarian bookstore in Denver just before Christmas last year and faking a record of your child's history, or misleading your son into thinking that you were incompetent when it came to computers, or sending your tame thug up to Montana to talk to a little girl, or half the other sins the feds had tagged the man with. There was no evidence that Jamie had ever been locked in that bare, windowless room adjoining his father's, nor that he had been parked in a remote cabin during one of the times when a target in Reno or Cincinnati had been hit. Oh sure, CPS would hold on to the boy for a while, but Allen did not imagine that a foster placement would deter Mark O'Connell for two minutes, once he was out.

Everyone knew that from the purchase of the diary to the smashing of the potentially incriminating hard drive on Jamie's computer—Jamie's, but which his father also used when he wanted to hide the evidence of his activities—the man's meticulous planning was aimed at closing down his operation and providing Jamie as a suspect for murder. Everyone but Jamie knew this, but so far the accumulated charges were all financial, and sooner or later O'Connell's lawyers were going to hit on a judge with no imagination and a hefty respect for defendants' rights, who would grant the man bail. And then he'd vanish.

Only Jamie stood in his way. Jamie, who claimed he couldn't remember half the places he'd been, any of the times he'd been abandoned for a crucial day or two. Jamie, whose clever mind had pieced together the story he'd blurted out to Allen, Jerry, and Ed, but who had since that night proved uncertain on chapter and verse. Jamie, who loved his father and desperately longed for the man's blessing with all the passion in his confused, abused soul. Jamie, whom Allen would accompany to a confrontation with the father who had been setting him up, using him as a carpenter uses a nail or a hit man a scope (although the feds were proving wildly unsuccessful at proving that role too).

He'd talked it over endlessly, with Rachel and Jerry, Alice and Rae, and several highly competent psychologists, and not one of them could tell him any more than he knew. Seeing his father would be bad for the boy; not seeing him would in the long run be worse.

The feds were desperate enough that when Allen pointed out that he alone had a chance of prying the facts out of Jamie, they believed him. And when he told them that he would only do so if they allowed Jamie a visit with his father, they believed that as well. In fact, Allen had no intention of carrying out his half of the bargain. He did not for a moment doubt that he could break Jamie's silence, had no question at all that the boy would testify if Allen drove him to it. But he would not do that, because to force Jamie would be to lose him. He'd be saving Jamie from his father, by becoming the father himself.

As he'd snatched Mouse from one atrocity, by flinging him into another.

And so he'd told the boy, *Do what you think is right,* praying that it was enough, knowing that when the boy came face-to-face with the father he so craved, those six little words would probably blow up in Allen's face. Trip wires worked both ways.

But in the end, all Allen could do was trust.

At some point during that long and sleepless night, the realization stole into Allen's mind that he was, again, keeping watch over a sleeping platoon. All his life, he had been assembling a far-flung platoon composed of nervy women with thousand-yard stares and their shell-shocked children who knew firsthand the meaning of "friendly fire." He worked with them because it was the closest he could get to being with a bunch of vets: Until Rae, there was no bullshit with them, no need to explain hidden messages, no reason to pretend that life was pretty. They understood war stories, and although they didn't have any room in their minds for black humor at first, give them a few weeks of safety, they managed just fine. There was not one woman he'd ever slept with that he felt as close to as the women he'd helped to disappear, not a kid among his blood relations he'd choose over one of the beaten children he took in hand.

It was the reason, he supposed, that he loved Rae, who was as damaged as they come. And the reason he'd never felt as close to Jerry as he wanted to, because Jerry was basically a nice guy who knew the world's pain from the outside.

Thing was, a person needed a community that spoke the same language. People who had been there, whom he could trust not to get it wrong. People who could come to trust him, through shared ordeals. People like Jamie O'Connell.

All that night, Allen Carmichael kept vigil at the side of a boy twenty miles away, thinking of green things, sitting between The Wolf and a man with a streak in his dark hair, seeing before him a black hand gentling a blond head. And the next morning, driving through the rain, the whirl of Allen's mind calmed and grew still, until it seemed that he was traveling through a great and ringing silence. It persisted all the way to the jail, through the gates and the check-ins, into the conference room with its long table and forest of chairs, a room cleared of anything that might be adapted as a weapon, a private space set aside for their use. Jamie was already there, looking small and cold. Allen rested his hand on the boy's shoulder, said hello, asked if he was all right. Then he took a chair to the side, so as not to come between the boy and his father.

And with a rattle at the door, the man himself was there, wearing the ordinary shirt and jeans Allen had suggested instead of the orange jail-issue suit, the guards removing his handcuffs, his glance discarding Allen as he'd discarded the sight of Jerry's badge, seeking out the child with the huge, dark eyes filled with such terrible hope. The man rubbed his wrists and smiled, that warm, charming, self-assured expression he'd used so often, and his voice when he spoke resonated with affection, approval, and humor.

"Hello, son."

And Jamie stepped into his father's arms like the last piece of a puzzle, fitting home.

Chapter 36

THE TWO O'CONNELLS HELD EACH OTHER LONG AND HARD, BLOND HAIR bent over dark, a man's muscles around the boy's slimness. When O'Connell gently pushed his son from him, it was to look down into his eyes and say, "You've grown," with a crooked smile that acknowledged the past months even as it dismissed them.

Jamie tentatively returned the smile. "Almost half an inch."

"No, it's got to be more than that. Three-quarters, I'm sure."

Pleased, Jamie shook his head and said without thinking, "I just got measured. Maybe it's your shoes." Then he froze, catching too late his reference to the jail-issue footgear his father had on. But O'Connell only laughed, stretching out one leg to display the cheap canvas shoes he wore.

"You like the clothes, son?"

"They don't really look like you," Jamie agreed, and Allen flashed briefly on the half-empty closet, its custom suits cleared out and as yet undiscovered.

"You should see the jumpsuit I usually wear—makes me look like that Vegas mechanic. The one you like—what's his name?"

"Nick," Jamie provided. It was a flattery game—Allen would have bet his left hand that O'Connell remembered the man's name.

"Nick, that's right. The guy who wanted you to come work for him in the summer, thought he could pay Mark O'Connell's son minimum wages. Can you see that happening, Mr. Carmichael?"

He didn't look at Allen when he asked the question, nor did Allen look up from the contemplation of his own hands. "Nothing wrong with honest work. Teaches a man self-respect."

"He's right," O'Connell told his son. "You might even enjoy it for a couple of months, James, maybe during high school. Hey, that's only two years from now, isn't it? We ought to think about where you want to go. There are some great schools in the Bay Area. Or boarding schools, if you'd rather. But there's plenty of time to talk about that."

Jamie nodded, and his father, picking up on some faint hesitation, deflected it with physical movement, resting his hand on the boy's shoulder and walking with him to the chairs at the table.

He was good, Allen saw, watching as the con man maneuvered his son into a chair angling away from Allen. He touched Jamie's shoulders just enough to remind the boy of his hunger to be held, and then stood away, taking one of the other chairs and moving it so he and the boy were facing each other. Allen could see why the man had made such a success of bilking Silicon Valley entrepreneurs out of their money: His words and body language were enormously self-assured and letter-perfect, letting his son know that this was the most temporary of situations, one that they both needed to regard with good-tempered resignation. Allen fought down the urge to yank Jamie out before it went any further.

"Anyway, son, you look great. You've been taking care of yourself over the summer, I'm glad to see."

"I missed you."

"Oh, man, I've missed you, too. Oh, James, you can't imagine how awful it was, getting that call from Mrs. Mendez. I was . . . devastated. When I found you were alive last month, I was so happy."

"But I wrote you a letter, saying I ran away but I was safe."

"You wrote—I never got a letter." The look on O'Connell's face hastily arranged itself from puzzlement to dismay, but in between the two, Allen had seen the brief instant when the man remembered the letter. He didn't think Jamie had noticed his father's snap decision to lie.

"I wrote so you wouldn't worry, and so the police wouldn't look so hard. I didn't really say in it why I ran away, but I wanted to. And I want to now."

"Son, that's all in the past. It's time to move on."

"But Father, I—"

"Son, why don't you call me Dad, or Daddy? 'Father' is finished with. You're practically grown up." He reached out a finger to brush a lock of hair from Jamie's forehead; Allen felt a sudden urge to rip the finger off and stuff it down the man's throat. "I'll get this all straightened up and get out of here, and you and I will go off somewhere. Then we can talk and talk and figure out what went wrong and how to make it right. How about that?"

The pure, naked longing on Jamie O'Connell's face was obscene, as raw and tortured as a scream from out of the jungle night. *No, not this time, you bastard*—but the protest in Allen's mind was so weak, he was not even aware that it had passed through. For the first time he saw the physical resemblance between father and son, the shape of the mouth and chin, the way their shoulders leaned toward each other across the table, yearning. Oh Christ, oh shit, why had he imagined any good could come of this? O'Connell was as smooth and seductive as a polished stone, and in a minute Jamie would reach out and pick him up, and be lost.

But Jamie was looking down, a faint line puckering his forehead.

"I . . . I was thinking I should go back to Montana. I'm missing school."

"Why the hell would you want to go to Montana?" Halfway through the sentence O'Connell caught himself and modulated his voice from irritation to puzzlement, but that time, Allen saw Jamie's wince, and was grateful for it. O'Connell had seen it, too, and made haste to cover it over. "Well, if Montana is what you want, that's fine—they tell me you've found yourself a nice family there, lots of animals to fool around with. And I suppose I'll be pretty busy with legal problems for a few weeks. So sure, why don't you go back there and enjoy yourself, and when Christmas vacation comes we can see where we stand?"

Jamie was silent, his head bowed. His father leaned forward, too, bending over until they were nearly touching, and he spoke in a quiet voice.

"It's just, son, that you're going to need to be really careful what you say to those policemen, and especially the FBI. They have a way of twisting a person's words around, and you'd hate to have something unimportant you've said turned into some major piece of evidence, now wouldn't you? James?"

The boy took a shaky breath, loud in the bare room, and pushed back his chair to reach for his father. O'Connell was startled, but as soon as his arms had closed around his son, his gaze locked on to Allen, his pale eyes triumphant and amused as he held the boy to his heart, murmuring endearments into the dark hair.

The boy pulled back a little, to say to his father, "From now on, I'm going to use the name Jamie. Like Mommy used to call me."

"What? Oh, sure, son. Jamie it is. And you promise you won't tell those men anything, Jamie?"

But something was wrong. The boy was continuing to pull away from his father's arms, disengaging himself from the insistent hands, taking a step back, then another. O'Connell's face changed as he felt his son slipping away from him; his eyes blazed with disbelief and fury, and only the presence of Allen in the room and guards behind the glass kept him in his chair. Watching him, Allen thought it was a near thing. Jamie backed quickly away, exquisitely sensitive to his father's moods, and circled the long table until he was beyond reach of those hands, standing in front of Allen. Only then did he transfer his gaze from his father to Allen. The child's face looked like a man fresh from combat, haggard beyond his years with experience and understanding. He spoke to Allen, for the first time since he'd come into the room, his voice rough with emotion, but sure.

"He'd never give way like that," he whispered to Allen. "He'd never let me live in Montana unless he wanted something. The only reason he says I can go there is because he thinks that if he does, then I won't talk before he can get someone to come after me." He took a shaky breath, and the tears slipped down his face. "You can tell your brother that I'll tell him what he wants to know."

After

ALLEN CARMICHAEL AND JAMIE O'CONNELL SAT ON THE ROCK PROMONtory of Sanctuary Island, waiting for the morning fog to lift. The late October sun was out there somewhere, but down here by the water the swirls of gray and blue persisted, and the boy leaned in to the man as much for warmth as for shared solidarity. Jamie wore on his head a red baseball cap embroidered with the words ORCAS ISLAND. His suitcase waited on the boards of Rae's dock.

Neither of them had spoken for several minutes. They had talked so much over the past few days, about all that had happened and all that would come next, it was a relief just to sit on the cold boulders, small waves lapping near their feet, wrapped in mist and stillness.

It was Jamie who broke the silence, to say in a dreamy voice, "When I was a kid, I used to believe that if I tried hard enough, I could conjure up a magical cloak that would make me invisible. I even had a name for it: *The Quiet*. It was just those colors, gray and white and silver."

Classic dissociative technique, Allen noted—but picturing the shattered frame of the boy's door, that small and bloodstained storage room between his room and his father's, he could well imagine how appealing such a garment would have been to the child. He still didn't know precisely what had gone on inside that small room, although Jamie had gone so far as to admit that it was something he didn't want to talk about with Allen, which in itself was a big admission. Better to leave it in the hands of the expert, scheduled to meet with Jamie twice a week for a long time. It was not Allen's business. He was not the boy's therapist, nor his rescuer any longer; just his friend.

He wrapped his arm around the thin shoulders and hugged the child to him.

"He really doesn't love me, does he?" Jamie asked.

How to answer a question like that? *He loves you like the hawk loves the squirrel? Like a mad platoon leader adores the men he wields? Like a bullet cleaves to flesh?*

"I think he does, in his way. But he's just not equipped for anything more. I suppose you could call him an emotional cripple." More comfort than truth, but sometimes that's what was needed.

"And I'm not."

Allen's arm tightened, and he rested his face on Jamie's red hat. "No, thank God, you're not." Hugely handicapped, yes, but not entirely crippled.

The mist was thinning, lifting free of the water's surface. Not long before Ed came, to take them to the mainland.

"You're really sure about going back to Montana?" he asked Jamie. The bending of fostering procedures and the government's willingness to overlook the wildly illicit nature of the Johnson link was directly tied to Jamie's willingness to testify. Allen wasn't about to tell the boy what to do, but he was very good at telling him how to get it done. And the boy had proved remarkably unencumbered by blood relatives to take the Johnsons' place.

"You sure I can't stay with you?"

"Jamie," Allen began; they'd been over this before, more than once.

"I know, I know," the boy cut him off. " 'Maybe I can come visit during summer vacation.' No, I'll go back there. I don't have anywhere else I want to go. Anyway, I can see what it's like to have a real winter."

"Even if it means only half an hour of online time a day?"

Jamie ducked his head. "Yeah. I don't even know if I'll play for a while. The whole thing, knowing that my father was one of the players—

it's just too creepy to think about. I somehow feel like, every time another player comes on I'll be wondering, *Is that him?*"

Silverfish, the ubiquitous, had been O'Connell's online name, the
man's means of keeping track of his son, of coaxing out information,
entering the boy's mind and life as surreptitiously as the insect occupied a house. Creepy, indeed.

Allen raised his head, hearing the first vibrations of a familiar engine across the water. As his head moved, the corner of his eye caught
a dark shape on the opposite side of the cove. He looked closely, startled, but after a moment relaxed: only a tree trunk, enshrouded by the
mist. Not a squatting figure in jungle fatigues, gazing approvingly
across the water at him. Not a man with a white streak in his hair.
Allen smiled to himself, and turned to the boy. "I think that's the *Orca
Queen.*"

Jamie was hunched over, arms wrapped around his knees, and
seemed not to have heard. "I've been . . . remembering," he said. "It's
like, there were things I knew, but I sort of forgot. Like I didn't want to
see them or something. One of them is, my father did kill my dog, I
know he did. His name was Snowflake—Mom named him, kind of a
dumb name because he was always so dirty, but he was an okay dog.
And then one day he peed on the rug and Father just kicked him and
kicked him until he died. I was right there. And he made me clean it
up, the blood and the pee, and made me bury Snowy. I never told anyone, because who'd believe me? But the weirdest thing was, he acted
like I'd done it. Used to whisper that my secret was safe with him and
then he'd laugh. It almost got to the point that I believed him, I could
almost remember my foot kicking Snowy."

"The mind is a mysterious thing, isn't it?" It was the only comment
Allen could come up with. But Jamie didn't seem to hear; he wasn't
finished.

"And I'm not sure, but I think maybe my father was there, the day
my mother . . . when she died. I don't know why, but it just came to me
the other day, I suddenly remembered walking down the block, going
home from school. I remembered hearing this big noise just after I'd
crossed the street, a bang that I thought was somebody backing into a
garbage can or something. But when I got home, I was just sure there
was someone else in the house. I don't remember why I thought that,
whether I heard someone walking around or what, but when I went up
and found her, somewhere in the back of my mind, I *knew* someone
was there, 'cause I remember thinking, 'Why didn't he stop her?' And

Father had the only other key, and everything was locked, and when the police went looking there was nobody else inside. I never said anything, and after a while I just . . . forgot about it. How could I forget something like that?"

Because you'd taught yourself to forget, Allen answered silently. One trauma in a happy childhood gets remembered; after a lifetime of them, the habit of repression is strong. Too bad his own childhood had been happy, Allen reflected with black humor; there were a few things he could have done with erasing from his memory, only he'd learned the techniques too late. "Talk to Dr. Marian about that," he suggested. "She'll help you figure it out."

The *Orca Queen*'s engine was near enough now for Jamie to raise his head and watch for the shape to emerge from the fog. Allen gave the skinny shoulders a last squeeze, then rose, but Jamie, his eyes on the fading mist, said, "I never cried, you know. Not when he hit me, not since I was really small. Not even when . . . in the hunting game, when he'd drive off and leave me, even then I didn't cry, not after the first couple of times. I knew he'd come back, he wouldn't let me starve or freeze to death or anything. It was only when he hugged me that I couldn't help myself. He'd pick me up and hug me and kiss my hair and call me 'son,' and I couldn't help it, I'd start to cry. I hated it and I'd tell myself, *Not this time,* but I couldn't stop. And it always felt then like he'd won."

Allen's impulse was to pick the boy up and hug him and kiss his hair and call him *son,* to overlay one man's acts with another's; instead, he squatted down in front of the boy, to take hold of his shoulders and meet his eyes. "Jamie, you cried because you're human. Not because your father won, but because you couldn't let him. You cried because you were missing your mother, and because you were waiting for us to find you, me and Alice, and Rachel and Pete and the kids, and for Ed and Jerry and Rae and everyone. He never won, Jamie, you did. You won because you never forgot what your mother taught you: that you're worth loving."

You won because you didn't kill the pale-eyed bastard, Allen added to himself. *You won because you were strong enough not to go along with his game, because even though he carved a great fissure down the middle of your soul, a wound that will never, ever completely heal, and even though you'll never take a single step in your whole life when your feet don't expect the ground to fall out from under you and swallow you up, you've managed not to let it twist you. Somehow, you've managed to make the right choice every time.*

All that was too much. So Allen simply leaned forward to give the boy's cold cheek a kiss, and say, "Jamie, you're very possibly the bravest person I've ever met."

The boy didn't believe him, but that didn't matter as much as having said the words. Allen reached down to pull Jamie to his feet, and walked with him down the promontory to the future.

Glossary of Vietnam war terms

AK47—Soviet rifle used by *NVA* and *VC*
C4—plastic explosives (chunks also burned to heat *C-rations*)
C-rations—Combat rations, canned and eaten cold or heated
    individually
Charlie—from Victor Charlie, call letters for *VC*
Claymore—portable antipersonnel mines
DEROS—Dates Eligible Return from OverSeas
didi; didi mau—run; run fast
dinky dau—crazy
FNG—Fucking New Guy
Grunt—foot soldier
KIA—Killed In Action
LAW—Light Antitank Weapon, single-shot rocket in fiberglass
    tube
LZ—landing zone

M16—semiautomatic rifle issued to American troops from
    1967 on
M60—American machine gun
NDP—Night Defensive Position
NVA—North Vietnamese Army (collective or individual)
REMF—Rear Echelon Mother Fucker, who fights his war behind the
    lines
VC—Viet Cong (South Vietnamese insurgent, usually guerilla fighter)